Assassin's

Robin Hobb is one of ███████ ████ ███████ ██
She was born in California in 1952 but raised ██ ███ ██████, where
she learned how to raise a wolf cub, to skin a moose and to survive
in the wilderness. When she married a fisherman who fished herring
and the Kodiak salmon-run for half the year, these skills would
stand her in good stead. She raised her family, ran a smallholding,
delivered post to her remote community, all at the same time as
writing stories and novels. She succeeded on all fronts, raising four
children and becoming an internationally best-selling writer. She
lives in Tacoma, Washington State.

ROBIN HOBB

Book One of The Farseer Trilogy

HARPER
Voyager

Harper*Voyager*
An imprint of HarperCollins*Publishers*
1 London Bridge Street
London SE1 9GF

www.harpercollins.co.uk

This paperback edition 2014
10

First published in Great Britain by
HarperCollins*Publishers* 1995

Copyright © Robin Hobb 1995

Robin Hobb asserts the moral right to
be identified as the author of this work

A catalogue record for this book
is available from the British Library

ISBN: 978 0 00 756225 1

Set in Goudy by Palimpsest Book Production Limited,
Falkirk, Stirlingshire

Printed and bound in Great Britain by
CPI Group (UK) Ltd, Croydon CR0 4YY

MIX
Paper from
responsible sources
FSC **FSC** C007454

For Giles
And for Raphael and Freddy,
the Princes of Assassins

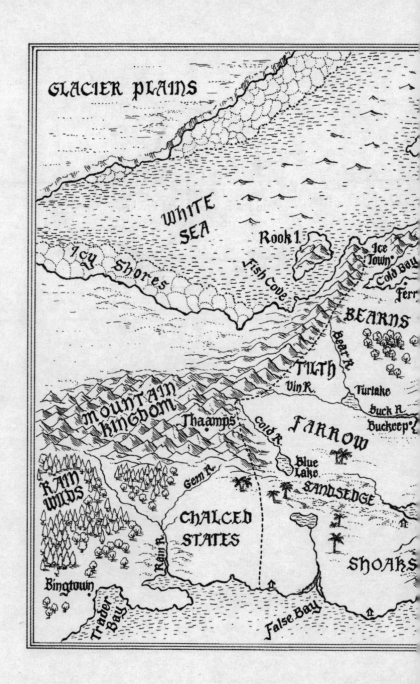

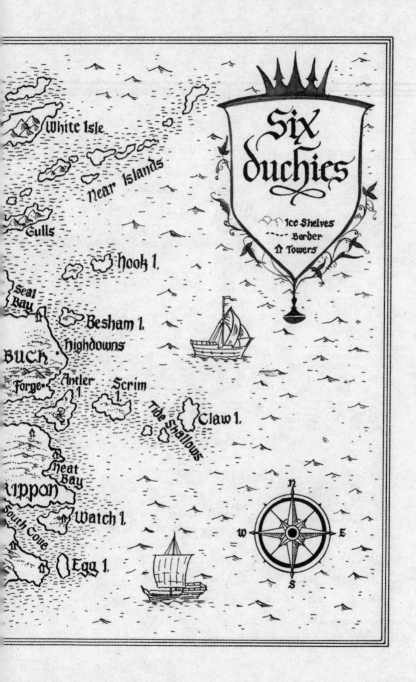

Six
duchies

Ice Shelves
Border
Towers

White Isle

Near Islands

Gulls

Hook I.

Seal Bay

Besham I.

highdowns

BUCK

Forge

Antler
I.

Scrim
I.

Tide Shallows

Claw I.

heat Bay

RIPPON

South Cove

Watch I.

Egg I.

N
W   E
S

ONE

The Earliest History

A history of the Six Duchies is of necessity a history of its ruling family, the Farseers. A complete telling would reach back beyond the founding of the First Duchy, and if such names were remembered, would tell us of Outislanders raiding from the Sea, visiting as pirates a shore more temperate and gentler than the icy beaches of the Out Islands. But we do not know the names of these earliest forebears.

And of the first real king, little more than his name and some extravagant legends remain. Taker his name was, quite simply, and perhaps with that naming began the tradition that daughters and sons of his lineage would be given names that would shape their lives and beings. Folk beliefs claim that such names were sealed to the newborn babes by magic, and that these royal offspring were incapable of betraying the virtues whose names they bore. Passed through fire and plunged through salt water and offered to the winds of the air; thus were names sealed to these chosen children. So we are told. A pretty fancy, and perhaps once there was such a ritual, but history shows us this was not always sufficient to bind a child to the virtue that named it . . .

My pen falters, then falls from my knuckly grip, leaving a worm's trail of ink across Fedwren's paper. I have spoiled another leaf of the fine stuff, in what I suspect is a futile endeavour. I wonder if I can write this history, or if on every page there will be some sneaking show of a bitterness I thought long dead. I think myself cured of all spite, but when I touch pen to paper, the hurt of a boy bleeds out with the sea-spawned ink, until I suspect each carefully formed black letter scabs over some ancient scarlet wound.

Both Fedwren and Patience were so filled with enthusiasm whenever a written account of the history of the Six Duchies was discussed that I persuaded myself the writing of it was a worthwhile effort. I convinced myself that the exercise would turn my thoughts aside from my pain and help the time to pass. But each historical event I consider only awakens my own personal shades of loneliness and loss. I fear I will have to set this work aside entirely, or else give in to reconsidering all that has shaped what I have become. And so I begin again, and again, but always find that I am writing of my own beginnings rather than the beginnings of this land. I do not even know to whom I try to explain myself. My life has been a web of secrets, secrets that even now are unsafe to share. Shall I set them all down on fine paper, only to create from them flame and ash? Perhaps.

My memories reach back to when I was six years old. Before that, there is nothing, only a blank gulf no exercise of my mind has ever been able to pierce. Prior to that day at Moonseye, there is nothing. But on that day they suddenly begin, with a brightness and detail that overwhelms me. Sometimes it seems too complete, and I wonder if it is truly mine. Am I recalling it from my own mind, or from dozens of retellings by legions of kitchen maids and ranks of scullions and herds of stable-boys as they explained my presence to each other? Perhaps I have heard the story so many times, from so many sources, that I now recall it as an actual memory of my own. Is the detail the result of a six-year-old's open absorption of all that goes on around him? Or could the completeness of the memory be the bright overlay of the Skill, and the later drugs a man takes to control his addiction to it, the drugs that bring on pains and cravings of their own? The last is most possible. Perhaps it is even probable. One hopes it is not the case.

The remembrance is almost physical; the chill greyness of the fading day, the remorseless rain that soaked me, the icy cobbles of the strange town's streets, even the callused roughness of the huge hand that gripped my small one. Sometimes I wonder about that grip. The hand was hard and rough, trapping mine within it. And yet it was warm, and not unkind, as it held mine. Only firm. It did not let me slip on the icy streets, but it did not let me escape my fate, either. It was as implacable as the freezing grey rain that glazed the trampled snow and ice of the gravelled pathway outside the huge wooden doors of the fortified building that stood like a fortress within the town itself.

The doors were tall, not just to a six-year-old boy, but tall enough to admit giants, to dwarf even the rangy old man who towered over me. And they looked strange to me, although I cannot summon up what type of door or dwelling would have looked familiar. Only that these, carved and bound with black iron hinges, decorated with a buck's head and knocker of gleaming brass, were beyond my experience. I recall that slush had soaked through my clothes, so that my feet and legs were wet and cold. And yet, again, I cannot recall that I had walked far through winter's last curses, nor that I had been carried. No, it all starts there, right outside the doors of the stronghouse, with my small hand trapped inside the tall man's.

Almost, it is like a puppet show beginning. Yes, I can see it thus. The curtains parted, and there we stood before that great door. The old man lifted the brass knocker and banged it down, once, twice, thrice, on the plate that resounded to his pounding. And then, from off-stage, a voice sounded. Not from within the doors, but from behind us, back the way we had come. 'Father, please,' the woman's voice begged. I turned to look at her, but it had begun to snow again, a lacy veil that clung to eyelashes and coatsleeves. I can't recall that I saw anyone. Certainly, I did not struggle to break free of the old man's grip on my hand, nor did I call out, 'Mother, Mother!' Instead I stood, a spectator, and heard the sound of boots within the keep, and the unfastening of the door hasp within.

One last time she called. I can still hear the words perfectly, the desperation in a voice that now would sound young to my ears. 'Father, please, I beg you!' A tremor shook the hand that gripped mine, but whether of anger or some other emotion, I shall never know. As swift as a black crow seizes a bit of dropped bread, the old man stooped and snatched up a frozen chunk of dirty ice. Wordlessly he flung it, with great force and fury, and I cowered where I stood. I do not recall a cry, nor the sound of struck flesh. What I do remember is how the doors swung outward, so that the old man had to step hastily back, dragging me with him.

And there is this: the man who opened the door was no house-servant, as I might imagine if I had only heard this story. No, memory shows me a man-at-arms, a warrior, gone a bit to grey and with a belly more of hard suet than muscle, but not some mannered house-servant. He looked both the old man and me up and down with a soldier's practised suspicion, and then stood there silently, waiting for us to state our business.

I think it rattled the old man a bit, and stimulated him, not to fear, but to anger. For he suddenly dropped my hand and instead gripped me by the back of my coat and swung me forward, like a whelp offered to a prospective new owner. 'I've brought the boy to you,' he said in a rusty voice.

And when the house-guard continued to stare at him, without judgement or even curiosity, he elaborated. 'I've fed him at my table for six years, and never a word from his father, never a coin, never a visit, though my daughter gives me to understand he knows he fathered a bastard on her. I'll not feed him any longer, nor break my back at a plough to keep clothes on his back. Let him be fed by him what got him. I've enough to tend to of my own, what with my woman getting on in years, and this one's mother to keep and feed. For not a man will have her now, not a man, not with this pup running at her heels. So you take him, and give him to his father.' And he let go of me so suddenly that I sprawled to the stone doorstep at the guard's feet. I scrabbled to a sitting position, not much hurt that I recall, and looked up to see what would happen next between the two men.

The guard looked down at me, lips pursed slightly, not in judgement but merely considering how to classify me. 'Whose get?' he asked, and his tone was not one of curiosity, but only that of a man who asks for more specific information on a situation, in order to report well to a superior.

'Chivalry's,' the old man said, and he was already turning his back on me, taking his measured steps down the flagstoned pathway. 'Prince Chivalry,' he said, not turning back as he added the qualifier. 'Him what's King-in-Waiting. That's who got him. So let him do for him, and be glad he managed to father one child, somewhere.'

For a moment the guard watched the old man walking away. Then he wordlessly stooped to seize me by the collar and drag me out of the way so that he could close the door. He let go of me for the brief time it took him to secure the door. That done, he stood looking down on me. No real surprise, only a soldier's stoic acceptance of the odder bits of his duty. 'Up, boy, and walk,' he said.

So I followed him, down a dim corridor, past rooms spartanly furnished, with windows still shuttered against winter's chill, and finally to another set of closed doors, these of rich, mellow wood embellished with carvings. There he paused, and straightened his own garments briefly. I remember quite clearly how he went down on one knee, to tug my shirt straight and smooth my hair with a rough pat or two, but whether this was from some kind-hearted impulse that I make a good impression, or merely a concern that his package look well-tended, I will never know. He stood again, and knocked once at the double doors. Having knocked, he did not wait for a reply, or at least I never heard one. He pushed the doors open, herded me in before him, and shut the doors behind him.

This room was as warm as the corridor had been chill, and alive as the other chambers had been deserted. I recall a quantity of furniture in it, rugs and hangings, and shelves of tablets and scrolls overlain with the scattering of clutter that any well-used and comfortable chamber takes on. There was a fire burning in a massive fireplace, filling the room with heat and a pleasantly rosinous scent. An immense table was placed at an angle to the fire, and behind it sat a stocky man, his brows knit as he bent over a sheaf of papers in front of him. He did not look up immediately, and so I was able to study his rather bushy disarray of dark hair for some moments.

When he did look up, he seemed to take in both myself and the guard in one quick glance of his black eyes. 'Well, Jason?' he asked, and even at that age I could sense his resignation to a messy interruption. 'What's this?'

The guard gave me a gentle nudge on the shoulder that propelled me a foot or so closer to the man. 'An old ploughman left him, Prince Verity, sir. Says it's Prince Chivalry's bastid, sir.'

For a few moments the harried man behind the desk continued to regard me with some confusion. Then something very like an amused smile lightened his features and he rose and came around the desk to stand with his fists on his hips, looking down on me. I did not feel threatened by his scrutiny; rather it was as if something about my appearance pleased him inordinately. I looked up at him curiously. He wore a short dark beard, as bushy and disorderly as his hair, and his cheeks were weathered above it. Heavy brows were raised above his dark eyes. He had a barrel of a chest, and shoulders that strained the fabric of his shirt. His fists were square and work-scarred, yet ink stained the fingers of his right hand. As he stared at me, his grin gradually widened, until finally he gave a snort of laughter.

'Be damned,' he finally said. 'Boy does have Chiv's look to him, doesn't he? Fruitful Eda. Who'd have believed it of my illustrious and virtuous brother?'

The guard made no response at all, nor was one expected from him. He continued to stand alertly, awaiting the next command. A soldier's soldier.

The other man continued to regard me curiously. 'How old?' he asked the guard.

'Ploughman says six.' The guard raised a hand to scratch at his cheek, then suddenly seemed to recall he was reporting. He dropped his hand. 'Sir,' he added.

The other didn't seem to notice the guard's lapse in discipline. The dark eyes roved over me, and the amusement in his smile grew broader. 'So make it seven years or so, to allow for her belly to swell. Damn. Yes. That was the first year the Chyurda tried to close the pass. Chivalry was up this way for three, four months, chivvying them into opening it to us. Looks like it wasn't the only thing he chivvied open. Damn. Who'd have thought it of him?' He paused, then, 'Who's the mother?' he demanded suddenly.

The guardsman shifted uncomfortably. 'Don't know, sir. There was only the old ploughman on the doorstep, and all him said was that this was Prince Chivalry's bastid, and he wasn't going to feed him ner put clothes on his back no more. Said him what got him could care for him now.'

The man shrugged as if the matter were of no great importance. 'The boy looks well tended. I give it a week, a fortnight at most before she's whimpering at the kitchen door because she misses her pup. I'll find out then if not before. Here, boy, what do they call you?'

His jerkin was closed with an intricate buckle shaped like a buck's head. It was brass, then gold, then red as the flames in the fireplace moved. 'Boy,' I said. I do not know if I were merely repeating what he and the guardsman had called me, or if I truly had no name besides the word. For a moment the man looked surprised and a look of what might have been pity crossed his face. But it disappeared as swiftly, leaving him looking only discomfited, or mildly annoyed. He glanced back at the map that still awaited him on the table.

'Well,' he said into the silence. 'Something's got to be done with him, at least until Chiv gets back. Jason, see the boy's fed and bedded somewhere, at least for tonight. I'll give some thought to what's to be done with him tomorrow. Can't have royal bastards cluttering up the countryside.'

'Sir,' said Jason, neither agreeing nor disagreeing, but merely accepting the order. He put a heavy hand on my shoulder and turned me back toward the door. I went somewhat reluctantly, for the room was bright and pleasant and warm. My cold feet had started to tingle, and I knew if I could stay a little longer, I would be warmed through. But the guardsman's hand was inexorable, and I was steered out of the warm chamber and back into the chill dimness of the drear corridors.

They seemed all the darker after the warmth and light, and endless as I tried to match the guard's stride as he wound through them. Perhaps I whimpered, or perhaps he grew tired of my slower pace, for he spun suddenly, seized me, and tossed me up to sit on his shoulder as casually as if I weighed nothing at all. 'Soggy little pup, you,' he observed, without rancour, and then bore me down corridors and around turns and up and down steps and finally into the yellow light and space of a large kitchen.

There half a dozen other guards lounged on benches and ate and drank at a big scarred table before a fire fully twice as large as the one in the study. The room smelled of food, of beer and men's sweat, of wet wool garments and the smoke of the wood and drip of grease into flames. Hogsheads and small casks ranged against the wall, and smoked joints of meats were dark shapes hung from the rafters. The table bore a clutter of food and dishes. A chunk of meat on a spit was swung back from the flames and dripped fat onto the stone hearth. My stomach clutched my ribs suddenly at the rich smell. Jason set me rather firmly on the corner of the table closest to the fire's warmth, jogging the elbow of a man whose face was hidden by a mug.

'Here, Burrich,' Jason said matter-of-factly. 'This pup's for you, now.' He turned away from me. I watched with interest as he broke a corner as big as his fist off a dark loaf, and then drew his belt knife to take a wedge of cheese off a wheel. He pushed these into my hands, and then stepping to the fire, began sawing a man-sized portion of meat off the joint. I wasted no time in filling my mouth with bread and cheese. Beside me, the man called Burrich set down his mug and glared around at Jason.

'What's this?' he asked, sounding very much like the man in the warm chamber. He had the same unruly blackness to his hair and beard, but his face was angular and narrow. His face had the colour of a man much outdoors. His eyes were brown rather than black, and his hands were long-fingered and clever. He smelled of horses and dogs and blood and leathers.

'He's yours to watch over, Burrich. Prince Verity says so.'

'Why?'

'You're Chivalry's man, ain't you? Care for his horse, his hounds, and his hawks?'

'So?'

'So, you got his little bastid, at least until Chivalry gets back and does otherwise with him.' Jason offered me the slab of dripping meat. I looked from the bread to the cheese I gripped, loth to surrender either, but longing for the hot meat, too. He shrugged at seeing my dilemma, and with a fighting man's practicality, flipped the meat casually onto the table beside my hip. I stuffed as much bread into my mouth as I could, and shifted to where I could watch the meat.

'Chivalry's bastard?'

Jason shrugged, busy with getting himself bread and meat and cheese of his own. 'So said the old ploughman what left him here.' He layered the meat and cheese onto a slab of bread, took an immense bite, and then spoke through it. 'Said Chivalry ought to be glad he'd seeded one child, somewhere, and should feed and care for him himself now.'

An unusual quiet bloomed suddenly in the kitchen. Men paused in their eating, gripping bread or mugs or trenchers, and turned eyes to the man called Burrich. He himself set his mug carefully away from the edge of the table. His voice was quiet and even, his words precise. 'If my master has no heir, 'tis Eda's will, and no fault of his manhood. The Lady Patience has always been delicate, and . . .'

'Even so, even so,' Jason was quickly agreeing. 'And there sits the very proof that there's nowt wrong with him as a man, is all I was saying, that's all.' He wiped his mouth hastily on his sleeve. 'As like to Prince Chivalry as can be, as even his brother said but a while ago. Not the Crown Prince's fault if his Lady Patience can't carry his seed to term . . .'

But Burrich had stood suddenly. Jason backed a hasty step or two before he realized I was Burrich's target, not him. Burrich gripped my shoulders and turned me to the fire. When he firmly took my jaw in his hand and lifted my face to his, he startled me so that I dropped both bread and cheese. Yet he paid no mind to this as he turned my face toward the fire and studied me as if I were a map. His eyes met mine, and there was a sort of wildness in them, as if what he saw in my face were an injury I'd done him. I started to draw away from that look, but his grip wouldn't let me. So I stared back at him with as much defiance as I could muster, and saw his upset masked suddenly with a sort of reluctant wonder. And lastly he closed his eyes for a second, hooding them against some pain. 'It's a thing that will try her lady's will to the edge of her very name,' Burrich said softly.

He released my jaw, and stooped awkwardly to pick up the bread and cheese I'd dropped. He brushed them off and handed them back to me. I stared at the thick bandaging on his right calf and over his knee that had kept him from bending his leg. He reseated himself and refilled his mug from a pitcher on the table. He drank again, studying me over the rim of his mug.

'Who'd Chivalry get him on?' a man at the other end of the table asked incautiously.

Burrich swung his gaze to the man as he set his mug down. For a moment he didn't speak, and I sensed that silence hovering again. 'I'd say it was Prince Chivalry's business who the mother was, and not for kitchen talk,' Burrich said mildly.

'Even so, even so,' the guard agreed abruptly, and Jason nodded like a courting bird in agreement. Young as I was, I still wondered what kind of man this was who, with one leg bandaged, could quell a room full of rough men with a look or a word.

'Boy don't have a name,' Jason volunteered into the silence. 'Just goes by "boy".'

This statement seemed to put everyone, even Burrich, at a loss for words. The silence lingered as I finished bread and cheese and meat, and washed it down with a swallow or two of beer that Burrich offered me. The other men left the room gradually, in twos and threes, and still he sat there, drinking and looking at me. 'Well,' he said at long last. 'If I know your father, he'll face up to it square and do what's right. But Eda only knows what he'll think is the right thing to do. Probably whatever hurts the most.' He watched me silently a moment longer. 'Had enough to eat?' he asked at last.

I nodded, and he stood stiffly, to swing me off the table and onto the floor. 'Come on, then, fitz,' he said, and moved out of the kitchen and down a different corridor. His stiff leg made his gait ungainly, and perhaps the beer had something to do with it as well. Certainly I had no trouble in keeping up. We came at last to a heavy door, and a guard who nodded us through with a devouring stare at me.

Outside, a chill wind was blowing. All the ice and snow that had softened during the day had gone back to sharpness with the coming of night. The path cracked under my feet, and the wind seemed to find every crack and gap in my garments. My feet and leggings had been warmed by the kitchen's fire, but not quite dried, so the cold seized on them. I remember darkness, and the sudden tiredness that came over me, a terrible weepy sleepiness that dragged at me as I followed the strange man with the bandaged leg through the chill, dark courtyard. There were tall walls around us, and guards moved intermittently on top of them, dark shadows visible only as they blotted the stars occasionally from the sky. The cold bit at me, and I stumbled and slipped on the icy pathway. But something about Burrich did not permit me to whimper or beg quarter from him. Instead I followed him doggedly. We reached a building and he dragged open a heavy door.

Warmth and animal smells and a dim yellow light spilled out. A sleepy stable-boy sat up in his nest of straw, blinking like a rumpled fledgling. At a word from Burrich he lay down again, curling up small in the straw and closing his eyes. We moved past him, Burrich dragging the door to behind us. He took the lantern that burned dimly by the door and led me on.

I entered a different world then, a night world where animals shifted and breathed in stalls, where hounds lifted their heads from their crossed forepaws to regard me with lambent eyes green or yellow in the lantern's glow. Horses stirred as we passed their stalls. 'Hawks are down at the far end,' Burrich said as we passed stall after stall. I accepted it as something he thought I should know.

'Here,' he said finally. 'This'll do. For now, anyway. I'm jigged if I know what else to do with you. If it weren't for the Lady Patience, I'd be thinking this a fine god's jest on the master. Here, Nosy, you just move over and make this boy a place in the straw. That's right, you cuddle up to Vixen, there. She'll take you in, and give a good slash to any that think to bother you.'

I found myself facing an ample box-stall, populated with three hounds. They had roused and lay, stick tails thumping in the straw at Burrich's voice. I moved uncertainly in amongst them, and finally lay down next to an old bitch with a whitened muzzle and one torn ear. The older male regarded me with a certain suspicion, but the third was a half-grown pup, and Nosy welcomed me with ear lickings, nose nipping and much pawing. I put an arm around him to settle him, and then cuddled in amongst them as Burrich had advised. He threw a thick blanket that smelled much of horse down over me. A very large grey beast in the next stall stirred suddenly, thumping a heavy hoof against the partition, and then hanging his head over to see what the night excitement was about. Burrich calmed him absently with a touch.

'It's rough quarters here for all of us at this outpost. You'll find Buckkeep a more hospitable place. But for tonight, you'll be warm here, and safe.' He stood a moment longer, looking down at us. 'Horse, hound, and hawk, Chivalry. I've minded them all for you for many a year, and minded them well. But this by-blow of yours; well, what to do with him is beyond me.'

I knew he wasn't speaking to me. I watched him over the edge of the blanket as he took the lantern from its hook and wandered off, muttering to himself. I remember that first night well, the warmth of the hounds, the prickling straw, and even the sleep that finally came as the pup cuddled close beside me. I drifted into his mind and shared his dim dreams of an endless chase, pursuing a quarry I never saw, but whose hot scent dragged me onward through nettle, bramble and scree.

And with the hound's dream, the precision of the memory wavers like the bright colours and sharp edges of a drug dream. Certainly the days that follow that first night have no such clarity in my mind.

I recall the spitting wet days of winter's end as I learned the route from my stall to the kitchen. I was free to come and go there as I pleased. Sometimes there was a cook in attendance, setting meat onto the hearth-hooks or pummelling bread dough or breaching a cask of drink. More often, there was not, and I helped myself to whatever had been left out on the table, and shared generously with the pup that swiftly became my constant companion. Men came and went, eating and drinking, and regarding me with a speculative curiosity that I came to accept as normal. The men had a sameness about them, with their rough wool cloaks and leggings, their hard bodies and easy movements, and the crest of a leaping buck that each bore over his heart. My presence made some of them uncomfortable. I grew accustomed to the mutter of voices that began whenever I left the kitchen.

Burrich was a constant in those days, giving me the same care he gave to Chivalry's beasts; I was fed, watered, groomed and exercised, said exercise usually coming in the form of trotting at his heels as he performed his other duties. But those memories are blurry and details, such as those of washing or changing garments, have probably faded with a six-year-old's calm assumptions of such things as normal. Certainly I remember the hound pup, Nosy. His coat was red and slick and short, and bristly in a way that prickled me through my clothes when we shared the horse blanket at night. His eyes were green as copper ore, his nose the colour of cooked liver, and the insides of his mouth and tongue were mottled pink and black. When we were not eating in the kitchen, we wrestled in the courtyard or in the straw of the box-stall. Such was my world for however long it was I was there. Not too long, I think, for I do not recall the weather changing. All my memories of that time are of raw days and blustery wind, and snow and ice that partially melted each day but were restored by night's freezes.

One other memory I have of that time, but it is not sharp-edged. Rather it is warm and softly tinted, like a rich old tapestry seen in a dim room. I recall being roused from sleep by the pup's wriggling and the yellow light of a lantern being held over me. Two men bent over me, but Burrich stood stiffly behind them and I was not afraid.

'Now you've wakened him,' warned the one, and he was Prince Verity, the man from the warmly-lit chamber of my first evening.

'So? He'll go back to sleep as soon as we leave. Damn him, he has his father's eyes as well. I swear, I'd have known his blood no matter where I saw him. There'll be no denying it to any that see him. But have neither you nor Burrich the sense of a flea? Bastard or not, you don't stable a child among beasts. Was there no where else you could put him?'

The man who spoke was like Verity around the jaw and eyes, but there the resemblance ended. This man was younger by far. His cheeks were beardless, and his scented and smoothed hair was finer and brown. His cheeks and forehead had been stung to redness by the night's chill, but it was a new thing, not Verity's weathered ruddiness. And Verity dressed as his men dressed, in practical woollens of sturdy weave and subdued colours. Only the crest on his breast showed brighter, in gold and silver thread. But the younger man with him gleamed in scarlets and primrose, and his cloak drooped with twice the width of cloth needed to cover a man. The doublet that showed beneath it was a rich cream, and laden with lace. The scarf at his throat was secured with a leaping stag done in gold, its single eye a winking green gem. And the careful turn of his words were like a twisted chain of gold compared to the simple links of Verity's speech.

'Regal, I had given it no thought. What do I know of children? I turned him over to Burrich. He is Chivalry's man, and as such he's cared for . . .'

'I meant no disrespect to the blood, sir,' Burrich said in honest confusion. 'I am Chivalry's man, and I saw to the boy as I thought best. I could make him up a pallet in the guardroom, but he seems small to be in the company of such men, with their comings and goings at all hours, their fights and drinking and noise.' The tone of his words made his own distaste for their company obvious. 'Bedded here, he has quiet, and the pup has taken to him. And with my Vixen to watch over him at night, no one could do him harm without her teeth taking a toll. My lords, I know little of children myself, and it seemed to me . . .'

'It's fine, Burrich, it's fine,' Verity said quietly, cutting him off. 'If it had to be thought about, I should have done the thinking. I left it to you, and I don't find fault with it. It's better than a lot of children have in this village, Eda knows. For here, for now, it's fine.'

'It will have to be different when he comes back to Buckkeep.' Regal did not sound pleased.

'Then our father wishes him to return with us to Buckkeep?' The question came from Verity.

'Our father does. My mother does not.'

'Oh.' Verity's tone indicated he had no interest in further discussing that. But Regal frowned and continued.

'My mother the Queen is not at all pleased about any of this. She has counselled the King long, but in vain. Mother and I were for putting the boy . . . aside. It is only good sense. We scarcely need more confusion in the line of succession.'

'I see no confusion in it now, Regal,' Verity spoke evenly. 'Chivalry, me, and then you. Then our cousin August. This bastard would be a far fifth.'

'I am well aware that you precede me; you need not flaunt it at me at every opportunity,' Regal said coldly. He glared down at me. 'I still think it would be better not to have him about. What if Chivalry never does get a legal heir on Patience? What if he chooses to recognize this . . . boy? It could be very divisive to the nobles. Why should we tempt trouble? So say my mother and I. But our father the King is not a hasty man, as well we know. Shrewd is as Shrewd does, as the common folk say. He forbade any settling of the matter. "Regal," he said, in that way he has. "Don't do what you can't undo, until you've considered what you can't do once you've done it." Then he laughed.' Regal himself gave a short, bitter laugh. 'I weary so of his humour.'

'Oh,' said Verity again, and I lay still and wondered if he were trying to sort out the King's words, or refraining from replying to his brother's complaint.

'You discern his real reason, of course,' Regal informed him.

'Which is?'

'He still favours Chivalry.' Regal sounded disgusted. 'Despite everything. Despite his foolish marriage and his eccentric wife. Despite this mess. And now he thinks this will sway the people, make them warmer toward him. Prove he's a man, that Chivalry can father a child. Or maybe prove he's a human, and can make mistakes like the rest of them.' Regal's tone betrayed that he agreed with none of this.

'And this will make the people like him more, support his future kingship more? That he fathered a child on some wild woman before he married his queen?' Verity sounded confused by the logic.

I heard the sourness in Regal's voice. 'So the King seems to think. Does he care nothing for the disgrace? But I suspect Chivalry will feel differently about using his bastard in such a way. Especially as it regards dear Patience. But the King has ordered that the bastard be brought to Buckkeep when you return.' Regal looked down on me as if ill satisfied.

Verity looked briefly troubled, but nodded. A shadow lay over Burrich's features that the yellow lamplight could not lift.

'Has my master no say in this?' Burrich ventured to protest. 'It seems to me that if he wants to settle a portion on the family of the boy's mother, and set him aside, then, why surely for the sake of my Lady Patience's sensibilities, he should be allowed that discretion . . .'

Prince Regal broke in with a snort of disdain. 'The time for discretion was before he rolled the wench. The Lady Patience is not the first woman to have to face her husband's bastard. Everyone here knows of his existence; Verity's clumsiness saw to that. There's no point to trying to hide him. And as far as a royal bastard is concerned, none of us can afford to have such sensibilities, Burrich. To leave such a boy in a place like this is like leaving a weapon hovering over the King's throat. Surely even a houndsman can see that. And even if you can't, your master will.'

An icy harshness had come into Regal's voice, and I saw Burrich flinch from his voice as I had seen him cower from nothing else. It made me afraid, and I drew the blanket up over my head and burrowed deeper into the straw. Beside me, Vixen growled lightly in the back of her throat. I think it made Regal step back, but I cannot be sure. The men left soon after, and if they spoke any more than that, no memory of it lies within me.

Time passed, and I think it was two, or perhaps three weeks later that I found myself clinging to Burrich's belt and trying to wrap my short legs around a horse behind him as we left that chill village and began what seemed to me an endless journey down to warmer lands. I suppose at some point Chivalry must have come to see the bastard he had sired, and must have passed some sort of judgement on himself as regarded me. But I have no memory of such a meeting with my father. The only image I carry of him in my mind is from his portrait on the wall in Buckkeep. Years later I was given to understand that his diplomacy had gone well indeed, securing a treaty and peace that lasted well into my teens and earning the respect and even fondness of the Chyurda.

In truth, I was his only failure that year, but I was a monumental one. He preceded us home to Buckkeep, where he abdicated his claim to the throne. By the time we arrived, he and Lady Patience were gone from court, to live as the Lord and Lady of Withywoods. I have been to Withywoods. Its name bears no relationship to its appearance. It is a warm valley, centred on a gently flowing river that carves a wide plain that nestles between gently rising and rolling foothills. A place to grow grapes and grain and plump children. It is a soft holding, far from the borders, far from the politics of court, far from anything that had been Chivalry's life up to then. It was a pasturing out, a gentle and genteel exile for a man who would have been king. A velvet smothering for a warrior and a silencing of a rare and skilled diplomat.

And so I came to Buckkeep, sole child and bastard of a man I'd never know. Prince Verity became King-in-Waiting and Prince Regal moved up a notch in the line of succession. If all I had ever done was to be born and discovered, I would have left a mark across all the land for all time. I grew up fatherless and motherless in a court where all recognized me as a catalyst. And a catalyst I became.

TWO

Newboy

There are many legends about Taker, the first Outislander to claim Buckkeep as the First Duchy and the founder of the royal line. One is that the raiding voyage he was on was his first and only foray out from whatever cold harsh island bore him. It is said that upon seeing the timbered fortifications of Buckkeep, he had announced, 'If there's a fire and a meal there, I shan't be leaving again.' And there was, and he didn't.

But family rumour says that he was a poor sailor, made sick by the heaving water and salt-fish rations that other Outislanders throve upon. He and his crew had been lost for days upon the water, and if he had not managed to seize Buckkeep and make it his own, his crew would have drowned him. Nevertheless, the old tapestry in the Great Hall shows him as a well-thewed stalwart grinning fiercely over the prow of his vessel as his oarsmen propel him toward an ancient Buckkeep of logs and poorly dressed stone.

Buckkeep had begun its existence as a defensible position on a navigable river at the mouth of a bay with excellent anchorage. Some petty landchief, whose name has been lost in the mists of history, saw the potential for controlling trade on the river and built the first stronghold there. Ostensibly, he had built it to defend both river and bay from the Outislander raiders who came every summer to plunder up and down the river. What he had not reckoned on were the raiders that infiltrated his fortifications by treachery. The towers and walls became their toehold. They moved their occupations and domination up the river, and, rebuilding his timber fort into towers and walls of dressed stone, finally made Buckkeep the heart of the First Duchy, and eventually the capital of the kingdom of the Six Duchies.

The ruling house of the Six Duchies, the Farseers, were descended from those Outislanders. They had, for several generations, kept up their ties with the Outislanders, making courting voyages and returning home with plump dark brides of their own folk. And so the blood of the Outislanders still ran strong in the royal lines and the noble houses, producing children with black hair and dark eyes and muscled, stocky limbs. And with those attributes went a predilection for the Skill, and all the dangers and weaknesses inherent in such blood. I had my share of that heritage, too.

But my first experience of Buckkeep held nothing of history or heritage. I knew it only as an end place for a journey, a panorama of noise and people, carts and dogs and buildings and twisting streets that led finally to an immense stone stronghold on the cliffs that overlooked the city sheltered below it. Burrich's horse was weary, and his hooves slipped on the often slimy cobbles of the city streets. I held on grimly to his belt, too weary and aching even to complain. I craned my head up once to stare at the tall grey towers and walls of the keep above us. Even in the unfamiliar warmth of the sea breeze, it looked chill and forbidding. I leaned my forehead against his back and felt ill in the brackish iodine smell of the immense water. And that was how I came to Buckkeep.

Burrich had quarters over the stables, not far from the mews. It was there he took me, along with the hounds and Chivalry's hawk. He saw to the hawk first, for it was sadly bedraggled from the trip. The dogs were overjoyed to be home, and were suffused with a boundless energy that was very annoying to anyone as weary as I. Nosy bowled me over half a dozen times before I could convey to his thick-skulled hound's mind that I was weary and half-sick and in no mood for play. He responded as any pup would, by seeking out his former litter-mates and immediately getting himself into a semi-serious fight with one of them that was quelled by a shout from Burrich. Chivalry's man he might be, but when he was at Buckkeep, he was the Master for hounds, hawks, and horses.

His own beasts seen to, he proceeded to walk through the stables, surveying all that had been done, or left undone, in his absence. Stable-boys, grooms, and falconers appeared as if by magic to defend their charges from any criticisms. I trotted at his heels for as long as I could keep up. It was only when I finally surrendered, and sank wearily onto a pile of straw, that he appeared to notice me. A look of irritation, and then great weariness passed across his face.

'Here, you, Cob. Take young fitz there to the kitchens and see that he's fed, and then bring him back up to my quarters.'

Cob was a short, dark dog-boy, perhaps ten years old, who had just been praised over the health of a litter that had been whelped in Burrich's absence. Moments before he had been basking in Burrich's approval. Now his grin faltered, and he looked at me dubiously. We regarded one another as Burrich moved off down the line of stalls with his entourage of nervous caretakers. Then the boy shrugged, and went into a half-crouch to face me. 'Are you hungry, then, fitz? Shall we go find you a bite?' he asked invitingly, in exactly the same tone as he had used to coax his puppies out where Burrich could see them. I nodded, relieved that he expected no more from me than from a puppy, and followed him.

He looked back often to see if I were keeping up. No sooner were we outside the stables than Nosy came frolicking up to join me. The hound's evident affection for me raised me in Cob's estimation, and he continued to speak to both of us in short encouraging phrases, telling us there was food just ahead, come along now, no, don't go off sniffing after that cat, come along now, there's some good fellows.

The stables had been bustling, with Verity's men putting up their horses and gear and Burrich finding fault with all that had not been done up to his standards in his absence. But as we drew closer to the inner keep, the foot traffic increased. Folk brushed by us on all manner of errands: a boy carrying an immense slab of bacon on his shoulder, a giggling cluster of girls, arms heavy with stewing reeds and heather, a scowling old man with a basket of flopping fish, and three young women in motley and bells, their voices ringing as merrily as their chimes.

My nose informed me that we were getting closer to the kitchens, but the traffic increased proportionately until we drew near a door with a veritable crush of people going in and out. Cob stopped, and Nosy and I paused behind him, noses working appreciatively. He regarded the press of folk at the door, and frowned to himself. 'Place is packed. Everyone's getting ready for the welcoming feast tonight, for Verity and Regal. Anyone who's anyone has come into Buckkeep for it; word spread fast about Chivalry ducking out on the kingship. All the dukes have come or sent a man to counsel about it. I hear even the Chyurda sent someone, to be sure Chivalry's treaties will be honoured if Chivalry is no longer about . . .'

He halted, suddenly embarrassed, but whether it was because he was speaking of my father to the cause of his abdication, or because he was addressing a puppy and a six-year-old as if they had intelligence, I am not sure. He glanced about, reassessing the situation. 'Wait here,' he told us finally. 'I'll slip in and bring something out for you. Less chance of me getting stepped on . . . or caught. Now stay.' And he reinforced his command with a firm gesture of his hand. I backed up to a wall and crouched down there, out of traffic's way, and Nosy sat obediently beside me. I watched admiringly as Cob approached the door, and slipped between the clustered folk, eeling smoothly into the kitchens.

With Cob out of sight, the more general populace claimed my attention. Largely the folk that passed us were serving people and cooks, with a scattering of minstrels and merchants and delivery folk. I watched them come and go with a weary curiosity. I had already seen too much that day to find them of great interest. Almost more than food I desired a quiet place away from all this activity. I sat flat on the ground, my back against the sun-warmed wall of the keep, and put my forehead on my knees. Nosy leaned against me.

Nosy's stick tail beating against the earth roused me. I lifted my face from my knees, to perceive a tall pair of brown boots before me. My eyes travelled up rough leather pants and over a coarse wool shirt to a shaggy, bearded face thatched with pepper-grey hair. The man staring down at me balanced a small keg on one shoulder.

'You the bastid, hey?'

I had heard the word often enough to know it meant me, without grasping the fullness of its meaning. I nodded slowly. The man's face brightened with interest.

'Hey,' he said loudly, no longer speaking to me but to the folk coming and going. 'Here's the bastid. Stiff-as-a-stick Chivalry's by-blow. Looks a fair bit like him, don't you say? Who's your mother, boy?'

To their credit, most of the passing people continued to come and go, with no more than a curious stare at the six-year-old sitting by the wall. But the cask-man's question was evidently of great interest, for more than a few heads turned, and several tradesmen who had just exited from the kitchen drew nearer to hear the answer.

But I did not have an answer. Mother had been mother, and whatever I had known of her was already fading. So I made no reply, but only stared up at him.

'Hey. What's your name then, boy?' And turning to his audience, he confided, 'I heard he ain't got no name. No high-flown royal name to shape him, nor even a cottage name to scold him by. That right, boy? You got a name?'

The group of onlookers was growing. A few showed pity in their eyes, but none interfered. Some of what I was feeling passed to Nosy, who dropped over onto his side and showed his belly in supplication while thumping his tail in that ancient canine signal that always means, 'I'm only a puppy. I cannot defend myself. Have mercy.' Had they been dogs they would have sniffed me over and then drawn back. But humans have no such inbred courtesies. So when I didn't answer, the man drew a step nearer, and repeated, 'You got a name, boy?'

I stood slowly, and the wall that had been warm against my back a moment ago was now a chill barrier to retreat. At my feet, Nosy squirmed in the dust on his back and let out a pleading whine. 'No,' I said softly, and when the man made as if to lean closer to hear my words, 'NO!' I shouted, and *repelled* at him, while crabbing sideways along the wall. I saw him stagger a step backwards, losing his grip on his cask so that it fell to the cobbled path and cracked open. No one in the crowd could have understood what had happened. I certainly didn't. For the most part, folk laughed to see a grown man cower back from a child. In that moment my reputation for both temper and spirit were made, for before nightfall the tale of the bastard standing up to his tormentor was all over the town. Nosy scrabbled to his feet and fled with me. I had one glimpse of Cob's face, taut with confusion as he emerged from the kitchen, pies in hands, and saw Nosy and me flee. Had he been Burrich, I probably would have halted and trusted my safety to him. But he was not, and so I ran, letting Nosy take the lead.

We fled through the trooping servants, just one more small boy and his dog racing about in the courtyard, and Nosy took me to what he obviously regarded as the safest place in the world. Far from the kitchen and the inner keep was a hollow Vixen had scraped out under a corner of a rickety outbuilding where sacks of peas and beans were stored. Here Nosy had been whelped, in total defiance of Burrich and here she had managed to keep her pups hidden for almost three days. Burrich himself had found her there. His smell was the first human smell Nosy could recall. It was a tight squeeze to get under the building, but once within, the den was warm and dry and semi-dark. Nosy huddled close to me and I put my arm around him. Hidden there, our hearts soon eased down from their wild thumpings, and from calmness we passed into the deep, dreamless sleep reserved for warm spring afternoons and puppies.

I came awake shivering, hours later. It was full dark and the tenuous warmth of the early spring day had fled. Nosy was awake as soon as I was, and together we scraped and slithered out of the den.

There was a high night sky over Buckkeep, with stars shining bright and cold. The smell of the bay was stronger as if the day-smells of men and horses and cooking were temporary things that had to surrender each night to the ocean's power. We walked down deserted pathways, through exercise yards and past granaries and the winepress. All was still and silent. As we drew closer to the inner keep, I saw torches still burning, and heard voices still raised in talk. But it all seemed tired somehow, the last vestiges of revelry winding down before dawn came to lighten the skies. Still, we skirted the inner keep by a wide margin, having had enough of people.

I found myself following Nosy back to the stables. As we drew near the heavy doors, I wondered how we would get in. But Nosy's tail began to wag wildly as we got closer, and then even my poor nose picked up Burrich's scent in the dark. He rose from the wooden crate he'd been seated on by the door. 'There you are,' he said soothingly. 'Come along then. Come on.' And he stood and opened the heavy doors for us and led us in.

We followed him through darkness, between rows of stalls, past grooms and handlers put up for the night in the stables, and then past our own horses and dogs and the stable-boys who slept amongst them, and then to a staircase that climbed the wall which separated the stables from the mews. We followed Burrich up its creaking wooden treads, and then he opened another door. Dim yellow light from a guttering candle on a table blinded me temporarily. We followed Burrich into a slant-roofed chamber that smelled of Burrich and leather and the oils and salves and herbs that were part of his trade. He shut the door firmly behind us, and as he came past us to kindle a fresh candle from the nearly spent one on the table, I smelled the sweetness of wine on him.

The light spread, and Burrich seated himself on a wooden chair by the table. He looked different, dressed in fine thin cloth of brown and yellow, with a bit of silver chain across his jerkin. He put his hand out, palm up, on his knee and Nosy went to him immediately. Burrich scratched his hanging ears, and then thumped his ribs affectionately, grimacing at the dust that rose from his coat. 'You're a fine pair, the two of you,' he said, speaking more to the pup than to me. 'Look at you. Filthy as beggars. I lied to my king today for you. First time ever in my life I've done that. Appears as if Chivalry's fall from grace will take me down as well. Told him you were washed up and sound asleep, exhausted from your journey. He was not pleased he would have to wait to see you, but luckily for us, he had weightier things to handle. Chivalry's abdication has upset a lot of lords. Some are seeing it as a chance to push for an advantage, and others are disgruntled to be cheated of a king they admired. Shrewd's trying to calm them all. He's letting it be noised about that Verity was the one who negotiated with the Chyurda this time. Those as will believe that shouldn't be allowed to walk about on their own. But they came, to look at Verity anew, and wonder if and when he'd be their next king, and what kind of a king he would be. Chivalry's throwing it over and leaving for Withywood has stirred all the Duchies as if he'd poked a stick in a hive.'

Burrich lifted his eyes from Nosy's eager face. 'Well, fitz. Guess you got a taste of it today. Fair scared poor Cob to death, your running off like that. Now, are you hurt? Did anyone rough you up? I should have known there would be those would blame all the stir on you. Come here, then. Come on.'

When I hesitated, he moved over to a pallet of blankets made up near the fire and patted it invitingly. 'See. There's a place here for you, all ready. And there's bread and meat on the table for both of you.'

His words made me aware of the covered platter on the table. *Flesh*, Nosy's senses confirmed, and I was suddenly full of the smell of the meat. Burrich laughed at our rush to the table, and silently approved how I shared a portion out to Nosy before filling my own jaws. We ate to repletion, for Burrich had not under-estimated how hungry a pup and a boy would be after the day's misadventures. And then, despite our long nap earlier, the blankets so close to the fire were suddenly immensely inviting. Bellies full, we curled up with the flames baking our backs and slept.

When we awoke the next day, the sun was well risen and Burrich already gone. Nosy and I ate the heel of last night's loaf and gnawed the leftover bones clean before we descended from Burrich's quarters. No one challenged us or appeared to take any notice of us.

Outside, another day of chaos and revelry had begun. The keep was, if anything, more swollen with people. Their passage stirred the dust and their mixing voices were an overlay to the shushing of the wind and the more distant muttering of the waves. Nosy drank it all in, every scent, every sight, every sound. The doubled sensory impact dizzied me. As I walked, I gathered from snatches of conversation that our arrival had coincided with some spring rite of merriment and gathering. Chivalry's abdication was still the main topic, but it did not prevent the puppet shows and jugglers from making every corner a stage for their antics. At least one puppet show had already incorporated Chivalry's fall from grace into its bawdy comedy, and I stood anonymous in the crowd and puzzled over dialogue about sowing the neighbour's fields that had the adults roaring with laughter.

But very soon the crowds and the noise became oppressive to both of us, and I let Nosy know I wished to escape it all. We left the keep, passing out of the thick-walled gate past guards intent upon flirting with the merrymakers as they came and went. One more boy and dog leaving on the heels of a fish-mongering family were nothing to notice. And with no better distraction in sight, we followed the family as they wound their way down the streets away from the keep and towards the town of Buckkeep. We dropped further and further behind them as new scents demanded that Nosy investigate and then urinate at every corner, until it was just him and me wandering in the city.

Buckkeep then was a windy, raw place. The streets were steep and crooked, with paving stones that rocked and shifted out of place under the weight of passing carts. The wind blasted my inland nostrils with the scent of beached kelp and fish guts while the keening of the gulls and sea-birds were an eerie melody above the rhythmic shushing of the waves. The town clings to the rocky black cliffs much like limpets and barnacles cling to the pilings and quays that venture out into the bay. The houses were of stone and wood, with the more elaborate wooden ones built higher up the rocky face and cut more deeply into it.

Buckkeep Town was relatively quiet compared to the festivity and crowds up in the keep. Neither of us had the sense or experience to know the waterfront town was not the best place for a six-year-old and a puppy to wander. Nosy and I explored eagerly, sniffing our way down Baker's Street and through a near-deserted market and then along the warehouses and boat-sheds that were the lowest level of the town. Here the water was close, and we walked on wooden piers as often as we did on sand and stone. Business here was going on as usual with little allowance for the carnival atmosphere up in the keep. Ships must dock and unload as the rising and falling of the tides allow, and those who fish for a living must follow the schedules of the finned creatures, not those of men.

We soon encountered children, some busy at the lesser tasks of their parents' crafts, but some idlers like ourselves. I fell in easily with them, with little need for introductions or any of the adult pleasantries. Most of them were older than I, but several were as young or younger. None of them seemed to think it odd I should be out and about on my own. I was introduced to all the important sights of the city, including the swollen body of a cow that had washed up at the last tide. We visited a new fishing boat under construction at a dock littered with curling shavings and strong-smelling pitch spills. A fish-smoking rack left carelessly untended furnished a mid-day repast for a half-dozen of us. If the children I was with were more ragged and boisterous than those who passed at their chores, I did not notice. And had anyone told me I was passing the day with a pack of beggar brats denied entrance to the keep because of their light-fingered ways, I would have been shocked. At the time, I knew only that it was suddenly a lively and pleasant day, full of places to go and things to do.

There were a few youngsters, larger and more rambunctious, who would have taken the opportunity to set the newcomer on his ear had Nosy not been with me and showing his teeth at the first aggressive shove. But as I did not show any signs of wanting to challenge their leadership, I was allowed to follow. I was suitably impressed by all their secrets, and I would venture that by the end of the long afternoon, I knew the poorer quarter of town better than many who had grown up above it.

I was not asked for a name, but simply was called Newboy. The others had names as simple as Dick or Kerry, or as descriptive as Netpicker and Nosebleed. The last might have been a pretty little thing in better circumstances. She was a year or two older than I, but very outspoken and quickwitted. She got into one dispute with a big boy of twelve, but she showed no fear of his fists, and her sharp-tongued taunts soon had everyone laughing at him. She took her victory calmly and left me awed by her toughness. But the bruises on her face and thin arms were layered in shades of purple, blue and yellow, while a crust of dried blood below one ear belied her name. Even so, Nosebleed was a lively one, her voice shriller than the gulls that wheeled above us. Late afternoon found Kerry, Nosebleed and me on a rocky shore beyond the net-menders' racks, with Nosebleed teaching me to scour the rocks for tight-clinging sheels. These she levered off expertly with a sharpened stick. She was showing me how to use a nail to pry the chewy inmates out of their shells when another girl hailed us with a shout.

The neat blue cloak that blew around her and the leather shoes on her feet set her apart from my companions. Nor did she come to join our harvesting, but only came close enough to call, 'Molly, Molly, he's looking for you, high and low. He waked up near sober an hour ago, and took to calling you names as soon as he found you gone and the fire out.'

A look mixed of defiance and fear passed over Nosebleed's face. 'Run away, Kittne, but take my thanks with you. I'll remember you next time the tides bare the kelpcrabs' beds.'

Kittne ducked her head in a brief acknowledgement and immediately turned and hastened back the way she had come.

'Are you in trouble?' I asked Nosebleed when she did not go back to turning over stones for sheels.

'Trouble?' She gave a snort of disdain. 'That depends. If my father can stay sober long enough to find me, I might be in for a bit of it. More than likely he'll be drunk enough tonight that not a one of whatever he hurls at me will hit. More than likely!' she repeated firmly when Kerry opened his mouth to object to this. And with that she turned back to the rocky beach and our search for sheel.

We were crouched over a many-legged grey creature that we found stranded in a tide pool when the crunch of a heavy boot on the barnacled rocks brought all our heads up. With a shout Kerry fled down the beach, never pausing to look back. Nosy and I sprang back, Nosy crowding against me, teeth bared bravely as his tail tickled his cowardly little belly. Molly Nosebleed was either not so fast to react, or resigned to what was to come. A gangly man caught her a smack on the side of the head. He was a skinny man, rednosed and raw-boned, so that his fist was like a knot at the end of his bony arm, but the blow was still enough to send Molly sprawling. Barnacles cut into her wind-reddened knees, and when she crabbed aside to avoid the clumsy kick he aimed at her, I winced at the salty sand that packed the new cuts.

'Faithless little musk-cat! Didn't I tell you to stay and tend to the dipping! And here I find you mucking about on the beach, with the tallow gone hard in the pot. They'll be wanting more tapers up at the keep this night, and what am I to sell them?'

'The three dozen I set this morning. That was all you left me wicking for, you drunken old sot!' Molly got to her feet and stood bravely despite her brimming eyes. 'What was I to do? Burn up all the fuel to keep the tallow soft so that when you finally gave me wicking we'd have no way to heat the kettle?'

The wind gusted and the man swayed shallowly against it. It brought us a whiff of him. Sweat and beer, Nosy informed me sagely. For a moment the man looked regretful, but then the pain of his sour belly and aching head hardened him. He stooped suddenly and seized a whitened branch of driftwood. 'You won't talk to me like that, you wild brat! Down here with the beggar boys, doing El knows what! Stealing from the smoke racks again, I'll wager, and bringing more shame to me! Dare to run, and you'll have it twice when I catch you.'

She must have believed him, for she only cowered as he advanced on her, putting up her thin arms to shield her head and then seeming to think better of it, and hiding only her face with her hands. I stood transfixed in horror while Nosy yelped with my terror and wet himself at my feet. I heard the swish of the driftwood knob as the club descended. My heart leaped sideways in my chest and I *pushed* at the man, the force jerking out oddly from my belly.

He fell, as had the keg-man the day before. But this man fell clutching at his chest, his driftwood weapon spinning harmlessly away. He dropped to the sand, gave a twitch that spasmed his whole body, and then was still.

An instant later Molly unscrewed her eyes, shrinking from the blow she still expected. She saw her father collapsed on the rocky beach, and amazement emptied her face. She leaped toward him crying, 'Papa, Papa, are you all right? Please, don't die, I'm sorry

I'm such a wicked girl! Don't die, I'll be good, I promise I'll be good.' Heedless of her bleeding knees, she knelt beside him, turning his face so he wouldn't breathe in sand, and then vainly trying to sit him up.

'He was going to kill you,' I told her, trying to make sense of the whole situation.

'No. He hits me, a bit, when I am bad, but he'd never kill me. And when he is sober and not sick, he cries about it and begs me not to be bad and make him angry. I should take more care not to anger him. Oh, Newboy, I think he's dead.'

I wasn't sure myself, but in a moment he gave an awful groan and opened his eyes a bit. Whatever fit had felled him seemed to have passed. Dazedly he accepted Molly's self-accusations and anxious help, and even my reluctant aid. He leaned on the two of us as we wove our way down the rocky beach over the uneven footing. Nosy followed us, by turns barking and racing in circles around us.

The few folk who saw us pass paid no attention to us. I guessed that the sight of Molly helping her papa home was not strange to any of them. I helped them as far as the door of a small chandlery, Molly sniffling apologies every step of the way. I left them there, and Nosy and I found our way back up the winding streets and hilly road to the keep, wondering every step at the ways of folk.

Having found the town and the beggar children once, I was drawn like a magnet to them every day afterwards. Burrich's days were taken up with his duties, and his evenings with the drink and merriment of the Springfest. He paid little mind to my comings and goings, as long as each evening found me on my pallet before his hearth. In truth, I think he had little idea of what to do with me, other than to see that I was fed well enough to grow heartily and that I slept safe within doors at night. It could not have been a good time for him. He had been Chivalry's man, and now that Chivalry had cast himself down, what was to become of him? That must have been much on his mind. And there was the matter of his leg. Despite his knowledge of poultices and bandaging, he could not seem to work the healing on himself that he so routinely served to his beasts. Once or twice I saw the injury unwrapped and winced at the ragged tear that refused to heal smoothly but remained swollen and oozing. Burrich cursed it roundly at first, and set his teeth grimly each night as he cleaned and re-dressed it, but as the days passed he regarded it with more of a sick despair than anything else. Eventually he did get it to close, but the ropy scar twisted his leg and disfigured his walk. Small wonder he had little mind to give to a young bastard deposited in his care.

So I ran free in the way that only small children can, unnoticed for the most part. By the time Springfest was over, the guards at the keep's gate had become accustomed to my daily wanderings. They probably thought me an errand boy, for the keep had many of those, only slightly older than I. I learned to pilfer early from the keep's kitchen enough for both Nosy and myself to breakfast heartily. Scavenging other food – burnt crusts from the baker's, sheel and seaweed from the beach, smoked fish from untended racks – was a regular part of my day's activities. Molly Nosebleed was my most frequent companion. I seldom saw her father strike her after that day; for the most part he was too drunk to find her, or to make good his threats when he did. To what I had done that day, I gave little thought, other than to be grateful that Molly had not realized I was responsible.

The town became the world to me, with the keep a place I went to sleep. It was summer, a wonderful time in a port town. No matter where I went, Buckkeep Town was alive with comings and goings. Goods came down the Buck River from the Inland Duchies, on flat river barges manned by sweating bargemen. They spoke learnedly about shoals and bars and landmarks and the rising and falling of the river waters. Their freight was hauled up into the town shops or warehouses, and then down again to the docks and into the holds of the sea ships. Those were manned by swearing sailors who sneered at the rivermen and their inland ways. They spoke of tides and storms and nights when not even the stars would show their faces to guide them. And fishermen tied up to Buckkeep docks as well, and were the most genial of the group. At least, so they were when the fish were running well.

Kerry taught me the docks and the taverns, and how a quick-footed boy might earn three or even five pence a day, running messages up the steep streets of the town. We thought ourselves sharp and daring, to thus undercut the bigger boys who asked two pence or even more for just one errand. I don't think I have ever been as brave since as I was then. If I close my eyes, I can smell those glorious days. Oakum and tar and fresh wood shavings from the dry-docks where the shipwrights wielded their drawknives and mallets. The sweet smell of very fresh fish, and the poisonous odour of a catch held too long on a hot day. Bales of wool in the sun added their own note to the scent of oak kegs of mellow Sandsedge brandy. Sheaves of fevergone hay waiting to sweeten a forepeak mingled scents with crates of hard melons. And all of these smells were swirled by a wind off the bay, seasoned with salt and iodine. Nosy brought all he scented to my attention as his keener senses overrode my duller ones.

Kerry and I would be sent to fetch a navigator gone to say goodbye to his wife, or to bear a sampling of spices to a buyer at a shop. The harbourmaster might send us running to let a crew know some fool had tied the lines wrong and the tide was about to abandon their ship. But I liked best the errands that took us into the taverns. There the storytellers and gossips plied their trades. The storytellers told the classic tales, of voyages of discovery and crews who braved terrible storms and of foolish captains who took down their ships with all hands. I learned many of the traditional ones by heart, but the tales I loved best came not from the professional storytellers but from the sailors themselves. These were not the tales told at the hearths for all to hear, but the warnings and tidings passed from crew to crew as the men shared a bottle of brandy or a loaf of yellow pollen-bread.

They spoke of catches they'd made, nets full to sinking the boat, or of marvellous fish and beasts glimpsed only in the path of a full moon as it cut a ship's wake. There were stories of villages raided by Outislanders, both on the coast and on the outlying islands of our duchy, the tales of pirates and battles at sea and ships taken by treachery from within. Most gripping were the tales of the Red Ship Raiders, Outislanders who both raided and pirated, and attacked not only our ships and towns but even other Outislander ships. Some scoffed at the notion of the red-keeled ships, and mocked those who told of Outislander pirates turning against others like themselves.

But Kerry and I and Nosy would sit under the tables with our backs braced against the legs, nibbling penny sweetloaves, and listen wide-eyed to tales of red-keeled ships with a dozen bodies swinging from their yardarms, not dead, no, but bound men who jerked and shrieked when the gulls came down to peck at them. We would listen to deliciously scary tales until even the stuffy taverns seemed chilling cold, and then we would race down to the docks again, to earn another penny.

Once Kerry, Molly and I built a raft of driftwood logs and poled it about under the docks. We left it tied up there, and when the tide came up, it battered loose a whole section of dock and damaged two skiffs. For days we dreaded that someone would discover we were the culprits. And one time a tavern-keeper boxed Kerry's ears and accused us both of stealing. Our revenge was the stinking herring we wedged up under the supports of his table-tops. It rotted and stank and made flies for days before he found it.

I learned a smattering of trades in my travels: fish-buying, net-mending, boat-building and idling. I learned even more of human nature. I became a quick judge of who would actually pay the promised penny for a message delivered, and who would just laugh at me when I came to collect. I knew which baker could be begged from, and which shops were easiest to thieve from. And through it all, Nosy was at my side, so bonded to me now that I seldom separated my mind completely from his. I used his nose, his eyes and his jaws as freely as my own, and never thought it the least bit strange.

So the better part of the summer passed. But one fine day, with the sun riding a sky bluer than the sea, my good fortune came at last to an end. Molly, Kerry and I had pilfered a fine string of liver sausages from a smoke-house and were fleeing down the street with the rightful owner in pursuit. Nosy was with us, as always. The other children had come to accept him as a part of me. I don't think it ever occurred to them to wonder at our singleness of mind. Newboy and Nosy we were, and they probably thought it but a clever trick that Nosy would know before I threw where to be to catch our shared bounty. Thus there were actually four of us, racing down the cluttered street, passing the sausages from grubby hand to damp jaws and back to hand again while behind us the owner bellowed and chased us in vain.

Then Burrich stepped out of a shop.

I was running toward him. We recognized one another in a moment of mutual dismay. The blackness of the look that appeared on his face left me no doubts about my conduct. Flee, I decided in a breath, and dodged away from his reaching hands, only to discover in sudden befuddlement that I had somehow run right into him.

I do not like to dwell on what happened next. I was soundly cuffed, not only by Burrich but by the enraged owner of the sausages. All my fellow culprits save Nosy evaporated into the nooks and crannies of the street. Nosy came bellying up to Burrich, to be cuffed and scolded. I watched in agony as Burrich took coins from his pouch to pay the sausage man. He kept a grip on the back of my shirt that nearly lifted me off my feet. When the sausage man had departed and the little crowd who had gathered to watch my discomfiture were dispersing, he finally released me. I wondered at the look of disgust he gave me. With one more backhanded cuff on the back of my head, he commanded, 'Get home. Now.'

We did, more speedily than ever we had before. We found our pallet before the hearth, and waited in trepidation. And waited, and waited, through the long afternoon and into early evening. Both of us got hungry, but knew better than to leave. There had been something in Burrich's face more frightening than even the anger of Molly's papa.

When Burrich did come, full night was in place. We heard his step on the stair, and I did not need Nosy's keener senses to know that Burrich had been drinking. We shrank in on ourselves as he let himself into the dimmed room. His breathing was heavy, and it took him longer than usual to kindle several tapers from the single one I had set out. That done, he dropped onto a bench and regarded the two of us. Nosy whined, and then fell over on his side in puppy supplication. I longed to do the same, but contented myself with looking up at him fearfully. After a moment, he spoke.

'Fitz. What's to come of you? What's to come of us both?

Running with beggar-thieves in the streets, with the blood of kings in your veins. Packing up like animals.'

I didn't speak.

'And me as much to blame as you, I suppose. Come here, then. Come here, boy.'

I ventured a step or two closer. I didn't like coming too close. Burrich frowned at my caution. 'Are you hurt, boy?'

I shook my head.

'Then come here.'

I hesitated, and Nosy whined in an agony of indecision.

Burrich glanced down at him in puzzlement. I could see his mind working through a wine-induced haze. His eyes went from the pup to me and back again, and a sickened look spread across his face. He shook his head. Slowly he stood and walked away from the table and the pup, favouring his damaged leg. In the corner of the chamber there was a small rack, supporting an assortment of dusty tools and objects. Slowly Burrich reached up and took one down. It was made of wood and leather, stiff with disuse. He swung it, and the short leather lash smacked smartly against his leg. 'Know what this is, boy?' he asked gently, in a kind voice.

I shook my head mutely.

'Dog whip.'

I looked at him blankly. There was nothing in my experience or Nosy's to tell me how to react to this. He must have seen my confusion. He smiled genially and his voice remained friendly, but I sensed something hidden in his manner, something waiting.

'It's a tool, fitz. A teaching device. When you get a pup that won't mind – when you say to a pup, "come here", and the pup refuses to come – well, a few sharp lashes from this and the pup learns to listen and obey the first time. Just a few sharp cuts is all it takes to make a pup learn to mind.' He spoke casually as he lowered the whip and let the short lash dance lightly over the floor. Neither Nosy nor I could take our eyes off it, and when he suddenly flipped the whole object at Nosy, the pup gave a yelp of terror and leaped back from it, and then rushed to cower behind me.

And Burrich sank down slowly, covering his eyes as he folded himself onto a bench by the fireplace. 'Oh, Eda,' he breathed, between a curse and a prayer. 'I guessed, I suspected, when I saw you running together like that, but damn El's eyes, I didn't want to be right. I didn't want to be right. I've never hit a pup with that damn thing in my life. Nosy had no reason to fear it. Not unless you'd been sharing minds with him.'

Whatever the danger had been, I sensed that it had passed. I sank down to sit beside Nosy, who crawled up into my lap and nosed at my face anxiously. I quieted him, suggesting we wait to see what happened next. Boy and pup, we sat, watching Burrich's stillness. When he finally raised his face, I was astounded to see that he looked as if he had been crying. 'Like my mother,' I remember thinking, but oddly I cannot now recall an image of her weeping. Only of Burrich's grieved face.

'Fitz. Boy. Come here,' he said softly, and this time there was something in his voice that could not be disobeyed. I rose and went to him, Nosy at my heels. 'No,' he said to the pup, and pointed to a place by his boot, but me he lifted onto the bench beside him.

'Fitz,' he began, and then paused. He took a deep breath and started again. 'Fitz, this is wrong. It's bad, very bad, what you've been doing with this pup. It's unnatural. It's worse than stealing or lying. It makes a man less than a man. Do you understand me?'

I looked at him blankly. He sighed, and tried again.

'Boy, you're of the royal blood. Bastard or not, you're Chivalry's own son, of the old line. And this thing you're doing, it's wrong. It's not worthy of you. Do you understand?'

I shook my head mutely.

'There, you see. You're not talking any more. Now talk to me. Who taught you to do this?'

I tried. 'Do what?' My voice felt creaky and rough.

Burrich's eyes grew rounder. I sensed his effort at control. 'You know what I mean. Who taught you to be with the dog, in his mind, seeing things with him, letting him see with you, telling each other things?'

I mulled this over for a moment. Yes, that was what had been happening. 'No one,' I answered at last. 'It just happened. We were together a lot,' I added, thinking that might explain it.

Burrich regarded me gravely. 'You don't speak like a child,' he observed suddenly. 'But I've heard that was the way of it, with those who had the old Wit. That from the beginning, they were never truly children. They always knew too much, and as they got older, they knew even more. That was why it was never accounted a crime, in the old days, to hunt them down and burn them. Do you understand what I'm telling you, fitz?'

I shook my head, and when he frowned at my silence, I forced myself to add, 'But I'm trying. What is the old Wit?'

Burrich looked incredulous, then suspicious. 'Boy!' he threatened me, but I only looked at him. After a moment, he conceded my ignorance.

'The Wit,' he began slowly. His face darkened, and he looked down at his hands as if remembering an ancient sin. 'It's the power of the beast blood, just as the Skill comes from the line of kings. It starts out like a blessing, giving you the tongues of the animals. But then it seizes you and draws you down, makes you a beast like the rest of them. Until finally there's not a shred of humanity in you, and you run and give tongue and taste blood, as if the pack were all you had ever known. Until no man could look on you and think you had ever been a man.' His voice had become lower and lower as he spoke, and he had not looked at me, but had turned to the fire and stared into the failing flames there. 'There's some as say a man takes on the shape of a beast then, but he kills with a man's passion rather than a beast's simple hunger. Kills for the killing . . .

'Is that what you want, fitz? To take the blood of kings that's in you, and drown it in the blood of the wild hunt? To be as a beast among beasts, simply for the sake of the knowledge it brings you? Worse yet, think on what comes before. Will the scent of fresh blood touch off your temper, will the sight of prey shut down your thoughts?' His voice grew softer still, and I heard the sickness he felt as he asked me, 'Will you wake fevered and asweat because somewhere a bitch is in season and your companion scents it? Will that be the knowledge you take to your lady's bed?'

I sat small beside him. 'I do not know,' I said in a little voice.

He turned to face me, outraged. 'You don't know?' he growled. 'I tell you where it will lead, and you say you don't know?'

My tongue was dry in my mouth and Nosy cowered at my feet. 'But I don't know,' I protested. 'How can I know what I'll do, until I've done it? How can I say?'

'Well, if you can't say, I can!' he roared, and I sensed then in full how he had banked the fires of his temper, and also how much he'd drunk that night. 'The pup goes and you stay. You stay here, in my care, where I can keep an eye on you. If Chivalry will not have me with him, it's the least I can do for him. I'll see that his son grows up a man, and not a wolf. I'll do it if it kills both of us!'

He lurched from the bench to seize Nosy by the scruff of the neck. At least, such was his intention. But the pup and I sprang clear of him. Together we rushed for the door, but the latch was fastened and before I could work it, Burrich was upon us. Nosy he shoved aside with his boot; me he seized by a shoulder and propelled me away. 'Come here, pup,' he commanded, but Nosy fled to my side. Burrich stood panting and glaring by the door, and I caught the growling undercurrent of his thoughts, the fury that taunted him to smash us both and be done with it. Control overlay it, but that brief glimpse was enough to terrify me. And when he suddenly sprang at us, I *repelled* at him with all the force of my fear.

He dropped as suddenly as a bird stoned in flight, and sat for a moment on the floor. I stooped and clutched Nosy to me. Burrich slowly shook his head as if shaking raindrops from his hair. He stood, towering over us. 'It's in his blood,' I heard him mutter to himself. 'From his damned mother's blood, and I shouldn't be surprised. But the boy has to be taught.' And then, as he looked me full in the eye, he warned me, 'Fitz. Never do that to me again. Never. Now, give me that pup.'

He advanced on us again, and as I felt the lap of his hidden wrath, I could not contain myself. I *repelled* at him again. But this time my defence was met by a wall that hurled it back at me, so that I stumbled and sank down, almost fainting, my mind pressed down by blackness. Burrich stooped over me. 'I warned you,' he said softly, and his voice was like the growling of a wolf. Then, for the last time, I felt his fingers grip Nosy's scruff. He lifted the pup bodily, and carried him, not roughly, to the door.

The latch that had eluded me he worked swiftly, and in moments I heard the heavy tromp of his boots down the stair.

In a moment I had recovered and was up, flinging myself against the door. But Burrich had locked it somehow, for I scrabbled vainly at the catch. My sense of Nosy receded as he was carried farther and farther from me, leaving in its place a desperate loneliness. I whimpered, then howled, clawing at the door, and seeking after my contact with him. There was a sudden flash of red pain, and Nosy was gone. As his canine senses deserted me completely, I screamed and cried as any six-year-old might, and hammered vainly at the thick wood planks.

It seemed hours before Burrich returned. I heard his step, and lifted my head from where I lay panting and exhausted on the doorstep. He opened the door, and then caught me deftly by the back of my shirt as I tried to dart past him. He jerked me back into the room, and then slammed the door and fastened it again. I flung myself wordlessly against it, and a whimpering rose in my throat. Burrich sat down wearily.

'Don't even think it, boy,' he cautioned me, as if he could hear my wild plans for the next time he let me out. 'He's gone. The pup's gone, and a damn shame, for he was good blood. His line was nearly as long as yours. But I'd rather waste a hound than a man.' When I did not move, he added, almost kindly, 'Let go of longing after him. It hurts less, that way.'

But I did not, and I could hear in his voice that he hadn't really expected me to. He sighed, and moved slowly as he readied himself for bed. He didn't speak to me again, just extinguished the lamp and settled himself on his bed. But he did not sleep, and it was still hours short of morning when he rose and lifted me from the floor and placed me in the warm place his body had left in the blankets. He went out again, and did not return for some hours.

As for me, I was heartsick and feverish for days. Burrich, I believe, let it be known that I had some childish ailment, and so I was left in peace. It was days before I was allowed out again, and then it was not on my own.

Afterward, Burrich was at pains to see that I was given no chance to bond with any beast. I am sure he thought he'd succeeded, and to some extent he did, in that I did not form an exclusive bond with any hound or horse. I know he meant well. But I did not feel protected by him, but confined. He was the warden that ensured my isolation with fanatical fervour. Utter loneliness was planted in me then, and sent its deep roots down into me.

THREE

Covenant

The original source of the Skill will probably remain forever shrouded in mystery. Certainly a penchant for it runs remarkably strong within the royal family, and yet it is not solely confined to the King's household. There does seem to be some truth to the folk saying, 'When the sea blood flows with the blood of the plains, the Skill will blossom'. It is interesting to note that the Outislanders seem to have no predilection for the Skill, nor the folk descended solely from the original inhabitants of the Six Duchies.

Is it the nature of the world that all things seek a rhythm, and in that rhythm a sort of peace? Certainly it has always seemed so to me. All events, no matter how earth-shaking or bizarre, are diluted within moments of their occurrence by the continuance of the necessary routines of day-to-day living. Men walking a battlefield to search for wounded among the dead will still stop to cough, to blow their noses, still lift their eyes to watch a V of geese in flight. I have seen farmers continue their ploughing and planting, heedless of armies clashing but a few miles away.

So it proved for me. I look back on myself and wonder. Separated from my mother, dragged off to a new city and clime, abandoned by my father to the care of his man, and then bereft of my puppy companion, I still rose from my bed one day and resumed a small boy's life. For me, that meant rising when Burrich awoke me, and following him to the kitchens, where I ate beside him. After that, I was Burrich's shadow. He seldom allowed me out of his sight. I'd dog his heels, watching him at his tasks, and eventually assisting him in many small ways. Evening brought a meal during which I sat at his side on a bench and ate, my manners supervised by his sharp eyes. Then it was up to his quarters, where I might spend the rest of the evening watching the fire in silence while he drank, or watching the fire in silence awaiting his return. He worked while he drank, mending or making harness, compounding a salve, or rendering down a physic for a horse. He worked, and I learned, watching him, though few words passed between us that I recall. Odd to think of two years, and most of another one passed in such a way.

I learned to do as Molly did, stealing bits of time for myself on the days when Burrich was called away to assist in a hunt or help a mare birth. Once in a great while I dared to slip out when he had drunk more than he could manage, but those were dangerous outings. When I was free, I would hastily seek out my young companions in the city and run with them for as long as I dared. I missed Nosy with a keenness as great as if Burrich had severed a limb from my body. But neither of us ever spoke of that.

Looking back, I suppose he was as lonely as I. Chivalry had not allowed Burrich to follow him into his exile. Instead, he had been left to care for a nameless bastard, and found that the bastard had a penchant for what he regarded as a perversion. And even after his leg healed he discovered he would never ride nor hunt nor even walk as well as he once had; all that had to be hard, hard for a man such as Burrich. He never whined about it to anyone, that I heard. But again, in looking back, I cannot imagine to whom he could have made complaint. Locked into loneliness were we two, and looking at one another every evening, we each saw the one we blamed for it.

Yet all things must pass, but especially time, and with the months and then the years, I came slowly to have a place in the scheme of things. I fetched for Burrich, bringing before he had thought to ask for it, and tidied up after his ministrations to the beasts, and saw to clean water for the hawks and picked ticks off dogs come home from the hunt. Folk got used to seeing me, and no longer stared. Some seemed not to see me at all. Gradually Burrich relaxed his watch on me. I came and went more freely, but still took care that he should not know of my sojourns into town.

There were other children within the keep, many about my own age. Some were even related to me, second cousins or third. Yet I never formed any real bonds with any of them. The younger ones were kept by their mothers or caretakers, the older ones had their own tasks and chores to occupy them. Most were not cruel to me; I was simply outside their circles. So, although I might not see Dick or Kerry or Molly for months, they remained my closest friends. In my explorations of the keep, and on winter evenings when all gathered in the Great Hall for minstrels, or puppet shows or indoor games, I swiftly learned where I was welcome and where I was not.

I kept myself out of the Queen's view, for whenever she saw me, she would always find some fault with my behaviour and have Burrich reproached with it. Regal, too, was a source of danger. He had most of his man's growth, but did not scruple to shove me out of his path or walk casually through whatever I had found to play with. He was capable of a pettiness and vindictiveness that I never encountered in Verity. Not that Verity ever took time with me, but our chance encounters were never unpleasant. If he noticed me, he would tousle my hair, or offer me a penny. Once a servant brought to Burrich's quarters some little wooden toys, soldiers and horses and a cart, their paint much worn, with a message that Verity had found them in a corner of his clothing chest and thought I might enjoy them. I cannot think of any other possession I ever valued more.

Cob in the stables was another danger zone. If Burrich were about, he spoke me fair and treated me evenly, but had small use for me at other times. He gave me to understand he did not want me about and underfoot where he was working. I found out eventually that he was jealous of me, and felt my care had replaced the interest Burrich had once taken in him. He was never overtly cruel, never struck me or scolded me unfairly; but I could sense his distaste for me, and avoided him.

All the men-at-arms showed a great tolerance for me. After

the street children of Buckkeep Town, they were probably the closest I had to friends. But no matter how tolerant men may be of a boy of nine or ten, there is precious little in common. I watched their bone games and listened to their stories, but for every hour I spent among their company, there were days when I did not go amongst them at all. And while Burrich never forbade me the guardroom, he did not conceal that he disapproved of the time I spent there.

So I was and was not a member of the keep community. I avoided some and I observed some and I obeyed some. But with none did I feel a bond.

Then one morning, when I was still a bit shy of my tenth year I was at play under the tables in the Great Hall, tumbling and teasing with the puppies. It was quite early in the day. There had been an occasion of some sort the day before, and the feasting had lasted the whole day and well into the night. Burrich had drunk himself senseless. Almost everyone, noble or servants, was still abed, and the kitchen had not yielded up much to my hungry venturing that morning. But the tables in the Great Hall were a trove of broken pastries and dishes of meat. There were bowls of apples as well, slabs of cheese; in short, all a boy could wish for plundering. The great dogs had taken the best bones and retreated to their own corners of the hall, leaving various pups to scrabble for the smaller bits. I had taken a rather large meat pasty under the table and was sharing it out with my chosen favourites among the pups. Ever since Nosy, I had taken care that Burrich should not see me to have too great an affinity with any one puppy. I still did not understand why he objected to my closeness to a hound, but I would not risk the life of a puppy to dispute it with him. So I was alternating bites with three whelps when I heard slow footsteps threshing across the reed-strewn floor. Two men were speaking, discussing something in low tones.

I thought it was the kitchen servants, come to clear away. I scrabbled from beneath the table to snare a few more choice leavings before they were gone.

But it was no servant who startled at my sudden appearance but the old King, my grandfather, himself. A scant step behind him, at his elbow, was Regal. His bleary eyes and rumpled doublet attested to his participation in last night's revelries. The King's new Fool, but recently acquired, pattered after them, pale eyes agoggle in an eggshell face. He was so strange a creature, with his pasty skin and motley all of blacks and whites, that I scarce dared to look at him. In contrast, King Shrewd was clear of eye, his beard and hair freshly groomed and his clothing immaculate. For an instant he was surprised, and then remarked, 'You see, Regal, it is as I was telling you. An opportunity presents itself, and someone seizes it; often someone young, or someone driven by the energies and hungers of youth. Royalty has no leisure to ignore such opportunities, or to let them be created for others.'

The King continued his stroll past me, expounding on his theme while Regal gave me a baleful look from bloodshot eyes. A flap of his hand indicated that I should disappear myself. I indicated my understanding with a quick nod, but darted first to the table. I stuffed two apples into my jerkin, and took up a mostly whole gooseberry tart when the King suddenly rounded and gestured at me. His Fool mimed an imitation. I froze where I stood.

'Look at him,' the old King commanded.

Regal glared at me, but I dared not move.

'What will you make of him?'

Regal looked perplexed. 'Him? It's the fitz. Chivalry's bastard. Sneaking and thieving as always.'

'Fool.' King Shrewd smiled, but his eyes remained flinty. The Fool, thinking himself addressed, smiled sweetly. 'Are your ears stopped with wax? Do you hear nothing I say? I asked you, not "what do you make of him?" but "what will you make of him?". There he stands, young, strong, and resourceful. His lines are every bit as royal as yours, for all that he was born on the wrong side of the sheets. So, what will you make of him? A tool? A weapon? A comrade? An enemy? Or will you leave him lying about, for someone else to take up and use against you?'

Regal squinted at me, then glanced past me and, finding no one else in the hall, returned his puzzled gaze to me. At my ankle, a pup whined a reminder that earlier we had been sharing. I warned him to hush.

'The bastard? He's only a child.'

The old King sighed. 'Today. This morning and now, he is a child. When next you turn around he will be a youth, or worse, a man, and then it will be too late for you to make anything of him. But take him now, Regal, and shape him, and a decade hence you will command his loyalty. Instead of a discontented bastard who may be persuaded to become a pretender to the throne, he will be a henchman, united to the family by spirit as well as blood. A bastard, Regal, is a unique thing. Put a signet ring on his hand and send him forth, and you have created a diplomat no foreign ruler will dare to turn away. He may safely be sent where a prince of the blood may not be risked. Imagine the uses for one who is and yet is not of the royal bloodline. Hostage exchanges. Marital alliances. Quiet work. The diplomacy of the knife.'

Regal's eyes grew round at the King's last words. For a pause, we all breathed in silence, regarding one another. When Regal spoke, he sounded as if he had dry bread caught in his throat. 'You speak of these things in front of the boy. Of using him, as a tool, a weapon. You think he will not remember your words when he is grown?'

King Shrewd laughed, and the sound rang against the stone walls of the Great Hall. 'Remember them? Of course he will. I count on it. Look at his eyes, Regal. There is intelligence there, and possibly potential Skill. I'd be a fool to lie to him. More stupid still simply to begin his training and education with no explanation, for that would leave his mind fallow for whatever seeds others might plant there. Isn't it so, boy?'

He was regarding me steadily and I suddenly realized I was returning his look. For all of his speech our gazes had been locked as we read one another. In the eyes of the man who was my grandfather was honesty, of a rocky, bony sort. There was no comfort in it, but I knew I could always count on it to be there. I nodded slowly.

'Come here.'

I walked to him slowly. When I reached him, he got down on one knee, to be eye-to-eye with me. The Fool knelt solemnly beside us, looking earnestly from face to face. Regal glared down at all of us. At the time I never grasped the irony of the old

King genuflecting to his bastard grandson. So I was solemn as he took the tart from my hands and tossed it to the puppies who had trailed after me. He drew a pin from the folds of silk at his throat and solemnly pushed it through the simple wool of my shirt.

'Now you are mine,' he said, and made that claiming of me more important than any blood we shared. 'You need not eat any man's leavings. I will keep you, and I will keep you well. If any man or woman ever seeks to turn you against me by offering you more than I do, then, come to me, and tell me of the offer, and I shall meet it. You will never find me a stingy man, nor be able to cite ill-use as a reason for treason against me. Do you believe me, boy?'

I nodded, in the mute way that was still my habit, but his steady brown eyes demanded more.

'Yes, sir.'

'Good. I will be issuing some commands regarding you. See that you comply with them. If any seem strange to you, speak to Burrich. Or to myself. Simply come to the door of my chamber, and show that pin. You'll be admitted.'

I glanced down at the red stone that winked in a nest of silver. 'Yes, sir,' I managed again.

'Ah,' he said softly, and I sensed a trace of regret in his voice, and wondered what it was for. His eyes released me, and suddenly I was once more aware of my surroundings, of the puppies and the Great Hall and Regal watching me with fresh distaste on his face, and the Fool nodding enthusiastically in his vacant way. Then the King stood. When he turned away a chill went over me, as if I had suddenly shed a cloak. It was my first experience of the Skill at the hands of a master.

'You don't approve, do you, Regal?' The King's tone was conversational.

'My King may do whatever he wishes.' Sulky.

King Shrewd sighed. 'That is not what I asked you.'

'My mother and Queen will certainly not approve. Favouring the boy will only make it appear that you recognize him. It will give him ideas, and others.'

'Faugh!' The King chuckled as if amused.

Regal was instantly incensed. 'My mother the Queen will not agree with you, nor will she be pleased. My mother –'

'Has not agreed with me, nor been pleased with me for some years. I scarcely notice it any more, Regal. She will flap and squawk and tell me again that she would return to Farrow, to be Duchess there, and you Duke after her. And if very angry, she will threaten that if she did, Tilth and Farrow would rise up in rebellion, and become a separate kingdom, with her as the Queen.'

'And I as King after her!' Regal added defiantly.

Shrewd nodded to himself. 'Yes, I thought she had planted such festering treason in your mind. Listen, boy. She may scold and fling crockery at the servants, but she will never do more than that. Because she knows it is better to be queen of a peaceful kingdom than duchess of a duchy in rebellion. And Farrow has no reason to rise up against me, save the ones she invents in her head. Her ambitions have always exceeded her abilities.' He paused, and looked directly at Regal. 'In royalty, that is a most lamentable failing.'

I could feel the waves of anger Regal suppressed as he looked at the floor.

'Come along,' the King said, and Regal heeled after him, obedient as any hound. But the parting glance he cast me was venomous.

I stood and watched as the old King departed the hall. I felt an echoing loss. Strange man. Bastard though I was, he could have declared himself my grandfather, and had for the asking what he instead chose to buy. At the door, the pale Fool paused. For an instant he looked back at me, and made an incomprehensible gesture with his narrow hands. It could have been an insult or a blessing. Or simply the fluttering of a Fool's hands. Then he smiled, waggled his tongue at me, and turned to hurry after the King.

Despite the King's promises, I stuffed my jerkin front with sweet cakes. The pups and I shared them all in the shade behind the stables. It was a bigger breakfast than any of us were accustomed to, and my stomach murmured unhappily for hours afterward. The pups curled up and slept, but I wavered between dread and anticipation. Almost I hoped that nothing would come of it, that the King would forget his words to me. But he did not.

Late that evening I finally wandered up the steps and let myself into Burrich's chamber. I had spent the day pondering what the morning's words might mean for me. I could have saved myself the trouble. For as I entered, Burrich set aside the bit of harness he was mending and focused all his attention on me. He considered me in silence for a bit, and I returned his stare. Something had changed, and I feared. Ever since he had disappeared Nosy, I had believed that Burrich had the power of life and death over me as well; that a fitz could be disposed of as easily as a pup. That hadn't stopped me from developing a feeling of closeness for him; one needn't love in order to depend. That sense of being able to rely on Burrich was the only real stability I had in my life, and now I felt it trembling under me.

'So.' He spoke at last, and put a finality into the word. 'So. You had to put yourself before his eyes, did you? Had to call attention to yourself. Well. He's decided what to do with you.' He sighed, and his silence changed. For a brief time, I almost felt he pitied me. But after a bit, he spoke.

'I'm to choose a horse for you tomorrow. He suggested that it be a young one, that I train you up together. But I talked him into starting you with an older, steadier beast. One student at a time, I told him. But I've my own reasons for putting you with an animal that's . . . less impressionable. See that you behave; I'll know if you're playing about. Do we understand one another?'

I gave him a quick nod.

'Answer, fitz. You'll have to use your tongue if you'll be dealing with tutors and masters.'

'Yes, sir.'

It was so like Burrich. Entrusting a horse to me had been uppermost in his mind. With his own concern attended to, he announced the rest quite casually.

'You'll be up with the sun from now on, boy. You'll learn from me in the morning. Caring for a horse, and mastering it. And how to hunt your hounds properly, and have them mind you. A man's way of controlling beasts is what I'll teach you.' The last he emphasized heavily, and paused to be sure I understood. My heart sank, but I began a nod, then amended it to, 'Yes, sir.'

'Afternoons, they've got you. For weapons and such. Probably the Skill, eventually. In winter months, there will be indoor learning. Languages and signs. Writing and reading and numbers, I don't doubt. Histories, too. What you'll do with it all I've no idea, but mind you learn it well to please the King. He's not a man to displease, let alone cross. Wisest course of all is not to have him notice you. But I didn't warn you about that, and now it's too late.'

He cleared his throat suddenly and took a breath. 'Oh, and there's another thing that's to change.' He took up the bit of leather he'd been working on and bent over it again. He seemed to speak to his fingers. 'You'll have a proper room of your own, now. Up in the keep where all those of noble blood sleep. You'd be sleeping there right now, if you'd bothered to come in on time.'

'What? I don't understand. A room?'

'Oh, so you can be swift spoken, when you've a mind? You heard me, boy. You'll have a room of your own, up at the keep.' He paused, then went on heartily. 'I'll finally get my privacy back. Oh, and you're to be measured for clothes tomorrow as well. And boots. Though what's the sense of putting a boot on a foot that's still growing, I don't . . .'

'I don't want a room up there.' As oppressive as living with Burrich had become, I suddenly found it preferable to the unknown. I imagined a large, cold, stone room, with shadows lurking in the corners.

'Well, you're to have one,' Burrich announced relentlessly. 'And it's time and past time for it. You're Chivalry's get, even if you're not a proper-born son, and to put you down here in the stable, like a stray pup, well, it's just not fitting.'

'I don't mind it,' I ventured desperately.

Burrich lifted his eyes and regarded me sternly. 'My, my. Positively chatty tonight, aren't we?'

I lowered my eyes from his. 'You live down here,' I pointed out sullenly. 'You aren't a stray pup.'

'I'm not a prince's bastard, either,' he said tersely. 'You'll live in the keep now, fitz, and that's all.'

I dared to look at him. He was speaking to his fingers again.

'I'd rather I was a stray pup,' I made bold to say. And then all my fears broke my voice as I added, 'You wouldn't let them do this to a stray pup, changing everything all at once. When they gave the bloodhound puppy to Lord Grimsby, you sent your old shirt with it, so it would have something that smelled of home until it settled in.'

'Well,' he said, 'I didn't . . . come here, fitz. Come here, boy.'

And puppy-like, I went to him, the only master I had, and he thumped me lightly on the back and rumpled up my hair, very much as if I had been a hound.

'Don't be scared, now. There's nothing to be afraid of. And, anyway,' he said, and I heard him relenting, 'they've only told us that you're to have a room up at the keep. No one's said that you've got to sleep in it every night. Some nights, if things are a bit too quiet for you, you can find your way down here. Eh, fitz? Does that sound right to you?'

'I suppose so,' I muttered.

Change rained fast and furious on me for the next fortnight. Burrich had me up at dawn, and I was tubbed and scrubbed, the hair cut back from my eyes and the rest bound down my back in a tail such as I had seen on the older men of the keep. He told me to dress in the best clothing I had, then clicked his tongue over how small it had become on me. With a shrug he said it would have to do.

Then it was into the stables, where he showed me the mare that now was mine. She was grey, with a hint of dapple in her coat. Her mane and tail, nose and stockings were blackened as if she'd got into soot. And that, too, was her name. She was a placid beast, well shaped and well cared for. A less challenging mount would be hard to imagine. Boyish, I had hoped for at least a spirited gelding. But Sooty was my mount instead. I tried to conceal my disappointment, but Burrich must have sensed it. 'You don't think she's much, do you? Well, how much of a horse did you have yesterday, fitz, that you'd turn up your nose at a willing, healthy beast like Sooty? She's with foal by that nasty bay stallion of Lord Temperance, so see you treat her gently. Cob's had her training until now; he'd hoped to make a chase horse out of her. But I decided she'd suit you better.

He's a bit put out over it, but I've promised him he can start again with the foal.'

Burrich had adapted an old saddle for me, vowing that regardless of what the King might say, I'd have to show myself a horseman before he'd let a new one be made for me. Sooty stepped out smoothly and answered the reins and my knees promptly. Cob had done wonderfully with her. Her temperament and mind reminded me of a quiet pond. If she had thoughts, they were not about what we were doing, and Burrich was watching me too closely for me to risk trying to know her mind. So I rode her blind, talking to her only through my knees and the reins and the shifting of my weight. The physical effort of it exhausted me long before my first lesson was over, and Burrich knew it. But that did not mean he excused me from cleaning and feeding her, and then cleaning my saddle and tack. Every tangle was out of her mane, and the old leather shone with oil before I was allowed to go to the kitchens and eat.

But as I darted away to the kitchen's back door, Burrich's hand fell on my shoulder.

'No more of that for you,' he told me firmly. 'That's fine for men-at-arms and gardeners and such. But there's a hall where the high folk and their special servants eat. And that is where you eat now.'

And so saying, he propelled me into a dim room dominated by a long table, with another, higher table at the head of it. There were all manner of foods set out upon it, and folk busy at various stages of their meals. For when the King and Queen and Princes were absent from the high table, as was the case today, no one stood upon formalities.

Burrich nudged me to a place on the left side of the table, above the mid-point but not by much. He himself ate on the same side, but lower. I was hungry, and no one was staring hard enough to unnerve me, so I made short work of a largish meal. Food pilfered directly from the kitchen had been hotter and fresher. But such matters do not count to a growing boy, and I ate well after my empty morning.

My stomach full, I was thinking of a certain sandy embankment, warmed by the afternoon sun and replete with rabbit holes,

where the hound pups and I often spent sleepy afternoons. I
started to rise from the table, but immediately there was a boy
behind me, saying, 'Master?'

I looked around to see who he was speaking to, but everyone
else was busy at trenchers. He was taller than I was, and older
by several summers, so I stared up at him in amazement when he
looked me in the eye and repeated, 'Master? Have you finished
eating?'

I bobbed my head in a nod, too surprised to speak.

'Then you're to come with me. Hod's sent me. You're expected
for weapons practice on the court this afternoon. If Burrich is
finished with you, that is.'

Burrich suddenly appeared by my side and astonished me by
going down on one knee beside me. He tugged my jerkin straight
and smoothed my hair back as he spoke.

'As finished as I'm likely to be for a while. Well, don't look
so startled, fitz. Did you think the King was not a man of his
word? Wipe your mouth and be on your way. Hod is a sterner
master than I am; tardiness will not be tolerated on the weapons
court. Hurry along with Brant, now.'

I obeyed him with a sinking heart. As I followed the boy from
the hall, I tried to imagine a master stricter than Burrich. It was
a frightening idea.

Once outside the hall, the boy quickly dropped his fine
manners. 'What's your name?' he demanded as he led me down
the gravelled pathway to the armoury and the practice courts that
fronted it.

I shrugged and glanced aside, pretending a sudden interest in
the shrubbery that bordered the path.

Brant snorted knowingly. 'Well, they got to call you something.
What's old game-leg Burrich call you?'

The boy's obvious disdain for Burrich so surprised me that I
blurted out, 'Fitz. He calls me fitz.'

'Fitz?' He snickered. 'Yeah, he would. Direct spoken is the old
gimper.'

'A boar savaged his leg,' I explained. This boy spoke as if
Burrich's limp were something foolish he did for show. For some
reason, I felt stung by his mockery.

'I know that!' He snorted disdainfully. 'Ripped him right down to the bone. Big old tusker, was going to take Chiv down, until Burrich got in the way. Got Burrich instead, and half a dozen of the hounds, is what I hear.' We went through an opening in an ivy-covered wall, and the exercise courts suddenly spread out before us. 'Chiv had gone in thinking he just had to finish the pig, when up it jumped and came after him. Snapped the Prince's lance turning on him, too, is what I hear.'

I'd been following at the boy's heels, hanging on his words when he suddenly rounded on me. I was so startled I all but fell, scrambling backwards. The older boy laughed at me. 'Guess it must have been Burrich's year for taking on Chivalry's fortunes, hey? That's what I hear the men saying. That Burrich took Chivalry's death and changed it into a lame leg for himself, and that he took on Chiv's bastard, and made a pet of him. What I'd like to know is, how come you're to have arms training all of a sudden? Yes, and a horse too, from what I hear?'

There was something more than jealousy in his tone. I have since come to know that many men always see another's good fortune as a slight to themselves. I felt his rising hostility as if I'd entered a dog's territory unannounced. But a dog I could have touched minds with and reassured of my intentions. With Brant there was only the hostility, like a storm rising. I wondered if he were going to hit me, and if he expected me to fight back or retreat. I had nearly decided to run when a portly figure dressed all in grey appeared behind Brant and took a firm grip on the back of his neck.

'I hear the King said he was to have training, yes, and a horse to learn horsemanship on. And that is enough for me, and it should be more than enough for you, Brant. And, from what I hear, you were told to fetch him here, and then to report to Master Tullume, who has errands for you. Isn't that what you heard?'

'Yes, ma'am.' Brant's pugnaciousness was suddenly transformed into bobbing agreement.

'And while you're "hearing" all this vital gossip, I might point out to you that no wise man tells all he knows. And that he who carries tales has little else in his head. Do you understand me, Brant?'

'I think so, ma'am.'

'You think so? Then I shall be plainer. Stop being a nosy little gossip and attend to your chores. Be diligent and willing, and perhaps folk will start gossiping that you are my "pet". I could see that you are kept too busy for gossip.'

'Yes, ma'am.'

'You, boy.' Brant was already hurrying up the path as she rounded on me. 'Follow me.'

The old woman didn't wait to see if I obeyed or not. She simply set out at a businesslike walk across the open practice fields that had me trotting to keep up. The packed earth of the field was baked hard and the sun beat down on my shoulders. Almost instantly, I was sweating. But the woman appeared to find no discomfort in her rapid pace.

She was dressed all in grey: a long, dark grey over-tunic, lighter grey leggings, and over all a grey apron of leather that came nearly to her knees. A gardener of some sort, I surmised, though I wondered at the soft grey boots she wore.

'I've been sent for lessons . . . with Hod,' I managed to pant out.

She nodded curtly. We reached the shade of the armoury and my eyes widened gratefully after the glare of the open courts.

'I'm to be taught arms and weaponry,' I told her, just in case she had mistaken my original words.

She nodded again and pushed open a door in the barn-like structure that was the outer armoury. Here, I knew, the practice weapons were kept. The good iron and steel were up in the keep itself. Within the armoury was a gentle halflight, and a slight coolness, along with a smell of wood and sweat and fresh strewn reeds. She did not hesitate, and I followed her to a rack that supported a supply of peeled poles.

'Choose one,' she told me, the first words she'd spoken since directing me to follow her.

'Hadn't I better wait for Hod?' I asked timidly.

'I am Hod,' she replied impatiently. 'Now pick yourself a stave, boy. I want a bit of time alone with you, before the others come. To see what you're made of and what you know.'

It did not take her long to establish that I knew next to nothing, and was easily daunted. After but a few knocks and parries with her own brown rod, she easily caught mine a clip that sent it spinning from my stung hands.

'Hm,' she said, not harshly nor kindly. The same sort of noise a gardener might make over a seed potato that had a bit of blight on it. I quested out toward her, and found the same sort of quietness I'd encountered in the mare. She had none of Burrich's guardedness toward me. I think it was the first time I realized that some people, like some animals, were totally unaware of my reaching out toward them. I might have quested further into her mind, except that I was so relieved at not finding any hostility that I feared to stir any. So I stood small and still before her inspection.

'Boy, what are you called?' she demanded suddenly.

Again. 'Fitz.'

She frowned at my soft words. I drew myself up straighter and spoke louder. 'Fitz is what Burrich calls me.'

She flinched slightly. 'He would. Calls a bitch a bitch, and a bastard a bastard, does Burrich. Well . . . I suppose I see his reasons. Fitz you are, and Fitz you'll be called by me as well. Now. I shall show you why the pole you selected was too long for you, and too thick. And then you shall select another.'

And she did, and I did, and she took me slowly through an exercise that seemed infinitely complex then, but by the end of the week was no more difficult than braiding my horse's mane. We finished just as the rest of her students came trooping in. There were four of them, all within a year or two of my age, but all more experienced than I. It made for an awkwardness, as there were now an odd number of students, and no one particularly wanted the new one as a sparring partner.

Somehow I survived the day, though the memory of how fades into a blessedly vague haze. I remember how sore I was when she finally dismissed us; how the others raced up the path and back to the keep while I trailed dismally behind them, berating myself for ever coming to the King's attention. It was a long climb to the keep, and the hall was crowded and noisy. I was too weary to eat much. Stew and bread, I think, were all I had, and I had left the table and was limping toward the door, thinking only of the warmth and quiet of the stables, when Brant again accosted me.

'Your chamber is ready,' was all he said.

I shot a desperate look at Burrich, but he was engaged in conversation with the man next to him. He didn't notice my plea at all. So once more I found myself following Brant, this time up a wide flight of stone steps, into a part of the keep I had never explored.

We paused on a landing, and he took up a candelabrum from a table there and kindled its tapers. 'Royal family lives down this wing,' he casually informed me. 'The King has a bedroom big as the stable down at the end of this hallway.'

I nodded, blindly believing all he told me, though I later discovered that an errand boy such as Brant would never have penetrated the royal wing. That would be for more important lackeys. Up another flight he took me, and again paused. 'Visitors get rooms here,' he said, gesturing with the light so that the wind of his motion set the flames to streaming. 'Important ones, that is.'

And up another flight we went, the steps perceptibly narrowing from the first two. At the next landing we paused again, and I looked with dread up an even narrower and steeper flight of steps. But Brant did not take me that way. Instead we went down this new wing, three doors down, and then he slid a latch on a plank door and shouldered it open. It swung heavily and not smoothly. 'Room hasn't been used in a while,' he observed cheerily. 'But now it's yours and you're welcome to it.' And with that he set the candelabrum down on a chest, plucked one candle from it and left. He pulled the heavy door closed behind him as he went, leaving me in the semi-darkness of a large and unfamiliar room.

Somehow I refrained from running after him or opening the door. Instead, I took up the candelabrum and lit the wall sconces. Two other sets of candles set the shadows writhing back into the corners. There was a fireplace with a pitiful effort at a fire in it. I poked it up a bit, more for light than for heat, and set to exploring my new quarters.

They consisted of a simple square room with a single window. Stone walls, of the same stone as that under my feet, were softened only by a tapestry hung on one wall. I held my candle high to study it, but could not illuminate much. I could make out a gleaming and winged creature of some sort, and a kingly personage in supplication before it. I was later informed it was King Wisdom being befriended by the Elderling. At the time it seemed menacing to me. I turned aside from it.

Someone had made a perfunctory effort at freshening the room. There was a scattering of clean reeds and herbs on the floor, and the feather bed had a fat, freshly shaken look to it. The two blankets on it were of good wool. The bed curtains had been pulled back and the chest and bench that were the other furnishings had been dusted. To my inexperienced eyes, it was a rich room indeed. A real bed, with coverings and hangings about it, and a bench with a cushion, and a chest to put things in were more furniture than I could recall having to myself before. There was also the fireplace, that I boldly added another piece of wood to, and the window, with an oak seat before it, shuttered now against the night air, but probably looking out over the sea.

The chest was a simple one, cornered with brass fittings. The outside of it was dark, but when I opened it, the interior was light-coloured and fragrant. Inside I found my limited wardrobe, brought up from the stables. Two nightshirts had been added to it, and a woollen blanket was rolled up in the corner of the chest. That was all. I took out a nightshirt and closed the chest.

I set the nightshirt down on the bed, and then clambered up myself. It was early to be thinking of sleep, but my body ached and there seemed nothing else for me to do. Down in the stable room by now Burrich would be sitting and drinking and mending harness or whatever. There would be a fire in the hearth, and the muffled sounds of horses as they shifted in their stalls below. The room would smell of leather and oil and Burrich himself, not dank stone and dust. I pulled the nightshirt over my head and nudged my clothes to the foot of the bed. I nestled into the feather bed; it was cool and my skin stood up in goose-bumps. Slowly my body heat warmed it and I began to relax. It had been a full and strenuous day. Every muscle I possessed seemed to be both aching and tired. I knew I should rise once more, to put the candles out, but I could not summon the energy.

Nor the will-power to blow them out and let a deeper darkness flood the chamber. So I drowsed, half-lidded eyes watching the struggling flames of the small hearthfire. I wished idly for something else, for any situation that was neither this forsaken chamber nor the tenseness of Burrich's room. For a restfulness that perhaps I had once known somewhere else but could no longer recall. And so I drowsed into an oblivion.

FOUR

Apprenticeship

A story is told of King Victor, he who conquered the inland territories that became eventually the Duchy of Farrow. Very shortly after adding the lands of Sandsedge to his rulings, he sent for the woman who would, had Victor not conquered her land, have been the Queen of Sandsedge. She travelled to Buckkeep in much trepidation, fearing to go, but fearing more the consequences to her people if she appealed to them to hide her. When she arrived, she was both amazed and somewhat chagrined that Victor intended to use her, not as a servant, but as a tutor to his children, that they might learn both the language and customs of her folk. When she asked him why he chose to have them learn of her folk's ways, he replied, 'A ruler must be ruler of all his people, for one can only rule what one knows.' Later, she became the willing wife of his eldest son, and took the name Queen Graciousness at her coronation.

I awoke to sunlight in my face. Someone had entered my chamber and opened the window shutters to the day. A basin, cloth and jug of water had been left on top of the chest. I was grateful for them, but not even washing my face refreshed me. Sleep had left me sodden and I recall feeling uneasy that someone could enter my chamber and move freely about without awakening me.

As I had guessed, the window looked out over the sea, but I didn't have much time to devote to the view. A glance at the sun told me that I had overslept. I flung on my clothes and hastened down to the stables without pausing for breakfast.

But Burrich had little time for me that morning. 'Get back up to the keep,' he advised me. 'Mistress Hasty already sent Brant down here to look for you. She's to measure you for clothing. Best go find her quickly; she lives up to her name, and won't appreciate your upsetting her morning routine.'

My trot back up to the keep reawakened all my aches of the day before. Much as I dreaded seeking out this Mistress Hasty and being measured for clothing I was certain I didn't need, I was relieved not to be on horseback again this morning.

After querying my way up from the kitchens, I finally found Mistress Hasty in a room several doors down from my bedchamber. I paused shyly at the door and peered in. Three tall windows were flooding the room with sunlight and a mild salt breeze. Baskets of yarn and dyed wool were stacked against one wall, while a tall shelf on another wall held a rainbow of cloth goods. Two young women were talking over a loom, and in the far corner a lad not much older than I was rocking to the gentle pace of a spinningwheel. I had no doubt that the woman with her broad back to me was Mistress Hasty.

The two young women noticed me and paused in their conversation. Mistress Hasty turned to see where they stared, and a moment later I was in her clutches. She didn't bother with names or explaining what she was about. I found myself up on a stool, being turned and measured and hummed over, with no regard for my dignity or indeed my humanity. She disparaged my clothes to the young women, remarked very calmly that I quite reminded her of young Chivalry, and that my measurements and colouring were much the same as his had been when he was my age. She then demanded their opinions as she held up bolts of different goods against me.

'That one,' said one of the loom-women. 'That blue quite flatters his darkness. It would have looked well on his father. Quite a mercy that Patience never has to see the boy. Chivalry's stamp is much too plain on his face to leave her any pride at all.'

And as I stood there, draped in woolgoods, I heard for the first time what every other person in Buckkeep knew full well. The weaving-women discussed in detail how the word of my existence reached Buckkeep and Patience long before my father could tell her himself, and of the deep anguish it caused her. For Patience was barren, and though Chivalry had never spoken a word against her, all guessed how difficult it must be for an heir such as he to have no child eventually to assume his title. Patience took my existence as the ultimate rebuke, and her health, never sound after so many miscarriages, completely broke along with her spirit. It was for her sake as well as for propriety that Chivalry had given up his throne, and taken his invalid wife back to the warm and gentle lands that were her home province. Word was that they lived well and comfortably there, that Patience's health was slowly mending, and that Chivalry, substantially quieter a man than he had been before, was gradually learning stewardship of his vineyard-rich valley. A pity that Patience blamed Burrich as well for Chivalry's lapse in morals, and had declared she could no longer abide the sight of him. For between the injury to his leg and Chivalry's abandonment of him, old Burrich just wasn't the man he had been. Was a time when no woman of the keep walked quickly past him; to catch his eye was to make yourself the envy of nearly anyone old enough to wear skirts. And now? Old Burrich, they called him, and him still in his prime – so unfair, as if any manservant had any say over what his master did. But it was all to the good anyway, they supposed. And didn't Verity, after all, make a much better King-in-Waiting than had Chivalry? So rigorously noble was Chivalry that he made all others feel slatternly and stingy in his presence; he'd never allowed himself a moment's respite from what was right, and while he was too chivalrous to sneer at those who did, one always had the feeling that his perfect behaviour was a silent reproach to those with less self-discipline. Ah, but then here was the bastard, now, though, after all those years, and well, here was the proof that he hadn't been the man he'd pretended to be. Verity, now there was a man among men, a king folk could look to and see as royalty. He rode hard, and soldiered alongside his men, and if he was occasionally drunk or had at times been less than discreet, well, he owned up to it, honest as his name. Folk could understand a man like that, and follow him.

To all this I listened avidly, if mutely, while several fabrics were held against me, debated and selected. I gained a much deeper understanding of why the keep children left me to play alone. If the women considered that I might have thoughts or feelings about their conversation, they showed no sign of it. The only remark I remember Mistress Hasty making to me specifically was that I should take greater care in washing my neck. Then Mistress Hasty shooed me from the room as if I were an annoying chicken, and I found myself finally heading to the kitchens for some food.

That afternoon I was back with Hod, practising until I was sure my stave had mysteriously doubled its weight. Then food, and bed, and up again in the morning and back to Burrich's tutelage. My learning filled my days, and any spare time I found was swallowed up with the chores associated with my learning, whether it was tack-care for Burrich, or sweeping the armoury and putting it back in order for Hod. In due time I found not one, or even two, but three entire sets of clothing, including stockings, set out one afternoon on my bed. Two were of fairly ordinary stuff, in a familiar brown that most of the children my age seemed to wear, but one was of thin blue cloth, and on the breast was a buck's head, done in silver thread. Burrich and the other men-at-arms wore a leaping buck as their emblem. I had only seen the buck's head on the jerkins of Regal and Royal. So I looked at it and wondered, but wondered too, at the slash of red stitching that cut it diagonally, marching right over the design.

'It means you're a bastard,' Burrich told me bluntly when I asked him about it. 'Of acknowledged royal blood, but a bastard all the same. That's all. It's just a quick way of showing you've royal blood, but aren't of the true line. If you don't like it, you can change it. I am sure the King would grant it. A name and a crest of your own.'

'A name?'

'Certainly. It's a simple enough request. Bastards are rare in the noble houses, especially so in the King's own. But they aren't unheard of.' Under the guise of teaching me the proper care of a saddle, we were going through the tack room, looking over all the old and unused tack. Maintaining and salvaging old tack was one of Burrich's odder fixations. 'Devise a name and a crest for yourself, and then ask the King . . .'

'What name?'

'Why, any name you like. This looks as if it's ruined; someone put it away damp and it mildewed. But we'll see what we can do with it.'

'It wouldn't feel real.'

'What?'

He held an armload of smelly leather out toward me. I took it.

'A name I just put to myself. It wouldn't feel as if it was really mine.'

'Well, what do you intend to do, then?'

I took a breath. 'The King should name me. Or you should.' I steeled myself. 'Or my father. Don't you think?'

Burrich frowned. 'You get the most peculiar notions. Just think about it yourself for a while. You'll come up with a name that fits.'

'Fitz,' I said sarcastically, and I saw Burrich clamp his jaw.

'Let's just mend this leather,' he suggested quietly.

We carried it to his workbench and started wiping it down. 'Bastards aren't that rare,' I observed. 'And in town, their parents name them.'

'In town, bastards aren't so rare,' Burrich agreed after a moment. 'Soldiers and sailors whore around. It's a common way for common folk. But not for royalty. Or for anyone with a bit of pride. What would you have thought of me, when you were younger, if I'd gone out whoring at night, or brought women up to the room? How would you see women now? Or men? It's fine to fall in love, Fitz, and no one begrudges a young woman or man a kiss or two. But I've seen what it's like down in Bingtown. Traders bring pretty girls or well-made youths to the market like so many chickens or potatoes. And the children they end up bearing may have names, but they don't have much else. And even when they marry, they don't stop their . . . habits. If ever I find the right woman, I'll want her to know I won't be looking at another. And I'll want to know all my children are mine.' Burrich was almost impassioned.

I looked at him miserably. 'So what happened with my father?'

He looked suddenly weary. 'I don't know, boy. I don't know. He was young, just twenty or so. And far from home, and trying to shoulder a heavy burden. Those are neither reasons nor excuses. But it's as much as either of us will ever know.'

And that was that.

My life went round in its settled routine. There were evenings that I spent in the stables, in Burrich's company, and more rarely, evenings that I spent in the Great Hall when some travelling minstrel or puppet show arrived. Once in a great while, I could slip out for an evening down in town, but that meant paying the next day for missed sleep. Afternoons were inevitably spent with some tutor or instructor. I came to understand that these were my summer lessons, and that in winter I would be introduced to the kind of learning that came with pens and letters. I was kept busier than I had ever been in my young life. But despite my schedule, I found myself mostly alone.

Loneliness.

It found me every night as I vainly tried to find a small and cosy spot in my big bed. When I had slept above the stables in Burrich's rooms, my nights had been muzzy, my dreams heathery with the warm and weary contentment of the well-used animals that slept and shifted and thudded in the night below me. Horses and dogs dream, as anyone who has ever watched a hound yipping and twitching in dream pursuit knows. Their dreams had been like the sweet-rising waft from a baking of good bread. But now, isolated in a room walled with stone, I finally had time for all those devouring, aching dreams that are the portion of humans. I had no warm dam to cosy against, no sense of siblings or kin stabled nearby. Instead I would lie awake and wonder about my father and my mother, and how both could have dismissed me from their lives so easily. I heard the talk that others exchanged so carelessly over my head, and interpreted their comments in my own terrifying way. I wondered what would become of me when I was grown and old King Shrewd dead and gone. I wondered, occasionally, if Molly Nosebleed and Kerry missed me, or if they accepted my sudden disappearance as easily as they had accepted my coming. But mostly I ached with loneliness, for in all that great keep, there were none I sensed as friend. None save the beasts, and Burrich had forbidden me to have any closeness with them.

One evening I had gone wearily to bed, only to torment myself with my fears until sleep grudgingly pulled me under. Light in my face awoke me, but I came awake knowing something was wrong. I hadn't slept long enough, and this light was yellow and wavering, unlike the whiteness of the sunlight that usually spilled in my window. I stirred unwillingly and opened my eyes.

He stood at the foot of my bed, holding aloft a lamp. This in itself was a rarity at Buckkeep, but more than the buttery light from the lamp held my eyes. The man himself was strange. His robe was the colour of undyed sheep's wool that had been washed, but only intermittently and not recently. His hair and beard were about the same hue and their untidiness gave the same impression. Despite the colour of his hair, I could not decide how old he was. There are some poxes that will scar a man's face with their passage. But I had never seen a man marked as he was, with scores of tiny pox scars, angry pinks and reds like small burns, and livid even in the lamp's yellow light. His hands were all bones and tendons wrapped in papery white skin. He was peering at me, and even in the lamplight his eyes were the most piercing green I had ever seen. They reminded me of a cat's eyes when it is hunting; the same combination of joy and fierceness. I pulled my quilt up higher under my chin.

'You're awake,' he said. 'Good. Get up and follow me.'

He turned abruptly from my bedside and walked away from the door, to a shadowed corner of my room between the hearth and the wall. I didn't move. He glanced back at me, held the lamp higher. 'Hurry up, boy,' he said irritably and rapped the stick he leaned on against my bed post.

I got out of bed, wincing as my bare feet hit the cold floor. I reached for my clothes and shoes, but he wasn't waiting for me. He glanced back once, to see what was delaying me, and the piercing look was enough to make me drop my clothes and quake.

I followed, wordlessly, in my nightshirt, for no reason I could explain to myself, except that he had suggested it. I followed him to a door that had never been there, and up a narrow flight of winding steps that were lit only by the lamp he held above his head. His shadow fell behind him and over me, so that I walked in a shifting darkness, feeling each step with my feet. The stairs were cold stone, worn and smooth and remarkably even. And they went up, and up, and up, until it seemed to me that we had climbed past the height of any tower the keep possessed. A chill breeze flowed up those steps and up my nightshirt, shrivelling me with more than mere cold. And we went up, and then finally he was pushing open a substantial door that nonetheless moved silently and easily. We entered a chamber.

It was lit warmly by several lamps, suspended from an unseen ceiling on fine chains. The chamber was large, certainly three times the size of my own. One end of it beckoned me. It was dominated by a massive wooden bedframe fat with feather mattresses and cushions. There were carpets on the floor, overlapping one another with their scarlets and verdant greens and blues both deep and pale. There was a table made of wood the colour of wild honey, and on it sat a bowl of fruits so perfectly ripe that I could smell their fragrances. Parchment books and scrolls were scattered about carelessly as if their rarity were of no concern. All three walls were draped with tapestries that depicted open, rolling country with wooded foothills in the distance. I started toward it.

'This way,' said my guide, and relentlessly led me to the other end of the chamber.

Here was a different spectacle. A stone slab of a table dominated it, its surface much stained and scorched. Upon it were various tools, containers and implements, a scale, a mortar and pestle, and many things I couldn't name. A fine layer of dust overlay much of it, as if projects had been abandoned in midcourse, months or even years ago. Beyond the table was a rack which held an untidy collection of scrolls, some edged in blue or gilt. The scent of the room was at once pungent and aromatic; bundles of herbs were drying on another rack. I heard a rustling and caught a glimpse of movement in a far corner, but the man gave me no time to investigate. The fireplace that should have warmed this end of the room gaped black and cold. The old embers in it looked damp and settled. I lifted my eyes from my perusal to look at my guide. The dismay on my face seemed to surprise him. He turned from me and slowly surveyed the room himself. He considered it for a bit, and then I sensed an embarrassed disgruntlement from him.

'It is a mess. More than a mess, I suppose. But, well. It's been a while, I suppose. And longer than a while. Well. It's soon put to rights. But first, introductions are in order. And I suppose it is a bit nippy to be standing about in just a nightshirt. This way, boy.'

I followed him to the comfortable end of the room. He seated himself in a battered wooden chair that was overdraped with blankets. My bare toes dug gratefully into the nap of a woollen rug. I stood before him, waiting, as those green eyes prowled over me. For some minutes the silence held. Then he spoke.

'First, let me introduce you to yourself. Your pedigree is written all over you. Shrewd chose to acknowledge it, for all his denials wouldn't have sufficed to convince anyone otherwise.' He paused for an instant, and smiled as if something amused him. 'A shame Galen refuses to teach you the Skill; but years ago, it was restricted, for fear it would become too common a tool. I'll wager if old Galen were to try to teach you, he'd find you apt. But we have no time to worry about what won't happen.' He sighed meditatively, and was silent for a moment. Abruptly he went on, 'Burrich's shown you how to work, and how to obey. Two things that Burrich himself excels at. You're not especially strong, or fast, or bright. Don't think you are. But you'll have the stubbornness to wear down anyone stronger, or faster or brighter than yourself. And that's more of a danger to you than to anyone else. But that is not what is now most important about you.

'You are the King's man now. And you must begin to understand, now, right now, that that is the most important thing about you. He feeds you, he clothes you, he sees you are educated. And all he asks in return, for now, is your loyalty. Later he will ask your service. Those are the conditions under which I will teach you. That you are the King's man, and loyal to him completely. For if you are otherwise, it would be too dangerous to educate you in my art.' He paused and for a long moment we simply looked at one another. 'Do you agree?' he asked, and it was not a simple question but the sealing of a bargain.

'I do,' I said, and then, as he waited, 'I give you my word.'

'Good.' He spoke the word heartily. 'Now. On to other things. Have you ever seen me before?'

'No.' I realized for an instant how strange that was. For, though there were often strangers in the keep, this man had obviously been a resident for a long, long time. And almost all those who lived there I knew by sight if not by name.

'Do you know who I am, boy? Or why you're here?'

I shook my head a quick negative to each question. 'Well, no one else does either. So you mind it stays that way. Make yourself clear on that: you speak to no one of what we do here, nor of anything you learn. Understand that?'

My nod must have satisfied him, for he seemed to relax in the chair. His bony hands gripped the knobs of his knees through his woollen robe. 'Good. Good. Now. You can call me Chade. And I shall call you?' He paused and waited, but when I did not offer a name, he filled in, 'Boy. Those are not names for either of us, but they'll do, for the time we'll have together. So. I'm Chade, and I'm yet another teacher that Shrewd has found for you. It took him a while to remember I was here, and then it took him a space to nerve himself to ask me. And it took me even longer to agree to teach you. But all that's done now. As to what I'm to teach you . . . well.'

He rose and moved to the fire. He cocked his head as he stared into it, then stooped to take a poker and stir the embers to fresh flames. 'It's murder, more or less. Killing people. The fine art of diplomatic assassination. Or blinding, or deafening. Or a weakening of the limbs, or a paralysis or a debilitating cough or impotency. Or early senility, or insanity or . . . but it doesn't matter. It's all been my trade. And it will be yours, if you agree. Just know, from the beginning, that I'm going to be teaching you how to kill people. For your king. Not in the showy way Hod is teaching you, not on the battlefield where others see and cheer you on. No. I'll be teaching you the nasty, furtive, polite ways to kill people. You'll either develop a taste for it, or not. That isn't something I'm in charge of. But I'll make sure you know how. And I'll make sure of one other thing, for that was the stipulation I made with King Shrewd: that you know what you are learning, as I never did when I was your age. So. I'm to teach you to be an assassin. Is that all right with you, boy?'

I nodded again, uncertain, but not knowing what else to do.

He peered at me. 'You can speak, can't you? You're not a mute as well as a bastard, are you?'

I swallowed. 'No, sir. I can speak.'

'Well, then, do speak. Don't just nod. Tell me what you think of all this. Of who I am and what I just proposed that we do.'

Invited to speak, I yet stood dumb. I stared at the poxed face, the papery skin of his hands, and felt the gleam of his green eyes on me. I moved my tongue inside my mouth, but found only silence. His manner invited words, but his visage was still more terrifying than anything I had ever imagined.

'Boy,' he said, and the gentleness in his voice startled me into meeting his eyes. 'I can teach you even if you hate me, or if you despise the lessons. I can teach you if you are bored, or lazy or stupid. But I can't teach you if you're afraid to speak to me. At least, not the way I want to teach you. And I can't teach you if you decide this is something you'd rather not learn. But you have to tell me. You've learned to guard your thoughts so well, you're almost afraid to let yourself know what they are. But try speaking them aloud, now, to me. You won't be punished.'

'I don't much like it,' I blurted suddenly. 'The idea of killing people.'

'Ah.' He paused. 'Neither did I, when it came down to it. Nor do I, still.' He sighed suddenly, deeply. 'As each time comes, you'll decide. The first time will be hardest. But know, for now, that that decision is many years away. And in the meantime, you have much to learn.' He hesitated. 'There is this, boy – and you should remember it in every situation, not just this one – learning is never wrong. Even learning how to kill isn't wrong. Or right. It's just a thing to learn, a thing I can teach you. That's all. For now, do you think you could learn how to do it, and later decide if you wanted to do it?'

Such a question to put to a boy. Even then, something in me raised its hackles and sniffed at the idea, but child that I was, I could find no objection to raise. And curiosity was nibbling at me.

'I can learn it.'

'Good.' He smiled, but there was a tiredness to his face and he didn't seem as pleased as he might have. 'That's well enough, then. Well enough.' He looked around the room. 'We may as well begin tonight. Let's start by tidying up. There's a broom over there. Oh, but first, change out of your nightshirt into something . . . ah, there's a ragged old robe over there. That'll do for now. Can't have the washerfolk wondering why your nightshirts smell of camphor and pain's ease, can we? Now, you sweep up the floor a bit while I put away a few things.'

And so passed the next few hours. I swept, then mopped the stone floor. He directed me as I cleared the paraphernalia from the great table. I turned the herbs on their drying rack. I fed the three lizards he had caged in the corner, chopping up some sticky old meat into chunks that they gulped whole. I wiped clean a number of pots and bowls and stored them. And he worked alongside me, seeming grateful for the company, and chatted to me as if we were both old men. Or both young boys.

'No letters as yet? No ciphering. Bagrash! What's the old man thinking? Well, I shall see that remedied swiftly. You've your father's brow, boy, and just his way of wrinkling it. Has anyone ever told you that before? Ah, there you are, Slink, you rascal! What mischief have you been up to now?'

A brown weasel appeared from behind a tapestry, and we were introduced to one another. Chade let me feed Slink quails' eggs from a bowl on the table, and laughed when the little beast followed me about begging for more. He gave me a copper bracelet that I found under the table, warning that it might make my wrist green, and cautioning that if anyone asked me about it, I should say I had found it behind the stables.

At some time we stopped for honey cakes and hot, spiced wine. We sat together at a low table on some rugs before the fireplace, and I watched the firelight dancing over his scarred face and wondered why it had seemed so frightening. He noticed me watching him, and his face contorted in a smile. 'Seems familiar, doesn't it, boy? My face, I mean.'

It didn't. I had been staring at the grotesque scars on the pasty white skin. I had no idea what he meant. I stared at him questioningly, trying to figure it out.

'Don't trouble yourself about it, boy. It leaves its tracks on all of us, and sooner or later, you'll get the tumble of it. But now, well . . .' He rose, stretching so that his cassock bared his skinny white calves. 'Now it's mostly later. Or earlier, depending on which end of the day you fancy most. Time you headed back to your bed. Now. You'll remember that this is all a very dark secret, won't you? Not just me and this room, but the whole thing, waking up at night and lessons in how to kill people, and all of it.'

'I'll remember,' I told him, and then, sensing that it would mean something to him, I added, 'You have my word.'

He chuckled, and then nodded almost sadly. I changed back into my nightshirt, and he saw me down the steps. He held his glowing light by my bed as I clambered in, and then smoothed the blankets over me as no one had done since I'd left Burrich's chambers. I think I was asleep before he had even departed my bedside.

Brant was sent to wake me the next morning, so late was I in arising. I came awake groggy, my head pounding painfully. But as soon as he left the room, I sprang from my bed and raced to the corner of my room. Cold stone met my hands as I pushed against the wall there, and no crack in mortar or stone gave any sign of the secret door I felt sure must be there. Never for one instant did I think Chade had been a dream, and even if I had, there remained the simple copper bracelet on my wrist to prove he wasn't.

I dressed hurriedly and passed through the kitchens for a slab of bread and cheese that I was still eating when I got to the stables. Burrich was out of sorts with my tardiness, and found fault with every aspect of my horsemanship and stable tasks. I remember well how he berated me: 'Don't think that because you've a room up in the castle, and a crest on your jerkin, you can turn into some sprawlabout rogue who snores in his bed until all hours and then only rises to fluff at his hair. I'll not have it. Bastard you may be, but you're Chivalry's bastard, and I'll make you a man he'll be proud of.'

I paused, the grooming brushes still in my hands. 'You mean Regal, don't you?'

My unwonted question startled him. 'What?'

'When you talk about rogues who stay in bed all morning and do nothing except fuss about hair and garments, you mean how Regal is.'

Burrich opened his mouth and then shut it. His wind-reddened cheeks grew redder. 'Neither you nor I,' he muttered at last, 'are in a position to criticize any of the princes. I meant only as a general rule, that sleeping the morning away ill befits a man, and even less so a boy.'

'And never a prince.' I said this, and then stopped, to wonder where the thought had come from.

'And never a prince,' Burrich agreed grimly. He was busy in the next stall with a gelding's hot leg. The animal winced suddenly, and I heard Burrich grunt with the effort of holding him. 'Your father never slept past the sun's midpoint because he'd been drinking the night before. Of course, he had a head for wine such as I've never seen since, but there was discipline to it, too. Nor did he have some man standing by to rouse him. He got himself out of bed, and then expected those in his command to follow his example. It didn't always make him popular, but his soldiers respected him. Men like that in a leader, that he demands of himself the same thing he expects of them. And I'll tell you another thing: your father didn't waste coin on decking himself out like a peacock. When he was a younger man, before he was wed to Lady Patience, he was at dinner one evening, at one of the lesser keeps. They'd seated me not too far below him, a great honour to me, and I overheard some of his conversation with the daughter they'd seated so hopefully next to the King-in-Waiting. She'd asked him what he thought of the emeralds she wore, and he had complimented her on them. "I had wondered, sir, if you enjoyed jewels, for you wear none of them yourself tonight," she said flirtatiously. And he replied, quite seriously, that his jewels shone as brilliantly as hers, and much larger. "Oh, and where do you keep such gems, for I should dearly like to see them?" Well, he replied he'd be happy to show them to her later that evening, when it was darker. I saw her blush, expecting a tryst of some kind. And later he did invite her out onto the battlements with him, but he took with them half the dinner guests as well. And he pointed out the lights of the coast-watch towers, shining clearly in the dark, and told her that he considered those his best and dearest jewels, and that he spent the coin from her father's taxes to keep them shining so. And then he pointed out to the guests the winking lights of that lord's own watchmen in the fortifications of his keep, and told them that when they looked at their Duke, they should see those shining lights as the jewels on his brow. It was quite a compliment to the Duke and Duchess, and the other nobles there took note of it. The Outislanders had very few successful raids that summer. That was how Chivalry ruled. By example, and by the grace of his words. So should any real prince do.'

'I'm not a real prince. I'm a bastard.' It came oddly from my mouth, that word I heard so often and so seldom said.

Burrich sighed softly. 'Be your blood, boy, and ignore what anyone else thinks of you.'

'Sometimes I get tired of doing the hard things.'

'So do I.'

I absorbed this in silence for a while as I worked my way down Sooty's shoulder. Burrich, still kneeling by the grey, spoke suddenly. 'I don't ask any more of you than I ask of myself. You know that's true.'

'I know that,' I replied, surprised that he'd mentioned it further.

'I just want to do my best by you.'

This was a whole new idea to me. After a moment I asked, 'Because if you could make Chivalry proud of me, of what you'd made me into, then maybe he would come back?'

The rhythmic sound of Burrich's hands working liniment into the gelding's leg slowed, then ceased abruptly. But he remained crouched down by the horse, and spoke quietly through the wall of the stall. 'No. I don't think that. I don't suppose anything would make him come back. And even if he did,' and Burrich spoke more slowly, 'even if he did, he wouldn't be who he was. Before, I mean.'

'It's all my fault he went away, isn't it?' The words of the weaving-women echoed in my head. *But for the boy, he'd still be in line to be king.*

Burrich paused long. 'I don't suppose it's any man's fault that he's born . . .' He sighed, and the words seemed to come more reluctantly. 'And there's certainly no way a babe can make itself not a bastard. No. Chivalry brought his downfall on himself, though that's a hard thing for me to say.' I heard his hands go back to work on the gelding's leg.

'And your downfall, too.' I said it to Sooty's shoulder, softly, never dreaming he'd hear.

But a moment or two later, I heard him mutter, 'I do well enough for myself, Fitz. I do well enough.'

He finished his task and came around into Sooty's stall. 'Your tongue's wagging like the town gossip today, Fitz. What's got into you?'

It was my turn to pause and wonder. Something about Chade, I decided. Something about someone who wanted me to understand and have a say in what I was learning had freed up my tongue finally to ask all the questions I'd been carrying about for years. But because I couldn't very well say so, I shrugged, and truthfully replied, 'They're just things I've wondered about for a long time.'

Burrich grunted his acceptance of the answer. 'Well. It's an improvement that you ask, though I won't always promise you an answer. It's good to hear you speak like a man. Makes me worry less about losing you to the beasts.' He glared at me over the last words, and then gimped away. I watched him go, and remembered that first night I had seen him, and how a look from him had been enough to quell a whole room full of men. He wasn't the same man. And it wasn't just the limp that had changed the way he carried himself and how men looked at him. He was still the acknowledged master in the stables and no one questioned his authority there. But he was no longer the right hand of the King-in-Waiting. Other than watching over me, he wasn't Chivalry's man at all any more. No wonder he couldn't look at me without resentment. He hadn't sired the bastard that had been his downfall. For the first time since I had known him, my wariness of him was tinged with pity.

FIVE

Loyalties

In some kingdoms and lands, it is the custom that male children will have precedence over female in matters of inheritance. Such has never been the case in the Six Duchies. Titles are inherited solely by order of birth.

The one who inherits a title is supposed to view it as a stewardship. If a lord or lady were so foolish as to cut too much forest at once, or neglect vineyards or let the quality of the cattle become too inbred, the people of the duchy could rise up and come to ask the King's Justice. It has happened, and every noble is aware it can happen. The welfare of the people belongs to the people, and they have the right to object if their duke stewards it poorly.

When the title-holder weds, he is supposed to keep this in mind. The partner chosen must be willing to be a steward likewise. For this reason, the partner holding a lesser title must surrender it to the next younger sibling. One can only be a true steward of one holding. On occasion this has led to divisions. King Shrewd married Lady Desire, who would have been Duchess of Farrow, had she not chosen to accept his offer and become Queen instead. It is said she came to regret her decision, and convinced herself that, had she remained Duchess, her power would have been greater. She married Shrewd knowing well that she was his second queen, and that the first had already borne him two heirs. She never concealed her disdain for the two older princes, and often pointed out that as she was much higher born than King Shrewd's first queen, she considered her son Regal to be more royal than his two half-brothers. She attempted to instil this idea in others

*by her choice of name for her son. Unfortunately for her plans, most
saw this ploy as being in poor taste. Some even mockingly referred to
her as the Inland Queen, when, intoxicated, she would ruthlessly claim
that she had the political influence to unite Farrow and Tilth into a
new kingdom, one that would shrug off King Shrewd's rule at her
behest. But most put her claims down to her fondness for intoxicants,
both alcoholic and herbal. It is true, however, that before she finally
succumbed to her addictions, she was responsible for nurturing the rift
between the Inland and Coastal Duchies.*

I grew to look forward to my dark-time encounters with Chade.
They never had a schedule, nor any pattern that I could discern.
A week, even two, might go by between meetings, or he might
summon me every night for a week straight, leaving me staggering
about my day-time chores. Sometimes he summoned me as soon as
the castle was abed; at other times, he called upon me in the wee
hours of the morning. It was a strenuous schedule for a growing boy,
yet I never thought of complaining to Chade or refusing one of his
calls. Nor do I think it ever occurred to him that my night lessons
presented a difficulty for me. Nocturnal himself, it must have seemed
a perfectly natural time for him to be teaching me. And the lessons
I learned were oddly suited to the darker hours of the world.

There was tremendous scope to his lessons. One evening might
be spent in laborious study of the illustrations in a great herbal
he kept, with the requirement that the next day I was to collect
six samples that matched those illustrations. He never saw fit to
hint as to whether I should look in the kitchen garden or the
darker nooks of the forest for those herbs, but find them I did,
and learned much of observation in the process.

There were games we played, too. For instance, he would tell
me that I must go on the morrow to Sara the cook and ask her
if this year's bacon were leaner than last year's. And then I must
that evening report the entire conversation back to Chade, as
close to word perfect as I could, and answer a dozen questions
for him about how she stood, and was she left-handed and did
she seem hard of hearing and what she was cooking at the time.
My shyness and reticence were never accounted a good enough

excuse for failing to execute such an assignment, and so I found myself meeting and coming to know a good many of the lesser folk of the keep. Even though my questions were inspired by Chade, every one of them welcomed my interest and was more than willing to share expertise. Without intending it, I began to garner a reputation as a 'sharp youngster' and a 'good lad'. Years later I realized that the lesson was not just a memory exercise but also instruction in how to befriend the commoner folk, and to learn their minds. Many's the time since then that a smile, a compliment on how well my horse had been cared for, and a quick question put to a stable-boy brought me information that all the coin in the kingdom couldn't have bribed out of him.

Other games built my nerve as well as my powers of observation. One day Chade showed me a skein of yarn, and told me that, without asking Mistress Hasty, I must find out exactly where she kept the supply of yarn that matched it, and what herbs had been used in the dyeing of it. Three days later I was told I must spirit away her best shears, conceal them behind a certain rack of wines in the wine cellar for three hours, and then return them to where they had been, all undetected by her or anyone else. Such exercises initially appealed to a boy's natural love of mischief, and I seldom failed at them. When I did, the consequences were my own look-out. Chade had warned me that he would not shield me from anybody's wrath, and suggested that I have a worthy tale ready to explain away being where I should not be, or possessing that which I had no business possessing.

I learned to lie very well. I do not think it was taught me accidentally.

These were the lessons in my assassin's primer. And more. Sleight of hand and the art of moving stealthily. Where to strike a man to render him unconscious. Where to strike a man so that he dies without crying out. Where to stab a man so that he dies without too much blood welling out. I learned it all rapidly and well, thriving under Chade's approval of my quick mind.

Soon he began to use me for small jobs about the keep. He never told me, ahead of time, if they were tests of my skill, or actual tasks he wished accomplished. To me it made no difference; I pursued them all with a single-minded devotion to Chade and anything he commanded. In spring of that year, I treated the wine cups of a visiting delegation from the Bingtown traders so that they became much more intoxicated than they had intended. Later that same month, I concealed one puppet from a visiting puppeteer's troupe, so that he had to present the Incidence of the Matching Cups, a light-hearted little folk tale instead of the lengthy historical drama he had planned for the evening. At the High-Summer Feast, I added a certain herb to a serving-girl's afternoon pot of tea, so that she and three of her friends were stricken with loose bowels and could not wait the tables that night. In the autumn I tied a thread around the fetlock of a visiting noble's horse, to give the animal a temporary limp that convinced the noble to remain at Buckkeep two days longer than he had planned. I never knew the underlying reasons for the tasks Chade set me. At that age, I set my mind to how I would do a thing, rather than why. And that, too, was a thing that I believe it was intended I learn: to obey without asking why an order was given.

There was one task that absolutely delighted me. Even at the time, I knew that the assignment was more than a whim of Chade's. He summoned me for it in the last bit of dark before dawn. 'Lord Jessup and his lady have been visiting this last two weeks. You know them by sight; he has a very long moustache, and she constantly fusses with her hair, even at the table. You know who I mean?'

I frowned. A number of nobles had gathered at Buckkeep, to form a council to discuss the increase in raids from the Outislanders. I gathered that the Coastal Duchies wanted more warships, but the Inland Duchies opposed sharing the taxes for what they saw as a purely coastal problem. Lord Jessup and Lady Dahlia were Inlanders. Jessup and his moustaches both seemed to have fitful temperaments and to be constantly impassioned. Lady Dahlia, on the other hand, seemed to take no interest at all in the council, but spent most of her time exploring Buckkeep.

'She wears flowers in her hair, all the time? They keep falling out?'

'That's the one,' Chade replied emphatically. 'Good. You know her. Now, here's your task, and I've no time to plan it with you.

Some time today, at any moment today, she will send a page to Prince Regal's room. The page will deliver something; a note, a flower, an object of some kind. You will remove the object from Regal's room before he sees it. You understand?'

I nodded and opened my mouth to say something, but Chade stood abruptly and almost chased me from the room. 'No time; it is nearly dawn!' he declared.

I contrived to be in Regal's room, in hiding, when the page arrived. From the way the girl slipped in, I was convinced this was not her first mission. She set a tiny scroll and a flower bud on Regal's pillow, and slipped out of the room. In a moment both were in my jerkin, and later under my own pillow. I think the most difficult part of the task was refraining from opening the scroll. I turned scroll and flower over to Chade late that night.

Over the next few days, I waited, certain there would be some sort of furore, and hoping to see Regal thoroughly discomfited. But to my surprise, there was none. Regal remained his usual self, save that he was even sharper than usual, and seemed to flirt even more outrageously with every lady. As for Lady Dahlia, she suddenly took an interest in the council proceedings, and confounded her husband by becoming an ardent supporter of warship taxes. The Queen expressed her displeasure over this change of alliance by excluding Lady Dahlia from a wine-tasting in her chambers. The whole thing mystified me, but when I at last mentioned it to Chade, he rebuked me.

'Remember, you are the King's man. A task is given you, and you do it. And you should be well satisfied with yourself that you completed the given task. That is all you need to know. Only Shrewd may plan the moves and plot his game. You and I, we are playing pieces, perhaps. But we are the best of his markers; be assured of that.'

But early on, Chade found the limits of my obedience. In laming the horse, he had suggested I cut the frog of the animal's foot. I never even considered doing that. I informed him, with all the worldly wisdom of one who has grown up around horses, that there were many ways to make a horse limp without actually harming him, and that he should trust me to choose an appropriate one. To this day, I do not know how Chade felt about my refusal. He said nothing at the time to condemn it, or to suggest he approved my actions. In this as in many things, he kept his own counsel.

Once every three months or so, King Shrewd would summon me to his chambers. Usually the call for me came in the very early morning. I would stand before him, often-times while he was in his bath, or having his hair bound back in the gold-wired queue that only the King could wear, or while his man was laying out his clothes. Always the ritual was the same. He would look me over carefully, studying my growth and grooming as if I were a horse he was considering buying. He would ask a question or two, usually about my horsemanship or weapons study, and listen gravely to my brief answer. And then he would ask, almost formally, 'And do you feel I am keeping my bargain with you?'

'Sir, I do,' I would always answer.

'Then see that you keep your end of it as well,' was always his reply and my dismissal. And whatever servant attending him or opening the door for me to enter or leave never appeared to take the slightest notice of me or of the King's words at all.

Come late autumn of that year, on the very cusp of winter's tooth, I was given my most difficult assignment. Chade had summoned me up to his chambers almost as soon as I had blown out my night candle. We were sharing sweetmeats and a bit of spiced wine, sitting in front of Chade's hearth. He had been lavishly praising my latest escapade, one that required me turning inside out every shirt hung to dry on the laundry courtyard's drying-lines without getting caught. It had been a difficult task, the hardest part of which had been to refrain from laughing aloud and betraying my hiding place within a dyeing-vat when two of the younger laundry-lads had declared my prank the work of water sprites and refused to do any more washing that day. Chade, as usual, knew of the whole scenario even before I reported to him. He delighted me by letting me know that Master Lew of the launderers had decreed that Sinjon's Wort was to be hung at every corner of the court-yard and garlanded about every well to ward off sprites from tomorrow's work.

'You've a gift for this, boy,' Chade chuckled and tousled

my hair. 'I almost think there's no task I could set you that you couldn't do.'

He was sitting in his straight-backed chair before the fire, and I was on the floor beside him, leaning my back against one of his legs. He patted me the way Burrich might pat a young bird dog that had done well, and then leaned forward to say softly, 'But I've a challenge for you.'

'What is it?' I demanded eagerly.

'It won't be easy, even for one with as light a touch as yours,' he warned me.

'Try me!' I challenged him in return.

'Oh, in another month or two, perhaps, when you've had a bit more teaching. I've a game to teach you tonight, one that will sharpen your eye and your memory.' He reached into a pouch and drew out a handful of something. He opened his hand briefly in front of me; coloured stones. The hand closed. 'Were there any yellow ones?'

'Yes. Chade, what is the challenge?'

'How many?'

'Two that I could see. Chade, I bet I could do it now.'

'Could there have been more than two?'

'Possibly, if some were concealed completely under the top layer. I don't think it likely. Chade, what is the challenge?'

He opened his bony old hand, stirred the stones with his long forefinger. 'Right you were. Only two yellow ones. Shall we go again?'

'Chade, I can do it.'

'You think so, do you? Look again, here's the stones. One, two, three, and gone again. Were there any red ones?'

'Yes. Chade, what is the task?'

'Were there more red ones than blue? To bring me something personal from the King's night-table.'

'What?'

'Were there more red stones than blue ones?'

'No, I mean, what was the task?'

'Wrong, boy!' Chade announced it merrily. He opened his fist. 'See, three red and three blue. Exactly the same. You'll have to look quicker than that if you're to meet my challenge.'

'And seven green. I knew that, Chade. But . . . you want me to steal from the King?' I still couldn't believe I had heard it.

'Not steal, just borrow. As you did Mistress Hasty's shears. There's no harm in a prank like that, is there?'

'None except that I'd be whipped if I were caught. Or worse.'

'And you're afraid you'd be caught. See, I told you it had best wait a month or two, until your skills are better.'

'It's not the punishment. It's that if I were caught . . . the King and I . . . we made a bargain . . .' My words dwindled away. I stared at him in confusion. Chade's instruction was a part of the bargain Shrewd and I had made. Each time we met, before he began instructing me, he formally reminded me of that bargain. I had given to Chade, as well as to the King, my word that I would be loyal. Surely he could see that if I acted against the King, I'd be breaking my part of the bargain.

'It's a game, boy,' Chade said patiently. 'That's all. Just a bit of mischief. It's not really as serious as you seem to think it. The only reason I'm choosing it as a task is that the King's room and his things are so closely watched. Anyone can make off with a seamstress's shears. We're talking about a real bit of stealth now, to enter the King's own chambers and take something that belongs to him. If you could do that, I'd believe I'd spent my time well in teaching you. I'd feel you appreciated what I'd taught you.'

'You know I appreciate what you teach me,' I said quickly. That wasn't it at all. Chade seemed to be completely missing my point. 'I'd feel . . . disloyal. As if I was using what you'd taught me to trick the King. Almost as if I were laughing at him.'

'Ah!' Chade leaned back in his chair, a smile on his face. 'Don't let that bother you, boy. King Shrewd can appreciate a good jest when he's shown one. Whatever you take, I'll return myself to him. It will be a sign to him of how well I've taught you and how well you've learned. Take something simple if it worries you so; it needn't be the crown off his head or the ring from his finger! Just his hairbrush, or any bit of paper that's about – even his glove or belt would do. Nothing of any great value. Just a token.'

I thought I should pause to think, but I knew I didn't need to. 'I can't do it. I mean, I won't do it. Not from King Shrewd.

Name any other, anyone else's room, and I'll do it. Remember when I took Regal's scroll? You'll see, I can creep in anywhere and . . .'

'Boy?' Chade's voice came slowly, puzzled. 'Don't you trust me? I tell you it's all right. It's just a challenge we're talking about; not high treason. And this time, if you're caught, I promise I'll step right in and explain it all. You won't be punished.'

'That's not it,' I said frantically. I could sense Chade's growing puzzlement over my refusal. I scrabbled frantically within myself to find a way to explain to him. 'I promised to be loyal to Shrewd. And this . . .'

'There's nothing disloyal about this!' Chade snapped. I looked up to see angry glints in his eyes. Startled, I drew back from him. I'd never seen him glare so. 'What are you saying, boy? That I'm asking you to betray your king? Don't be an idiot. This is just a simple little test, my way of measuring you and showing Shrewd himself what you've learned, and you balk at it. And try to cover your cowardice by prattling about loyalty. Boy, you shame me. I thought you had more backbone than this, or I'd never have begun teaching you.'

'Chade!' I began in horror. His words had left me reeling. He pulled away from me, and I felt my small world rocking around me as his voice went on coldly.

'Best you get back to your bed, little boy. Think exactly how you've insulted me tonight. To insinuate I'd somehow be disloyal to our King. Crawl down the stairs, you little craven. And the next time I summon you . . . Hah, if I summon you again, come prepared to obey me. Or don't come at all. Now go.'

Never had Chade spoken to me so. I could not recall that he had even raised his voice to me. I stared, almost without comprehension, at the thin pock-scarred arm that protruded from the sleeve of his robe, at the long finger that pointed so disdainfully toward the door and the stairs. As I rose, I felt physically sick. I reeled, and had to catch hold of a chair as I passed. But I went, doing as he told me, unable to think of anything else to do. Chade, who had become the central pillar of my world, who had made me believe I was something of value, was taking it all away.

Not just his approval, but our time together, my sense that I was going to be something in my lifetime.

I stumbled and staggered down the stairs. Never had they seemed so long or so cold. The bottom door grated shut behind me, and I was left in total darkness. I groped my way to my bed, but my blankets could not warm me, nor did I find any trace of sleep that night. I tossed in agony. The worst part was that I could find no indecision in myself. I could not do the thing Chade asked of me. Therefore, I would lose him. Without his instruction, I would be of no value to the King. But that was not the agony. The agony was simply the loss of Chade from my life. I could not remember how I had managed before when I had been so alone. To return to the drudgery of living day to day, going from task to task seemed impossible.

I tried desperately to think of something to do. But there seemed no solution. I could go to Shrewd himself, show my pin and be admitted, and tell him of my dilemma. But what would he say? Would he see me as a silly little boy? Would he say I should have obeyed Chade? Worse, would he say I was right to disobey Chade and be angry with Chade? These were very difficult questions for a boy's mind, and I found no answers that helped me.

When morning finally came, I dragged myself from my bed and reported to Burrich as usual. I went about my tasks in a grey listlessness that first brought me scoldings, and then an inquiry as to the state of my belly. I told him simply that I had not slept well, and he let me off without the threatened tonic. I did no better at weapons. My state of distraction was such that I let a much younger boy deliver a stout clout to my skull. Hod scolded us both for recklessness and told me to sit down for a bit.

My head was pounding and my legs were shaky when I returned to the keep. I went to my room, for I had no stomach for the noon meal or the loud conversations that went with it. I lay on my bed, intending to close my eyes for just a moment, but fell into a deep sleep. I awoke halfway through the afternoon, and thought of the scoldings I would face for missing my afternoon lessons. But it wasn't enough to rouse me and I dropped off, only to be awakened at supper time by a serving-girl who had come to inquire after me at Burrich's behest. I staved her off by telling her I had a sour gut and was going to fast until it cleared. After she left, I drowsed but did not sleep. I couldn't. Night deepened in my unlit room, and I heard the rest of the keep go off to rest. In darkness and stillness, I lay waiting for a summons I would not dare answer. What if the door opened? I could not go to Chade, for I could not obey him. Which would be worse: if he did not summon me, or if he opened the door for me and I dared not go? I tormented myself from rock to stone, and in the grey creeping of morning I had the answer. He hadn't even bothered to call for me.

Even now, I do not like to recall the next few days. I hunched through them, so sick at heart that I could not properly eat or rest. I could not focus my mind on any task, and took the rebukes that my teachers gave me with bleak acceptance. I acquired a headache that never ceased, and my stomach stayed so clenched on itself that food held no interest for me. The very thought of eating made me weary. Burrich put up with it for two days before he cornered me, and forced down me both a worming draught and a blood tonic. The combination made me vomit up what little I'd eaten that day. He made me wash out my mouth with plum wine afterwards, and to this day I cannot drink plum wine without gagging. Then, to my weary amazement, he dragged me up the stairs to his loft and gruffly ordered me to rest there for the day. When evening came, he chivvied me up to the keep, and under his watchful eye I was forced to consume a watery bowl of soup and a hunk of bread. He would have taken me back to his loft again, had I not insisted that I wanted my own bed. In reality, I had to be in my room. I had to know whether Chade at least tried to call me, whether I could go or not. Through another sleepness night, I stared in blackness at a darker corner of my room.

But he didn't summon me.

Morning greyed my window. I rolled over and kept to my bed. The depth of bleakness that settled over me was too solid for me to fight. All of my possible choices led to grey ends. I could not face the futility of getting out of bed. A headachey sort of near-sleep claimed me. Any sound seemed too loud, and I was either too hot or too cold no matter how I fussed with my covers. I closed my eyes, but even my dreams were bright and annoying. Arguing voices, as loud as if they were in the bed with me, and all the more frustrating because it sounded like one man arguing with himself and taking both sides. 'Break him as you broke the other one!' he'd mutter angrily. 'You and your stupid tests!' and then, 'Can't be too careful. Can't put your trust in just anyone. Blood will tell. Test his mettle, that's all.' 'Metal! You want a brainless blade, go hammer it out yourself. Beat it flat.' And more quietly, 'I've got no heart for this. I'll not be used again. If you wanted to test my temper, you've done it.' Then, 'Don't talk to me about blood and family. Remember who I am to you! It isn't his loyalty she's worrying about, or mine.'

The angry voice broke up, merged, became another argument, this one shriller. I cracked open my eyelids. My chamber had become the scene of a brief battle. I woke to a spirited disagreement between Burrich and Mistress Hasty as to whose jurisdiction I fell under. She had a wicker basket, from which protruded the necks of several bottles. The scents of mustard in a plaster and chamomile wafted over me so strongly that I wanted to retch. Burrich stood stoically between her and my bed. His arms were crossed on his chest and Vixen sat at his feet. Mistress Hasty's words rattled in my head like pebbles. 'In the keep', 'Those clean linens', 'Know about boys', 'That smelly dog'. I don't recall that Burrich said a word. He just stood there so solidly that I could feel him with my eyes closed.

Later, he was gone, but Vixen was on the bed, not at my feet, but beside me, panting heavily but refusing to abandon me for the cooler floor. I opened my eyes again, later, to early twilight. Burrich had tugged free my pillow, shook it a bit, and was awkwardly stuffing it back under my head, cool side up. He then sat down heavily on the bed.

He cleared his throat. 'Fitz, there's nothing the matter with you that I've ever seen before. At least, whatever's the matter with you isn't in your guts or your blood. If you were a bit older, I'd suspect you had woman problems. You act like a soldier on a three-day drunk, but without the wine. Boy, what's the matter with you?'

He looked down on me with sincere worry. It was the same look he wore when he was afraid a mare was going to miscarry, or when hunters brought back dogs that boars had gored. It reached me, and without meaning to, I quested out toward him. As always, the wall was there, but Vixen whined lightly and put her muzzle against my cheek. I tried to express what was inside me without betraying Chade. 'I'm just so alone now,' I heard myself say, and even to me it sounded like a feeble complaint.

'Alone?' Burrich's brows knit. 'Fitz, I'm right here. How can you say you're alone?'

And there the conversation ended, with both of us looking at one another and neither understanding at all. Later he brought me food, but didn't insist I eat it. And he left Vixen with me for the night. A part of me wondered how she would react if the door opened, but a larger part of me knew I didn't have to worry. That door would never open again.

Morning came again, and Vixen nosed at me and whined to go out. Too broken to care if Burrich caught me, I quested toward her. Hungry and thirsty and her bladder was about to burst. And her discomfort was suddenly my own. I dragged on a tunic and took her down the stairs and outside, and then back to the kitchen to eat. Cook was more pleased to see me than I had imagined anyone could be. Vixen was given a generous bowl of last night's stew, while Cook insisted on giving me six rashers of thick-cut bacon on the warm crust of the day's first baking of bread. Vixen's keen nose and sharp appetite sparked my own senses, and I found myself eating, not with my normal appetite, but with a young creature's sensory appreciation for food.

From there she led me to the stables, and though I pulled my mind back from her before we went inside, I felt somewhat rejuvenated from the contact. Burrich straightened up from some task as I came in, looked me over, glanced at Vixen, grunted wryly to himself, and then handed me a suckle bottle and wick. 'There isn't much in a man's head,' he told me, 'that can't be cured by working and taking care of something else. The rat-dog whelped a few days ago, and there's one pup too weak to compete with the others. See if you can keep him alive today.'

It was an ugly little pup, pink skin showing through his brindle fur. His eyes were shut tight still, and the extra skin he'd use up as he grew was piled on top of his muzzle. His skinny little tail looked just like a rat's, so that I wondered his mother didn't worry her own pups to death just for the resemblance's sake. He was weak and passive, but I bothered him with the warm milk and wicking until he sucked a little, and got enough all over him that his mother was inspired to lick and nuzzle him. I took one of his stronger sisters off her teat and plugged him into her place. Her little belly was round and full anyway; she had only been sucking for the sake of obstinacy. She was going to be white with a black spot over one eye. She caught my little finger and suckled at it, and already I could feel the immense strength those jaws would someday hold. Burrich had told me stories about rat-dogs that would latch onto a bull's nose and hang there no matter what the bull did. He had no use for men that would teach a dog to do so, but could not contain his respect for the courage of a dog that would take on a bull. Our rat-dogs were kept for ratting, and taken on regular patrols of the corn cribs and grain barns.

I spent the whole morning there, and left at noon with the gratification of seeing the pup's small belly round and tight with milk. The afternoon was spent mucking out stalls. Burrich kept me at it, adding another chore as soon as I completed one, with no time for me to do anything but work. He didn't talk with me or ask me questions, but he always seemed to be working only a dozen paces away. It was as if he had taken my complaint about being alone quite literally, and was resolved to be where I could see him. I wound up my day back with my puppy who was substantially stronger than he had been that morning. I cradled him against my chest and he crept up under my chin, his blunt little muzzle questing there for milk. It tickled. I pulled him down and looked at him. He was going to have a pink nose. Men said the rat-dogs with the pink noses were the most savage ones when they fought. But his little mind now was only a muzzy warmth of security and milk-want and affection for my smell. I wrapped him in my protection of him, praised him for his new strength. He wiggled in my fingers. And Burrich leaned over the side of the stall and rapped me on the head with his knuckles, bringing twin yelps from the pup and me.

'Enough of that,' he warned sternly. 'That's not a thing for a man to do. And it won't solve whatever is chewing on your soul. Give the pup back to his mother, now.'

So I did, but reluctantly, and not at all sure that Burrich was right that bonding with a puppy wouldn't solve anything. I longed for his warm little world of straw and siblings and milk and mother. At that moment, I could imagine no better one.

Then Burrich and I went up to eat. He took me into the soldiers' mess, where manners were whatever you had and no one demanded talk. It was comforting to be casually ignored, to have food passed over my head with no one being solicitous of me. Burrich saw that I ate, though, and then afterwards we sat outside beside the kitchen's back door and drank. I'd had ale and beer and wine before, but I had never drunk in the purposeful way that Burrich now showed me. When Cook dared to come out and scold him for giving strong spirits to a mere boy, he gave her one of his quiet stares that reminded me of the first night I had met him, when he'd faced down a whole room of soldiers over Chivalry's good name. And she left.

He walked me up to my room, dragged my tunic off over my head as I stood unsteadily beside my bed, and then casually tumbled me into the bed and tossed a blanket over me. 'Now you'll sleep,' he informed me in a thick voice. 'And tomorrow we'll do the same again. And again. Until one day you get up and find out that whatever it was didn't kill you after all.'

He blew out my candle and left. My head reeled and my body ached from the day's work. But still I didn't sleep. What I found myself doing was crying. The drink had loosened whatever knot held my control, and I wept. Not quietly. I sobbed, and hiccuped and then wailed with my jaw shaking. My throat closed up, my nose ran, and I cried so hard I felt I couldn't breathe. I think I cried every tear I had never shed since the day my grandfather forced my mother to abandon me. 'Mere!' I heard myself call out, and suddenly there were arms around me, holding me tight.

Chade held me and rocked me as if I were a much younger child. Even in the darkness I knew those bony arms and the herb-and-dust smell of him. Disbelieving, I clung to him and cried until I was hoarse, and my mouth so dry no sound would come at all. 'You were right,' he said into my hair, quietly, calmingly. 'You were right. I was asking you to do something wrong, and you were right to refuse it. You won't be tested that way again. Not by me.' And when I was finally still, he left me for a time, and then brought back to me a drink, lukewarm and almost tasteless, but not water. He held the mug to my mouth and I drank it down without questions. Then I lay back so suddenly sleepy that I don't even remember Chade leaving my room.

I awoke near dawn and reported to Burrich after a hearty breakfast. I was quick at my chores and attentive to my charges and could not at all understand why he had awakened so headachey and grumpy. He muttered something once about 'his father's head for spirits', and then dismissed me early, telling me to take my whistling elsewhere.

Three days later, King Shrewd summoned me in the dawn. He was already dressed, and there was a tray and food for more than one person set out on it. As soon as I arrived, he sent away his man and told me to sit. I took a chair at the small table in his room, and without asking me if I were hungry, he served me food with his own hand and then sat down across from me to eat. The gesture was not lost on me, but even so I could not bring myself to eat much. He spoke only of the food, and said nothing of bargains or loyalty or keeping one's word. When he saw I had finished eating, he pushed his own plate away. He shifted uncomfortably.

'It was my idea,' he said suddenly, almost harshly. 'Not his. He never approved of it. I insisted. When you're older, you'll understand. I can take no chances, not on anyone. But I promised him that you'd know this right from me. It was all my own idea, never his. And I will never ask him to try your mettle in such a way again. On that you have a king's word.'

He made a motion that dismissed me. And I rose, but as I did so, I took from his tray a little silver knife, all engraved, that he had been using to cut fruit with. I looked him in the eyes as I did so, and quite openly slipped it up my sleeve. King Shrewd's eyes widened, but he said not a word.

Two nights later, when Chade summoned me, our lessons resumed as if there had never been a pause. He talked, I listened,

I played his stone game and never made an error. He gave me an assignment, and we made small jokes together. He showed me how Slink the weasel would dance for a sausage. All was well between us again. But before I left his chambers that night, I walked to his hearth. Without a word, I placed the knife on the centre of his mantel-shelf. Actually, I drove it, blade first, into the wood of the shelf. Then I left without speaking of it or meeting his eyes. In fact, we never spoke of it.

I believe that the knife is still there.

SIX

Chivalry's Shadow

There are two traditions about the custom of giving royal offspring names suggestive of virtues or abilities. The one that is most commonly held is that somehow these names are binding; that when such a name is attached to a child who will be trained in the Skill, somehow the Skill melds the name to the child, and the child cannot help but grow up to practise the virtue ascribed to him or her by name. This first tradition is most doggedly believed by those same ones most prone to doff their caps in the presence of minor nobility.

A more ancient tradition attributes such names to accident, at least initially. It is said that King Taker and King Ruler, the first two of the Outislanders to rule what would become the Six Duchies, had no such names at all. Rather that their names in their own foreign tongue were very similar to the sounds of such words in the duchies' tongue, and thus came to be known by their homonyms rather than by their true names. But for the purposes of royalty, it is better to have the common folk believe that a boy given a noble name must grow to have a noble nature.

'Boy!'

I lifted my head. Of the half-dozen or so other lads lounging about before the fire, no one else even flinched. The girls took even less notice as I moved up to take my place at the opposite side of the low table where Master Fedwren knelt. He had mastered some trick of inflection that let all know when Boy meant 'boy' and when it meant 'the bastard'.

I tucked my knees under the low table and sat on my feet, then presented Fedwren with my sheet of pith-paper. As he ran his eyes down my careful columns of letters, I let my attention wander.

Winter had harvested us and stored us here in the Great Hall. Outside, a sea storm lashed the walls of the keep while breakers pounded the cliffs with a force that occasionally sent a tremor through the stone floor beneath us. The heavy overcast had stolen even the few hours of watery daylight that winter had left us. It seemed to me that a darkness lay over us like a fog, both outside and within. The dimness penetrated my eyes, so that I felt sleepy without feeling tired. For a brief moment, I let my senses expand, and felt the winter sluggishness of the hounds where they dozed and twitched in the corners. Not even there could I find a thought or image to interest me.

Fires burned in all three of the big hearths, and different groups had gathered before each. At one, fletchers busied themselves with their work, lest tomorrow be a clear enough day to allow for a hunt. I longed to be there, for Sherf's mellow voice was rising and falling in the telling of some tale, broken frequently with appreciative laughter from her listeners. At the end hearth, children's voices piped along in the chorus of a song. I recognized it as the Shepherd's Song, a counting tune. A few watchful mothers tapped toes as they tatted at their lacemaking while Jerdon's withered old fingers on the harp strings kept the young voices almost in tune.

Here, at our hearth, children old enough to sit still and learn letters, did. Fedwren saw to that. His sharp blue eyes missed nothing. 'Here,' he said to me, pointing. 'You've forgotten to cross their tails. Remember how I showed you? Justice, open your eyes and get back to your penwork. Doze off again and I'll let you bring us another log for the fire. Charity, you can help him if you smirk again. Other than that,' and his attention was suddenly back on my work again, 'your lettering is much improved, not only on these Duchian characters, but on the Outislander runes as well. Though those can't really be properly brushed onto such poor paper. The surface is too porous, and takes the ink too well. Good, pounded bark sheets are what you want for runes,' and he ran a finger appreciatively over the sheet he was working on. 'Continue to show this type of work, and before winter's out I'll let you make me a copy of Queen Bidewell's Remedies. What do you say to that?'

I tried to smile and be properly flattered. Copywork was not usually given to students; good paper was too rare, and one careless brushstroke could ruin a sheet. I knew the Remedies was a fairly simple set of herbal properties and prophecies but any copying was an honour to aspire to. Fedwren gave me a fresh sheet of pith-paper. As I rose to return to my place, he lifted a hand to stop me. 'Boy?'

I paused.

Fedwren looked uncomfortable. 'I don't know who to ask this of, except you. Properly, I'd ask your parents, but . . .' Mercifully he let the sentence die. He scratched his beard meditatively with his ink-stained fingers. 'Winter's soon over, and I'll be on my way again. Do you know what I do in summer, boy? I wander all the Six Duchies, getting herbs and berries and roots for my inks, and making provisions for the papers I need. It's a good life, walking free on the roads in summers and guesting at the keep here all winter. There's much to be said for scribing for a living.' He looked at me meditatively. I looked back, wondering what he was getting at.

'I take an apprentice, every few years. Some of them work out, and go on to do scribing for the lesser keeps. Some don't. Some don't have the patience for the detail, or the memory for the inks. I think you would. What would you think about becoming a scribe?'

The question caught me completely off-guard, and I stared at him mutely. It wasn't just the idea of becoming a scribe; it was the whole notion that Fedwren would want me to be his apprentice, to follow him about and learn the secrets of his trade. Several years had passed since I had begun my bargain with the old King. Other than the nights I spent in Chade's company or my stolen afternoons with Molly and Kerry, I had never thought of anyone finding me companionable, let alone good material for an apprentice. Fedwren's proposal left me speechless. He must have sensed my confusion, for he smiled his genial young-old smile.

'Well, think on it, boy. Scribing's a good trade, and what other prospects do you have? Between the two of us, I think that some time away from Buckkeep might do you good.'

'Away from Buckkeep?' I repeated in wonder. It was like someone opening a curtain. I had never considered the idea. Suddenly the roads leading away from Buckkeep gleamed in my mind, and the weary maps I had been forced to study became places I could go. It transfixed me.

'Yes,' Fedwren said softly. 'Leave Buckkeep. As you grow older, Chivalry's shadow will grow thinner. It will not always shelter you. Better you were your own man, with your own life and calling to content you before his protection is entirely gone. But you don't have to answer me now. Think about it. Discuss it with Burrich, perhaps.'

And he handed me my pith-paper and sent me back to my place. I thought about his words, but it was not Burrich I took them to. In the feeble hours of a new day, Chade and I were crouched, head to head, I picking up the red shards of a broken crock that Slink had overset while Chade salvaged the fine black seeds that had scattered in all directions. Slink clung to the top of a sagging tapestry and chirred apologetically, but I sensed his amusement.

'Come all the way from Kalibar, these seeds, you skinny little pelt!' Chade scolded him.

'Kalibar,' I said, and dredged out, 'A day's travel past our border with Sandsedge.'

'That's right, my boy,' Chade muttered approvingly.

'Have you ever been there?'

'Me? Oh, no. I meant that they came from that far. I had to send to Fircrest for them. They've a large market there, one that draws trade from all six duchies and many of our neighbours as well.'

'Oh. Fircrest. Have you ever been there?'

Chade considered. 'A time or two, when I was a younger man. I remember the noise, mostly, and the heat. Inland places are like that: too dry, too hot. I was glad to return to Buckkeep.'

'Was there any other place you ever went that you liked better than Buckkeep?'

Chade straightened slowly, his pale hand cupped full of fine black seed. 'Why don't you just ask me your question instead of beating around the bush?'

So I told him of Fedwren's offer, and also of my sudden realization that maps were more than lines and colours. They were places and possibilities, and I could leave here and be someone else, be a scribe, or . . .

'No.' Chade spoke softly but abruptly. 'No matter where you went, you would still be Chivalry's bastard. Fedwren is more perspicacious than I believed him to be, but he still doesn't understand. Not the whole picture. He sees that here at court you must always be a bastard, must always be something of a pariah. What he doesn't realize is that here, partaking of King Shrewd's bounty, learning your lessons, under his eye, you are not a threat to him. Certainly, you are under Chivalry's shadow here. Certainly it does protect you. But were you away from here, far from being unneedful of such protection, you would become a danger to King Shrewd, and a greater danger to his heirs after him. You would have no simple life of freedom as a wandering scribe. Rather you would be found in your inn bed with your throat cut some morning, or with an arrow through you on the high road.'

A coldness shivered through me. 'But why?' I asked softly.

Chade sighed. He dumped the seeds into a dish, dusted his hands lightly to shake loose those that clung to his fingers. 'Because you're a royal bastard, and hostage to your own blood-lines. For now, as I say, you're no threat to Shrewd. You're too young, and besides, he has you right where he can watch you. But he's looking down the road. And you should be, too. These are restless times. The Outislanders are getting braver about their raids. The coast folk are beginning to grumble, saying we need more patrol ships, and some say warships of our own, to raid as we are raided. But the Inland Duchies want no part of paying for ships of any kind, especially not warships that might precipitate us into a full-scale war. They complain the coast is all the king thinks of, with no care for their farming. And the mountain folk are becoming more chary about the use of their passes. The trade fees grow steeper every month. So the merchants mumble and complain to each other. To the south, in Sandsedge and beyond, there is drought, and times are hard. Everyone there curses, as if the King and Verity were to blame for that as well. Verity is a fine fellow to have a mug with, but he is neither the soldier nor the diplomat that Chivalry was. He would rather hunt winter buck, or listen to a minstrel by the fireside than travel winter roads in raw weather, just to stay in touch with the other duchies. Sooner or later, if things do not improve, people will look about and say, "Well, a bastard's not so large a thing to make a fuss over. Chivalry should have come to power; he'd soon put a stop to all this. He might have been a bit stiff about protocol, but at least he got things done, and didn't let foreigners trample all over us".'

'So Chivalry might yet become King?' The question sent a queer thrill through me. Instantly I was imagining his triumphant return to Buckkeep, our eventual meeting, and . . . What then?

Chade seemed to be reading my face. 'No, boy. Not likely at all. Even if the folk all wanted him to, I doubt that he'd go against what he set upon himself, or against the King's wishes. But it would cause mumblings and grumblings, and those could lead to riots and skirmishes, oh, and a generally bad climate for a bastard to be running around free in. You'd have to be settled one way or another. Either as a corpse, or as the King's tool.'

'The King's tool. I see.' An oppression settled over me. My brief glimpse of blue skies arching over yellow roads and me travelling down them astride Sooty suddenly vanished. I thought of the hounds in their kennels instead, or of the hawk, hooded and strapped, that rode on the King's wrist and was loosed only to do the King's will.

'It doesn't have to be that bad,' Chade said quietly. 'Most prisons are of our own making. A man makes his own freedom, too.'

'I'm never going to get to go anywhere, am I?' Despite the newness of the idea, travelling suddenly seemed immensely important to me.

'I wouldn't say that.' Chade was rummaging about for something to use as a stopper on the dish full of seeds. He finally contented himself with putting a saucer on top of it. 'You'll go to many places. Quietly, and when the family interests require you to go there. But that's not all that different for any prince of the blood. Do you think Chivalry got to choose where he would go to work his diplomacy? Do you think Verity likes being sent off to view towns raided by Outislanders, to hear the complaints of folks who insist that if only they'd been better fortified or better manned, none of this would have happened? A true prince has very little freedom when it comes to where he will go or how he will spend his time. Chivalry has probably more of both now than he ever had before.'

'Except that he can't come back to Buckkeep?' The flash of insight made me freeze, my hands full of shards.

'Except he can't come back to Buckkeep. It doesn't do to stir folks up with visits from a former King-in-Waiting. Better he faded quietly away.'

I tossed the shards into the hearth. 'At least he gets to go somewhere,' I muttered. 'I can't even go to town . . .'

'And it's that important to you? To go down to a grubby, greasy little port like Buckkeep Town?'

'There are other people there . . .' I hesitated. Not even Chade knew of my town friends. I plunged ahead. 'They call me Newboy. And they don't think "the bastard" every time they look at me.' I had never put it into words before, but suddenly the attraction of town was quite clear to me.

'Ah,' said Chade, and his shoulders moved as if he sighed, but he was silent. And a moment later he was telling me how one could sicken a man just by feeding him rhubarb and spinach at the same sitting, sicken him even to death if the portions were sufficient, and never set a bit of poison on the table at all. I asked him how to keep others at the same table from also being sickened, and our discussion wandered from there. Only later did it seem to me that his words regarding Chivalry had been almost prophetic.

Two days later I was surprised to be told that Fedwren had requested my services for a day or so. I was surprised even more when he gave me a list of supplies he required from town, and enough silver to buy them, with two extra coppers for myself. I held my breath, expecting that Burrich or one of my other masters would forbid it, but instead I was told to hurry on my way. I went out of the gates with a basket on my arm and my brain giddy with sudden freedom. I counted up the months since I had last been able to slip away from Buckkeep, and was shocked to find it had been a year or better. Immediately I planned to renew my old familiarity with the town. No one had told me when I had to return, and I was confident I could snatch an hour or two to myself and no one the wiser.

The disparity of the items on Fedwren's list took me all over the town. I had no idea what use a scribe had for dried Sea-Maid's Hair, or for a peck of forester's nuts. Perhaps he used them to make his coloured inks, I decided, and when I could not find them in the usual shops, I took myself down to the harbour bazaar, where anyone with a blanket and something to sell could declare himself a merchant. The seaweed I found swiftly enough there, and learned it was a common ingredient in chowder. The nuts took longer, for those were something that would have come from inland rather than from the sea, and there were fewer traders who dealt in such things.

But find them I did, alongside baskets of porcupine quills and carved wooden beads and nutcones and pounded bark fabric. The woman who presided over the blanket was old, and her hair had gone silver rather than white or grey. She had a strong, straight nose and her eyes were on bony shelves over her cheeks. It was a racial heritage both strange and oddly familiar to me, and a shiver walked down my back when I suddenly knew she was from the mountains.

'Keppet,' said the woman at the next mat as I completed my purchase. I glanced at her, thinking she was addressing the woman I had just paid. But she was staring at me. 'Keppet,' she said, quite insistently, and I wondered what it meant in her language. It seemed a request for something, but the older woman only stared coldly out into the street, so I shrugged at her younger neighbour apologetically and turned away as I stowed the nuts in my basket.

I hadn't gone more than a dozen steps when I heard her shriek, 'Keppet!' yet again. I looked back to see the two women engaged in a struggle. The older one gripped the younger one's wrists and the younger one thrashed and kicked to be free of her. Around her, other merchants were getting to their feet in alarm and snatching their own merchandise out of harm's way. I might have turned back to watch had not another more familiar face met my eyes.

'Nosebleed!' I exclaimed.

She turned to face me full-on, and for an instant I thought I had been mistaken. A year had passed since I'd last seen her. How could a person change so much? The dark hair that used to be in sensible braids behind her ears now fell free past her shoulders. And she was dressed not in a jerkin and loose trousers but in blouse and skirt. The adult garments put me at a loss for words. I might have turned aside and pretended I addressed someone else had her dark eyes not challenged me as she asked me coolly, 'Nosebleed?'

I stood my ground. 'Aren't you Molly Nosebleed?'

She lifted a hand to brush some hair back from her cheek. 'I'm Molly Chandler.' I saw recognition in her eyes, but her voice was chill as she added, 'I'm not sure that I know you. Your name, sir?'

Confused, I reacted without thinking. I quested toward her, found her nervousness, and was surprised by her fears. Thought and voice I sought to soothe it. 'I'm Newboy,' I said without hesitation.

Her eyes widened with surprise, and then she laughed at what she construed as a joke. The barrier she had erected between us burst like a soap bubble, and suddenly I knew her as I had before. There was the same warm kinship between us that reminded me of nothing so much as Nosy. All awkwardness disappeared. A crowd was forming about the struggling women, but we left it behind us as we strolled up the cobbled street. I admired her skirts, and she calmly informed that she had been wearing skirts for several months now and that she quite preferred them to trousers. This one had been her mother's; she was told that one simply couldn't get wool woven this fine any more, or a red as bright as it was dyed. She admired my clothes, and I suddenly realized that perhaps I appeared to her as different as she to me. I had my best shirt on, my trousers had been washed only a few days ago and I wore boots as fine as any man-at-arms, despite Burrich's objections about how rapidly I outgrew them. She asked my business and I told her I was on errands for the writing master at the keep. I told her too that he was in need of two beeswax tapers, a total fabrication on my part, but one that allowed me to remain by her side as we strolled up the winding street. Our elbows bumped companionably and she talked. She was carrying a basket of her own on her arm. It had several packets and bundles of herbs in it, for scenting candles, she told me. Beeswax took the scent much better than tallow, in her opinion. She made the best scented candles in Buckkeep; even the two other chandlers in town admitted it. This, smell this, this was lavender, wasn't it lovely? Her mother's favourite, and hers, too. This was crushsweet, and this beebalm. This was thresher's root, not her favourite, no, but some said it made a good candle to cure headaches and winter-glooms. Mavis Threadsnip had told her that Molly's mother had mixed it with other herbs and made a wonderful candle, one that would calm even a colicky baby. So Molly had decided to try, by experimenting, to see if she could find the right herbs to re-create her mother's recipe.

Her calm flaunting of her knowledge and skills left me burning to distinguish myself in her eyes. 'I know the thresher's root,' I told her. 'Some use it to make an ointment for sore shoulders and backs. That's where the name comes from. But if you distil a tincture from it and mix it well in wine it's never tasted, and it will make a grown man sleep a day and a night and a day again, or make a child die in his sleep.'

Her eyes widened as I spoke, and at my last words a look of horror came over her face. I fell silent and felt the sharp awkwardness again. 'How do you know such things?' she demanded breathlessly.

'I . . . I heard an old travelling midwife talking to our midwife up at the keep,' I improvised. 'It was . . . a sad story she told, of an injured man given some to help him rest, but his baby got into it as well. A very, very sad story.' Her face was softening and I felt her warming toward me again. 'I only tell it to be sure you are careful of the root. Don't leave it about where any child can get at it.'

'Thank you. I shan't. Are you interested in herbs and roots? I didn't know a scriber cared about such things.'

I suddenly realized that she thought I was the scriber's

help-boy. I didn't see any reason to tell her otherwise. 'Oh, Fedwren uses many things for his dyes and inks. Some copies he makes quite plain, but others are fancy, all done with birds and cats and turtles and fish. He showed me a Herbal with the greens and flowers of each herb done as the border for the page.'

'That I should dearly love to see,' she said in a heartfelt way, and I instantly began thinking of ways to purloin it for a few days.

'I might be able to get you a copy to read . . . not to keep, but to study for a few days,' I offered hesitantly.

She laughed, but there was a slight edge in it. 'As if I could read! Oh, but I imagine you've picked up some letters, running about for the scribe's errands.'

'A few,' I told her, and was surprised at the envy in her eyes when I showed her my list and confessed I could read all seven words on it.

A sudden shyness came over her. She walked more slowly, and I realized we were getting close to the chandlery. I wondered if her father still beat her, but dared not ask about it. Her face, at least, showed no sign of it. We reached the chandlery door and paused there. She made some sudden decision, for she put her hand on my sleeve, took a breath and then asked, 'Do you think you could read something for me? Or even any part of it?'

'I'll try,' I offered.

'When I . . . now that I wear skirts, my father has given me my mother's things. She had been dress-help to a lady up at the keep when she was a girl, and had letters taught her. I have some tablets she wrote. I'd like to know what they say.'

'I'll try,' I repeated.

'My father's in the shop.' She said no more than that, but something in the way her consciousness rang against mine was sufficient.

'I'm to get Scribe Fedwren two beeswax tapers,' I reminded her. 'I dare not go back to the keep without them.'

'Be not too familiar with me,' she cautioned me, and then opened the door.

I followed her, but slowly, as if coincidence brought us to the door together. I need not have been so circumspect. Her father slept quite soundly in a chair beside the hearth. I was shocked at the change in him. His skinniness had become skeletal, the flesh on his face reminding me of an undercooked pastry over a lumpy fruit pie. Chade had taught me well. I looked to the man's fingernails and lips, and even from across the room, I knew he could not live much longer. Perhaps he no longer beat Molly because he no longer had the strength. Molly motioned me to be quiet. She vanished behind the hangings that divided their home from their shop, leaving me to explore the store.

It was a pleasant place, not large, but the ceiling was higher than in most of the shops and dwellings in Buckkeep Town. I suspected it was Molly's diligence that kept it swept and tidy. The pleasant smells and soft light of her industry filled the room. Her wares hung in pairs by their joined wicks from long dowels on a rack. Fat sensible candles for ships' use filled another shelf. She even had three glazed pottery lamps on display, for those able to afford such things. In addition to candles, I found she had pots of honey, a natural by-product of the beehives she tended behind the shop that furnished the wax for her finest products.

Then Molly reappeared and motioned to me to come and join her. She brought a branch of tapers and a set of tablets to a table and set them out on it. Then she stood back and pressed her lips together as if wondering if what she did were wise.

The tablets were done in the old style. Simple slabs of wood had been cut with the grain of the tree and sanded smooth. The letters had been brushed in carefully, and then sealed to the wood with a yellowing rosin layer. There were five, excellently lettered. Four were carefully precise accounts of herbal recipes for healing candles. As I read each one softly aloud to Molly, I could see her struggling to commit them to memory. At the fifth tablet, I hesitated. 'This isn't a recipe,' I told her.

'Well, what is it?' she demanded in a whisper.

I shrugged and began to read it to her. '"On this day was born my Molly Nosegay, sweet as any bunch of posies. For her birth labours, I burned two tapers of bayberry and two cup-candles scented with two handfuls of the small violets that grow near Dowell's Mill and one handful of redroot, chopped very fine. May she do likewise when her time comes to bear a child, and her labour will be as easy as mine, and the fruit of it as perfect. So I believe."'

That was all, and when I had read it, the silence grew and blossomed. Molly took that last tablet from my hands and held it in her two hands and stared at it, as if reading things in the letters that I had not seen. I shifted my feet, and the scuffing recalled to her that I was there. Silently she gathered up all her tablets and disappeared with them once more.

When she came back, she walked swiftly to the shelf and took down two tall beeswax tapers, and then to another shelf whence she took two fat pink candles.

'I only need . . .'

'Shush. There's no charge for any of these. The sweetberry blossom ones will give you calm dreams. I very much enjoy them, and I think you will, too.' Her voice was friendly, but as she put them into my basket, I knew she was waiting for me to leave. Still, she walked to the door with me, and opened it softly lest it wake her father. 'Goodbye, Newboy,' she said, and then gave me one real smile. 'Nosegay. I never knew she called me that. Nosebleed, they called me on the streets. I suppose the older ones who knew what name she had given me thought it was funny. And after a while they probably forgot it had ever been anything else. Well. I don't care. I have it now. A name from my mother.'

'It suits you,' I said in a sudden burst of gallantry, and then, as she stared and the heat rose in my cheeks, I hurried away from the door. I was surprised to find that it was late afternoon, nearly evening. I raced through the rest of my errands, begging the last item on my list, a weasel's skin, through the shutters of the merchant's window. Grudgingly he opened his door to me, complaining that he liked to eat his supper hot, but I thanked him so profusely he must have believed me a little daft.

I was hurrying up the steepest part of the road back to the keep when I heard the unexpected sound of horses behind me. They were coming up from the dock section of town, ridden hard. It was ridiculous. No one kept horses in town, for the roads were too steep and rocky to make them of much use. Also, the town was crowded into such a small area as to make riding a horse a vanity rather than a convenience. So these must be horses from the keep's stables. I stepped to one side of the road and waited, curious to see who would risk Burrich's wrath by riding horses at such speed on slick and uneven cobbles in poor light.

To my shock it was Regal and Verity on the matched blacks that were Burrich's pride. Verity carried a plumed baton, such as messengers to the keep carried when the news they bore was of the utmost importance. At the sight of me standing quietly beside the road they both pulled in their horses so violently that Regal's spun aside and nearly went down on his knees.

'Burrich will have fits if you break that colt's knees!' I cried out in dismay and ran toward him.

Regal gave an inarticulate cry, and a half-instant later, Verity laughed at him shakily. 'You thought he was a ghost, same as I. Whoah, lad, you gave us a turn, standing so quiet as that. And looking so much like him. Eh, Regal?'

'Verity, you're a fool. Hold your tongue.' Regal gave his mount's mouth a vindictive jerk, and then tugged his jerkin smooth again. 'What are you doing out on this road so late, bastard? Just what do you think you're up to, sneaking away from the keep and into town at this hour?'

I was used to Regal's disdain for me. This sharp rebuke was something new, however. Usually, he did little more than avoid me, or hold himself away from me as if I were fresh manure. The surprise made me answer quickly, 'I'm on my way back, not to, sir. I've been running errands for Fedwren.' And I held up my basket as proof.

'Of course you have,' he sneered. 'Such a likely tale. It's a bit too much of a coincidence, bastard.' Again he flung the word at me.

I must have looked both hurt and confused, for Verity snorted in his bluff way and said, 'Don't mind him, boy. You gave us both a bit of a turn. A river ship just came into town, flying the pennant for a special message. And when Verity and I rode down to get it, lo and behold, it's from Patience, to tell us Chivalry's dead. Then, as we come up the road, what do we see but the very image of him as a boy, standing silent before us and of course we were in that frame of mind and—'

'You are such an idiot, Verity!' Regal spat. 'Trumpet it out for the whole town to hear before the King's even been told. And don't put ideas in the bastard's head that he looks like Chivalry. From what I hear, he has ideas enough, and we can thank our dear father for that. Come on. We've got a message to deliver.'

Regal jerked his mount's head up again, and then set spurs to him. I watched him go, and for an instant I swear all I thought was that I should go to the stable when I got back to the keep, to check on the poor beast and see how badly his mouth was bruised. But for some reason I looked up at Verity and said, 'My father's dead.'

He sat still on his horse. Bigger and bulkier than Regal, he still always sat a horse better. I think it was the soldier in him. He looked at me in silence for a moment. Then he said, 'Yes. My brother's dead.' He granted me that, my uncle, that instant of kinship, and I think that ever after it changed how I saw him. 'Up behind me, boy, and I'll take you back to the keep,' he offered.

'No, thank you. Burrich would take my hide off for riding a horse double on this road.'

'That he would, boy,' Verity agreed kindly. Then, 'I'm sorry you found out this way. I wasn't thinking. It does not seem it can be real.' I caught a glimpse of his true grief, and then he leaned forward and spoke to his horse and it sprang forward. In moments I was alone on the road again.

A fine misting rain began and the last natural light died, and still I stood there. I looked up at the keep, black against the stars, with here and there a bit of light spilling out. For a moment I thought of setting my basket down and running away, running off into the darkness and never coming back. Would anyone ever come looking for me? I wondered. But instead I shifted my basket to my other arm and began my slow trudge back up the hill.

SEVEN

An Assignment

There were rumours of poison when Queen Desire died. I choose to put in writing here what I absolutely know as truth. Queen Desire did die of poisoning, but it had been self-administered, over a long period of time, and was none of her king's doing. Often he had tried to dissuade her from using intoxicants as freely as she did. Physicians had been consulted, as well as herbalists, but no sooner had he persuaded her to desist from one than she discovered another to try.

Towards the end of the last summer of her life, she became even more reckless, using several kinds simultaneously and no longer making any attempts to conceal her habits. Her behaviours were a great trial for Shrewd, for when she was drunk with wine or incensed with smoke, she would make wild accusations and inflammatory statements with no heed at all as to who was present or what the occasion was. One would have thought that her excesses toward the end of her life would have disillusioned her followers. To the contrary, they declared either that Shrewd had driven her to self-destruction, or poisoned her himself. But I can say with complete knowledge that her death was not of the King's doing.

Burrich cut my hair for mourning. He left it only a finger's width long. He shaved his own head, even his beard and eyebrows for his grief. The pale parts of his head contrasted sharply with his ruddy cheeks and nose; it made him look very strange, stranger even than the forest men who came to town with their hair stuck down with pitch and their teeth dyed red and black. Children stared at those wild men and whispered to one another behind their hands as they passed, but they cringed silently from Burrich. I think it was his eyes. I've seen holes in a skull that had more life in them than Burrich's eyes had during those days.

Regal sent a man to rebuke Burrich for shaving his head and cutting my hair. That was mourning for a crowned king, not for a man who had abdicated the throne. Burrich stared at the man until he left. Verity cut a hand's width from his hair and beard, as that was mourning for a brother. Some of the keep guards cut varying lengths from their braided queues of hair, as a fighting man does for a fallen comrade. But what Burrich had done to himself and to me was extreme. People stared. I wanted to ask him why I should mourn for a father I had never even seen; for a father who had never come to see me, but a look at his frozen eyes and mouth and I hadn't dared. No one mentioned to Regal the mourning lock he cut from each horse's mane, or the stinking fire that consumed all the sacrificial hair. I had a sketchy idea that meant Burrich was sending parts of our spirits along with Chivalry's; it was some custom he had from his grandmother's people.

It was as if Burrich had died. A cold force animated his body, performing all his tasks flawlessly but without warmth or satisfaction. Underlings who had formerly vied for the briefest nod of praise from him now turned aside from his glance, as if shamed for him. Only Vixen did not forsake him. The old bitch slunk after him wherever he went, unrewarded by any look or touch, but always there. I hugged her once, in sympathy, and even dared to quest toward her, but I encountered only a numbness frightening to touch minds with. She grieved with her master.

The winter storms cut and snarled around the cliffs. The days possessed a lifeless cold that denied any possibility of spring. Chivalry was buried at Withywoods. There was a Grieving Fast at the keep, but it was brief and subdued. It was more an observation of correct form than a true Grieving. Those who truly mourned him seemed to be judged guilty of poor taste. His public life should have ended with his abdication; how tactless of him to draw further attention to himself by actually dying.

A full week after my father died I awoke to the familiar draught from the secret staircase and the yellow light that beckoned me. I rose and hastened up the stairs to my refuge. It would be good to get away from all the strangeness, to mingle herbs and make strange smokes with Chade again. I needed no more of the odd suspension of self that I'd felt since I'd heard of Chivalry's death.

But the worktable end of his chamber was dark, its hearth was cold. Instead, Chade was seated before his own fire. He beckoned to me to sit beside his chair. I sat and looked up at him, but he was staring at the fire. He lifted his scarred hand and let it come to rest on my quillish hair. For a while we just sat like that, watching the fire together.

'Well, here we are, my boy,' he said at last, and then nothing more, as if he had said all he needed to. He ruffled my short hair.

'Burrich cut my hair,' I told him suddenly.

'So I see.'

'I hate it. It prickles against my pillow and I can't sleep. My hood won't stay up. And I look stupid.'

'You look like a boy mourning his father.'

I was silent a moment. I had thought of my hair as being a longer version of Burrich's extreme cut. But Chade was right. It was the length for a boy mourning his father, not a subject mourning a king. That only made me angrier.

'But why should I mourn him?' I asked Chade as I hadn't dared to ask Burrich. 'I didn't even know him.'

'He was your father.'

'He got me on some woman. When he found out about me, he left. A father. He never cared about me.' I felt defiant finally saying it out loud. It made me furious, Burrich's deep wild mourning and now Chade's quiet sorrow.

'You don't know that. You only hear what the gossips say. You aren't old enough to understand some things. You've never seen a wild bird lure predators away from its young by pretending to be injured.'

'I don't believe that,' I said, but I suddenly felt less confident saying it. 'He never did anything to make me think he cared about me.'

Chade turned to look at me and his eyes were older, sunken and red. 'If you had known he'd cared, so would others. When you are a man, maybe you'll understand just how much that cost him. To not know you in order to keep you safe. To make his enemies ignore you.'

'Well, I'll "not know" him to the end of my days, now,' I said sulkily.

Chade sighed. 'And the end of your days will come a great deal later than they would have had he acknowledged you as an heir.' He paused, then asked cautiously, 'What do you want to know about him, my boy?'

'Everything. But how would you know?' The more tolerant Chade was, the more surly I felt.

'I've known him all his life. I've . . . worked with him. Many times. Hand in glove, as the saying goes.'

'Were you the hand or the glove?'

No matter how rude I was, Chade refused to get angry. 'The hand,' he said after a brief consideration. 'The hand that moves unseen, cloaked by the velvet glove of diplomacy.'

'What do you mean?' Despite myself, I was intrigued.

'Things can be done.' Chade cleared his throat. 'Things can happen that make diplomacy easier. Or that make a party more willing to negotiate. Things can happen . . .'

My world turned over. Reality burst on me as suddenly as a vision, the fullness of what Chade was and what I was to be. 'You mean one man can die, and his successor can be easier to negotiate with because of it. More amenable to our cause, because of fear or because of . . .'

'Gratitude. Yes.'

A cold horror shook me as all the pieces suddenly fell into place. All the lessons and careful instructions and this is what they led to. I started to rise, but Chade's hand suddenly gripped my shoulder.

'Or a man can live, two years or five or a decade longer than any thought he could, and bring the wisdom and tolerance of age to the negotiations. Or a babe can be cured of a strangling cough, and the mother suddenly see with gratitude that what we offer can be beneficial to all involved. The hand doesn't always deal death, my boy. Not always.'

'Often enough.'

'I never lied to you about that.' I heard two things in Chade's voice that I had never heard before. Defensiveness. And hurt. But youth is merciless.

'I don't think I want to learn any more from you. I think I'm going to go to Shrewd and tell him to find someone else to kill people for him.'

'That is your decision to make. But I advise you against it, for now.'

His calmness caught me off-guard. 'Why?'

'Because it would negate all Chivalry tried to do for you. It would draw attention to you. And right now, that is not a good idea.' His words came ponderously slow, freighted with truth.

'Why?' I found I was whispering.

'Because some will be wanting to write *finis* to Chivalry's story completely. And that would be best done by eliminating you. Those ones will be watching how you react to your father's death. Does it give you ideas and make you restless? Will you become a problem now, the way he was?'

'What?'

'My boy,' he said, and pulled me close against his side. For the first time I heard the possession in his words. 'It is a time for you to be quiet and careful. I understand why Burrich cut your hair, but in truth I wish he had not. I wish no one had been reminded that Chivalry was your father. You are such a hatchling yet . . . but listen to me. For now, change nothing that you do. Wait six months, or a year. Then decide. But for now . . .'

'How did my father die?'

Chade's eyes searched my face. 'Did you not hear that he fell from a horse?'

'Yes. And I heard Burrich curse the man who told it, saying that Chivalry would not fall, nor would that horse throw him.'

'Burrich needs to guard his tongue.'

'Then how did my father die?'

'I don't know. But like Burrich, I do not believe he fell from a horse.' Chade fell silent. I sank down to sit by his bony bare feet and stare into his fire.

'Are they going to kill me, too?'

He was silent a long while. 'I don't know. Not if I can help it. I think they must first convince King Shrewd it is necessary. And if they do that, I shall know of it.'

'Then you think it comes from within the keep.'

'I do.' Chade waited long but I was silent, refusing to ask. He answered anyway. 'I knew nothing of it before it happened. I had no hand in it in any way. They didn't even approach me about it. Probably because they know I would have done more than just refused. I would have seen to it that it never happened.'

'Oh.' I relaxed a little. But already he had trained me too well in the ways of court thinking. 'Then they probably won't come to you if they decide they want me done. They'd be afraid of your warning me as well.'

He took my chin in his hand and turned my face so that I looked into his eyes. 'Your father's death should be all the warning you need, now or ever. You're a bastard, Fitz. We're always a risk and a vulnerability. We're always expendable. Except when we are an absolute necessity to their own security. I've taught you quite a bit, these last few years. But hold this lesson closest and keep it always before you. If ever you make it so they don't need you, they will kill you.'

I looked at him wide-eyed. 'They don't need me now.'

'Don't they? I grow old. You are young, and tractable, with the face and bearing of the royal family. As long as you don't show any inappropriate ambitions, you'll be fine.' He paused, then carefully emphasized, 'We are the *King's*, boy. His exclusively, in a way perhaps you have not thought about. No one knows what I do and most have forgotten who I am. Or was. If any know of us, it is from the King.'

I sat putting it cautiously together. 'Then . . . you said it came from within the keep. But if you were not used, then it was not from the King . . . the Queen!' I said it with sudden certainty.

Chade's eyes guarded his thoughts. 'That's a dangerous assumption to make. Even more dangerous if you think you must act on it in some way.'

'Why?'

Chade sighed. 'When you spring to an idea, and decide it is truth, without evidence, you blind yourself to other possibilities. Consider them all, boy. Perhaps it was an accident. Perhaps Chivalry was killed by someone he had offended at Withywoods. Perhaps it had nothing to do with him being a prince. Or, perhaps the King has another assassin, one I know nothing about, and it was the King's own hand against his son.'

'You don't believe any of those,' I said with certainty.

'No. I don't. Because I have no evidence to declare them truth. Just as I have no evidence to say your father's death was the Queen's hand striking.'

That is all I remember of our conversation then. But I am sure that Chade had deliberately led me to consider who might have acted against my father, to instil in me a greater wariness of the Queen. I held the thought close to me, and not just in the days that immediately followed. I kept myself to my chores, and slowly my hair grew, and by the beginning of real summer all seemed to have returned to normal. Once every few weeks, I would find myself sent off to town on errands. I soon came to see that no matter who sent me, one or two items on the list wound up in Chade's quarters, so I guessed who was behind my little bouts of freedom. I did not manage to spend time with Molly every time I went to town, but it was enough for me that I would stand outside the window of her shop until she noticed me, and at least exchanged a nod. Once I heard someone in the market talking about the quality of her scented candles, and how no one had made such a pleasant and healthful taper since her mother's day, and I smiled for her and was glad.

Summer came, bringing warmer weather to our coasts, and with it the Outislanders. Some came as honest traders, with cold-land goods to trade – furs and amber and ivory and kegs of oil – and tall tales to share, ones that still could prickle my neck just as they had when I was small. Our sailors did not trust them, and called them spies and worse. But their goods were rich, and the gold they brought to purchase our wines and grains was solid and heavy, and our merchants took it.

Other Outislanders also visited our shores, though not too close to Buckkeep Hold. They came with knives and torches, with bows and rams, to plunder and rape the same villages they had been plundering and raping for years. Sometimes it seemed an elaborate and bloody contest: for them to find villages unaware or underarmed and for us to lure them in with seemingly vulnerable targets and then to slaughter and plunder the pirates themselves. But if it were a contest, it went very badly for us that summer. My every visit to town was heavy with the news of destruction and the mutterings of the people.

Up at the keep, among the men-at-arms, there was a collective feeling of doltishness that I shared. The Outislanders eluded our warships with ease, and never fell into our traps. They struck where we were undermanned and least expecting it. Most discomfited of all was Verity, for to him had fallen the task of defending the kingdom once Chivalry had abdicated. I heard it muttered in the taverns that since he had lost his elder brother's good counsel, all had gone sour. No one spoke against Verity yet; but it was unsettling that no one spoke out strongly for him either.

Boyishly, I viewed the raids as a thing impersonal to me. Certainly they were bad things, and I felt sorry in a vague way for those villagers whose homes were torched or plundered. But secure at Buckkeep, I had very little feeling for the constant fear and vigilance that other seaports endured, or for the agonies of villagers who rebuilt each year, only to see their efforts torched the next. I was not to keep my ignorant innocence long.

I went down to Burrich for my 'lesson' one morning; though I spent as much time doctoring animals and teaching young colts and fillies as I did in being taught. I had very much taken over Cob's place in the stables, while he had gone on to being Regal's groom and dog man. But that day, to my surprise, Burrich took me upstairs to his room and sat me down at his table. I dreaded spending a tedious morning repairing tack.

'I'm going to teach you manners today,' Burrich announced suddenly. There was doubt in his voice, as if he were sceptical of my ability to learn such.

'With horses?' I asked incredulously.

'No. You've those already. With people. At table, and afterwards, when folk sit and talk with one another. Those sorts of manners.'

'Why?'

Burrich frowned. 'Because, for reasons I don't understand, you're to accompany Verity when he goes to Neatbay to see Lord Kelvar of Rippon. Lord Kelvar has not been cooperating with Lord Shemshy in manning the coastal towers. Shemshy accuses him of leaving towers completely without watches, so that the Outislanders are able to sail past and even anchor outside Watch Island, and from there raid Shemshy's villages in Shoaks Duchy. Prince Verity is going to consult with Kelvar about these allegations.'

I grasped the situation completely. It was common gossip around Buckkeep Town. Lord Kelvar of Rippon Duchy had three watch towers in his keeping. The two that bracketed the points of Neatbay were always well-manned, for they protected the best harbour in Rippon Duchy. But the tower on Watch Island protected little of Rippon that was worth much to Lord Kelvar; his high and rocky coastline sheltered few villages, and would-be raiders would have a hard time keeping their ships off the rocks while raiding. His southern coast was seldom bothered. Watch Island itself was home to little more than gulls, goats and a hefty population of clams. Yet the tower there was critical to the early defence of Southcove in Shoaks Duchy. It commanded views of both the inner and outer channels, and was placed on a natural summit that allowed its beacon fires to be easily seen from the mainland. Shemshy himself had a watch tower on Egg Island, but Egg was little more than a bit of sand that stuck up above the waves on high tide. It commanded no real view of the water, and was constantly in need of repair from the shifting of the sands and the occasional storm tide that overwhelmed it. But it could see a watch fire warning light from Watch Island and send the message on. As long as Watch Island tower lit such a fire.

Traditionally, the fishing grounds and clamming beaches of Watch Island were the territory of Rippon Duchy, and so the manning of the watch tower there had fallen to Rippon Duchy as well. But maintaining a garrison there meant bringing in men and their victuals, and also supplying wood and oil for the beacon fires, and maintaining the tower itself from the savage ocean storms that swept across the barren little island. It was an unpopular duty station for men-at-arms, and rumour had it that to be stationed there was a subtle form of punishment for unruly or unpolitical garrisons. More than once when in his cups, Kelvar had declaimed that if manning the tower was so important to Shoaks Duchy, then Lord Shemshy should do it himself. Not that Rippon Duchy was interested in surrendering the fishing grounds off the island or the rich shellfish beds.

So when Shoaks villages were raided, without warning, in an early spring spree that destroyed all hopes of the fields being planted on time, as well as seeing most of the pregnant sheep either slaughtered, stolen or scattered, Lord Shemshy had protested loudly to the King that Kelvar had been lax in manning his towers. Kelvar denied it, and asserted that the small force he had installed there was suitable for a location that seldom needed to be defended. 'Watchers, not soldiers, are what Watch Island tower requires,' he had declared. And for that purpose, he had recruited a number of elderly men and women to man the tower. A handful of them had been soldiers, but most were refugees from Neatbay; debtors and pickpockets and ageing whores, some declared, while supporters of Kelvar asserted they were but elderly citizens in need of secure employment.

All this I knew better from tavern gossip and Chade's political lectures than Burrich could imagine. But I bit my tongue and sat through his detailed and strained explanation. Not for the first time, I realized he considered me slightly slow. My silences he mistook for a lack of wit rather than a lack of any need to speak.

So now, laboriously, Burrich began to instruct me in the manners that, he told me, most other boys picked up simply by being around their elders. I was to greet people when I first encountered them each day, or if I walked into a room and found it occupied; melting silently away was not polite. I should call folk by their names, and if they were older than me or of higher political station, as, he reminded me, almost anyone I met on this journey would be, I should address them by title as well. Then he inundated me with protocol; who could precede me out of a room, and under what circumstances (almost anyone, and under almost all conditions, had precedence over me). And on to the manners of the table. To pay attention to where I was seated; to pay attention to whoever occupied the high seat at that table and pace my dining accordingly; how to drink a toast, or a series of toasts without overindulging myself. And how to speak engagingly, or more likely, to listen attentively, to whoever might be seated near me at dinner. And on. And on. Until I began to daydream wistfully of endlessly cleaning tack.

Burrich recalled my attention with a sharp poke. 'And you're not to do that, either. You look an imbecile, sitting there nodding with your mind elsewhere. Don't fancy no one notices when you do that. And don't glare like that when you're corrected. Sit up straight, and put a pleasant expression on your face. Not a vacuous smile, you dolt. Ah, Fitz, what am I to do with you? How can I protect you when you invite troubles on yourself? And why do they want to take you off like this anyway?'

The last two questions, put to himself, betrayed his real concern. Perhaps I was a trifle stupid not to have seen it. He wasn't going. I was. For no good reason that he could discern. Burrich had lived long enough near court to be very cautious. For the first time since he had been entrusted with my care, I was being removed from his watchfulness. It had not been so long since my father had been buried. And so he wondered, though he didn't dare say, whether I would be coming back or if someone was making the opportunity to dispose of me quietly. I realized what a blow to his pride and reputation it would be if I were to be 'vanished'. So I sighed, and then carefully commented that perhaps they wanted an extra hand with the horses and dogs. Verity went nowhere without Leon, his wolfhound. Only two days before he had complimented me on how well I managed him. This I repeated to Burrich, and it was gratifying to see how well this small subterfuge worked. Relief flooded his face, then pride that he had taught me well. The topic instantly shifted from manners to the correct care of the wolfhound. If the lectures on manners had wearied me, the repetition of hound lore was almost painfully tedious. When he released me to go to my other lessons, I left with winged feet.

I went through the rest of the day in a distracted haze that had Hod threatening me with a good whipping if I didn't attend to what I was doing. Then she shook her head over me, sighed, and told me to run along and come back when I had a mind again. I was only too happy to obey her. The thought of actually leaving Buckkeep and journeying, journeying all the way to

Neatbay was all I could fit inside my head. I knew I should wonder why I was going, but felt sure Chade would advise me soon. Would we go by land or by sea? I wished I had asked Burrich. The roads to Neatbay were not the best, I'd heard, but I wouldn't mind. Sooty and I had never been on a long journey together. But a sea trip, on a real ship . . .

I took the long way back to the keep, up a path that went through a lightly wooded bit of rocky hillside. Paper birches struggled there, and a few alder, but mostly it was nondescript brush. Sunlight and a light breeze were playing together in the higher branches, giving the day a fey and dappled air. I lifted my eyes to the dazzle of sun through the birch leaves, and when I looked down, the King's Fool stood before me.

I stopped in my tracks, astonished. Reflexively, I looked for the King, despite how ridiculous it would have been to find him here. But the Fool was alone. And outside, in the daylight! The thought made the hair on my arms and neck stand up in my tightened skin. It was common knowledge in the keep that the King's Fool could not abide the light of day. Common knowledge. Yet, despite what every page and kitchen maid nattered knowingly, there stood the Fool, pale hair floating in the light breeze. The blue and red silk of his motley jacket and trousers were startlingly bright against his paleness. But his eyes were not as colourless as they were in the dim passages of the keep. As I received their stare from only a few feet away in the light of day, I perceived there was a blueness to them, very pale, as if a single drop of pale blue wax had fallen onto a white platter. The whiteness of his skin was an illusion also, for out here in the dappling sunlight I could see a pinkness suffused him from within. 'Blood,' I realized with a sudden quailing. 'Red blood showing through layers of skin.'

The Fool took no notice of my whispered comment. Instead, a finger was held aloft, as if to pause not only my thoughts but the very day around us. But I could not have focused my attention more completely on anything, and when he was satisfied of this, the Fool smiled, showing small, white separate teeth, like a baby's new smile in a boy's mouth.

'Fitz!' he intoned in a piping voice. 'Fitz fitz fice fitz. Fatz sfitz.'

He stopped abruptly, and again gave me that smile. I stared back uncertainly, without word or movement.

Again the finger soared aloft, and this time was shaken at me. 'Fitz! Fitz fix fice fitz. Fats sfitzes.' He cocked his head at me, and the movement sent the dandelion fluff of his hair wafting in a new direction.

I was beginning to lose my fear of him. 'Fitz,' I said carefully, and tapped my chest with my forefinger. 'Fitz, that's me. Yes. My name is Fitz. Are you lost?' I tried to make my voice gentle and reassuring so as not to alarm the poor creature. For surely he had somehow wandered off from the keep, and that was why he seemed so delighted to find a familiar face.

He took a breath through his nose, and then shook his head violently, until his hair stood out all around his skull like a flame around a wind-blown candle. 'Fitz!' he said emphatically, his voice cracking a little. 'Fitz fitzes fyces fitz. Fatzafices.'

'It's all right,' I said soothingly. I crouched a bit, though in reality I was not that much taller than the Fool. I made a soft beckoning motion with my open hand. 'Come along, then. Come along. I'll show you the way back home. All right? Don't be afraid now.'

Abruptly the Fool dropped his hands to his sides. Then he lifted his face and rolled his eyes at the heavens. He looked back at me fixedly, and poked his mouth out as if he wanted to spit.

'Come along, now.' I beckoned to him again.

'No,' he said, quite plainly in an exasperated voice. 'Listen to me, you idiot. Fitz fixes fyces fitz. Fatsafices.'

'What?' I asked, startled.

'I said,' he enunciated elaborately. 'Fitz fixes fyce fits. Fat suffices.' He bowed, turned, and began to walk away from me, up the trail.

'Wait!' I demanded. My ears were turning red with my embarrassment. How do you politely explain to someone that you had believed for years that he was a moron as well as a Fool? I couldn't. So, 'What does all that fitzy-ficeys stuff mean? Are you making fun of me?'

'Hardly.' He paused long enough to turn, and say, 'Fitz fixes feists fits. Fat suffices. It's a message, I believe. A calling for a significant act. As you are the only one I know who endures being called Fitz, I believe it's for you. As for what it means, how should I know? I'm a Fool, not an interpreter of dreams. Good day.' Again he turned away from me, but this time instead of continuing up the path, he stepped off it, into a clump of buckbrush. I hurried after him, but when I got to where he had left the path, he was gone. I stood still, peering into the open, sun-dappled woods, thinking I should see a bush still swaying from his passage, or catch a glimpse of his motley jacket. But there was no sign of him.

And no sense at all to his silly message. I mulled over the strange encounter all the way back to the keep, but in the end I set it aside as a strange but random occurrence.

Not that night, but the next, Chade called me. Burning with curiosity, I raced up the stairs. But when I reached the top I halted, knowing that my questions would have to wait. For there sat Chade at the stone table, Slink perched on top of his shoulders, and a new scroll half unwound on the table before him. A glass of wine weighted one end as his crooked finger travelled slowly down some sort of listing. I glanced at it as I passed. It was a list of villages and dates. Beneath each village name was a tally: so many warriors, so many merchants, so many sheep or casks of ale or measures of grain, and so on. I sat down on the opposite side of the table and waited. I had learned not to interrupt Chade.

'My boy,' he said softly, without looking up from the scroll. 'What would you do if some ruffian walked up behind you and rapped you on the head? But only when your back was turned. How would you handle it?'

I thought briefly. 'I'd turn my back and pretend to be looking at something else. Only I'd have a long, thick stick in my hands. So when he rapped me, I'd spin around and break his head.'

'Hmm. Yes. Well, we tried that. But no matter how nonchalant we are, the Outislanders always seem to know when we are baiting them and never attack. Well, actually, we've managed to fool one or two of the ordinary raiders. But never the Red Ship Raiders. And those are the ones we want to hurt.'

'Why?'

'Because they are the ones that are hurting us the worst. You see, boy, we are used to being raided. You could almost say that we've adapted to it. Plant an extra acre, weave another bolt of cloth, raise an extra steer. Our farmers and townsfolk always try to put a bit extra by, and when someone's barn gets burned or a warehouse is torched in the confusion of a raid, everyone turns out to raise the beams again. But the Red Ship Raiders aren't just stealing, and destroying in the process of stealing. They're destroying, and what they actually carry off with them seems almost incidental.' Chade paused and stared at a wall as if seeing through it.

'It makes no sense,' he continued bemusedly, more to himself than to me. 'Or at least no sense that I can unravel. It's like killing a cow that bears a good calf every year. Red Ship Raiders torch the grain and hay still standing in the fields. They slaughter the stock they can't carry off. Three weeks ago, in Tornsby, they set fire to the mill and slashed open the sacks of grain and flour there. Where's the profit in that for them? Why do they risk their lives simply to destroy? They've made no effort to take and hold territory; they have no grievance against us that they've ever uttered. A thief you can guard against, but these are random killers and destroyers. Tornsby won't be rebuilt; the folk that survived have neither the will nor the resources. They've moved on, some to family in other towns, others to be beggars in our cities. It's a pattern we're seeing too often.'

He sighed, and then shook his head to clear it. When he looked up, he focused on me totally. It was a knack Chade had. He could set aside a problem so completely you would swear he had forgotten it. Now he announced, as if it were his only care, 'You'll be accompanying Verity when he goes to reason with Lord Kelvar at Neatbay.'

'So Burrich told me. But he wondered, and so do I. Why?'

Chade looked perplexed. 'Didn't you complain a few months ago that you had wearied of Buckkeep and wished to see more of the Six Duchies?'

'Certainly. But I rather doubt that that is why Verity is taking me.'

Chade snorted. 'As if Verity paid any attention as to who

makes up his retinue. He has no patience with the details; and hence none of Chivalry's genius for handling people. Yet Verity is a good soldier, and in the long run, perhaps that will be what we need. No, you are right. Verity has no inkling as to why you're going. But your King does. He and I have consulted together upon this. Are you ready to begin repaying all he has done for you? Are you ready to begin your service for the family?'

He said it so calmly and looked at me so openly that it was almost easy to be calm as I asked, 'Will I have to kill someone?'

'Perhaps.' He shifted in his chair. 'You'll have to decide that. Deciding and then doing it . . . it's different from simply being told, "That is the man and it must be done." It's much harder, and I'm not all that sure you're ready.'

'Would I ever be ready?' I tried to smile, and grinned like a muscle spasm. I tried to wipe it away, and couldn't. A strange quiver passed through me.

'Probably not.' Chade fell silent, and then decided that I had accepted the mission. 'You'll go as an attendant for an elderly noblewoman who is also going along, to visit relatives in Neatbay. It will not be too heavy a task for you. She is very elderly and her health is not good. Lady Thyme travels in a closed litter. You will ride beside it, to see she is not jolted too much, to bring her water if she asks for it, and to see to any other such small requests.'

'It doesn't sound too different from caring for Verity's wolfhound.'

Chade paused, then smiled. 'Excellent. That will fall to you as well. Become indispensable to everyone on this journey. Then you will have reasons to go everywhere and hear everything, and no one will question your presence.'

'And my real task?'

'To listen and learn. It seems to both Shrewd and me that these Red Ship Raiders are too well-acquainted with our strategies and strengths. Kelvar has recently begrudged the funds to staff the Watch Island tower properly. Twice he has neglected it, and twice have the coastal villages of Shoaks Duchy paid for his negligence. Has he gone beyond negligence to treachery? Does Kelvar confer with the enemy to his profit? We want you to sniff about and see what you can discover. If all you find is innocence, or if you have but strong suspicions, bring news back to us. But if you discover treachery, and you are certain of it, then we cannot be rid of him too soon.'

'And the means?' I was not sure that was my voice. It was so casual, so contained.

'I have prepared a powder, tasteless in a dish, colourless in a wine. We trust to your ingenuity and discretion in applying it.' He lifted a cover from an earthenware dish on the table. Within was a packet made of very fine paper, thinner and finer than anything Fedwren had ever shown me. Odd, how my first thought was how much my scribe master would love to work with paper like that. Inside the packet was the finest of white powders. It clung to the paper and floated in the air. Chade shielded his mouth and nose with a cloth as he tapped a careful measure of it into a twist of oiled paper. He held it out to me, and I took death upon my open palm.

'And how does it work?'

'Not too quickly. He will not fall dead at the table, if that is what you are asking. But if he lingers over his cup, he will feel ill. Knowing Kelvar, I suspect he will take his bubbling stomach to bed, and never awaken in the morning.'

I slipped it into my pocket. 'Does Verity know anything of this?'

Chade considered. 'Verity is as good as his name. He could not sit at table with a man he was poisoning and conceal it. No, in this endeavour, stealth will serve us better than truth.' He looked me directly in the eyes. 'You will work alone, with no counsel other than your own.'

'I see.' I shifted on my tall wooden stool. 'Chade?'

'Yes?'

'Is this how it was for you? Your first time?'

He looked down at his hands, and for a moment he fingered the angry red scars that dotted the back of his left hand. The silence grew long, but I waited.

'I was a year older than you are,' he said at last. 'And it was simply the doing of it, not the deciding if it should be done. Is that enough for you?'

I was suddenly embarrassed without knowing why. 'I suppose,' I mumbled.

'Good. I know you meant no harm by it, boy. But men don't

talk about times spent among the pillows with a lady. And assassins don't talk about . . . our business.'

'Not even teacher to pupil?'

Chade looked away from me, to a dark corner of the ceiling. 'No.' After a moment more he added, 'Two weeks from now, you'll perhaps understand why.'

And that was all we ever said about it.

By my count, I was thirteen years old.

EIGHT

Lady Thyme

A history of the duchies is a study of their geography. The Court Scribe of King Shrewd, one Fedwren, was very fond of this saying. I cannot say I have ever found it wrong. Perhaps all histories are recountings of natural boundaries. The seas and ice that stood between us and the Outislanders made us separate peoples and the rich grasslands and fertile meadows of the duchies created the riches that made us enemies; perhaps that would be the first of a history of the duchies. The Bear and the Vin rivers are what created the rich vineyards and orchards of Tilth, as surely as the Painted Edges Mountains rising above Sandsedge both sheltered and isolated the folk there and left them vulnerable to our organized armies.

I jerked awake before the moon had surrendered her reign over the sky, amazed that I had slept at all. Burrich had supervised my travel preparations so thoroughly the night before that, had it been left to me, I would have departed a minute after I had swallowed my morning porridge.

But such is not the way when a group of folk set out together to do anything. The sun was well over the horizon before we were all assembled and ready. 'Royalty,' Chade had warned me, 'never travels light. Verity goes on this journey with the weight of the King's sword behind him. All folk who see him pass know that without being told. The news must run ahead to Kelvar, and to Shemshy. The imperial hand is about to reconcile their differences. They must both be left wishing they had never had any differences at all. That is the trick of good government. To make folk desire to live in such a way that there is no need for its intervention.'

So Verity travelled with a pomp that clearly irritated the soldier in him. His picked troop of men wore his colours as well as the Farseer buck badges, and rode ahead of the regular troops. To my young eyes, that was impressive enough. But to keep the impact from being too martial, Verity brought with him noble companions to provide conversation and diversion at the end of the day. Hawks and hounds with their handlers, musicians and bards, one puppeteer, those who fetched and carried for the lords and ladies, those who saw to their garments and hair and the cooking of favourite dishes; baggage beasts; all trailed behind the well-mounted nobles, and made the tail of our procession.

My place was about midway in the procession. I sat a restive Sooty beside an ornate litter borne between two sedate grey geldings. Hands, one of the brighter stable-boys, had been assigned a pony and given charge of the horses bearing the litter. I would manage our baggage mule, and see to the litter's occupant. This was the very elderly Lady Thyme whom I had never met before. When she at last appeared to mount her litter, she was so swathed in cloaks, veils and scarves that I received only the impression that she was elderly in a gaunt rather than plump way, and that her perfume caused Sooty to sneeze. She settled herself in the litter amidst a nest of cushions, blankets, furs and wraps, then immediately ordered that the curtains be drawn and fastened despite the fineness of the morning. The two little maids who had attended her darted happily away, and I was left, her sole servant. My heart sank. I had expected at least one of them to travel within the litter with her. Who was going to see to her personal needs when her pavilion was set up? I had no notion as to waiting on a woman, let alone a very elderly one. I resolved to follow Burrich's advice for a young man dealing with elderly women: be attentive and polite, cheerful and pleasant of mien. Old women were easily won over by a personable young man. Burrich said so. I approached the litter.

'Lady Thyme? Are you comfortable?' I inquired. A long interval passed with no response. Perhaps she was slightly deaf. 'Are you comfortable?' I asked more loudly.

'Stop bothering me, young man!' was the surprisingly vehement response. 'If I want you, I'll tell you.'

'I beg pardon,' I quickly apologized.

'Stop bothering me, I said!' she rasped indignantly. And added in an undertone, 'Stupid churl.'

At this, I had the sense to be quiet, though my dismay increased tenfold. So much for a merry and companionable ride. Eventually I heard the horns cry out and saw Verity's pennant lifted far ahead of us. Dust drifting back told me that our foreguard had begun the journey. Long minutes passed before the horses in front of us moved. Hands started the litter horses and I chirruped to Sooty. She stepped out eagerly and the mule followed resignedly.

I well recall that day. I remember the dust hanging thick in the air from all those who preceded us, and how Hands and I conversed in lowered voices, for the first time we laughed aloud, Lady Thyme scolded, 'Stop that noise!' I also remember bright blue skies arching from hill to hill as we followed the gentle undulations of the coast road. There were breathtaking views of the sea from the hilltops, and flower-scented air thick and drowsy in the vales. There were also the shepherdesses, all in a row on top of a stone wall to giggle and point and blush at us while we passed. Their fleecy charges dotted the hillside behind them, and Hands and I exclaimed softly at the way they had bundled their bright skirts to one side and knotted them up, leaving their knees and legs bare to the sun and wind. Sooty was restive and bored with our slow pace, while poor Hands was constantly nudging his old pony in the ribs to make it keep up.

We stopped twice during the day, to allow riders to dismount and stretch, and to let the horses water. Lady Thyme did not emerge from her litter, but one time tartly reminded me that I should have brought her water by now. I bit my tongue and fetched her a drink. It was as close as we came to conversation.

We halted when the sun was still above the horizon. Hands and I erected Lady Thyme's small pavilion while she dined within her litter from a wicker basket of cold meat, cheese and wine that she had thoughtfully provided for herself. Hands and I fared more poorly, on soldier's rations of hard bread and harder cheese and dried meat. In the midst of my meal, Lady Thyme demanded that I escort her from the litter to her pavilion. She emerged draped and veiled as if for a blizzard. Her finery was of varying colours and degrees of age, but all had been both expensive and well cut at one time. Now, as she leaned heavily on me and tottered along, I smelled a repulsive cacophony of dust and mildew and perfume, with an underlying scent of urine. She tartly dismissed me at the door, and warned me that she had a knife and would use it if I attempted to enter and bother her in any way. 'And well do I know how to use it, young man!' she threatened me.

Our sleeping accommodations were also the same as the soldiers': the ground and our cloaks. But the night was fine and we made a small fire. Hands teased and giggled about my supposed lust for Lady Thyme and the knife that awaited me if I should attempt to satisfy it. That led to a wrestling match between us, until Lady Thyme shrilled threats at us for keeping her awake. Then we spoke softly as Hands told me that no one had envied my assignment to her; that anyone who had ever journeyed with her avoided her ever after. He warned me also that my worst task was yet to come, but adamantly refused, though his eyes brimmed with tears of laughter, to let me know what it was. I fell asleep easily, for boy-like, I had put my true mission out of my head until I should have to face it.

I awoke at dawn to the twittering of birds and the overwhelming stench of a brimming chamberpot outside Lady Thyme's pavilion. Though my stomach had been hardened by cleaning stables and kennels, it was all I could force myself to do to dump it and cleanse it before returning it to her. By then she was harpying at me through the tent door that I had not yet brought her water, hot or cold, nor cooked her porridge whose ingredients she had set out. Hands had disappeared, to share the troop's fire and rations, leaving me to deal with my tyrant. By the time I had served her on a tray that she assured me was slovenly arranged, and cleaned the dishes and pot and returned all to her, the rest of the procession was almost ready to leave. But she would not allow her pavilion to be struck until she was safely within her litter. We accomplished that packing in a frantic haste and I found myself finally on my horse without a crumb of breakfast inside me.

I was ravenous after my morning's work. Hands regarded my glum face with some sympathy and motioned me to ride closer to him. He leaned over to speak to me.

'Everyone but us had heard of her before.' This with a furtive nod toward Lady Thyme's litter. 'The stench she makes every morning is a legend. Whitelock says she used to go along on a lot of Chivalry's trips . . . She has relatives all over the Six Duchies, and not much to do except visit them. All the men in the troop say they learned a long time ago to stay out of her range or she puts them to a bunch of useless errands. Oh, and Whitelock sent you this. He says not to expect to sit down and eat as long as you're tending her. But he'll try to set aside a bit for you each morning.'

Hands passed me a wad of camp-bread with three rashers of bacon greasily cold inside it. It tasted wonderful. I wolfed down the first few bites greedily.

'Churl!' shrilled Lady Thyme from inside her litter. 'What are you doing up there? Discussing your betters, I've no doubt. Get back to your position! How are you to see to my needs if you're gallivanting ahead like that?'

I quickly reined Sooty in and dropped back to a position alongside the litter. I swallowed a great lump of bread and bacon and managed to ask, 'Is there anything your ladyship requires?'

'Don't talk with your mouth full,' she snapped. 'And stop bothering me. Stupid clod.'

And so it went. The road followed the coastline, and at our laden pace it took us a full five days to reach Neatbay. Other than two small villages, our scenery consisted of windswept cliffs, gulls, meadows and occasional stands of twisted and stunted trees. Yet to me it seemed full of beauties and wonders, for every bend in the road brought me to a place I had never seen before.

As our journey wore on, Lady Thyme became more tyrannical. By the fourth day she had a constant stream of complaints, few of which I could do anything about. Her litter swayed too much; it was making her ill. The water I brought from a stream was too cold, that from my own water bags too warm. The men and horses ahead of us were raising too much dust; they were doing it on purpose, she was sure. And tell them to stop singing those rude songs. With her to deal with I had no time to think about killing or not killing Lord Kelvar, even if I had wanted to.

Early on the fifth day we saw the rising smoke of Neatbay. By noon we could pick out the larger buildings and the Neatbay watchtower on the cliffs above the town. Neatbay was a much gentler piece of land than Buckkeep. Our road wound down through a wide valley. The blue waters of Neatbay itself opened wide before us. The beaches were sandy, and their fishing fleet was all shallow draught vessels with flat bottoms, or spunky little dories that rode the waves like gulls. Neatbay didn't have the deep anchorage that Buckkeep did, so it was not the shipping and trading port that we were, but all the same it seemed to me it would have been a fine place to live.

Kelvar sent an honour guard to meet us, so there was a delay as they exchanged formalities with Verity's troops. 'Like two dogs sniffing each other's bung-holes,' Hands observed sourly. By standing in my stirrups, I was able to see far enough down the line to observe the official posturings, and grudgingly nodded my agreement. Eventually we got under way again, and were soon riding through the streets of Neatbay town itself.

Everyone else proceeded straight up to Kelvar's keep, but Hands and I were obliged to escort Lady Thyme's litter through several backstreets to reach the particular inn that she insisted on using. From the look on the chambermaid's face, she had guested there before. Hands took the litter horses and litter to the stables, but I had to endure her leaning heavily on my arm as I escorted her to her chamber. I wondered what she had eaten that had been so foully spiced as to make her every breath a trial to me. She dismissed me at the door, warning myriad punishments if I didn't return promptly in seven days. As I left, I felt sympathy for the chambermaid, for Lady Thyme's voice was lifted in a loud tirade about thieving maids she had encountered in the past, and exactly how she wanted the bed linens arranged on the bed.

With a light heart I mounted Sooty and called to Hands to make haste. We cantered through the streets of Neatbay, and managed to rejoin the tail of Verity's procession as they entered

Kelvar's keep. Bayguard was built on flat land that offered little natural defence, but was fortified by a series of walls and ditches that an enemy would have had to surmount before facing the stout stone walls of the keep. Hands told me that raiders had never got past the second ditch and I believed him. Workmen were doing maintenance on the walls and ditches as we passed, but they halted and watched in wonder as the King-in-Waiting came to Bayguard.

Once keep gates closed behind us, there was another interminable welcoming ceremony. Men and horses and all, we were kept standing in the midday sun while Kelvar and Bayguard welcomed Verity. Horns sounded and then the mutter of official voicings muted by shifting horses and men. But at last it was over. This was signalled by a sudden general movement of men and beasts as the formations ahead of us broke up.

Men dismounted and Kelvar's stable-folk were suddenly among us, directing us where to water our mounts, where we might rest for the night, and most important to any soldier, where we might ourselves wash and eat. I fell in beside Hands as we led Sooty and his pony toward the stables. I heard my name called and turned to see Sig from Buckkeep pointing me out to someone in Kelvar's colours.

'There he be: that's the fitz. Ho, Fitz! Sitswell here says you're summoned. Verity wants you in his chamber; Leon's sick. Hands, you take Sooty for the fitz.'

I could almost feel the food being snatched from my jaws. But I took a breath and presented a cheerful countenance to Sitswell, as Burrich had counselled me. I doubt that dour man even noticed. To him I was just one more boy underfoot on a hectic day. He took me to Verity's chamber and left me, obviously relieved to return to his stables. I tapped softly and Verity's man opened the door at once.

'Ah! Thank Eda it's you. Come in, then, for the beast won't eat and Verity's sure it's serious. Hurry up, Fitz.'

The man wore Verity's badge, but was no one I remembered having met. Sometimes it was disconcerting how many folk knew who I was when I had no inkling who they were. In an adjoining chamber Verity was splashing and instructing someone loudly about what garments he wished for the evening. But he was not my concern. Leon was.

Leon was Verity's wolfhound. I groped toward him, for I had no qualms about it when Burrich wasn't about. Leon lifted his bony head and regarded me with martyred eyes. He was lying on Verity's sweaty shirt in a corner by a cold hearth. He was too hot, he was bored, and if we weren't going to hunt anything he wanted to go home.

I made a show of running my hands over him and lifting his lips to examine his gums and then pressing my hand down firmly on his belly. I finished all this by scratching behind his ears and then told Verity's man, 'There's nothing wrong with him, he just isn't hungry. Let's give him a bowl of cold water and wait. When he wants to eat, he'll let us know. And let's take away all this, before it spoils in this heat and he eats it anyway and becomes really sick.' I referred to a dish already overfilled with scraps of pastries from a tray that had been set for Verity. None of it was fit for the dog, but I was so hungry I wouldn't have minded dining off the scraps myself; in fact my stomach growled at the sight of it. 'I wonder if I found the kitchens, perhaps they would have a fresh, beef bone for him? Something that's more toy than food is what he would welcome most now . . .'

'Fitz? Is that you? In here, boy! What's troubling my Leon?'

'I'll fetch the bone,' the man assured me, and I rose and stepped to the entrance of the adjoining room.

Verity rose dripping from his bath and took the proffered towel from his serving-man. He towelled his hair briskly and then again demanded as he dried himself, 'What's the matter with Leon?'

That was Verity's way. Months had passed since we had last spoken but he took no time for greetings. Chade said it was a lack in him, that he didn't make his men feel their importance to him. I think he believed that if anything significant had happened to me, someone would have told him. He had a bluff heartiness to him that I enjoyed, an attitude that things must be going well unless someone had told him otherwise.

'Not much is wrong with him, sir. He's a bit out of sorts from the heat and from travelling. A night's rest in a cool place will perk him up; but I'd not fill him full of pastry bits and suety things; not in this hot weather.'

'Well.' Verity bent down to dry his legs. 'Like as not, you're right, boy. Burrich says you've a way with the hounds, and I won't ignore what you say. It's just that he seemed so moony, and usually he has a good appetite for anything, but especially for anything from my plate.' He seemed abashed, as if caught cooing at an infant. I didn't know what to say.

'If that's all, sir, should I be returning to the stables?'

He glanced at me over his shoulder, puzzled. 'Seems a bit of a waste of time to me. Hands will see to your mount, won't he? You need to bathe and dress if you're to be on time for dinner. Charim? Have you water for him?'

The serving-man straightened from arranging Verity's garments on the bed. 'Right away, sir. And I'll lay out his clothes as well.'

In the space of the next hour, my place in the world seemed to shift topsy-turvy. I had known this was coming. Both Burrich and Chade had tried to prepare me for it. But to go suddenly from an insignificant hanger-on at Buckkeep to part of Verity's formal entourage was unnerving. Everyone else assumed I knew what was going on.

Verity was dressed and out of the room before I was into the tub. Charim informed me that he had gone to confer with his captain of guards. I was grateful that Charim was such a gossip. He did not consider my rank so lofty as to forbear from chatting and complaining in front of me.

'I'll make you up a pallet in here for the night. I doubt you'll be chill. Verity said he wanted you housed close by him, and not just to tend the hound. He has other chores for you as well?'

Charim paused hopefully. I covered my silence by ducking my head into the lukewarm water and soaping the sweat and dust from my hair. I came up for air.

He sighed. 'I'll lay out your clothes for you. Leave me those dirty ones. I'll wash them out for you.'

It seemed very strange to have someone waiting on me while I washed, and stranger still to have someone supervise my dressing. Charim insisted on straightening the seams on my jerkin and seeing the oversized sleeves on my new best shirt hung to their fullest and most annoying length. My hair had regrown long enough to have snarls in it and these he tugged out quickly and painfully. To a boy accustomed to dressing himself the primping and inspection seemed endless.

'Blood will tell,' said an awed voice from the entry. I turned to find Verity beholding me with a mixture of pain and amusement on his face.

'He's the image of Chivalry at that age, is he not, my lord?' Charim sounded immensely pleased with himself.

'He is.' Verity paused to clear his throat. 'No man can doubt who fathered you, Fitz. I wonder what my father was thinking when he told me to show you well? Shrewd he is called and shrewd he is; I wonder what he expects to gain. Ah, well.' He sighed. 'That is his kind of kingship, and I leave it to him. Mine is simply to ask a foppish old man why he cannot keep his watch towers properly manned. Come, boy. It's time we went down.'

He turned and left without waiting for me. As I hastened after him, Charim caught at my arm. 'Three steps behind him and on his left. Remember.' And that is where I fell in behind him. As he moved down the hallway, others of our entourage stepped out from their chambers and followed their prince. All were decked in their most elaborate finery, to maximize this chance to be seen and envied outside Buckkeep. The fullness of my sleeves was quite reasonable compared to what some were sporting. At least my shoes were not hung with tiny chiming bells or gently rattling amber beads.

Verity paused at the top of a stairway, and a hush fell over the folk gathered below. I looked out over the faces turned up to their prince, and had time to read on them every emotion known to mankind. Some women simpered while others appeared to sneer. Some young men struck poses that displayed their clothes; others, dressed more simply, straightened as if to be on guard. I read envy and love, disdain, fear, and on a few faces, hatred. But Verity gave none of them more than a passing glance before he descended. The crowd parted before us, to reveal Lord Kelvar himself waiting to conduct us into the dining hall.

Kelvar was not what I expected. Verity had called him foppish, but what I saw was a rapidly ageing man, thin and harried, who wore his extravagant clothes as if they were armour against time. His greying hair was pulled back in a thin tail as if he were still a man-at-arms, and he walked with that peculiar gait of the very good swordsman.

I saw him as Chade had taught me to see folk, and thought I understood him well enough even before we were seated. But it was after we had taken our places at table (and mine, to my surprise, was not so far down from the high folk) that I got my deepest glance into the man's soul. And this not by any act of his, but in the bearing of his lady as she arrived to join us.

I doubt if Kelvar's Lady Grace was much more than a hand of years older than I, and she was decked out like a magpie's nest. Never had I seen accoutrements before that spoke so garishly of expense and so little of taste. She took her seat in a flurry of flourishes and gestures that reminded me of a courting bird. Her scent rolled over me like a wave, and it too smelled of coin more than flowers. She had brought a little dog with her, a feist that was all silky hair and big eyes. She cooed over him as she settled him on her lap, and the little beast cuddled against her and set his chin on the edge of the table. And all the time, her eyes were on Prince Verity, trying to see if he marked her and was impressed. For my part, I watched Kelvar watch her perform her flirtations for the prince, and I thought to myself, there is more than half our problems with keeping Watch Island tower manned.

Dinner was a trial to me. I was ravenous, but manners forbade that I show it. I ate as I had been instructed, picking up my spoon when Verity did, and setting aside a course as soon as he showed disinterest in it. I longed for a good platter of hot meat with bread to sop up the juices, but what we were offered were tidbits of meat oddly spiced, exotic fruit compotes, pale breads, and vegetables cooked to pallor and then seasoned. It was an impressive display of good food abused in the name of fashionable cooking. I could see that Verity's appetite was as slack as mine, and wondered if all could see that the prince was not impressed.

Chade had taught me better than I had known. I was able to nod politely to my dinner companion, a freckled young woman, and follow her conversation about the difficulty of getting good linen fabric in Rippon these days, while letting my ears stray enough to pick up key bits of talk about the table. None of it was about the business that had brought us here. Verity and Lord Kelvar would closet themselves tomorrow for the discussion of that. But much of what I overheard touched on the manning of Watch Island's tower, and cast odd lights on it.

I overheard grumblings that the roads were not as well maintained as previously. Someone commented she was glad to see that repair on Bayguard's fortifications had been resumed. Another man complained that inland robbers were so common, he could scarcely count on two-thirds of his merchandise coming through from Farrow. This, too, seemed to be the basis of my dining companion's complaint about the lack of good fabric. I looked at Lord Kelvar, and how he doted upon his young wife's every gesture. As if Chade were whispering in my ear, I heard his judgement. 'There is a duke whose mind is not upon the governing of his duchy.' I suspected Lady Grace was wearing the required road repairs and the wages of those soldiers who would have kept his trade routes policed against brigands. Perhaps the jewels that dangled from her ears should have gone for pay to man Watch Island's towers.

Dinner finally ended. My stomach was full, but my hunger unabated, there had been so little substance to the meal. Afterwards, two minstrels and a poet entertained us, but I tuned my ears to the casual talk of folk rather than to the fine phrasings of the poet or the ballads of the musicians. Kelvar sat to the prince's right, while his lady sat to the left, her lap-dog sharing the chair.

Grace sat basking in the prince's presence. Her hands often strayed to touch first an earring, then a bracelet. She was not accustomed to wearing so much jewellery. My suspicion was that she had come of simple stock, and was awed by her own position. One minstrel sang 'Fair Rose amidst the Clover', his eyes on her face, and was rewarded with her flushed cheeks. But as the evening wore on and I grew weary, I could tell that Lady Grace was fading. She yawned once, lifting a hand too late to cover it. Her little dog had gone to sleep in her lap, and twitched and yipped occasionally in his small-brained dreams. As she grew sleepier, she reminded me of a child; she cuddled her dog as if it were a doll, and leaned her head back into the corner of her chair. Twice she started to nod off. I saw her surreptitiously pinching the skin on her wrists in an effort to wake herself up. She was visibly relieved when Kelvar summoned the minstrels and poet forward to reward them for their evening. She took her lord's arm to follow him off to their bedchamber while never relinquishing the dog she snuggled in her arm.

I was relieved to make my way up to Verity's antechamber. Charim had found me a featherbed and some blankets. My pallet was fully as comfortable as my own bed. I longed to sleep, but Charim gestured me into Verity's bedchamber. Verity, ever the soldier, had no use for lackeys to stand about and tug his boots off for him. Charim and I alone attended him. Charim clucked and muttered as he followed Verity about, picking up and smoothing the garments the Prince so casually shed. Verity's boots he immediately took off into a corner and began working more wax into the leather. Verity dragged a nightshirt on over his head and then turned to me.

'Well? What have you to tell me?'

And so I reported to him as I did to Chade, recounting all I had overheard, in as close to the words as I could manage, and noting who had spoken and to whom. At the last I added my own suppositions about the significance of it all. 'Kelvar is a man who has taken a young wife, one who is easily impressed with wealth and gifts,' I summarized. 'She has no idea of the responsibilities of her own position, let alone his. Kelvar diverts money, time and thought from his duties to enthralling her. Were it not disrespectful to say so, I would imagine that his manhood is failing him, and he seeks to satisfy his young bride with gifts as a substitute.'

Verity sighed heavily. He had flung himself onto the bed during the latter half of my recitation. Now he prodded at a too-soft pillow, folding it to give more support to his head. 'Damn Chivalry,' he said absently. "This is his kind of a knot, not mine. Fitz, you sound like your father. And were he here, he'd find some subtle way to handle this whole situation. Chiv would have had it solved by now, with one of his smiles and a kiss on someone's hand. But that's not my way, and I won't pretend to it.' He shifted about in his bed uncomfortably, as if he expected me to raise some argument to him about his duty. 'Kelvar's a man and a duke. And he has a duty. He's to man that tower properly. It's simple enough, and I intend to tell him that bluntly. Put decent soldiers in that tower, keep them there, and keep them happy enough to do a job. It seems simple to me. And I'm not going to make it into a diplomatic dance.'

He shifted heavily in the bed, then abruptly turned his back to me. 'Put out the light, Charim.' And Charim did, so promptly that I was left standing in the dark and had to blunder my way out of the chamber and back to my own pallet. As I lay down, I pondered that Verity saw so little of the whole. He could force Kelvar to man the tower, yes. But he couldn't force him to man it well, or take pride in it. That was a matter for diplomacy. And had he no heed for the roadwork and maintenance on the fortifications and the highwaymen problem? All that needed to be remedied now, in such a way that Kelvar's pride was kept intact, and that his position with Lord Shemshy was both corrected and affirmed. And someone had to undertake to teach Lady Grace her responsibilities. So many problems. But as soon as my head touched the pillow, I slept.

NINE

Fat Suffices

The Fool came to Buckkeep in the seventeenth year of King Shrewd's reign. This is one of the few facts that are known about the Fool. Said to be a gift from the Bingtown Traders, the origin of the Fool can only be surmised. Various stories have arisen. One is that the Fool was a captive of the Red Ship Raiders, and that the Bingtown Traders seized the Fool from them. Another is that the Fool was found as a babe, adrift in a small boat, shielded from the sun by a parasol of sharkskin and cushioned from the thwarts by a bed of heather and lavender. This can be dismissed as a creation of fancy. We have no real knowledge of the Fool's life before his arrival at King Shrewd's court.

The Fool was almost certainly born of the human race, though, not entirely of human parentage. Stories that he was born of the Other Folk are almost certainly false, for his fingers and toes are completely free of webbing and he has never shown the slightest fear of cats. The unusual physical characteristics of the Fool (lack of colouring, for instance) seem to be traits of his other parentage, rather than an individual aberration, though in this I well may be mistaken.

In the matter of the Fool, that which we do not know is almost more significant than that which we do. The age of the Fool at the time of his arrival at Buckkeep has been a matter for conjecture. From personal experience, I can vouch that the Fool appeared much younger, and in all ways more juvenile than at present. But as the Fool shows little sign of ageing it may be that he was not as young as he initially appeared, but rather was at the end of an extended childhood.

The gender of the Fool has been disputed. When directly questioned on this matter by a younger and more forward person than I am now, the Fool replied that it was no one's business but his own. So I concede.

In the matter of his prescience and the annoyingly vague forms that it takes, there is no consensus as to whether a racial or individual talent is being manifested. Some believe he knows all in advance, and even that he will always know if anyone, anywhere, speaks about him. Others say it is only his great love of saying, 'I warned you so!' and that he takes his most obscure sayings and twists them to have been prophecies. Perhaps sometimes this has been so, but in many well-witnessed cases, he has predicted, however obscurely, events that later came to pass.

Hunger woke me shortly after midnight. I lay awake, listening to my belly growl. I closed my eyes but my hunger was enough to make me nauseous. I got up and felt my way to the table where Verity's tray of pastries had been, but servants had cleared it away.

Easing open the chamber door, I stepped out into the dimly-lit hall. The two men Verity had posted there looked at me questioningly. 'Starving,' I told them. 'Did you notice where the kitchens were?'

I have never known a soldier who didn't know where the kitchens were. I thanked them, and promised to bring back some of whatever I found. I slipped off down the shadowy hall. As I descended the steps, it felt odd to have wood underfoot rather than stone. I walked as Chade had taught me, placing my feet silently, moving within the shadowiest parts of the passageways, walking to the sides where floorboards were less likely to creak. And it all felt natural.

The rest of the keep seemed well asleep. The few guards I passed were mostly dozing; none challenged me. At the time I put it down to my stealth; now I wonder if they considered a skinny, tousle-headed lad any threat worth bothering with.

I found the kitchens easily. It was a great open room, flagged and walled with stone as a defence against fires. There were three great hearths, fires well-banked for the night. Despite the lateness, or earliness, of the hour, the place was brightly lit. A keep's kitchen is never completely asleep.

I saw the covered pans and smelled the rising bread. A large pot of stew was being kept warm at the edge of one hearth. When I peeked under the lid, I saw it would not miss a bowl or two. I rummaged about and helped myself. Wrapped loaves on a shelf supplied me with an end crust and in another corner was a tub of butter kept cool inside a large keg of water. Not fancy, thank all, but the plain, simple food I had been craving all day.

I was halfway through my second bowl when I heard the light scuff of footsteps. I looked up with my most disarming smile, hoping that this cook would prove as soft-hearted as Buckkeep's. But it was a serving-girl, a blanket thrown about her shoulders over her nightrobe and her baby in her arms. She was weeping. I turned my eyes away in discomfort.

She scarcely gave me a glance anyway. She set her bundled baby down on top of the table, fetched a bowl and dipped it full of cool water, muttering all the time. She bent over the babe. 'Here, my sweet, my lamb. Here, my darling. This will help. Take a little. Oh, sweetie, can't you even lap? Open your mouth, then. Come now, open your mouth.'

I couldn't help but watch. She held the bowl awkwardly and tried to manoeuvre it to the baby's mouth. She was using her other hand to force the child's mouth open, and using a deal more force than I'd ever seen any other mother use on a child. She tipped the bowl, and the water slopped. I heard a strangled gurgle, and then a gagging sound. As I leapt up to protest, the head of a small dog emerged from the bundle.

'Oh, he's choking again! He's dying! My little Feisty is dying and no one but me cares. He just goes on snoring, and I don't know what to do and my darling is dying!'

She clutched the lap-dog to her as it gagged and strangled. It shook its little head wildly and then seemed to grow calmer. If I hadn't been able to hear its laboured breathing, I'd have sworn it had died in her arms. Its dark and bulgy eyes met mine, and I felt the force of the panic and pain in the little beast.

Easy. 'Here, now,' I heard myself saying. 'You're not helping him by holding him that tight. He can scarce breathe. Set him down. Unwrap him. Let him decide how he is most comfortable.

All wrapped up like that, he's too hot, so he's trying to pant and choke all at once. Set him down.'

She was a head taller than I and for a moment I thought I was going to have to struggle with her. But she let me take the bundled dog from her arms, and unwrap him from several layers of cloth. I set him on the table.

The little beast was in total misery. He stood with his head drooping between his front legs. His muzzle and chest were slick with saliva, his belly distended and hard. He began to retch and gag again. His small jaws opened wide, his lips writhed back from his tiny, pointed teeth. The redness of his tongue attested to the violence of his efforts. The girl squeaked and sprang forward, trying to snatch him up again, but I pushed her roughly back. 'Don't grab him,' I told her impatiently. 'He's trying to get something up, and he can't do it with you squeezing his guts.'

She stopped. 'Get something up?'

'He looks and acts as if he's got something lodged in his gullet, Could he have got into bones or feathers?'

She looked stricken. 'There were bones in the fish. But only tiny ones.'

'Fish? What idiot let him get into fish? Was it fresh or rotten?' I'd seen how sick a dog could get when it got into rotten, spawned-out salmon on a river bank. If that was what this little beast had gobbled, he didn't have a chance.

'It was fresh, and well-cooked. The same trout I had at dinner.'

'Well, at least it's not likely to be poisonous to him. Right now, it's just the bone. But if he gets it down, it's still likely to kill him.'

She gasped. 'No, it can't! He mustn't die. He'll be fine. He just has an upset stomach. I just fed him too much. He'll be fine! What do you know about it anyway, kitchen-boy?'

I watched the feist go through another round of convulsive retching. Nothing came up but yellow bile. 'I'm not a kitchen-boy. I'm a dog-boy. Verity's own dog-boy, if you must know. And if we don't help this little pup, he's going to die. Very soon.'

She watched, her face a mixture of awe and horror, as I gripped her little pet firmly. *I'm trying to help.* He didn't believe me. I prised his jaws open and forced my two fingers down his gullet.

The feist gagged even more fiercely, and pawed at me frantically. His claws needed cutting, too. With the tips of my fingers I could feel the bone. I twiddled my fingers against it, and felt it move, but it was wedged sideways in the little beast's throat. The dog gave a strangled howl and struggled frantically in my arms. I let him go. 'Well. He's not going to get rid of that without some help,' I observed.

I left her wailing and snivelling over him. At least she didn't snatch him up and squeeze him. I got myself a handful of butter from the keg and plopped it into my stew bowl. Now, I needed something hooked, or sharply curved, but not too large . . . I rattled through bins, and finally came up with a curved hook of metal with a handle on it. Possibly it was used to lift hot pots off the fire.

'Sit down,' I told the maid.

She gaped at me, and then sat obediently on the bench I'd pointed to.

'Now hold him firmly, between your knees. And don't let him go, no matter how he claws and wiggles or yelps. And hold onto his front feet, so he doesn't claw me to ribbons while I'm doing this. Understand?'

She took a deep breath, then gulped and nodded. Tears were streaming down her face. I set the dog on her lap and put her hands on him.

'Hold tight,' I told her. I scooped up a gobbet of butter. 'I'm going to use the fat to grease things up. Then I've got to force his jaws open, and hook the bone and jerk it out. Are you ready?'

She nodded. The tears had stopped flowing and her lips were set. I was glad to see she had some strength to her. I nodded back.

Getting the butter down was the easy part. It blocked his throat, though, and his panic increased, pounding at my self-control with his waves of terror. I had no time to be gentle as I forced his jaws open, and then put the hook down his throat. I hoped I wouldn't snag his flesh. But if I did, well, he would die anyway. I turned the tool in his throat as he wiggled and yelped and pissed all over his mistress. The hook caught on the bone and I pulled, evenly and firmly.

It came up in a welter of froth and bile and blood. A nasty

little bone, not a fish bone at all, but the partial breastbone of a small bird. I flipped it onto the table. 'And he shouldn't have poultry bones either,' I told her severely.

I don't think she even heard me. Doggie was wheezing gratefully on her lap. I picked up the dish of water and held it out to him. He sniffed it, lapped a bit, and then curled up, exhausted. She picked him up and cradled him in her arms, her head bent over his.

'There's something I want from you,' I began.

'Anything.' She spoke into his fur. 'Ask, and it's yours.'

'First, stop giving him your food. Give him only red meat and boiled grain for a while. And for a dog that size, no more than you can cup in your hand. And don't carry him everywhere. Make him run about, to give him some muscle and wear down his nails. And wash him. He smells foul, coat and breath, from too-rich food, or he won't live but another year or two.'

She looked up, stricken. Her hand went up to her mouth. And something in her motion, so like her self-conscious touching of her jewellery at dinner, suddenly made me realize who I was scolding. Lady Grace. And I had made her dog piss on her nightrobe.

Something in my face must have given me away. She smiled delightedly and held her feist closer. 'I'll do as you suggest, dog-boy. But for yourself? Is there nothing you'd ask as reward?'

She thought I'd ask for a coin or ring or even a position with her household. Instead, as steadily as I could, I looked at her and said, 'Please, Lady Grace. I ask that you ask your lord to man Watch Island's tower with the best of his men, to put an end to the strife between Rippon and Shoaks Duchies.'

'What?'

That single word question told me volumes about her. The accent and inflection hadn't been learned as Lady Grace.

'Ask your lord to man his towers well. Please.'

'Why does a dog-boy care about such things?'

Her question was too blunt. Wherever Kelvar had found her, she hadn't been high-born, or wealthy before this. Her delight when I recognized her, the way she had brought her dog down to the familiar comfort of a kitchen, by herself, wrapped in her blanket, told of a common girl elevated too quickly and too far above her previous station. She was lonely, and uncertain, and uneducated as to what was expected of her. Worse, she knew that she was ignorant, and that knowledge ate at her and soured her pleasures with fear. If she did not learn how to be a duchess before her youth and beauty faded, only years of loneliness and ridicule could await her. She needed a mentor, someone secret, like Chade. She needed the advice I could give her, right now. But I had to go carefully, for she would not accept advice from a dog-boy. Only a common girl might do that, and the only thing she knew about herself right now was that she was no longer a common girl, but a duchess.

'I had a dream,' I said, suddenly inspired. 'So clear. Like a vision. Or a warning. It woke me and I felt I must come to the kitchen.' I let my eyes unfocus. Her eyes went wide. I had her. 'I dreamed of a woman, who spoke wise words and turned three strong men into a united wall that the Red Ship Raiders could not breach. She stood before them, and jewels were in her hands, and she said, "Let the watchtowers shine brighter than the gems in these rings. Let the vigilant soldiers who man them encircle our coast as these pearls used to encircle my neck. Let the keeps be strengthened anew against those who threaten our people. For I would be glad to walk plain in the sight of both king and commoner, and let the defences that guard our people become the jewels of our land". And the King and his dukes were astounded at her wise heart and noble ways. But her people loved her best of all, for they knew she loved them better than gold or silver.'

It was awkward, not near as cleverly spoken as I had hoped to make it. But it caught her fancy. I could see her imagining herself standing straight and noble before the King and astonishing him with her sacrifice. I sensed in her the burning desire to distinguish herself, to be spoken of admiringly by the people she had come from. This would show them she was now a duchess in more than name. Lord Shemshy and his entourage would carry word of her deed back to Shoaks Duchy. Minstrels would celebrate her words in song. And her husband for once would be surprised by her. Let him see her as someone who cared for the land and folk, rather than the pretty little thing he had snared with his title. I could almost see the thoughts parade through her mind. Her eyes had gone distant and she wore an abstracted smile.

'Good night, dog-boy,' she said softly, and glided from the kitchen, her dog cuddled against her breast. She wore the blanket around her shoulders as if it were a cloak of ermine. She would play her role tomorrow very well. I grinned suddenly, wondering if I had accomplished my mission without poison. Not that I had really investigated whether or not Kelvar was guilty of treason; but I had a feeling that I had chopped the root of the problem. I was willing to bet that Watch Island tower would be well-manned before the week was out.

I made my way back up to my bed. I had pilfered a loaf of fresh bread from the kitchen and this I offered to the guards who readmitted me to Verity's bedchamber. In some distant part of Baykeep someone brayed out the hour. I didn't pay much attention. I burrowed back into my bedding, my belly satisfied and my spirit anticipating the spectacle that Lady Grace would present tomorrow. As I dozed off, I was wagering with myself that she would wear something straight and simple and white, and that her hair would be unbound.

I never got to find out. It seemed but moments later that I was shaken awake. I opened my eyes to find Charim crouched over me. A dim light from a lit candle made elongated shadows on the chamber walls. 'Wake up, Fitz,' he whispered hoarsely. 'A runner's come to the keep, from Lady Thyme. She requires you immediately. Your horse is being made ready.'

'Me?' I asked stupidly.

'Of course. I've laid out clothes for you. Dress quietly. Verity is still asleep.'

'What does she need me for?'

'Why, I don't know. The message wasn't specific. Perhaps she's taken ill, Fitz. The runner said only that she required you immediately. I suppose you'll find out when you get there.'

That was slim comfort. But it was enough to stir curiosity in me, and in any case, I had to go. I didn't know exactly what relation Lady Thyme was to the King, but she was far above me in importance. I didn't dare ignore her command. I dressed quickly by candlelight and left my room for the second time that night.

Hands had Sooty saddled and ready, along with a ribald jest or two about my summons. I suggested how he might amuse himself the rest of the night and then left. I was waved out of the keep and through the fortifications by guards who had been advised of my coming.

I turned wrong twice in the town. It all appeared different by night, and I had not paid much attention to where I had been going earlier. At last I found the inn-yard. A worried innkeeper was awake and had a light in the window. 'She's been groaning and calling for you for most of an hour now, sirrah,' she told me anxiously. 'I fear it's serious, but she will let no one in but you.'

I hurried down the hall to her door. I tapped cautiously, half-expecting her shrill voice to tell me to go away and stop bothering her. Instead, a quavering voice called out, 'Oh, Fitz, is that finally you? Hurry in, boy. I need you.'

I took a deep breath and lifted the latch. I went into the semi-darkness of the stuffy room, holding my breath against the various smells that assaulted my nostrils. Death-stench could hardly be worse than this, I thought to myself.

Heavy hangings draped the bed. The only light in the room came from a single candle guttering in its holder. I picked it up and ventured closer to the bed. 'Lady Thyme?' I asked softly. 'What's wrong?'

'Boy.' The voice came quietly from a dark corner of the room.

'Chade,' I said, and instantly felt more foolish than I care to remember.

'There's no time to explain all the reasons. Don't feel bad, boy. Lady Thyme has fooled many folk in her time, and will continue to. At least I hope so. Now. Trust me and don't ask questions. Just do what I tell you. First, go to the innkeeper. Tell her that Lady Thyme has had one of her attacks and must rest quietly for a few days. Tell her on no account to disturb her. Her great-grand-daughter will be coming in to care for her –'

'Who –'

'It's been arranged already. And her great-grand-daughter will be bringing in food for her and everything else she needs. Just emphasize that Lady Thyme needs quiet and to be left alone. Go and do that now.'

And I did, and I appeared jolted enough that I was very convincing. The innkeeper promised me that she would let no one so much as tap on a door, for she would be most reluctant to lose Lady Thyme's good opinion of her inn and her trade. By which I surmised that Lady Thyme paid her generously indeed.

I re-entered the room quietly, shutting the door softly behind me. Chade shot the bolt and kindled a fresh candle from the glimmering stump. He spread a small map on the table beside it. I noticed he was dressed for travelling – cloak, boots, jerkin and trousers all of black. He looked a different man, suddenly, very fit and energetic. I wondered if the old man in the worn robe was also a pose. He glanced up at me and for a moment I would have sworn it was Verity the soldier I was facing. He gave me no time to muse.

'Things will have to go here however they will go between Verity and Kelvar. You and I have business elsewhere. I received a message tonight. Red Ship Raiders have struck, here, at Forge. So close to Buckkeep that it's more than just an insult; it's a real threat. And done while Verity is at Neatbay. Don't tell me they didn't know he was here, away from Buckkeep. But that's not all. They've taken hostages, dragged them back to their ships. And they've sent words to Buckkeep, to King Shrewd himself. They're demanding gold, lots of it, or they'll return the hostages to the village.'

'Don't you mean they'll kill them if they don't get the gold?'

'No.' Chade shook his head angrily, a bear bothered by bees. 'No, the message was quite clear. If the gold is paid, they'll kill them. If not, they'll release them. The messenger was from Forge, a man whose wife and son had been taken. He insisted he had the threat correct.'

'I don't see that we have a problem,' I snorted.

'On the surface, neither do I. But the man who carried the message to Shrewd was still shaking, despite his long ride. He couldn't explain it, not even say if he thought the gold should be paid or not. All he could do was repeat, over and over again, how the ship's captain had smiled as he delivered the ultimatum, and how the other raiders had laughed and laughed at his words.

'So, we go to see, you and I. Now. Before the King makes any

official response, before Verity even knows. Now attend. This is
the road we came by. See how it follows the curve of the coast?
And this is the trail we go by. Straighter, but much steeper and
boggy in places, so that it has never been used by wagons. But
faster for men on horseback. Here, a small boat awaits us; crossing
the bay will cut a lot of miles and time from our journey. We'll
beach here, and then on up to Forge.'

I studied the map. Forge was north of Buckkeep; I wondered
how long our messenger had taken to reach us, and if by the time
we got there the Red Ship Raiders' threat would already have
been carried out. But it was no use wasting time on wondering.

'What about a horse for you?'

'That's been arranged, by the one who brought this message.
There's a bay outside with three white feet. He's for me. The
messenger will also provide a great-grand-daughter for Lady
Thyme, and the boat is waiting. Let's go.'

'One thing,' I said, and ignored his scowl at the delay. 'I have to
ask this, Chade. Were you here because you didn't trust me?'

'A fair question, I suppose. No. I was here to listen in the
town, to women's talk, as you were to listen in the keep.
Bonnet-makers and button-sellers may know more than a high
king's advisor, without even knowing they know it. Now. Do we
ride?'

We did. We left by the side entrance, and the bay was tethered
right outside. Sooty didn't much care for him, but she minded
her manners. I sensed Chade's impatience, but he kept the horses
to an easy pace until we had left the cobbled streets of Neatbay
behind us. Once the lights of the houses were behind us, we put
our horses to an easy canter. Chade led, and I wondered at how
well he rode, and how effortlessly he selected paths in the dark.
Sooty did not like this swift travelling by night. If it had not
been for a moon nearly at the full, I don't think I could have
persuaded her to keep up with the bay.

I will never forget that night ride. Not because it was a wild
gallop to the rescue, but because it was not. Chade guided us
and used the horses as if they were game-pieces on a board. He
did not play swiftly, but to win. And so there were times when
we walked the horses to breathe them, and places on the trail

where we dismounted and led them to get them safely past treacherous places.

As morning greyed the sky, we stopped to eat provisions from Chade's saddlebags. We were on a hilltop so thickly treed that the sky was barely glimpsed overhead. I could hear the ocean, and smell it, but could catch no sight of it. Our trail had become a sinuous path, little more than a deer-run, through these woods. Now that we were still, I could hear and smell the life all around us. Birds called, and I heard the movement of small animals in the underbrush and in the branches overhead. Chade had stretched, then sunk down to sit on deep moss with his back against a tree. He drank deeply from a water-skin, and then more briefly from a brandy flask. He looked tired, and the daylight exposed his age more cruelly than lamplight ever had. I wondered if he would last through the ride or collapse.

'I'll be fine,' he said when he caught me watching him. 'I've had to do more arduous duty than this, and on less sleep. Besides, we'll have a good five or six hours of rest on the boat, if the crossing is smooth. So there's no need to be longing after sleep. Let's go, boy.'

About two hours later our path diverged, and again we took the more obscure branching. Before long I was all but lying on Sooty's neck to escape the low sweeps of the branches. It was muggy under the trees and we were blessed with multitudes of tiny stinging flies that tortured the horses and crept into my clothes to find flesh to feast on. So thick were they that when I finally mustered the courage to ask Chade if we had gone astray, I near choked on the ones that rushed into my mouth.

By midday we emerged onto a windswept hillside that was more open. Once more I saw the ocean. The wind cooled the sweating horses and swept the insects away. It was a great pleasure simply to sit upright in the saddle again. The trail was wide enough that I could ride abreast of Chade. The livid spots stood out starkly against his pale skin; he looked more bloodless than the Fool. Dark circles underscored his eyes. He caught me watching him and frowned.

'Report to me, instead of staring at me like a simpleton,' he ordered me tersely, and so I did.

It was hard to watch the trail and his face at the same time, but the second time he snorted, I glanced over at him to find wry amusement on his face. I finished my report and he shook his head.

'Luck. Same luck your father had. Your kitchen-diplomacy may be enough to turn the situation around; if that is all there is to it. The little gossip I heard agreed. Well. Kelvar was a good duke before this, and it sounds as if all that happened was a young bride going to his head.' He sighed suddenly. 'Still, it's bad, with Verity there to rebuke a man for not minding his towers, and Verity himself with a raid on a Buckkeep town. Damn! There's so much we don't know. How did the Raiders get past our towers without being spotted? How did they know that Verity was away from Buckkeep at Neatbay? Or did they know? Was it luck for them? And what does that strange ultimatum mean? Is it a threat, or a mockery?' For a moment we rode silently.

'I wish I knew what action Shrewd was taking. When he sent me the messenger, he had not yet decided. We may get to Forge to find that all's been settled already. And I wish I knew exactly what message he Skilled to Verity. They say that in the old days, when more men trained in the Skill, a man could tell what his leader was thinking about just by being silent and listening for a while. But that may be no more than a legend. Not many are taught the Skill, any more. I think it was King Bounty who decided that. Keep the Skill more secret, more of an elite tool, and it becomes more valuable. That was the logic then. I never much understood it. What if they said that of good bowmen, or navigators? Still, I suppose the aura of mystery might give a leader more status with his men . . . or for a man like Shrewd, now, he'd enjoy having his underlings wondering if he can actually pick up what they were thinking without their uttering a word. Yes, that would appeal to Shrewd, that would.'

At first I thought Chade was very worried, or even angry. I had never heard him ramble so on a topic. But when his horse shied over a squirrel crossing his path, Chade was very nearly unseated. I reached out and caught at his reins. 'Are you all right? What's the matter?'

He shook his head slowly. 'Nothing. When we get to the boat,

I'll be all right. We just have to keep going. It's not much farther now.' His pale skin had become grey, and with every step his horse took, he swayed in his saddle.

'Let's rest a bit,' I suggested.

'Tides won't wait. And rest wouldn't help me, not the rest I'd get while I was worrying about our boat going on the rocks. No. We just have to keep going.' And he added, 'Trust me, boy. I know what I can do, and I'm not so foolish as to attempt more than that.'

And so we went on. There was very little else we could do. But I rode beside his horse's head, where I could take his reins if I needed to. The sound of the ocean grew louder, and the trail much steeper. Soon I was leading the way whether I would or no.

We broke clear of brush completely on a bluff overlooking a sandy beach.

'Thank Eda, they're here,' Chade muttered behind me, and then I saw the shallow-draught boat that was all but grounded near the point. A man on watch hallooed and waved his cap in the air. I lifted my arm in return greeting.

We made our way down, sliding more than riding, and then Chade boarded immediately. That left me with the horses. Neither was anxious to enter the waves, let alone heave themselves over the low rail and up onto deck. I tried to quest toward them, to let them know what I wanted. For the first time in my life, I found I was simply too tired. I could not find the focus I needed. So three deckhands, much cursing, and two duckings for me were required finally to get them loaded. Every bit of leather and every buckle on their harness had been doused with saltwater. How was I going to explain that to Burrich? That was the thought that was uppermost in my mind as I settled myself in the bow and watched the rowers in the dory bend their backs to the oars and tow us out to deeper water.

TEN

The Pocked Man

Time and tide wait for no man. There's an ageless adage. Sailors and fishermen mean it simply to say that a boat's schedule is determined by the ocean, not man's convenience. But sometimes I lie here, after the tea has calmed the worst of the pain, and wonder about it. Tides wait for no man, and that I know is true. But time? Did the times I was born into await my birth to be? Did the events rumble into place like the great wooden gears of the clock of Sayntanns, meshing with my conception and pushing my life along? I make no claim to greatness. And yet, had I not been born, had not my parents fallen before a surge of lust, so much would be different. So much. Better? I think not. And then I blink and try to focus my eyes, and wonder if these thoughts come from me or from the drug in my blood. It would be nice to hold council with Chade, one last time.

The sun had moved round to late afternoon when someone nudged me awake. 'Your master wants you,' was all he said, and I roused with a start. Gulls wheeling overhead, fresh sea air and the dignified waddle of the boat recalled me to where I was. I scrambled to my feet, ashamed to have fallen asleep without even wondering if Chade were comfortable. I hurried aft to the ship's house.

There I found Chade had taken over the tiny galley table. He was poring over a map spread out on it, but a large tureen of fish chowder was what got my attention. He motioned me to it without taking his attention from the map, and I was glad to fall to. There were ship's biscuits to go with it, and a sour red wine. I had not realized how hungry I was until the food was before me. I was scraping my dish with a bit of biscuit when Chade asked me, 'Better?'

'Much,' I said. 'How about you?'

'Better,' he said, and looked at me with his familiar hawk's glance. To my relief, he seemed totally recovered. He pushed my dishes to one side and slid the map before me. 'By evening,' he said, 'we'll be here. It'll be a nastier landing than the loading was. If we're lucky, we'll get wind when we need it. If not, we'll miss the best of the tide, and the current will be stronger. We may end up swimming the horses to shore while we ride in the dory. I hope not, but be prepared for it, just in case. Once we land . . .'

'You smell of carris seed.' I said it, not believing my own words. But I had caught the unmistakable sweet taint of the seed and oil on his breath. I'd had carris seed cakes, at Springfest, when everyone does, and I knew the giddy energy that even a sprinkling of the seed on a cake's top could bring. Everyone celebrated Spring's Edge that way. Once a year, what could it hurt? But I knew, too, that Burrich had warned me never to buy a horse that smelled of carris seed at all. And warned me further that if anyone were ever caught putting carris seed oil on any of our horse's grain, he'd kill him. With his bare hands.

'Do I? Fancy that. Now, I suggest that if you have to swim the horses, you put your shirt and cloak into an oilskin bag and give it to me in the dory. That way you'll have at least that much dry to put on when we reach the beach. From the beach, our road will . . .'

'Burrich says that once you've given it to an animal, it's never the same. It does things to horses. He says you can use it to win one race, or run down one stag, but after that, the beast will never be what it was. He says dishonest horse-traders use it to make an animal show well at a sale; it gives them spirit and brightens their eyes, but that soon passes. Burrich says that it takes away all their sense of when they're tired, so they go on, past the time when they should have dropped from exhaustion. Burrich told me that sometimes when the carris oil wears out, the horse just drops in its tracks.' The words spilled out of me, cold water over stones.

Chade lifted his gaze from the map. He stared at me mildly. 'Fancy Burrich knowing all that about carris seed. I'm glad you listened to him so closely. Now perhaps you'll be so kind as to give me equal attention as we plan the next stage of our journey.'

'But Chade . . .'

He transfixed me with his eyes. 'Burrich is a fine horse-master. Even as a boy he showed great promise. He is seldom wrong . . . when speaking about horses. Now attend to what I am saying. We'll need a lantern to get from the beach to the cliffs above. The path is very bad; we may need to bring one horse up at a time. But I am told it can be done. From there, we go overland to Forge. There isn't a road that will take us there quickly enough to be of any use. It's hilly country, but not forested. And we'll be going by night, so the stars will have to be our map. I am hoping to reach Forge by mid-afternoon. We'll go in as travellers, you and I. That's all I've decided so far; the rest will have to be planned from hour to hour . . .'

And the moment in which I could have asked him how he could use the seed and not die of it was gone, shouldered aside by his careful plans and precise details. For half an hour more he lectured me on details, and then he sent me from the cabin, saying he had other preparations to make and that I should check on the horses and get what rest I could.

The horses were forward, in a makeshift rope enclosure on deck. Straw cushioned the deck from their hooves and droppings. A sour-faced mate was mending a bit of railing that Sooty had kicked loose in the boarding. He didn't seem disposed to talk, and the horses were as calm and comfortable as could be expected. I roved the deck briefly. We were on a tidy little craft, an inter-island trader wider than she was deep. Her shallow draught let her go up rivers or right onto beaches without damage, but her passage over deeper water left a lot to be desired. She sidled along, with here a dip and there a curtsey, like a bundle-laden farm-wife making her way through a crowded market. We seemed to be the sole cargo. A deckhand gave me a couple of apples to share with the horses, but little talk. So after I had parcelled out the fruit,

I settled myself near them on their straw and took Chade's advice about resting.

The winds were kind to us, and the captain took us in closer to the looming cliffs than I'd have thought possible, but unloading the horses from the vessel was still an unpleasant task. All of Chade's lecturing and warnings had not prepared me for the blackness of night on the water. The lanterns on the deck seemed pathetic efforts, confusing me more with the shadows they threw than aiding me with their feeble light. In the end, a deck-hand rowed Chade to shore in the ship's dory. I went overboard with the reluctant horses, for I knew Sooty would fight a lead rope and probably swamp the dory. I clung to Sooty and encouraged her, trusting her common sense to take us toward the dim lantern on shore. I had a long line on Chade's horse, for I didn't want his thrashing too close to us in the water. The sea was cold, the night was black, and if I'd had any sense, I'd have wished myself elsewhere; but there is something in a boy that takes the mundanely difficult and unpleasant and turns it into a personal challenge and an adventure.

I came out of the water dripping, chilled and completely exhilarated. I kept Sooty's reins and coaxed Chade's horse in. By the time I had them both under control, Chade was beside me, lantern in hand, laughing exultantly. The dory man was already away and pulling for the ship. Chade gave me my dry things, but they did little good pulled on over my dripping clothes. 'Where's the path?' I asked, my voice shaking with my shivering.

Chade gave a derisive snort. 'Path? I had a quick look while you were pulling in my horse. It's no path, it's no more than the course the water takes when it runs off down the cliffs. But it will have to do.'

It was a little better than he had reported, but not much. It was narrow and steep and the gravel on it was loose underfoot. Chade went ahead with the lantern. I followed, with the horses in tandem. At one point Chade's bay acted up, tugging back, throwing me off-balance and nearly driving Sooty to her knees in her efforts to go the other direction. My heart was in my mouth until we reached the top of the cliffs.

Then the night and the open hillside spread out before us

under the sailing moon and the stars scattered wide overhead, and the spirit of the challenge caught me up again. I suppose it could have been Chade's attitude. The carris seed made his eyes wide and bright, even by lantern light, and his energy, unnatural though it was, was infectious. Even the horses seemed affected, snorting and tossing their heads. Chade and I laughed dementedly as we adjusted harness and then mounted. Chade glanced up to the stars, and then around the hillside that sloped down before us. With careless disdain he tossed our lantern to one side.

'Away!' he announced to the night, and kicked the bay, who sprang forward. Sooty was not to be outdone, and so I did as I had never dared before, galloping down unfamiliar terrain by night. It is a wonder we did not all break our necks. But there it is; sometimes luck belongs to children and madmen. That night I felt we were both.

Chade led and I followed. That night, I grasped another piece of the puzzle that Burrich had always been to me. For there is a very strange peace in giving over your judgement to someone else, to saying to them, 'You lead and I will follow, and I will trust entirely that you will not lead me to death or harm.' That night, as we pushed the horses hard, and Chade steered us solely by the night sky, I gave no thought to what might befall us if we went astray from our bearing, or if a horse were injured by an unexpected slip. I felt no sense of accountability for my actions. Suddenly, everything was easy and clear. I simply did whatever Chade told me to do, and trusted to him to have it turn out right. My spirit rode high on the crest of that wave of faith, and some-time during the night it occurred to me: this was what Burrich had had from Chivalry, and what he missed so badly.

We rode the entire night. Chade breathed the horses, but not as often as Burrich would have. And he stopped more than once to scan the night sky and then the horizon to be sure our course was true. 'See that hill there, against the stars? You can't see it too well, but I know it. By light, it's shaped like a buttermonger's cap. Keeffashaw, it's called. We keep it to the west of us. Let's go.'

Another time he paused on a hilltop. I pulled in my horse beside his. Chade sat still, very tall and straight. He could have been carved of stone. Then he lifted an arm and pointed. His hand shook slightly. 'See that ravine down there? We've come a bit too far to the east. We'll have to correct as we go.'

The ravine was invisible to me, a darker slash in the dimness of the starlit landscape. I wondered how he could have known it was there. It was perhaps half an hour later that he gestured off to our left, where on a rise of land a single light twinkled. 'Someone's up tonight in Woolcot,' he observed. 'Probably the baker, putting early-morning rolls to rise.' He half-turned in his saddle and I felt more than saw his smile. 'I was born less than a mile from here. Come, boy, let's ride. I don't like to think of Raiders so close to Woolcot.'

And on we went, down a hillside so steep that I felt Sooty's muscles bunch as she leaned back on her haunches and more than half-slid her way down.

Dawn was greying the sky before I smelled the sea again. And it was still early when we crested a rise and looked down on the little village of Forge. It was a poor place in some ways; the anchorage was good only on certain tides. The rest of the time the ships had to anchor further out and let small craft ply back and forth between them and shore. About all that Forge had to keep it on the map was iron ore. I had not expected to see a bustling city. But neither was I prepared for the rising tendrils of smoke from blackened, open-roofed buildings. Somewhere an unmilked cow was lowing. A few scuttled boats were just off the shore, their masts sticking up like dead trees.

Morning looked down on empty streets. 'Where are the people?' I wondered aloud.

'Dead, taken hostage, or hiding in the woods still.' There was a tightness in Chade's voice that drew my eyes to his face. I was amazed at the pain I saw there. He saw me staring at him and shrugged mutely. 'The feeling that these folk belong to you, that their disaster is your failure . . . it will come to you as you grow. It goes with the blood.' He left me to ponder that as he nudged his weary mount into a walk. We threaded our way down the hill and into the town.

Going more slowly seemed to be the only caution Chade was taking. There were two of us, weaponless, on tired horses, riding into a town where . . .

'The ship's gone, boy. A raiding ship doesn't move without a full complement of rowers. Not in the current off this piece of coast. Which is another wonder. How did they know our tides and currents well enough to raid here? Why raid here at all? To carry off iron ore? Easier by far for them to pirate it off a trading-ship. It doesn't make sense, boy. No sense at all.'

Dew had settled heavily the night before. There was a rising stench in the town, of burned, wet homes. Here and there a few still smouldered. In front of some, possessions were strewn out into the street, but I did not know if the inhabitants had tried to save some of their goods, or if the Raiders had begun to carry things off and then changed their minds. A salt-box without a lid, several yards of green woollen goods, a shoe, a broken chair: the litter spoke mutely but eloquently of all that was homely and safe broken forever and trampled in the mud. A grim horror settled on me.

'We're too late,' Chade said softly. He reined his horse in and Sooty stopped beside him.

'What?' I asked stupidly, jolted from my thoughts.

'The hostages. They returned them.'

'Where?'

Chade looked at me incredulously, as if I were insane or very stupid. 'There. In the ruins of that building.'

It is difficult to explain what happened to me in the next moment of my life. So much occurred, all at once. I lifted my eyes to see a group of people, all ages and sexes, within the burned-out shell of some kind of store. They were muttering among themselves as they scavenged in it. They were bedraggled, but seemed unconcerned by it. As I watched, two women picked up the same kettle at once, a large kettle, and then proceeded to slap at one another, each attempting to drive off the other and claim the loot. They reminded me of a couple of crows fighting over a cheese rind. They squawked and slapped and called one another vile names as they tugged at the opposing handles. The other folk paid them no mind, but went on with their own looting.

This was very strange behaviour for village folk. I had always heard of how after a raid, village folk banded together, cleaning out and making habitable what buildings were left standing, and then helping one another salvage cherished possessions, sharing and making do until cottages could be rebuilt, and store-buildings replaced. But these folk seemed completely careless that they had lost nearly everything and that family and friends had died in the raid. Instead, they had gathered to fight over what little was left.

This realization was horrifying enough to behold.

But I couldn't feel them either.

I hadn't seen or heard them until Chade pointed them out. I would have ridden right past them. And the other momentous thing that happened to me at that point was that I realized I was different from everyone else I knew. Imagine a seeing child growing up in a blind village, where no one else even suspects the possibility of such a sense. The child would have no words for colours, or for degrees of light. The others would have no conception of the way in which the child perceived the world. So it was in that moment, as we sat our horses and stared at the folk. For Chade wondered out loud, misery in his voice, 'What is wrong with them? What's got into them?'

I knew.

All the threads that run back and forth between folk, that twine from mother to child, from man to woman, all the kinships they extend to family and neighbour, to pets and stock, even to the fish of the sea and bird of the sky – all, all were gone.

All my life, without knowing it, I had depended on those threads of feelings to let me know when other live things were about. Dogs, horses, even chickens had them, as well as humans. And so I would look up at the door before Burrich entered it, or know there was one more new-born puppy in the stall, nearly buried under the straw. So I would wake when Chade opened the staircase. Because I could feel people. And that sense was the one that always alerted me first, that let me know to use my eyes and ears and nose as well, to see what they were about.

But these folk gave off no feelings at all.

Imagine water with no weight or wetness. That is how those folk were to me. Stripped of what made them not only human, but alive. To me, it was as if I watched stones rise up from the earth and quarrel and mutter at one another. A little girl found a pot of jam and stuck her fist in it and pulled out a handful to

lick. A grown man turned from the scorched pile of fabric he had
been rummaging through and crossed to her. He seized the pot
and shoved the child aside, heedless of her angry shouts.

No one moved to interfere.

I leaned forward and seized Chade's reins as he moved to
dismount. I shouted wordlessly at Sooty, and tired as she was, the
fear in my voice energized her. She leaped forward, and my jerk
on the reins brought Chade's bay with us. Chade was nearly
unseated, but he clung to the saddle, and I took us out of the dead
town as fast as we could go. I heard shouts behind us, colder than
the howling of wolves, cold as storm wind down a chimney, but
we were mounted and I was terrified. I didn't pull in or let Chade
have his own reins back until the houses were well behind us.
The road bent, and beside a small copse of trees, I pulled in at
last. I don't think I even heard Chade's angry demands for an
explanation until then.

He didn't get a very coherent one. I leaned forward on Sooty's
neck and hugged her. I could feel her weariness, and the trembling
of my own body. Dimly I felt that she shared my uneasiness. I
thought of the empty folk back in Forge and nudged Sooty with
my knees. She stepped out wearily and Chade kept pace,
demanding to know what was wrong. My mouth was dry and my
voice shook. I didn't look at him as I panted out my fear and a
garbled explanation of what I had felt.

When I was silent, our horses continued to pace down the
packed earth road. At length I got up my courage and looked at
Chade. He was regarding me as if I had sprouted antlers. Once
aware of this new sense, I couldn't ignore it. I sensed his scepti-
cism. But I also felt Chade distance himself from me, just a little
pulling-back, a little shielding of self from someone who had
suddenly become a bit of a stranger. It hurt all the more because
he had not pulled back that way from the folk in Forge. And
they were a hundred times stranger than I was.

'They were like marionettes,' I told Chade. 'Like wooden things
come to life and acting out some evil play. And if they had seen
us, they would not have hesitated to kill us for our horses or our
cloaks, or a piece of bread. They . . .' I searched for words. 'They
aren't even animals any more. There's nothing coming out of

them. Nothing. They're like little separate things. Like a row of books, or rocks or . . .'

'Boy,' Chade said, between gentleness and annoyance, 'you've got to get yourself in hand. It's been a long night of travel for us, and you're tired. Too long without a sleep, and the mind starts to play tricks, with waking dreams and . . .'

'No.' I was desperate to convince him. 'It's not that. It's not going without sleep.'

'We'll go back there,' he said reasonably. The morning breeze swirled his dark cloak around him, in a way so ordinary that I felt my heart would break. How could there be folk like those in that village, and a simple morning breeze in the same world? And Chade, speaking in so calm and ordinary a voice? 'Those folk are just ordinary folk, boy, but they've gone through a very bad time, and so they're acting oddly. I knew a girl who saw her father killed by a bear. She was like that, just staring and grunting, hardly even moving to care for herself, for more than a month. Those folk will recover, when they go back to their ordinary lives.'

'Someone's ahead!' I warned him. I had heard nothing, seen nothing, felt only that tug at the cobweb of sense I'd discovered. But as we looked ahead down the road, we saw that we were approaching the tail-end of a rag-tag procession of people. Some led laden beasts, others pushed or dragged carts of bedraggled possessions. They looked over their shoulders at us on our horses as if we were demons risen from the earth to pursue them.

'The Pocked Man!' cried a man close to the end of the line, and he lifted a hand to point at us. His face was drawn with weariness and white with fear. His voice cracked on the words. 'It's the legends come to life,' he warned the others who halted fearfully to stare back at us. 'Heartless ghosts walk embodied through our village ruins, and the black-cloaked pocked man brings his disease upon us. We have lived too soft, and the old gods punish us. Our fat lives will be the death of us all.'

'Oh, damn it all. I didn't mean to be seen like this,' Chade breathed. I watched his pale hands gather his reins, turning his bay. 'Follow me, boy.' He did not look toward the man who still pointed a quavering finger at us. He moved slowly, almost languorously, as he guided his horse off the road and up a tussocky hillside. It was the same unchallenging way of moving that Burrich had when confronting a wary horse or dog. His tired horse left the smooth trail reluctantly. Chade was headed up into a stand of birches on the hilltop. I stared at him uncomprehendingly. 'Follow me, boy,' he directed me over his shoulder when I hesitated. 'Do you want to be stoned in the road? It's not a pleasant experience.'

I moved carefully, swinging Sooty aside from the road as if I were totally unaware of the panicky folk ahead of us. They hovered there, between anger and fear. The feel of it was a black-red smear on the day's freshness. I saw a woman stoop, saw a man turn aside from his barrow.

'They're coming!' I warned Chade, even as they raced toward us. Some gripped stones, and others green staffs freshly taken from the forest. All had the bedraggled look of townsfolk forced to live in the open. Here were the rest of Forge's villagers, those not taken hostage by the Raiders. All of that I realized in the instant between digging in my heels and Sooty's weary plunge forward. Our horses were spent; their efforts at speed were grudging, despite the hail of rocks that thudded to the earth in our wake. Had the townsfolk been rested, or less fearful, they would have easily caught us. But I think they were relieved to see us flee. Their minds were more fixed on what walked the streets of their village than on fleeing strangers, no matter how ominous.

They stood in the road and shouted and waved their sticks until we were among the trees. Chade had taken the lead and I didn't question him as he took us on a parallel path that would keep us out of the sight of the folk leaving Forge. The horses had settled back into a grudging plod. I was grateful for the rolling hills and scattered trees that hid us from any pursuit. When I saw a stream glinting, I gestured to it without a word. Silently we watered the horses, and shook out for them some grain from Chade's supplies. I loosened harness, and wiped their draggled coats with handfuls of grass. For ourselves, there was cold stream-water and coarse travel-bread. I saw to the horses as best as I could. Chade seemed full of his own thoughts, and for a long time I respected their intensity. But finally I could contain my curiosity no longer and I asked the question.

'Are you really the Pocked Man?'

Chade startled, and then stared at me. There were equal parts amazement and ruefulness in that look. 'The Pocked Man? The legendary harbinger of disease and disaster? Oh, come, boy, you're not simple. That legend is hundreds of years old. Surely you can't believe I'm that ancient.'

I shrugged. I wanted to say, 'You are scarred, and you bring death', but I did not utter it. Chade did seem very old to me sometimes, and other times so full of energy that he seemed but a very young man in an old man's body.

'No, I am not the Pocked Man,' he went on, more to himself than to me. 'But after today, the rumours of him will be spread across the Six Duchies like pollen on the wind. There will be talk of disease and pestilence and divine punishments for imagined wrongdoing. I wish I had not been seen like this. The folk of the kingdom already have enough to fear. But there are sharper worries for us than superstitions. However you knew it, you were right. I have been thinking, most carefully, of everything I saw in Forge. And recalling the words of those villagers who tried to stone us. And the look of them all. I knew the Forge folk, in times past. They were doughty folk, not the type to flee in superstitious panic. But those folk we saw on the road, that was what they were doing. Leaving Forge, forever, or at least so they intend. Taking all that is left that they can carry. Leaving homes their grandfathers were born in. And leaving behind relatives who sift and scavenge in the ruins like witlings.

'The Raiders' threat was not an empty one. I think of those folk and I shiver. Something is sorely wrong, boy, and I fear what will come next. For if the Red Ships can capture our folk, and then demand that we pay them to kill them, for fear that they will otherwise return them to us like those ones were – what a bitter choice! And once more they have struck when we were least prepared to deal with it.' He turned to me as if to say more, then suddenly staggered. He sat down abruptly, his face greying. He bowed his head and covered his face with his hands.

'Chade!' I cried out in panic, and sprang to his side, but he turned aside from me.

'Carris seed,' he said through muffling hands. 'The worst part is that it abandons you so suddenly. Burrich was right to warn you about it, boy. But sometimes there are no choices but poor ones. Sometimes, in bad times like these.'

He lifted his head. His eyes were dull, his mouth almost slack. 'I need to rest now,' he said as piteously as a sick child. I caught him as he toppled and eased him to the ground. I pillowed his head on my saddlebags, and covered him with our cloaks. He lay still, his pulse slow and his breathing heavy, from that time until afternoon of the next day. I slept that night against his back, hoping to keep him warm, and the next day used what was left of our supplies to feed him.

By that evening he was recovered enough to travel, and we began a dreary journey. We went slowly, going by night. Chade chose our paths, but I led, and often he was little more than a load upon his horse. It took us two days to cover the distance we had traversed in that one wild night. Food was sparse, and talk was even scarcer. Just thinking seemed to weary Chade, and whatever he thought about, he found too bleak for words.

He pointed out where I should kindle the signal fire that brought the boat back to us. They sent a dory ashore for him, and he got into it without a word. That showed how spent he was: he simply assumed I would be able to get our weary horses aboard the ship. So my pride forced me to manage that task, and once aboard, I slept as I had not for days. Then again we offloaded, and made a weary trek back to Neatbay. We came in during the small hours of the morning and Lady Thyme once more took up residence in the inn.

By afternoon of the next day, I was able to tell the innkeeper that she was doing much better and would enjoy a tray from her kitchens if she would send one round to the rooms. Chade did seem better, though he sweated profusely at times, and at such times smelled rancidly sweet of carris seed. He ate ravenously, and drank great quantities of water. But in two days he had me tell the innkeeper that Lady Thyme would be leaving on the morrow.

I recovered more readily, and had several afternoons of wandering Neatbay, gawking at the shops and vendors and keeping my ears wide for the gossip that Chade so treasured. In this way we learned much what we had expected to. Verity's diplomacy had gone well, and Lady Grace was now the darling of the town. Already I could see an increase in the work on the roads and fortifications. Watch Island's tower was now manned with Kelvar's best men, and folk referred to it as Grace Tower now. But they gossiped, too, of how the Red Ships had crept past Verity's own towers, and of the strange events at Forge. I heard more than once about sightings of the Pocked Man. And the tales they told about the inn fire of those who lived in Forge now gave me nightmares.

Those who had fled Forge told soul-cleaving tales of kinfolk gone cold and heartless. They lived there now, just as if they were still human, but those who had known them best were the least capable of being deceived. Those folk did by day what had never been known to happen at any time in Buckkeep. The evils folk whispered were beyond my imaginings. Ships no longer stopped at Forge. Iron ore would have to be found elsewhere. It was said that no one even wanted to take in the folk that had fled, for who knew what taint they carried. After all, the Pocked Man had shown himself to them. Yet somehow it was harder still to hear ordinary folk say that soon it would be over, that the creatures of Forge would kill one another and thank all that was divine for that. The good folk of Neatbay wished death on those who had once been the good folk of Forge, and wished it as if it were the only good thing left that might befall them. As well it was.

On the night before Lady Thyme and I were to rejoin Verity's retinue to return to Buckkeep, I awoke to find a single candle burning and Chade sitting up, staring at the wall. Without my saying a word, he turned to me. 'You must be taught the Skill, boy,' he said as if it were a decision painfully come by. 'Evil times have come to us, and they will be with us for a long time. It is a time when good men must create whatever weapons they can. I will go to Shrewd yet again, and this time I will demand it. Hard times are here, boy. And I wonder if they will ever pass.'

In the years to come, I was to wonder that often.

ELEVEN

Forgings

The Pocked Man is a well-known figure in the folklore and drama of the Six Duchies. It is a poor troupe of puppeteers who does not possess a marionette of the Pocked Man, not only for his traditional roles, but also for his usefulness as an omen of disaster to come in original productions. Sometimes the Pocked Man puppet is merely displayed against the backdrop, to cast an ominous note to a scene. Among the Six Duchies, he is a universal symbol.

It is said the root of his legend reaches back to the first peopling of the duchies, not the conquering by the Farseer Outislanders, but the most ancient settling of the place by earlier immigrants. Even the Outislanders have a version of the most basic legend. It is a warning story, of the wrath of El the Sea God at being forsaken.

When the sea was young, El the first Elder believed in the people of the islands. To that folk he gave his sea, and with it all that swam within it, and all lands it touched for their own. For many years, the folk were grateful. They fished the sea, lived on its shores wherever they would, and raided any others who dared to take up abode where El had given them reign. Others who dared to sail their sea were the rightful prey of the folk as well. The folk prospered and grew tough and strong for El's sea winnowed them. Their lives were harsh and dangerous, but it made their boys grow to strong men and their maids fearless women at hearth or on deck. The folk respected El and to that Elder they offered their praises and only by him did they curse. And El took pride in his folk.

But in El's generosity, he blessed his folk too well. Not enough of

*them died in the harsh winters, and the storms he sent were too mild to
conquer their seamanship. So the folk grew in number. So grew also
their herds and flocks. In fat years, weak children did not die, but
grew, and stayed at home, and put land to the plough to feed the swollen
flocks and herds and other weaklings like themselves. The soil-grubbers
did not praise El for his strong winds and raiding currents. Instead,
they praised and cursed only by Eda, who is the Elder of those who
plough and plant and tend the beasts. So Eda blessed her weaklings
with the increase of their plants and beasts. This did not please El,
but he ignored them, for he still had the hardy folk of the ships and
the waves. They blessed by him and they cursed by him, and to
encourage their strength he sent them storms and cold winters.*

*But as time went on, those loyal to El dwindled. The soft folk
of the soil seduced the sailors, and bore them children fit only for
tending to the dirt. And the folk left the winter shores and icestrewn
pastures, and moved south, to the soft lands of grapes and grain.
Fewer and fewer folk came each year to plough the waves and to reap
the fish that El had decreed to them. Less and less often did El hear
his name in a blessing or a curse. Until at last there was a day when
there was only one left who only blessed or cursed in El's name. And
he was a skinny old man, too old for the sea, swollen and aching in
his joints with few teeth left in his head. His blessings and curses were
weak things and insulted more than pleased El, who had little use for
rickety old men.*

*At last there came a storm that should have ended the old man and
his small boat. But when the cold waves closed over him, he clung to
the wreckage of his craft, and dared to cry El for mercy, though all
know mercy is not in him. So enraged was El by this blasphemy that
he would not receive the old man in to his sea, but instead cast him
up upon the shore, and cursed him that he could never more sail, but
neither could he die. And when he crawled from the salt waves, his
face and body were pocked as if barnacles had clung to him, and
he staggered to his feet and went forth into the soft lands. And everywhere he went, he saw only soft soil-grubbers. And he warned them
of their folly, and that El would raise up a new and hardier folk and
give their heritage to them. But the folk would not listen, so soft and set
had they become. Yet everywhere the old man went, disease followed
in his wake. And it was all the pox diseases he spread, the ones that*

care not if a man is strong or weak, hard or soft, but take any and all that they touch. And this was fitting, for all know that the poxes come up from bad dust and are spread by the turning of the soil.

Thus is the tale told. And so the Pocked Man has become the harbinger of death and disease, and a rebuke to those who live soft and easily because their lands bear well.

Verity's return to Buckkeep was gravely marred by the events at Forge. Verity, pragmatic to a fault, had himself left Bayguard as soon as Dukes Kelvar and Shemshy had shown themselves in accord regarding Watch Island. Verity and his picked troops had actually left Bayguard before Chade and I returned to the inn. So the trek back had a hollow feel to it. During the days, and around the fires at night, folk spoke of Forge, and even within our caravan, the stories multiplied and embroidered themselves.

My journey home was spoiled by Chade's resumption of his noisome charade as the vile old lady. I had to fetch and wait upon her, right up to the time that her Buckkeep servants appeared to escort her back up to her chambers. 'She' lived in the women's wing, and though I devoted myself in the days to come to hear any and all gossip about her, I heard nothing except that she was reclusive and difficult. How Chade had created her and maintained her fictitious existence, I never completely discovered.

Buckkeep, in our absence, seemed to have undergone a tempest of new events, so that I felt as if we had been gone ten years rather than a matter of weeks. Not even Forge could completely eclipse Lady Grace's performance. The story was told and re-told, with minstrels vying to see whose recounting would become the standard. I heard that Duke Kelvar actually went down on one knee and kissed the tips of her fingers after she had spoken, very eloquently, about making the towers the grand jewels of their land. One source even told me that Lord Shemshy had personally thanked the lady and sought often to dance with her that evening, and thus nearly precipitated an entirely different disagreement between the neighbouring dukedoms.

I was glad of her success. I even heard it whispered, more than once, that Prince Verity should find himself a lady of like sentiments. As often as he was away, settling internal matters and chasing raiders, the people were beginning to feel the need of a strong ruler at home. The old King, Shrewd, was still nominally our sovereign. But, as Burrich observed, the people tended to look ahead. 'And', he added, 'folk like to know the King-in-Waiting has a warm bed to come home to. It gives them something to make their fancies about. Few enough of them can afford any romance in their lives, so they imagine all they can for their king. Or prince.'

But Verity himself, I knew, had no time to think about well-warmed beds, or any sort of bed at all. Forge had been both an example and a threat. Word of others followed, three in swift succession. Croft, up in the Near Islands, had apparently been 'Raider-Forged' as it came to be known, some weeks earlier. Word was slow to come from icy shores, but when it came, it was grim. Croft folk, too, had been taken hostage. The council of the town had, like Shrewd, been mystified by the Red Ships' ultimatum that they pay tribute or their hostages would be returned. They had not paid. And like Forge, their hostages had been returned, mostly sound of body, but bereft of any of the kinder emotions of humanity. The whispered word was that Croft had been more direct in their solution. The harsh climates of the Near Islands bred a harsh people. Yet even they had deemed it kindness when they took the sword to their now-heartless kin.

Two other villages were raided after Forge. At Rockgate the folk had paid the ransom. Parts of bodies had washed up the next day, and the village had gathered to bury them. The news came to Buckkeep with no apologies; only with the unvoiced assumption that had the King been more vigilant, they would have had warning of the raid at least.

Sheepmire met the challenge squarely. They refused to pay the tribute, but with the rumours of Forge running hot through the land, they prepared themselves. They had met their returned hostages with halters and shackles. They took their own folk back, clubbing them senseless in some cases, before tying them and taking them back into their rightful homes. The village was united in attempting to bring them back to their former selves. The tales from Sheepmire were the most told ones; of a mother who snapped at a child brought to her for nursing, declaring as she cursed at it that she had no use for the whimpering, wet creature. Of the little child who cried and screamed at his bonds, only to fly at his own father with a toasting fork as soon as the heartbroken sire released him. Some cursed and fought and spat at their kin. Others settled into a life of bondage and idleness, eating the food and drinking the ale set before them, but offering no words of thanks or affection. Freed of restraints, those ones did not attack their own families, but neither did they work, nor even join with them in their evening pastimes. They stole without remorse, even from their own children, and squandered coin and gobbled food like gluttons. No joy they gave to anyone, not even a kind word. But the word from Sheepmire was that the folk there intended to persevere until the 'Red Ship sickness' passed. They gave the nobles at Buckkeep a bit of hope to cling to. They spoke of the courage of the villagers with admiration, and vowed that they, too, would do the same, if kin of theirs were Raider-Forged.

Sheepmire and its brave inhabitants became a rallying point for the Six Duchies. King Shrewd levied more taxes in their name. Some went to provide grain for those so occupied with caring for bound kin that they had no time to rebuild their ravaged flocks or replant their burned fields. And some went to build more ships and hire more men to patrol the coastlines.

At first folk took pride in what they would do. Those who lived on the sea-cliffs began to keep volunteer watch. Runners and messenger birds and signal fires were kept in place. Some villages sent sheep and supplies to Sheepmire, to be given to those who needed help most. But as the long weeks passed, and there was no sign that any of the returned hostages had recovered their sensibilities, those hopes and devotions began to seem pathetic rather than noble. Those who had most supported those efforts now declared that, were they taken hostage, they would choose to be hacked to pieces and thrown into the sea rather than returned to cause their families such hardship and heartbreak.

Worst, I think, was that in such a time the throne itself had no firm idea of what to do. Had a royal edict been issued, to say either that folk must or must not pay the demanded tribute for hostages, it would have gone better. No matter which, some folk would have disagreed. But at least the King would have taken a stand, and people would have had some sense that this threat was being faced. Instead, the increased patrols and watches only made it seem that the Buckkeep itself was in terror of this new threat, but had no strategy for facing it. In the absence of royal edict, the coastal villages took things into their own hands. The councils met, to decide what they would do if Forged. And some decided one way, and some the other.

'But in every case,' Chade told me wearily, 'it matters not what they decide; it weakens their loyalty to the kingdom. Whether they pay the tribute or not, the Raiders may laugh over their blood-ale at us. For in deciding, our villagers are saying in their minds, not "if we are Forged" but "when we are Forged". And thus they already have been raped in spirit if not in flesh. They look at their kin, mother at child, man at parents, and already they have given them up, to death or Forging. And the kingdom fails, for as each town must decide alone, so it is separated from the whole. We will shatter into a thousand little townships, each worrying only about what it will do for itself if it is raided. If Shrewd and Verity do not act quickly, the kingdom will become a thing that exists only in name, and in the minds of its former rulers.'

'But what can they do?' I demanded. 'No matter what edict is passed, it will be wrong.' I picked up the tongs and pushed the crucible I was tending a bit deeper into the flames.

'Sometimes,' grumbled Chade, 'it is better to be defiantly wrong than silent. Look, boy, if you, a mere lad, can realize that either decision is wrong, so can all folk. But at least such an edict would give us a common response. It would not be as if each village were left to lick its own wounds. And in addition to such an edict, Shrewd and Verity should take other actions.' He leaned closer to peer at the bubbling liquid. 'More heat,' he suggested.

I picked up a small bellows, plied it carefully. 'Such as?'

'Organize raids on the Outislanders in return. Provide vessels and supplies to any willing to undertake such a raid. Forbid that herds and flocks be grazed so temptingly on the coast pastures. Supply more arms to the villages if we cannot give each one men to protect it. By Eda's plough, give them pellets of carris seed and nightshade, to carry in pouches about their wrists, so that if they are captured in a raid, they can take their own lives instead of being hostages. Anything, boy. Anything the King did at this point would be better than this damned indecisiveness.'

I sat staring at Chade. I had never heard him speak so forcefully, nor had I ever known him to criticize Shrewd so openly. It shocked me. I held my breath, hoping he'd say more but almost fearful of what I might hear. He seemed unaware of my stare. 'Poke that a bit deeper. But be careful. If it explodes, King Shrewd may have himself two Pocked Men instead of one.' He glanced at me. 'Yes, that's how I was marked. But it might have well and truly been a pox, for how Shrewd hears me lately. "Ill omens and warnings and cautions fill you," he said to me. "But I think you want the boy trained in the Skill simply because you were not. It's a bad ambition, Chade. Put it from you." There speaks the Queen's ghost with the King's tongue.'

Chade's bitterness filled me with stillness.

'Chivalry. That's who we need now,' he went on after a moment. 'Shrewd holds back, and Verity is a good soldier, but he listens to his father too much. Verity was raised to be second, not first. He does not take the initiative. We need Chivalry. He'd go into those towns, talk to the folk who have lost loved ones to Forging. Damn, he'd even talk to the Forged ones themselves . . .'

'Do you think it would do any good?' I asked softly. I scarcely dared to move. I sensed that Chade was talking more to himself than to me.

'It wouldn't solve it, no. But our folk would have a sense of their ruler's involvement. Sometimes that's all it takes, boy. But all Verity does is march his toy soldiers about and weigh strategies. And Shrewd watches it happen, and thinks not of his people, but only of how to assure that Regal can be kept safe and yet readied in power should Verity manage to get himself killed.'

'Regal?' I blurted in amazement. Regal, with his pretty clothes and cockerel posturings? Always he was at Shrewd's heels, but never had I thought of him as a real prince. To hear his name come up in such a discussion jolted me.

'He has become his father's favourite,' Chade growled. 'Shrewd has done nothing but spoil him since the Queen died. He tries to buy the boy's heart with gifts, now that his mother is no longer around to claim his allegiance. And Regal takes full advantage. He speaks only what the old man loves to hear. And Shrewd gives him too much rein. He lets him wander about, squandering coin on useless visits to Farrow and Tilth, where his mother's people fill Regal with ideas of his self-importance. The boy should be kept at home and made to give some account for how he spends his time. And the King's money. What he spends gallivanting about would have outfitted a warship.' And then, suddenly annoyed, 'That's too hot! You'll lose it, fish it out quickly.'

But his words came too late, for the crucible cracked with a noise like breaking ice and its contents filled Chade's tower room with an acrid smoke that brought all lessons and talk to an end for that night.

I was not soon summoned again. My other lessons went on, but I missed Chade as the weeks passed and he did not call for me. I knew he was not displeased with me, but only preoccupied. When, idle one day, I pushed my awareness towards him, I felt only secrecy and discordance. And a wallop to the back of my head when Burrich caught me at it.

'Stop it,' he hissed, and ignored my studied look of shocked innocence. He glanced about the stall I was mucking out as if he expected to find a dog or cat lurking.

'There's nothing here!' he exclaimed.

'Just manure and straw,' I agreed, rubbing the back of my head.

'Then what were you doing?'

'Daydreaming,' I muttered. 'That was all.'

'You can't fool me, Fitz,' he growled. 'And I won't have it. Not in my stables. You won't pervert my beasts that way. Or degrade Chivalry's blood. Mind what I've told you.'

I clenched my jaws and lowered my eyes and kept on working. After a time I heard him sigh and move away. I went on raking, inwardly seething and resolving never to let Burrich come up on me unawares again.

The rest of that summer was such a whirlpool of events that I find it hard to recall their progression. Overnight, the very feeling of the air seemed to change. When I went into town, all of the talk was of fortifications and readiness. Only two more towns were Forged that summer, but it seemed a hundred, for the stories of it were repeated and enlarged from lip to lip.

'Until it seems as if that is all folk talk about any more,' Molly complained to me.

We were walking on Long Beach, in the light of the summer evening sun. The wind off the water was a welcome bit of cool after a muggy day. Burrich had been called away to Springmouth to see if he could work out why all the cattle there were developing huge hide sores. It meant no morning lessons for me, but many, many more chores with the horses and hounds in his absence, especially as Cob had gone to Turlake with Regal, to manage his horses and hounds for a summer hunt.

But the opposite weight of the balance was that my evenings were less supervised, and I had more time to visit town.

My evening walks with Molly were almost a routine now. Her father's health was failing and he scarcely needed to drink to fall into an early and deep sleep each night. Molly would pack a bit of cheese and sausage for us, or a small loaf and some smoked fish, and we would take a basket and a bottle of cheap wine and walk out down the beach to the breakwater rocks. There we would sit on the rocks as they gave up the last heat of the day, and Molly would tell me about her day's work and the day's gossip and I would listen. Sometimes our elbows bumped as we walked.

'Sara, the butcher's daughter, told me that she positively yearns for winter to come. The winds and ice will beat the Red Ships back to their own shores for a bit, and give us a rest from fear, she says. But then Kelty up and says that maybe we'll be able to stop fearing more Forging, but that we'll still have to fear the Forged folk that are loose in our land. Rumour says that some from Forge have left there, now that there's nothing left for them to steal, and that they travel about as bandits, robbing travellers.'

'I doubt it. More than likely it's other folk doing the robbing, but trying to pass themselves off as Forged folk to send revenge looking elsewhere. Forged folk don't have enough kinship left in them to be a band of anything,' I contradicted her lazily. I was looking out across the bay, my eyes almost closed against the glare of the sun on the water. I didn't have to look at Molly to feel her there beside me. It was an interesting tension, one I didn't fully understand. She was sixteen, and I about fourteen, and those two years loomed between us like an unsurmountable wall. Yet she always made time for me, and seemed to enjoy my company. She seemed as aware of me as I was of her. But if I quested toward her at all, she would draw back, halting to shake a pebble from her shoe or suddenly speaking of her father's illness and how much he needed her. Yet if I drew my sensings back from that tension, she became uncertain and shyer of speech, and would try to look at my face and the set of my mouth and eyes. I didn't understand it, but it was as if we held a string taut between us. But now I heard an edge of annoyance in her speech.

'Oh. I see. And you know so much of Forged folk, do you, more than those who have been robbed by them?'

Her tart words caught me off-balance and it was a moment or two before I could speak. Molly knew nothing of Chade and me, let alone of my side trip with him to Forge. To her, I was an errand-boy for the keep, working for the stablemaster when I wasn't fetching for the scribe, I couldn't betray my first-hand knowledge, let alone how I had sensed what Forging was.

'I've heard the talk of the guards, when they're around the stables and kitchens at night. Soldiers like them have seen much of all kinds of folk, and they're the ones who say that the Forged ones have no friendships, no family, no kinship ties at all left. Still, I suppose if one of them took to robbing travellers, others would copy him, and it would be almost the same as a band of robbers.'

'Perhaps.' She seemed mollified by my comments. 'Look, let's climb up there to eat.'

'Up there' was a shelf on the cliff's edge rather than the breakwater. But I assented with a nod, and the next handful of minutes were spent in getting ourselves and our basket up there. It required more arduous climbing than our earlier expeditions had. I caught myself watching to see how Molly would manage her skirts, and taking opportunities to catch at her arm to balance her, or take her hand to help her up a steep bit while she kept hold of the basket. In a flash of insight I knew that Molly's suggestion that we climb had been her way of manipulating the situation to cause this. We finally gained the ledge and sat, looking out over the water with her basket between us, and I was savouring my awareness of her awareness of me. It reminded me of the clubs of the Springfest jugglers as they handed them back and forth, back and forth, more and more and faster and faster. The silence lasted until a time when one of us had to speak. I looked at her, but she looked aside. She looked into the basket and said, 'Oh, dandelion wine? I thought that wasn't any good until after midwinter.'

'It's last year's . . . it's had a winter to age,' I told her, and took it from her to work the cork loose with my knife. She watched me worry at it for a while, and then took it from me and, drawing her own slender sheath-knife, speared and twisted it out with a practised knack that I envied.

She caught my look and shrugged. 'I've been pulling corks for my father for as long as I can remember. It used to be because he was too drunk. Now he doesn't have the strength in his hands any more, even when he's sober.' Pain and bitterness mingled in her words.

'Ah.' I floundered for a more pleasant topic. 'Look, the *Rainmaiden*.' I pointed out over the water to a sleek-hulled ship coming into the harbour under oars. 'I've always thought her the most beautiful ship in the harbour.'

'She's been on patrol: The cloth merchants took up a collection. Almost every merchant in town contributed. Even I, although all I could spare was candles for her lanterns. She's manned with fighters now, and escorts the ships between here and Highdowns. The *Greenspray* meets them there and takes them further up the coast.'

'I hadn't heard that.' And it surprised me that I had not heard such a thing up in the keep itself. My heart sank in me, that even Buckkeep Town was taking measures independent of the King's advice or consent. I said as much.

'Well, folk have to do whatever they can if all King Shrewd is going to do is click his tongue and frown about it. It's well enough for him to bid us to be strong, when he sits secure up in his castle. It isn't as if his son or brother or little girl will be Forged.'

It shamed me that I could think of nothing to say in my King's defence. And shame stung me to say, 'Well, you're almost as safe as the King himself, living here below in Buckkeep Town.'

Molly looked at me levelly. 'I had a cousin, apprenticed out in Forge Town.' She paused, then said carefully, 'Will you think me cold when I say that we were relieved to hear he had only been killed? It was uncertain for a week or so, but finally we had word from one who had seen him die. And my father and I were both relieved. We could grieve, knowing that his life was simply over and we would miss him. We no longer had to wonder if he were still alive and behaving like a beast, causing misery to others and shame to himself.'

I was silent for a bit. Then, 'I'm sorry.' It seemed inadequate, and I reached out to pat her motionless hand. For a second it was almost as if I couldn't feel her there, as if her pain had shocked her into an emotional numbness the equal of a Forged one. But then she sighed and I felt her presence again beside me. 'You know,' I ventured, 'perhaps the King himself does not know what to do either. Perhaps he is at as great a loss for a solution as we are.'

'He is the King!' Molly protested. 'And named Shrewd to be shrewd. Folk are saying now he but holds back to keep the strings of his purse tight. Why should he pay out of his hoard, when desperate merchants will hire mercenaries of their own? But, enough of this . . .' she held up a hand to stop my words. 'This is not why we came out here into the peace and coolness, to talk of politics and fears. Tell me instead of what you've been doing. Has the speckled bitch had her pups yet?'

And so we spoke of other things, of Motley's puppies and of the wrong stallion getting at a mare in season, and then she told me of gathering greencones to scent her candles and picking blackberries, and how busy she would be for the next week, trying to make blackberry preserves for the winter while still tending the shop and making candles.

We talked and ate and drank and watched the late sun of summer as it lingered low on the horizon, almost but not quite setting. I felt the tension as a pleasant thing between us, as both a suspension and a wonder. I viewed it as an extension of my strange new sense, and so I marvelled that Molly seemed to feel and react to it as well. I wanted to speak to her about it, to ask her if she was aware of other folk in a similar way. But I feared that if I asked her, I might reveal myself as I had to Chade, or that she might be disgusted by it as I knew Burrich would be. So I smiled, and we talked, and I kept my thoughts to myself.

I walked her home through the quiet streets and bid her good night at the door of the chandlery. She paused a moment, as if thinking of something else she wanted to say, but then gave me only a quizzical look and a softly muttered, 'Good night, Newboy.'

I took myself home under a deeply blue sky pierced by bright stars, past the sentries at their eternal dice game and up to the stables. I made a quick round of the stalls, but all was calm and well there, even with the new puppies. I noticed two strange horses in one of the paddocks, and one lady's palfrey had been stabled. Some visiting noblewoman come to court, I decided. I wondered what had brought her here at the end of the summer, and admired the quality of her horses. Then I left the stables and headed up to the keep.

By habit my path took me through the kitchens. Cook was familiar with the appetites of stable-boys and men-at-arms, and knew that regular meals did not always suffice to keep one full. Especially lately I had found myself getting hungry at all hours, while Mistress Hasty had recently declared that if I didn't stop growing so rapidly, I should have to wrap myself in barkcloth like a wild man, for she had no idea how to keep me looking as if my clothes fitted. I was already thinking of the big earthenware bowl that Cook kept full of soft biscuits and covered with a cloth, and of a certain wheel of especially sharp cheese, and how well both would go with some ale, when I entered the kitchen door.

There was a woman at the table. She had been eating an apple and cheese, but at the sight of me coming in the door, she sprang up and put her hand over her heart as if she thought I were the Pocked Man himself. I paused. 'I did not mean to startle you, lady. I was merely hungry, and thought to get myself some food. Will it bother you if I stay?'

The lady slowly sank back into her seat. I wondered privately what someone of her rank was doing alone in the kitchen at night, for her high birth was something that could not be disguised by the simple cream robe she wore or the weariness in her face. This, undoubtedly, was the rider of the palfrey in the stable, and not some lady's maid. If she had awakened hungry at night, why hadn't she simply bestirred a servant to fetch something for her?

Her hand rose from clutching at her breast to pat at her lips, as if to steady her uneven breath. When she spoke, her voice was well-modulated, almost musical. 'I would not keep you from your food. I was simply a bit startled. You . . . came in so suddenly.'

'My thanks, lady.'

I moved around the big kitchen, from ale cask to cheese to bread, but everywhere I went, her eyes followed me. Her food lay ignored on the table where she had dropped it when I came in. I turned from pouring myself a mug of ale to find her eyes wide upon me. Instantly she dropped them away. Her mouth worked, but she said nothing.

'May I do something for you?' I asked politely. 'Help you find something? Would you care for some ale?'

'If you would be so kind.' She said the words softly. I brought her the mug I had just filled and set it on the table before her. She drew back when I came near her, as if I carried some contagion. I wondered if I smelled bad from my stable work earlier. I decided not, for Molly would have surely mentioned it. Molly was ever frank with me about such things.

I drew another mug for myself, and then, looking about, decided it would be better to carry my food up to my room. The lady's whole attitude bespoke her uneasiness at my presence. But as I was struggling to balance biscuits and cheese and mug, she gestured at the bench opposite her. 'Sit down,' she told me, as if she had read my thoughts. 'It is not right I should scare you away from your meal.'

Her tone was neither command nor invitation, but something in between. I took the seat she indicated, my ale slopping over a bit as I juggled food and mug into place. I felt her eyes on me as I sat. Her own food remained ignored before her. I ducked my head to avoid that gaze, and ate quickly, as furtively as a rat in a corner who suspects a cat is behind the door, waiting. She did not stare rudely, but openly watched me, with the sort of observation that made my hands clumsy, and led to my acute awareness that I had just unthinkingly wiped my mouth on the back of my sleeve.

I could think of nothing to say, and yet the silence jabbed at me. The biscuit seemed dry in my mouth, making me cough, and when I tried to wash it down with ale, I choked. Her eyebrows twitched, her mouth set more firmly. Even with my eyes lowered to my plate, I felt her gaze. I rushed through my food, wanting only to escape her hazel eyes and straight silent mouth. I pushed the last hunks of bread and cheese into my mouth and stood up quickly, bumping against the table and almost knocking the bench over in my haste. I headed toward the door, then remembered Burrich's instructions about excusing oneself from a lady's presence. I swallowed my half-chewed mouthful.

'Good night to you, lady,' I muttered, thinking the words not quite right, but unable to summon better. I crabbed toward the door.

'Wait,' she said, and when I paused, she asked, 'Do you sleep upstairs, or out in the stables?'

'Both. Sometimes. I mean, either. Ah, good night, then, lady.' I turned and all but fled. I was halfway up the stairs before I wondered at the strangeness of her question. It was only when I went to undress for bed that I realized I still gripped my empty ale mug. I went to sleep, feeling a fool, and wondering why.

TWELVE

Patience

The Red Ship Raiders were a misery and an affliction to their own folk long before they troubled the shores of the Six Duchies. From obscure cult beginnings, they rose to both religious and political power by means of ruthless tactics. Chiefs and Headmen who refused to align themselves with their beliefs often found that their wives and children had become the victims of what we have come to call Forging in memory of the ill-fated town of Forge. Hard-hearted and cruel as we consider the Outislanders to be, they have in their tradition a strong vein of honour, and heinous penalties for those who break the kin-rules. Imagine the anguish of the Outislander father whose son has been Forged. He must either conceal his son's crimes when the boy lies to him, steals from him, and forces himself upon the household women, or see the boy flayed alive for his crimes and suffer both the loss of his heir and the respect of the other Houses. The threat of Forging was a powerful detriment to opposing the political power of the Red Ship Raiders.

By the time the Raiders began to harry our shores seriously, they had subdued most opposition in the Out Islands. Those who openly opposed them died or fled. Others grudgingly paid tribute and clenched their teeth against the outrages of those who controlled the cult. But many gladly joined the ranks, and painted the hulls of their raiding vessels red and never questioned the rightness of what they did. It seems likely that these converts were formed mostly from the lesser Houses, who had never before been offered the opportunity to rise in influence. But he who controlled the Red Ship Raiders cared nothing for who a man's forebears had been, so long as he had the man's unswerving loyalty.

I saw the lady twice more before I discovered who she was. The second time I saw her was the next night, at about the same hour. Molly had been busy with her berries, so I had gone out for an evening of tavern music with Kerry and Dirk. I had had perhaps one or at most two glasses more of ale than I should have. I was neither dizzy nor sick, but I was placing my feet carefully for I had already taken one tumble in a pothole on the dusky road.

Separate but adjacent to the dusty kitchen courtyard with its cobbles and wagon docks is a hedged area. It is commonly referred to as the Women's Garden, not because it is exclusively their province but simply because they have the tending and the knowing of it. It is a pleasant place, with a pond in the middle, and many low beds of herbs set among flowering plantings, fruit-vines and green-stoned pathways. I knew better than to go straight to bed when I was in this condition. If I attempted to sleep now, the bed would begin to spin and sway, and within an hour, I would be puking sick. It had been a pleasant evening, and that seemed a wretched way to end it, so I took myself to the Women's Garden instead of to my room.

In one angle of the garden, between a sun-warmed wall and a smaller pond, there grew seven varieties of thyme. Their fragrances on a hot day can be giddying, but then, with evening verging on night, the mingling scents seemed to soothe my head. I splashed my face in the little pool, and then put my back to the rock wall that was still releasing the sun's heat back to the night. Frogs were chirruping to one another. I lowered my eyes and watched the pond's calm surface to keep myself from spinning.

Footsteps. Then a woman's voice asked tartly, 'Are you drunk?'

'Not quite,' I replied affably, thinking it was Tilly the orchard-girl. 'Not quite enough time or coin,' I added jokingly.

'I suppose you learned it from Burrich. The man is a sot and a lecher, and he has cultivated like traits in you. Ever he brings those around him down to his level.'

The bitterness in the woman's voice made me look up. I squinted through the dimming light to make out her features. It was the lady of the previous evening. Standing on the garden path, in a simple shift, she looked at first glance to be little more than a girl. She was slender, and less tall than I, though I was not overly tall for my fourteen years. But her face was a woman's, and right now her mouth was set in a condemning line echoed by the brows knit over her hazel eyes. Her hair was dark and curling, and though she had tried to restrain it, ringlets of it had escaped at her forehead and neck.

It was not that I felt compelled to defend Burrich; it was simply that my condition was no doing of his. So I made answer something to the effect that as he was some miles distant in a different town, he could scarcely be responsible for what I put in my mouth and swallowed.

The lady came two steps closer. 'But he has never taught you better, has he? He has never counselled you against drunkenness, has he?'

There is a saying from the southlands that there is truth in wine. There must be a bit of it in ale, also. I spoke it that night. 'Actually, my lady, he would be greatly displeased with me right now. First, he would berate me for not rising when a lady spoke to me.' And here I lurched to my feet. 'And then, he would lecture me long and severely about the behaviour expected from one who carries a prince's blood if not his titles.' I managed a bow, and when I succeeded, I distinguished myself by straightening up with a flourish. 'So, good evening to you, fair Lady of the Garden. I bid you good night, and I shall remove my oafish self from your presence.'

I was all the way to the arched entryway in the wall when she called out, 'Wait!' But my stomach gave a quietly protesting grumble, and I pretended not to hear. She did not come after me, but I felt sure she watched me, and so I kept my head up and my stride even until I was out of the kitchen courtyard. I took myself down to the stables, where I vomited into the manure pile, and ended up sleeping in a clean empty stall because the steps up to Burrich's loft looked entirely too steep.

But youth is amazingly resilient, especially when feeling

threatened. I was up at dawn the next day, for I knew Burrich was expected home by afternoon. I washed myself at the stables, and decided the tunic I had worn for the last three days needed to be replaced. I was doubly conscious of its condition when in the corridor outside my room the lady accosted me. She looked me up and down, and before I could speak, she addressed me.

'Change your shirt,' she told me. And then added, 'Those leggings make you look like a stork. Tell Mistress Hasty they need replacing.'

'Good morning, lady,' I said. It was not a reply, but those were the only words that came to me in my astonishment. I decided she was very eccentric, even more so than Lady Thyme. My best course was to humour her. I expected her to turn aside and go on her way. Instead she continued to hold me with her eyes.

'Do you play a musical instrument?' she demanded.

I shook my head mutely.

'You sing, then?'

'No, my lady.'

She looked troubled as she asked, 'Then perhaps you have been taught to recite the Epics and the knowledge verses, of herbs and healings and navigation . . . that sort of thing?'

'Only the ones that pertain to the care of horses, hawks and dogs,' I told her, almost honestly. Burrich had demanded I learn those. Chade had taught me a set about poisons and antidotes, but he had warned me they were not commonly known, and were not to be casually recited.

'But you dance, of course? And you have been instructed in the making of verse?'

I was totally confused. 'Lady, I think you have confused me with someone else. Perhaps you are thinking of August, the King's nephew. He is but a year or two younger than I and . . .'

'I am not mistaken. Answer my question!' she demanded, almost shrilly.

'No, my lady. The teachings you speak of are for those who are . . . well-born. I have not been taught them.'

At each of my denials, she had appeared more troubled. Her mouth grew straighter, and her hazel eyes clouded. 'This is not to be tolerated,' she declared, and turning in a flurry of skirts, she hastened off down the hallway. After a moment, I went into my room, changed my shirt, and put on the longest pair of leggings I owned. I dismissed the lady from my thoughts and threw myself into my chores and lessons for the day.

It was raining that afternoon when Burrich returned. I met him outside the stables, taking his horse's head as he swung stiffly down from the saddle. 'You've grown, Fitz,' he observed and looked me over with a critical eye, as if I were a horse or hound that was showing unexpected potential. He opened his mouth as if to say something more, then shook his head and gave a half-snort. 'Well?' he asked, and I began my report.

He had been gone scarcely more than a month, but Burrich liked to know things down to the smallest detail. He walked beside me, listening, as I led his horse to her stall and proceeded to care for her.

Sometimes it surprised me how much like Chade he could be. They were very alike in the way they expected me to recall exact details, and to be able to relate the doings of last week or last month in correct order. Learning to report for Chade had not been that difficult; he had merely formalized the requirements that Burrich had long expected of me. Years later I was to realize how similar it was to the reporting of a man-at-arms to his superior.

Another man would have gone off to the kitchens or the baths after hearing my summarized version of everything that had gone on in his absence. But Burrich insisted on walking through his stables, stopping here to chat with a groom and there to speak softly to a horse. When he came to the lady's old palfrey, he stopped. He looked at the horse for a few minutes in silence.

'I trained this beast,' he said abruptly, and at his voice the horse turned in the stall to face him and whickered softly. 'Silk,' he said softly, and stroked the soft nose. He sighed suddenly. 'So the Lady Patience is here. Has she seen you yet?'

Now there was a question difficult to answer. A thousand thoughts collided in my head at once. The Lady Patience, my father's wife, and by many accounts, the one most responsible for my father's withdrawal from the court and from me. That was who I had been chatting with in the kitchen, and drunkenly saluting. That was who had quizzed me this morning on my education. To Burrich I muttered, 'Not formally. But we've met.'

He surprised me by laughing. 'Your face is a picture, Fitz. I can see she hasn't changed much, just by your reaction. The first time I met her was in her father's orchard. She was sitting up in a tree. She demanded that I remove a splinter from her foot, and took her shoe and stocking off right there so I could do it. Right there in front of me. And she had no idea at all of who I was. Nor I, her. I thought she was a lady's maid. That was years ago, of course, and even a few years before my prince met her. I suppose I wasn't much older than you are now.' He paused, and his face softened. 'And she had a wretched little dog she always carried about with her in a basket. It was always wheezing and retching up wads of its own fur. Its name was Featherduster.' He paused a moment, and smiled almost fondly. 'What a thing to remember, after all these years.'

'Did she like you when she first met you?' I asked tactlessly.

Burrich looked at me and his eyes became opaque, the man disappearing behind the gaze. 'Better than she does now,' he said abruptly. 'But that's of small import. Let's hear it, Fitz. What does she think of you?'

Now there was a question. I plunged into an accounting of our meetings, glossing over details as much as I dared. I was halfway through my garden encounter when Burrich held up a hand.

'Stop,' he said quietly.

I fell silent.

'When you cut pieces out of the truth to avoid looking like a fool, you end up sounding like a moron instead. Let's start again.'

So I did, and spared him nothing, of either my behaviour or the lady's comments. When I was finished, I waited for his judgement. Instead, he reached out and stroked the palfrey's nose. 'Some things are changed by time,' he said at last. 'And others are not.' He sighed. 'Well, Fitz, you have a way of presenting yourself to the very people you should most ardently avoid. I am sure there will be consequences from this, but I have not the slightest idea what they will be. That being so, there's no point to worrying. Let's see the rat-dog's pups. You say she had six?'

'And all survived,' I said proudly, for the bitch had a history of difficult whelping.

'Let's just hope we do as well for ourselves,' Burrich muttered as we walked through the stables, but when I glanced up at him, surprised, he seemed not to have been talking to me at all.

'I'd have thought you'd have the good sense to avoid her,' Chade grumbled at me.

It was not the greeting I had looked for after more than two months' absence from his chambers. 'I didn't know it was the Lady Patience. I'm surprised there was no gossip about her arrival.'

'She strenuously objects to gossip,' Chade informed me. He sat in his chair before the small fire in the fireplace. Chade's chambers were chilly, and he was ever vulnerable to cold. He looked weary as well tonight, worn by whatever he had been doing in the weeks since I'd last seen him. His hands, especially, looked old, bony and lumpy about the knuckles. He took a sip of his wine and continued. 'And she has her eccentric little ways of dealing with those who talk about her behind her back. She has always insisted on privacy for herself. It is one reason she would have made a very poor queen. Not that Chivalry cared. That was a marriage he made for himself rather than for politics. I think it was the first major disappointment he dealt his father. After that, nothing he did ever completely pleased Shrewd.'

I sat still as a mouse. Slink came and perched on my knee. It was rare to hear Chade so talkative, especially about matters relating to the royal family. I scarcely breathed for fear of interrupting him.

'Sometimes I think there was something in Patience that Chivalry instinctively knew he needed. He was a thoughtful, orderly man, always correct in his manners, always aware of precisely what was going on around him. He was chivalrous, boy, in the best sense of that word. He did not give in to ugly or petty impulses. That meant he exuded a certain air of restraint at all times – so those who did not know him well thought him cold or cavalier.

'And then he met this girl . . . and she was scarcely more than a girl. And there was no more substance to her than to cobwebs and sea-foam. Thoughts and tongue always flying from this to that, nitterdy-natterdy, with never a pause or connection I could see. It used to exhaust me just to listen to her. But Chivalry would smile, and marvel. Perhaps it was that she had absolutely no awe of him. Perhaps it was that she didn't seem particularly eager to win him. But with a score of more eligible ladies, of better birth and brighter brains, pursuing him, he chose Patience. And it wasn't even timely for him to wed; when he took her to wife, he shut the gate on a dozen possible alliances that a wife could have brought him. There was no good reason for him to get married at that time. Not one.'

'Except that he wanted to,' I said, and then I could have bitten out my tongue. For Chade nodded, and then gave himself a bit of a shake. He took his gaze off the fire and looked at me.

'Well. Enough of that. I won't ask you how you made such an impression on her, or what changed her heart toward you. But last week, she came to Shrewd and demanded that you be recognized as Chivalry's son and heir and given an education appropriate to a prince.'

I was dizzied. Did the wall tapestries move before me, or was it a trick of my eyes?

'Of course he refused,' Chade continued mercilessly. 'He tried to explain to her why such a thing is totally impossible. All she kept saying was, "But you are the King. How can it be impossible for you?" "The nobles would never accept him. It would mean civil war. And think what it would do to an unprepared boy, to plunge him suddenly into this." So he told her.'

'Oh,' I said quietly. I couldn't remember what I had felt for the one instant. Elation? Anger? Fear? I only knew that the feeling was gone now, and I felt oddly stripped and humiliated that I had felt anything at all.

'Patience, of course, was not convinced at all. "Prepare the boy," she told the King. "And when he is ready, judge for yourself." Only Patience would ask such a thing, and in front of both Verity and Regal. Verity listened quietly, knowing how it must end, but Regal was livid. He becomes overwrought far too easily. Even an idiot should know Shrewd could not accede to Patience's demand.

But he knows when to compromise. In all else, he gave way to her, mostly I think to stop her tongue.'

'In all else?' I repeated stupidly.

'Some for our good, some for our detriment. Or at least, for our damned inconvenience.' Chade sounded both annoyed and elated. 'I hope you can find more hours in the day, boy, for I'm not willing to sacrifice any of my plans for hers. Patience has demanded that you be educated as befits your blood-lines. And she has vowed to undertake such educating herself. Music, poetry, dance, song, manners . . . I hope you've a better tolerance for it than I did. Though it never seemed to hurt Chivalry. Sometimes he even put such knowledge to good use. But it will take up a good part of your day. You'll be acting as page for Patience as well. You're old for it, but she insisted. Personally, I think she regrets much and is trying to make up for lost time, something that never works. You'll have to cut back your weapons-training. And Burrich will have to find himself another stable-boy.'

I didn't give a peg about the weapons-training. As Chade had often pointed out to me, a really good assassin worked close and quietly. If I learned my trade well, I wouldn't be swinging a long blade at anyone. But my time with Burrich – again I had the odd sensation of not knowing how I felt. I hated Burrich. Sometimes. He was overbearing, dictatorial and insensitive. He expected me to be perfect, yet bluntly told me that I would never be rewarded for it. But he was also open, and blunt, and believed I could achieve what he demanded . . .

'You're probably wondering what advantage she won us,' Chade went on obliviously. I heard suppressed excitement in his voice. 'It's something I've tried for twice for you, and been twice refused. But Patience nattered at Shrewd until he surrendered. It's the Skill, boy. You're to be trained in the Skill.'

'The Skill,' I repeated, without sense of what I was saying. It was all going too fast for me.

'Yes.'

I scrabbled to find thoughts. 'Burrich spoke of it to me, once. A long time ago.' Abruptly I remembered the context of that conversation. After Nosy accidentally betrayed us. He had spoken of it as the opposite of whatever was the sense I shared with animals. The same sense had revealed to me the change in the folk of Forge. Would training in one free me of the other? Or would it be a deprivation? I thought of the sense that I had shared with horses and dogs when I knew Burrich was not around. I remembered Nosy, in a mingling of warmth and grief. I had never been so close, before or since, to another living creature. Would this new training in the Skill take that away from me?

'What's the matter, boy?' Chade's voice was kindly, but concerned.

'I don't know.' I hesitated. But not even to Chade could I dare to reveal my fear. Or my taint. 'Nothing, I suppose.'

'You've been listening to old tales about the training,' he guessed, totally incorrectly. 'Listen, boy, it can't be that bad. Chivalry went through it. So did Verity. And with the threat of the Red Ships, Shrewd has decided to go back to the old ways, and extend the training to other likely candidates. He wants a coterie, or even two, to supplement what he and Verity can do with the Skill. Galen is not enthused, but I suspect it's a very good idea. Though, being a bastard myself, I was never allowed the training. So I've no real idea how the Skill might be employed to defend the land.'

'You're a bastard?' The words burst out of me. All my tangled thoughts were suddenly sliced through by this revelation. Chade stared at me, as shocked at my words as I by his.

'Of course. I thought you'd worked that out long ago. Boy, for someone as perceptive as you are, you've got some very odd blindspots.'

I looked at Chade as if for the first time. His scars, perhaps, had hidden it from me. The resemblance was there. The brow, the way his ears were set, the line of his lower lip. 'You're Shrewd's son,' I guessed wildly, going only by his appearance. Even before he spoke, I realized how foolish my words were.

'Son?' Chade laughed grimly. 'How he would scowl to hear you say that! But the truth makes him grimace even more. He is my younger half-brother, boy, though he was conceived in a wedded bed and I on a military campaign near Sandsedge.' Softly he added, 'My mother was a soldier when I was conceived. But she returned home to bear me, and later wedded a potter. When my mother died, her husband put me on a donkey, gave me a necklace she had worn, and told me to take it to the King at Buckkeep. I was ten. It was a long, hard road from Woolcot to Buckkeep, in those days.'

I couldn't think of anything to say.

'Enough of this.' Chade straightened himself up sternly. 'Galen will be instructing you in the Skill. Shrewd browbeat him into it. He finally acceded, but with reservations. No one is to interfere with any of his students during the training. I wish it were otherwise, but there's nothing I can do about it. You'll just have to be careful. You know of Galen, don't you?'

'A little,' I said. 'Only what other people say about him.'

'What do you know by yourself?' Chade quizzed me.

I took a breath and considered. 'He eats alone. I've never seen him at table, either with the men-at-arms, or in the dining-hall. I've never seen him just standing about and talking, not in the exercise yard or the washing-court or in any of the gardens. He's always going somewhere when I see him, and he's always in a hurry. He's bad with animals. The dogs don't like him, and he overcontrols the horses so much that he ruins their mouths and their temperaments. I imagine he's about Burrich's age. He dresses well, is almost as fancy as Regal. I've heard him called a Queen's man.'

'Why?' Chade asked quickly.

'Um, it was a long time ago. Gage. He's a man-at-arms. He came to Burrich one night, a bit drunk, a bit cut-up. He'd had a fight with Galen, and Galen had hit him in the face with a little whip or something. Gage asked Burrich to fix him up, because it was late, and he wasn't supposed to have been drinking that night. His watch was coming up, or something. Gage told Burrich that he'd overheard Galen say that Regal was twice as royal as Chivalry or Verity, and it was a stupid custom that kept him from the throne. Galen had said that Regal's mother was better-born than Shrewd's first queen. Which everyone knows is true. But what angered Gage enough to start the fight was that Galen said Queen Desire was more royal than Shrewd himself, for she'd Farseer blood from both her parents, and Shrewd's was just from his father. So Gage swung at him, but Galen sidestepped and struck him in the face with something.'

I paused.

'And?' Chade encouraged me.

'And so he favours Regal, over Verity or even the King. And Regal, well, accepts him. He's friendlier with him than he usually is with servants or soldiers. He seems to take counsel from him, the few times I've seen them together. It's almost funny to watch them together; you'd think Galen was aping Regal, from the way he dresses and walks as the prince does. Sometimes they almost look alike.'

'They do?' Chade leaned closer, waiting. 'What else have you noticed?'

I searched my memory for more first-hand knowledge of Galen. 'That's all, I think.'

'Has he ever spoken to you?'

'No.'

'I see.' Chade nodded as if to himself. 'And what do you know of him by reputation? What do you suspect?' He was trying to lead me to some conclusion, but I could not guess what.

'He's from Farrow. An Inlander. His family came to Buckkeep with King Shrewd's second queen. I've heard it said that he's afraid of the water, to sail or to swim. Burrich respects him, but doesn't like him. He says he's a man who knows his job and does it, but Burrich can't get along with anyone who mistreats an animal, even if it's out of ignorance. The kitchen folk don't like him. He's always making the younger ones cry. He accuses the girls of getting hair in his meals or having dirty hands, and he says the boys are too rowdy and don't serve food correctly. So the cooks don't like him either, because when the apprentices are upset they don't do their work well.' Chade was still looking at me expectantly, as if waiting for something very important. I racked my brains for other gossip.

'He wears a chain with three gems set in it. Queen Desire gave it to him, for some special service he did. Um. The Fool hates him. He told me once that if no one else is around Galen calls him a freak and throws things at him.'

Chade's brows went up. 'The Fool talks to you?'

His tone was more than incredulous. He sat up in his chair so suddenly that his wine leaped out of his cup and splashed on his knee. He rubbed at it distractedly with his sleeve.

'Sometimes,' I admitted cautiously. 'Not very often. Only when he feels like it. He just appears and tells me things.'

'Things? What kind of things?'

I realized suddenly that I had never recounted to Chade the Fitz-fits-fats riddle. It seemed too complicated to go into just then. 'Oh, just odd things. About two months ago, he stopped me and said the morrow was a poor day to hunt. But it was fine and clear. Burrich got that big buck that day. You remember. It was the same day that we came upon a wolverine. It tore up two of the dogs badly.'

'As I recall, it nearly got you.' Chade leaned forward, an oddly pleased look on his face.

I shrugged. 'Burrich rode it down. And then he cursed me down as if it were my fault, and told me that he'd have knocked me silly if the beast had hurt Sooty. As if I could have known it would turn on me.' I hesitated. 'Chade, I know the Fool is strange. But I like it when he comes to talk to me. He speaks in riddles, and he insults me, and makes fun of me, and gives himself leave to tell me things he thinks I should do, like wash my hair, or not wear yellow. But.'

'Yes?' Chade prodded as if what I was saying were very important.

'I like him,' I said lamely. 'He mocks me, but from him, it seems a kindness. He makes me feel, well, important. That he could choose me to talk to.'

Chade leaned back. He put his hand up to his mouth to cover a smile, but it was a joke I didn't understand. 'Trust your instincts,' he told me succinctly. 'And keep any counsels the Fool gives you. And, as you have, keep it private that he comes and speaks to you. Some could take it amiss.'

'Who?' I demanded.

'King Shrewd, perhaps. After all, the Fool is his. Bought and paid for.'

A dozen questions rose to my mind. Chade saw the expression on my face, for he held up a quelling hand. 'Not now. That's as much as you need to know right now. In fact, more than you need to know. But I was surprised by your revelation. It's not like me to tell secrets not my own. If the Fool wants you to know more, he can speak for himself. But, I seem to recall we were discussing Galen.'

I sank back in my chair with a sigh. 'Galen. So he is unpleasant to those who cannot challenge it, dresses well and eats alone. What else do I need to know, Chade? I've had strict teachers, and I've had unpleasant ones. I think I'll learn to deal with him.'

'You'd better.' Chade was deadly earnest. 'Because he hates you. He hates you more than he loved your father. The depth of emotion he felt for your father unnerved me. No man, not even a prince, merits such blind devotion, especially not so suddenly. And you he hates, with even more intensity. It frightens me.'

Something in Chade's tone brought a sick chill stalking up from my stomach. I felt an uneasiness that almost made me sick. 'How do you know?' I demanded.

'Because he told Shrewd so when Shrewd directed him to include you among his pupils. "Does not this bastard have to learn his place? Does he not have to be content with what you have decreed for him?" Then he refused to teach you.'

'He refused?'

'I told you. But Shrewd was adamant. And he is King, and Galen must obey him now, for all that he was a Queen's man. So Galen relented and said he would attempt to teach you. You will meet with him each day. Beginning a month from now. You are Patience's until then.'

'Where?'

'There is a tower top, called the Queen's Garden. You will be admitted there.' Chade paused, as if wanting to warn me, but not wishing to scare me. 'Be careful,' he said at last, 'for within the walls of the Garden, I have no influence. I am blind there.'

It was a strange warning, and one I took to heart.

THIRTEEN

Smithy

The Lady Patience established her eccentricity at an early age. As a small child, her nursemaids found her stubbornly independent, and yet lacking the common sense to take care of herself. One remarked, 'She would go all day with her laces undone because she could not tie them herself, yet would suffer no one to tie them for her.' Before the age of ten, she had decided to eschew the traditional trainings befitting a girl of her rank, and instead interested herself in handicrafts that were very unlikely to prove useful: pottery, tattooing, the making of perfumes, and the growing and propagation of plants, especially foreign ones.

She did not scruple to absent herself for long hours from supervision. She preferred the woodlands and orchards to her mother's courtyards and gardens. One would have thought this would produce a hardy and practical child. Nothing could be further from the truth. She seemed to be constantly afflicted with rashes, scrapes and stings, was frequently lost, and never developed any sensible wariness toward man or beast.

Her education came largely from herself. She mastered reading and ciphering at an early age, and from that time studied any scroll, book or tablet that came her way with avaricious and indiscriminate interest. Tutors were frustrated by her distractable ways and frequent absences that seemed to affect not at all her ability to learn almost anything swiftly and well. Yet the application of such knowledge interested her not at all. Her head was full of fancies and imaginings, she substituted poetry and music for logic and manners, she expressed no interest at all in social introductions and coquettish skills.

And yet she married a prince, one who had courted her with a single-minded enthusiasm that was to be the first scandal to befall him.

'Stand up straight!'

I stiffened.

'Not like that! You look like a turkey, drawn out and waiting for the axe. Relax more. No, put your shoulders back, don't hunch them. Do you always stand with your feet thrown out so?'

'Lady, he is only a boy. They are always so, all angles and bones. Let him come in and be at ease.'

'Oh, very well. Come in, then.'

I nodded my gratitude to a round-faced serving-woman who dimpled a smile at me in return. She gestured me toward a pewbench so bedecked with pillows and shawls that there was scarcely room left to sit. I perched on the edge of it and surveyed Lady Patience's chamber.

It was worse than Chade's. I would have thought it the clutter of years if I had not known that she had only recently arrived. Even a complete inventory of the room could not have described it, for it was the juxtaposition of objects that made them remarkable. A feather fan, a fencing glove and a bundle of cattails were all vased in a well-worn boot. A small black terrier with two fat puppies slept in a basket lined with a fur hood and some woollen stockings. A family of carved-ivory walruses perched on a tablet about horse-shoeing. But the dominant elements were the plants. There were fat puffs of greenery overflowing clay pots, teacups and goblets, and buckets of cuttings and cut-flowers, and vines spilling out of handle-less mugs and cracked cups. Failures were evident in bare sticks poking up out of pots of earth. The plants perched and huddled together in every location that would catch morning or afternoon sun from the windows. The effect was like a garden spilling in the windows and growing up around the clutter in the room.

'He's probably hungry, too, isn't he, Lacey? I've heard that about boys. I think there's some cheese and biscuits on the stand by my bed. Fetch them for him, would you, dear?'

Lady Patience stood slightly more than arm's distance away from me as she spoke past me to her lady.

'I'm not hungry, really, thank you,' I blurted out before Lacey could lumber to her feet. 'I'm here because I was told . . . to make myself available to you, in the mornings, for as long as you wanted me.'

That was a careful rephrasing. What King Shrewd had actually said to me was, 'Go to her chambers each morning, and do whatever it is she thinks you ought to be doing so that she leaves me alone. And keep doing it until she is as weary of you as I am of her.' His bluntness had astounded me, for I had never seen him so beleaguered as that day. Verity came in the door of the chamber as I was scuttling out, and he, too, looked much the worse for wear. Both men spoke and moved as if suffering from too much wine the night before, and yet I had seen them both at table last night, and there had been a marked lack of either merriness or wine. Verity tousled my head as I went past him. 'More like his father every day,' he remarked to a scowling Regal behind him. Regal glared at me as he entered the King's chamber and loudly closed the door behind him.

So here I was, in my lady's chamber, and she was skirting about me and talking past me as if I were an animal that might suddenly strike out at her or soil the carpets. I could tell that it afforded Lacey much amusement.

'Yes. I already knew that, you see, because I was the one who had asked the King that you be sent here,' Lady Patience explained carefully to me.

'Yes, ma'am.' I shifted on my bit of seat-space and tried to look intelligent and well-mannered. Recalling the earlier times we had met, I could scarcely blame her for treating me like a dolt.

A silence fell. I looked around at things in the room. Lady Patience looked toward a window. Lacey sat and smirked to herself and pretended to be tatting lace.

'Oh. Here.' Swift as a diving hawk, Lady Patience stooped down and seized the black terrier pup by the scruff of the neck. He yelped in surprise, and his mother looked up in annoyance as Lady Patience thrust him into my arms. 'This one's for you. He's yours now. Every boy should have a pet.'

I caught the squirming puppy and managed to support his body before she let go of him. 'Or maybe you'd rather have a bird? I have a cage of finches in my bedchamber. You could have one of them, if you'd rather.'

'Uh, no. A puppy's fine. A puppy is wonderful.' The second half of the statement was made to the pup. My instinctive response to his high-pitched yi-yi-yi had been to quest out to him with calm. His mother had sensed my contact with him, and approved. She settled back into her basket with the white pup with blithe unconcern. The puppy looked up at me and met my eyes directly. This, in my experience, was rather unusual. Most dogs avoided prolonged direct eye-contact. But also unusual was his awareness. I knew from surreptitious experiments in the stable that most puppies his age had little more than fuzzy self-awareness, and were mostly turned to mother and milk and immediate needs. This little fellow had a solidly-established identity within himself, and a deep interest in all that was going on around him. He liked Lacey, who fed him bits of meat, and was wary of Patience, not because she was cruel, but because she stumbled over him and kept putting him back in the basket each time he laboriously clambered out. He thought I smelled very exciting, and the scents of horses and birds and other dogs were like colours in my mind, images of things that as yet had no shape or reality for him, but that he nonetheless found fascinating. I imaged the scents for him and he climbed my chest, wriggling, sniffing and licking me in his excitement. *Take me, show me, take me.*

'. . . even listening?'

I winced, expecting a rap from Burrich, then came back to awareness of where I was and of the small woman standing before me with her hands on her hips.

'I think something's wrong with him,' she observed abruptly to Lacey. 'Did you see how he was sitting there, staring at the puppy? I thought he was about to go off into some sort of fit.'

Lacey smiled benignly and went on with her tatting. 'Fair reminded me of you, my lady, when you start pottering about with your leaves and bits of plants and end up staring at the dirt.'

'Well,' said Patience, clearly displeased. 'It is quite one thing for an adult to be pensive,' she observed firmly. 'And another for a boy to stand about looking daft.'

Later, I promised the pup. 'I'm sorry,' I said, and tried to look repentant. 'I was just distracted by the puppy.' He had cuddled into the crook of my arm and was casually chewing the edge of my jerkin. It is difficult to explain what I felt. I needed to pay attention to Lady Patience, but this small being snuggled against me was radiating delight and contentment. It is a heady thing to be suddenly proclaimed the centre of someone's world, even if that someone is an eight-week-old puppy. It made me realize how profoundly alone I had felt, and for how long. 'Thank you,' I said, and even I was surprised at the gratitude in my voice. 'Thank you very much.'

'It's just a puppy,' Lady Patience said, and to my surprise she looked almost ashamed. She turned aside and stared out the window. The puppy licked his nose and closed his eyes. *Warm. Sleep*. 'Tell me about yourself,' she demanded abruptly.

It took me aback. 'What would you like to know, lady?'

She made a small, frustrated gesture. 'What do you do each day? What have you been taught?'

So I attempted to tell her, but I could see that it didn't satisfy her. She folded her lips tightly at each mention of Burrich's name. She wasn't impressed with any of my martial training. Of Chade, I could say nothing. She nodded in grudging approval of my study of languages, writing and ciphering.

'Well,' she interrupted suddenly. 'At least you're not totally ignorant. If you can read, you can learn anything. If you've a will to. Have you a will to learn?'

'I suppose so.' It was a lukewarm answer, but I was beginning to feel badgered. Not even the gift of the puppy could outweigh her belittlement of my learning.

'I suppose you will learn, then. For I have a will that you will, even if you do not yet.' She was suddenly stern, in a shifting of attitude that left me bewildered. 'And what do they call you, boy?'

The question again. 'Boy is fine,' I muttered. The sleeping puppy in my arms whimpered in agitation. I forced myself to be calm for him.

I had the satisfaction of seeing a stricken look flit briefly across

Patience's face. 'I shall call you, oh, Thomas. Tom for everyday. Does that suit you?'

'I suppose so,' I said deliberately. Burrich gave more thought to naming a dog than that. We had no Blackies or Spots in the stables. Burrich named each beast as if they were royalty, with names that described them or traits he aspired to for them. Even Sooty's name masked a gentle fire I had come to respect. But this woman named me Tom after no more than an indrawn breath. I looked down so that she couldn't see my eyes.

'Fine, then,' she said, a trifle briskly. 'Come tomorrow at the same time. I shall have some things ready for you. I warn you, I shall expect willing effort from you. Good day, Tom.'

'Good day, lady.'

I turned and left. Lacey's eyes followed me, and then darted back to her mistress. I sensed her disappointment, but did not know what it was about.

It was still early in the day. This first audience had taken less than an hour. I wasn't expected anywhere; this time was my own. I headed for the kitchens, to wheedle scraps for my pup. It would have been easy to take him down to the stables, but then Burrich would have known about him. I had no illusions about what would happen next. The pup would stay in the stables. He would be nominally mine, but Burrich would see that this new bond was severed. I had no intention of allowing that to happen.

I made my plans. A basket from the launderers, an old shirt over straw for his bed. His messes now would be small, and as he got older, my bond with him would make him easy to train. For now, he'd have to stay by himself for part of each day. But as he got older, he could go about with me. Eventually, Burrich would find out about him. I resolutely pushed that thought aside. I'd deal with that later. For now, he needed a name. I looked him over. He was not the curly-haired yappy type of terrier. He would have a short smooth coat, a thick neck and a mouth like a coal scuttle. But, grown, he'd be less than knee-high, so it couldn't be too weighty a name. I didn't want him to be a fighter. So no Ripper or Charger. He would be tenacious, and alert. Grip, maybe. Or Sentry.

'Or Anvil. Or Forge.'

I looked up. The Fool stepped out of an alcove and followed me down the hall.

'Why?' I asked. I no longer questioned the way the Fool could guess what I was thinking.

'Because your heart will be hammered against him, and your strength will be tempered in his fire.'

'Sounds a bit dramatic to me,' I objected. 'And Forge is a bad word now. I don't want to mark my pup with it. Just the other day, down in town, I heard a drunk yell at a cut-purse, "May your woman be Forged!" Everyone in the street stopped and stared.'

The Fool shrugged. 'Well they might.' He followed me into my room. 'Smith, then. Or Smithy. Let me see him?'

Reluctantly I gave over my puppy. He stirred, awakened and then wiggled in the Fool's hands. *No smell, no smell.* I was astonished to agree with the pup. Even with his little black nose working for me, the Fool had no detectable scent. 'Careful. Don't drop him.'

'I'm a Fool, not a dolt,' said the Fool, but he sat on my bed and put the pup beside him. Smithy instantly began snuffling and rucking my bed. I sat on the other side of him lest he venture too near the edge.

'So,' the Fool asked casually. 'Are you going to let her buy you with gifts?'

'Why not?' I tried to be disdainful.

'It would be a mistake, for both of you.' The Fool tweaked Smithy's tiny tail, and he spun round with a puppy growl. 'She's going to want to give you things. You'll have to take them, for there's no polite way to refuse. But you'll have to decide whether they'll make a bridge between you, or a wall.'

'Do you know Chade?' I asked abruptly, for the Fool sounded so like him I suddenly had to know. I had never mentioned Chade to anyone else, save Shrewd, or heard talk of him from anyone around the keep.

'Shade or sunlight, I know when to keep a grip on my tongue. It would be a good thing for you to learn as well.' The Fool rose suddenly and went to the door. He lingered there a moment. 'She only hated you for the first few months. And it wasn't truly hate of you; it was blind jealousy of your mother, that she could bear a babe to Chivalry, but Patience could not. After that, her heart softened. She wanted to send for you, to raise you as her own. Some might say she merely wanted to possess anything that touched Chivalry. But I don't think so.'

I was staring at the Fool.

'You look like a fish, with your mouth open like that,' he observed. 'But of course, your father refused. He said it might appear he was formally acknowledging his bastard. But I don't think that was it at all. I think it would have been dangerous for you.' The Fool made an odd pass with his hand, and a stick of dried meat appeared in his fingers. I knew it had been up his sleeve, but I was unable to see how he accomplished his tricks. He flipped the meat onto my bed and the puppy sprang on it greedily.

'You can hurt her, if you choose,' he offered me. 'She feels such guilt at how alone you have been. And you look so like Chivalry, anything you say will be as if it came from his lips. She's like a gem with a flaw. One precise tap from you, and she will fly to pieces. She's half-mad as she is, you know. They would never have been able to kill Chivalry if she hadn't consented to his abdication. At least, not with such blithe dismissal of the consequences. She knows that.'

'Who is "they"?' I demanded.

'Who "are" they?' the Fool corrected me, and whisked out of sight. By the time I got to the door, he was gone. I quested after him, but got nothing. Almost as if he were Forged. I shivered at that thought, and went back to Smithy. He was chewing the meat to slimy bits all over my bed. I watched him. 'The Fool's gone,' I told Smithy. He wagged a casual acknowledgement and went on worrying his meat.

He was mine, given to me. Not a stable-dog I cared for, but mine, and beyond Burrich's knowledge or authority. Other than my clothes and the copper bracelet that Chade had given me, I had few possessions. But he made up for all lack I might ever have had.

He was a sleek and healthy pup. His coat was smooth now, but would grow bristly as he matured. When I held him up to the window, I could see faint mottlings of colour in his coat. He'd be a dark brindle, then. I discovered one white spot on his chin, and another on his left hind foot. He clamped his little jaws on my shirt-sleeve and shook it violently, uttering savage puppy growls. I tussled him on the bed until he fell into a deep, limp sleep. Then I moved him to his straw cushion and went reluctantly to my afternoon lessons and chores.

That initial week with Patience was a trying time for both of us. I learned to keep a thread of my attention always with Smithy, so he never felt alone enough to howl when I left him. But that took practice, so I felt somewhat distracted. Burrich frowned about it, but I persuaded him it was due to my sessions with Patience. 'I have no idea what that woman wants from me,' I told him by the third day. 'Yesterday it was music. In the space of two hours, she attempted to teach me to play the harp, the sea-pipes, and then the flute. Every time I came close to working out a few notes on one or the other of them, she snatched it away and commanded that I try a different one. She ended that session by saying that I had no aptitude for music. This morning it was poetry. She set herself to teaching me the one about Queen Healsall and her garden. It has a long bit, about all the herbs she grew and what each was for. And she kept getting it bungled, and got angry at me when I repeated it back to her that way, saying that I must know that catmint is not for poultices and that I was mocking her. It was almost a relief when she said I had given her such a headache that we must stop. And when I offered to bring her buds from the ladyshand bush for her headache, she sat right up and said, "There! I knew you were mocking me." I don't know how to please her, Burrich.'

'Why would you want to?' he growled, and I let the subject drop.

That evening, Lacey came to my room. She tapped, then entered, wrinkling her nose. 'You'd better bring up some strewing herbs if you're going to keep that pup in here. And use some vinegar and water when you scrub up his messes. It smells like a stable in here.'

'I suppose it does,' I admitted. I looked at her curiously and waited.

'I brought you this. You seemed to like it best.' She held out the sea-pipes. I looked at the short, fat tubes bound together with strips of leather. I had liked it best of the three instruments. The harp had far too many strings, and the flute had seemed shrill to me even when Patience had played it.

'Did Lady Patience send it to me?' I asked, puzzled.

'No. She doesn't know I've taken it. She'll assume it's lost in her litter, as usual.'

'Why did you bring it?'

'For you to practise on. When you've a little skill with it, bring it back and show her.'

'Why?'

Lacey sighed. 'Because it would make her feel better. And that would make my life much easier. There's nothing worse than being maid to someone as heartsick as Lady Patience. She longs desperately for you to be good at something. She keeps trying you out, hoping that you'll manifest some sudden talent, so that she can flout you about and tell folk, "There, I told you he had it in him." Now I've had boys of my own, and I know boys aren't that way. They don't learn, or grow, or have manners when you're looking at them. But turn away, and turn back, and there they are, smarter, taller, and charming everyone but their own mothers.'

I was a little lost. 'You want me to learn to play this, so that Patience will be happy?'

'So that she can feel she's given you something.'

'She gave me Smithy. Nothing she can ever give me will be better than him.'

Lacey looked surprised at my sudden sincerity. So was I. 'Well. You might tell her that. But you might also try to learn to play the sea-pipes or recite a ballad or sing one of the old prayers. That she might understand better.'

After Lacey left, I sat thinking, caught between anger and wistfulness. Patience wished me to be a success and felt she must discover something I could do. As if before her, I had never done or accomplished anything. But as I mulled over what I had done, and what she knew of me, I realized that her image of me must be a rather flat one. I could read and write, and take care of a horse or dog. I could also brew poisons, make sleeping-draughts, smuggle, lie and do sleight-of-hand; none of which would have pleased her even if she had known. So, was there anything to me, other than a spy or assassin?

The next morning I arose early and sought Fedwren. He was pleased when I asked to borrow brushes and colours from him. The paper he gave me was better than practice sheets, and he made me promise to show him my efforts. As I made my way up the stairs, I wondered what it would be like to apprentice with him. Surely it could not be any harder than what I had been set to lately.

But the task I had set myself proved harder than any Patience had put me to. I could see Smithy asleep on his cushion. How could the curve of his back be different from the curve of a rune, the shades of his ears so different from the shading of the herbal illustrations I painstakingly copied from Fedwren's work? But they were, and I wasted sheet after sheet of paper until I suddenly saw that it was the shadows around the pup that made the curve of his back and the line of his haunch. I needed to paint less, not more, and put down what my eye saw rather than what my mind knew.

It was late when I washed out my brushes and set them aside. I had two that pleased, and a third that I liked, though it was soft and muzzy, more like a dream of a puppy than a real puppy. More like what I sensed than what I saw, I thought to myself.

But when I stood outside Lady Patience's door, I looked down at the papers in my hand and suddenly saw myself as a toddler presenting crushed and wilted dandelions to his mother. What fitting pastime was this for a youth? If I were truly Fedwren's apprentice, then exercises of this sort would be appropriate, for a good scriber must illustrate and illuminate as well as scribe. But the door opened and there I was, my fingers smudged still with paint and the pages damp in my hand.

I was wordless when Patience irritably told me to come inside, that I was late enough already. I perched on the edge of a chair with a crumpled cloak and some half-finished bit of stitchery. I set my paintings to one side of me, on top of a stack of tablets.

'I think you could learn to recite verse, if you chose to,' she remarked with some asperity. 'And therefore you could learn to compose verse, if you chose to. Rhythm and meter are no more than . . . is that the puppy?'

'It's meant to be,' I muttered, and could not remember feeling more wretchedly embarrassed in my life.

She lifted the sheets carefully and examined each one in turn, holding them close and then at arm's length. She stared longest at the muzzy one. 'Who did these for you?' she asked at last. 'Not that it excuses your being late. But I could find good use for someone who can put on paper what the eye sees, with the colours so true. That is the trouble with all the herbals I have; all the herbs are painted the same green, no matter if they are grey or tinged pink as they grow. Such tablets are useless if you are trying to learn from them . . .'

'I suspect he's painted the puppy himself, ma'am,' Lacey interrupted benignly.

'And the paper, this is better than what I've had to . . .' Patience paused suddenly. 'You, Thomas?' (And I think that was the first time she remembered to use the name she had bestowed on me.) 'You paint like this?'

Before her incredulous look, I managed a quick nod. She held up the pictures again. 'Your father could not draw a curved line, save it was on a map. Did your mother draw?'

'I have no memories of her, lady.' My reply was stiff. I could not recall that anyone had ever been brave enough to ask me such a thing before.

'What, none? But you were five years old. You must remember something: the colour of her hair, her voice, what she called you . . .' Was that a pained hunger in her voice, a curiosity she could not quite bear to satisfy?

Almost, for a moment, I did remember. A smell of mint, or was it . . . it was gone. 'Nothing, lady. If she had wanted me to remember her, she would have kept me, I suppose.' I closed my heart. Surely I owed no remembrance to the mother who had not kept me, nor ever sought me since.

'Well.' For the first time, I think Patience realized she had taken our conversation into a difficult area. She stared out of the window at a grey day. 'Someone has taught you well,' she observed suddenly, too brightly.

'Fedwren.' When she said nothing, I added, 'The court scribe, you know. He would like me to apprentice to him. He is pleased with my letters, and works with me now on the copying of his images. When we have time, that is. I am often busy, and he is often out questing after new paper-reeds.'

'Paper-reeds?' she asked distractedly.

'He has a bit of paper. He had several measures of it, but little by little he has used it. He got it from a trader, who had it from another, and yet another before him, so he does not know where it first came from. But from what he was told, it was made of pounded reeds. The paper is a much better quality than any we make; it is thin, flexible and does not crumble so readily with age; yet it takes ink well, not soaking it up so that the edges of runes blur. Fedwren says that if we could duplicate it, it would change much. With a good, sturdy paper, any man might have a copy of tabletlore from the keep. Were paper cheaper, more children could be taught to write and read, or so he says. I do not understand why he is so . . .'

'I did not know any here shared my interest.' A sudden animation lit the lady's face. 'Has he tried paper made from pounded lily-root? I have had some success with that. And also with paper created by first weaving and then wet pressing sheets made with threads of bark from the kinue tree. It is strong and flexible, yet the surface leaves much to be desired. Unlike this paper . . .'

She glanced again at the sheets in her hand and fell silent. Then she asked hesitantly, 'You like the puppy this much?'

'Yes,' I said simply, and our eyes suddenly met. She stared into me in the same distracted way that she often stared out of the window. Abruptly, her eyes brimmed with tears.

'Sometimes, you are so like him that . . .' She choked. 'You should have been mine! It isn't fair, you should have been mine!'

She cried out the words so fiercely that I thought she would strike me. Instead, she leaped at me and caught me in a flying hug, at the same time treading upon her dog and overturning a vase of greenery. The dog sprang up with a yelp, the vase shattered on the floor, sending water and shards in all directions, while my lady's forehead caught me squarely under the chin, so that for a moment all I saw was sparks. Before I could react, she flung herself from me and fled into her bedchamber with a cry like a scalded cat. She slammed the door behind her.

And all the while Lacey kept on with her tatting.

'She gets like this, sometimes,' she observed benignly, and nodded me toward the door. 'Come again tomorrow,' she reminded me, and added, 'You know, Lady Patience has become quite fond of you.'

FOURTEEN

Galen

Galen, son of a weaver, came to Buckkeep as a boy. His father was one of Queen Desire's personal servants who followed her from Farrow. Solicity was then the Skillmaster at Buckkeep. She had instructed King Bounty and his son Shrewd in the Skill, so by the time Shrewd's sons were boys, she was ancient already. She petitioned King Bounty that she might take an apprentice, and he consented. Galen was greatly favoured by the Queen, and at Queen-in-Waiting Desire's energetic urging, Solicity chose the youth Galen as her apprentice. At that time, as now, the Skill was denied to bastards of the Farseer House, but when the talent bloomed, unexpected, among those not of royalty, it was cultivated and rewarded. No doubt Galen was such a one as this, a boy showing strange and unexpected talent that came abruptly to the attention of a Skillmaster.

By the time the Princes Chivalry and Verity were old enough to receive Skill instruction, Galen had advanced enough to assist in their instruction, though he was but a year or so older than they.

Once again, my life sought a balance and briefly found it. The awkwardness with Lady Patience gradually eroded into our acceptance that we would never become casual or overly familiar with one another. Neither of us felt a need to share feelings; instead we skirted one another at a formal distance, and nevertheless managed to gain a good understanding of one another. Yet in the formal dance of our relationship, there were occasional times of genuine merriment, and sometimes we even danced to the same piper.

Once she had given up the notion of teaching me everything that a Farseer prince should know, she was able to teach me a great deal. Very little of it was what she initially intended to teach me. I did gain a working knowledge of music, but this was by the loan of her instruments and many hours of private experimentation. I became more her runner than her page, and from fetching for her, I learned much of the perfumer's arts, as well as greatly increasing my knowledge of plants. Even Chade became enthused when he discovered my new talents for root and leaf propagation, and he followed with interest the experiments, few of them successful, that Lady Patience and I made into coaxing the buds of one tree to open to leaf when spliced into another tree. This was a magic she had heard rumoured, but did not scruple to attempt. To this day, in the Women's Garden, there is an apple tree, one branch of which bears pears. When I expressed a curiosity about the tattooer's art, she refused to let me mark my own body, saying I was too young for such a decision. But without the least qualm, she let me observe, and finally assist with the slow pricking of dye into her own ankle and calf that became a coiled garland of flowers.

But all of that evolved over months and years, not days. We had settled into a blunt-spoken courtesy toward one another by the end of ten days. She met Fedwren and enlisted him in her root-paper project. The pup was growing well, and was a greater pleasure to me every day. Lady Patience's errands to town gave me ample opportunities to see my town friends, especially Molly. She was an invaluable guide to the fragrant stalls where I purchased Lady Patience's perfume supplies. Forging and Red Ship Raiders might still threaten from the horizon, but for those few weeks they seemed a remote terror, like the remembered chill of winter on a midsummer day. For a very brief period, I was happy, and, an even rarer gift, I knew I was happy.

And then my lessons with Galen began.

The night before my lessons were to start, Burrich sent for me. I went to him wondering what chore I had done poorly and would be rebuked for. I found him waiting for me outside the stables, shifting his feet as restlessly as a confined stallion. He immediately beckoned me to follow him, and took me up to his chambers.

'Tea?' he offered, and when I nodded, poured me a mug from a pot still warm on his hearth.

'What's the matter?' I asked as I took it from him. He was strung as tight as I had ever seen him. This was so unlike Burrich that I feared some terrible news – that Sooty was ill, or dead, or that he had discovered Smithy.

'Nothing,' he lied, and did it so poorly that he himself immediately recognized it. 'It's this, boy,' he confessed suddenly. 'Galen came to me today. He told me that you were to be instructed in the Skill. And he charged me that while he was teaching you, I could interfere in no way: not to counsel, or ask chores of you, or even share a meal with you. He was most . . . direct about it.' Burrich paused, and I wondered what better word he had rejected. He looked away from me. 'There was a time when I'd hoped this chance would be offered to you, but when it wasn't, I thought, well, perhaps it's for the best. Galen can be a hard teacher. A very hard teacher. I've heard talk of it before. He drives his pupils, but he claims he expects no more of them than he does of himself. And, boy, I've heard that gossiped about me, too, if you can credit it.'

I permitted myself a small smile, that brought an answering scowl from Burrich.

'Listen to what I'm telling you. Galen makes no secret that he has no fondness for you. Of course, he doesn't know you at all, so it's not your fault. It's based solely on . . . what you are, and what you caused, and El knows that wasn't your fault. But if Galen admitted that, then he'd have to admit it was Chivalry's fault, and I've never known him to admit that Chivalry had any faults . . . but you can love a man and know better than that about him.' Burrich took a brisk turn around the room, then came back to the fire.

'Just tell me what you want to say,' I suggested.

'I'm trying,' he snapped. 'It's not easy to know what to say. I'm not even sure if I should be speaking to you. Is this interference, or counsel? But your lessons haven't started yet. So I say this now. Do your best for him. Don't talk back to Galen. Be respectful and courteous. Listen to all he says and learn it as well and quickly as you can.' He paused again.

'I hadn't intended to do otherwise,' I pointed out a bit tartly, for I could tell that none of this was what Burrich was trying to say.

'I know that, Fitz!' He sighed suddenly, and threw himself down at the table opposite me. With the heels of both hands he pressed at his temples as if pained. I had never seen him so agitated. 'A long time ago, I talked to you about that other . . . magic. The Wit. The being with the beasts, almost becoming one of them.' He paused and glanced about the room as if worried someone would hear. He leaned in closer to me and spoke softly but urgently. 'Stay clear of it. I've tried my best to get you to see it's shameful and wrong. But I've never really felt that you agreed. Oh, I know you've abided by my rule against it, most of the time. But a few times I've sensed, or suspected, that you were tinkering with things no good man touches. I tell you, Fitz, I'd sooner see . . . I'd sooner see you Forged. Yes, don't look so shocked, that's truly how I feel. And for Galen . . . Look, Fitz, don't even mention it to him. Don't speak of it, don't even think of it near him. It's little that I know about the Skill and how it works. But sometimes . . . oh, sometimes when your father touched me with it, it seemed he knew my heart before I did, and saw things that I kept buried even from myself.'

A sudden deep blush suffused Burrich's dark face, and almost I thought I saw tears stand in his dark eyes. He turned aside from me to the fire, and I sensed we were coming to the heart of what he needed to say. Needed, not wanted. There was a deep fear in him, one he denied himself. A lesser man, a man less stern with himself, would have trembled with it.

'. . . fear for you, boy.' He spoke to the stones above the mantelpiece, and his voice was so deep a rumble that I almost couldn't understand him.

'Why?' A simple question unlocks best, Chade had taught me.

'I don't know if he will see it in you. Or what he will do if he does. I've heard . . . no. I know it's true. There was a woman, actually, little more than a girl. She had a way with birds. She lived in the hills to the west of here, and it was said she could call a wild hawk from the sky. Some folk admired her, and said it was a gift. They took sick poultry to her, or called her in when hens wouldn't set their eggs. She did aught but good, for all I heard. But Galen spoke out against her. Said she was an abomination, and that it would be the worse for the world if she lived to breed. And one morning she was found beaten to death.'

'Galen did it?'

Burrich shrugged, a gesture most unlike him. 'His horse had been out of the stable that night. That much I know. And his hands were bruised, and he had scratches on his face and neck. But not the scratches a woman would have dealt him, boy. Talon marks, as if a hawk had tried to strike him.'

'And you said nothing?' I asked incredulously.

He barked a bitter laugh. 'Another spoke before I could. Galen was accused, by the girl's cousin, who happened to work here in the stables. Galen would not deny it. They went out to the Witness Stones, and fought one another for El's justice, which always prevails there. Higher than the King's court is the answer to a question settled there, and no one may dispute it. The boy died. Everyone said it was El's justice, that the boy had accused Galen falsely. One said it to Galen. And he replied that El's justice was that the girl had died before she bred, and her tainted cousin, too.'

Burrich fell silent. I was queasy with what he had told me, and a cold fear snaked through me. A question once decided at the Witness Stones could not be raised again. That was more than law, it was the very will of the gods. So I was to be taught by a man who was a murderer, a man who would try to kill me if he suspected I had the Wit.

'Yes,' Burrich said as if I had spoken aloud. 'Oh, Fitz, my son, be careful, be wise.' And for a moment I wondered, for it sounded as if he feared for me. But then he added, 'Don't shame me, boy. Or your father. Don't let Galen say that I've let my prince's son grow up a half-beast. Show him that Chivalry's blood runs true in you.'

'I'll try,' I muttered. And I went to bed that night wretched and afraid.

* * *

The Queen's Garden was nowhere near the Women's Garden or the kitchen garden or any other garden in Buckkeep. It was, instead, on top of a circular tower. The garden walls were high on the sides that faced the sea, but to the south and west, the walls were low and had seats along them. The stone walls captured the warmth of the sun and fended off the salt winds from the sea. The air was still there, almost as if hands were cupped over my ears. Yet there was a strange wildness to the garden founded on stone. There were rock basins, perhaps bird-baths or water gardens at one time, and various tubs and pots and troughs of earth, intermingled with statuary. At one time, the tubs and pots had probably overflowed with greenery and flowers. Of the plants, only a few stalks and the mossy earth in the tubs remained. The skeleton of a vine crawled over a half-rotted trellis. It filled me with an old sadness colder than the first chill of winter that was also here. Patience should have had this, I thought. She would bring life here again.

I was the first to arrive. August came soon after. He had Verity's broad build, much as I had Chivalry's height, and the dark Farseer colouring. As always, he was distant but polite. He dealt me a nod and then strolled about, looking at the statuary.

Others appeared rapidly after him. I was surprised at how many – over a dozen. Other than August, son of the King's sister, no one could boast as much Farseer blood as I could. There were cousins and second cousins, of both sexes and both younger and older than I. August was probably the youngest, at two years my junior, and Serene, a woman in her mid-twenties, was probably the oldest. It was an oddly subdued group. A few clustered, talking softly, but most drifted about, poking at the empty gardens or looking at the statues.

Then Galen came.

He let the door of the stairwell slam shut behind him. Several of the others jumped. He stood regarding us, and we in turn looked at him in silence.

There is something I have observed about skinny men. Some, like Chade, seem so preoccupied with their lives that they either forget to eat, or burn every bit of sustenance they take in the fires of their passionate fascination with life. But there is another type, one who goes about the world cadaverously, cheeks sunken, bones jutting, and one senses that he so disapproves of the whole of the world that he begrudges every bit of it that he takes inside himself. At that moment, I would have wagered that Galen had never truly enjoyed one bite of food or one swallow of drink in his life.

His dress puzzled me. It was opulently rich, with fur at his collar and neck, and amber beading so thick on his tunic it would have turned a sword. But the rich fabrics strained over him, the clothing tailored so snugly to him that one wondered if the maker had lacked sufficient fabric to finish the suit. At a time when full sleeves slashed with colours were the mark of a wealthy man, he wore his shirt as tight as a cat's skin. His boots were high and fitted to his calves, and he carried a little quirt, as if come straight from riding. His clothing looked uncomfortable and combined with his thinness to give an impression of stinginess.

His pale eyes swept the Queen's Garden dispassionately. He considered us, and immediately dismissed us as wanting. He breathed out through his hawk's nose, as does a man facing an unpleasant chore. 'Clear a space,' he directed us. 'Push all this rubbish to one side. Stack it there, against that wall. Quickly, now. I have no patience with sluggards.'

And so the last lines of the garden were destroyed. The arrangements of the pots and beds that had been shadows of the little walks and arbours that had once existed here were swept aside. The pots were moved to one side, the lovely little statues stacked crookedly on top of them. Galen spoke only once, to me. 'Hurry up, bastard,' he ordered me as I struggled with a heavy pot of earth, and he brought down his riding crop across my shoulders. It was not much of a blow, more a tap, but it seemed so contrived that I stopped in my efforts and looked at him. 'Didn't you hear me?' he demanded. I nodded, and went back to moving the pot. From the corner of my eye, I saw his odd look of satisfaction. The blow, I felt, had been a test, but I was not sure if I had passed or failed it.

The tower roof became a bare space, with only the green lines of moss and old runnels of dirt to indicate the garden that had been. He directed us to form ourselves into two lines. He ordered us by age and size, and then separated us by sex, putting the girls behind the boys and off to the right. 'I will tolerate no distractions or disruptive behaviour. You are here to learn, not dally,' he warned us. He then spaced us out, having us stretch our arms in all directions to show that there we could not touch one another, not even so much as a fingertip. From this, I expected physical exercises would follow, but instead he directed us to stand still, hands at our sides, and attend to him. So as we stood on the cold tower-top he lectured us.

'For seventeen years, I have been Skillmaster of this keep. Before this, my lessons were given to small groups, discreetly. Those who failed to show promise were turned away quietly. During that time the Six Duchies had no need for more than a handful to be trained. I trained only the most promising, wasting no time on those without talent or discipline. And, for the last fifteen years, I have not initiated any into the Skill.

'But evil times are upon us. The Outislanders ravage our shores and Forge our people. King Shrewd and Prince Verity turn their Skills to protecting us. Great are their efforts and many their successes, though the common folk never even guess at what they do. I assure you, against the minds I have trained, the Outislanders stand small chance. A few paltry victories they may have won, coming upon us unprepared, but the forces I have created to oppose them will prevail!'

His pale eyes burned and he lifted his hands to the heavens as he spoke. He held a long silence, staring upward, his arms stretched out above his head, as if he clawed down power from the sky itself. Then he let his arms slowly fall.

'This I know,' he went on in a calmer voice. 'This I know. The forces I have created will prevail. But our king, may all gods honour and bless him, doubts me. And as he is my king, I bow to his will. He requires that I seek amongst you of lesser blood, to see if there are any with the talent and will, the purity of purpose and sternness of soul, to be trained in the Skill. This I will do, for my king has commanded. Legends say in days of old there were many trained in the Skill, who worked alongside their kings to avert dangers from the land. Perhaps it was truly so; perhaps the old legends exaggerate. In any case, my king has commanded me to attempt to create such a surplus of Skilled ones, and so I will try.'

He totally ignored the five or so women of our group. Not once did his eyes turn toward them. The exclusion was so obvious that I wondered how they had offended him. I knew Serene slightly, for she also had been an apt pupil of Fedwren. I could almost feel the warmth of her displeasure. In the row beside me, one of the boys shifted. In a flash Galen had leaped in front of him.

'Bored, are we? Restless with an old man's talk?'

'Just a cramp in my calf, sir,' the boy rejoined, foolishly.

Galen slapped him, a backhand that rocked the boy's head. 'Be quiet, and stand still. Or leave. It's all one to me. It's already obvious that you lack the stamina to achieve the Skill. But the King has found you worthy to be here, and so I will attempt to teach you.'

I trembled inside. For when Galen spoke to the boy, it was me he stared at. As if the boy's movement had been my fault, somehow. A strong distaste for Galen flooded through me. I had taken blows from Hod in the course of my instruction in staves and swords, and endured discomfort even from Chade as he demonstrated touch-spots and strangling techniques, and ways to silence a man without disabling him. I'd had my share of cuffs, boots and swats from Burrich, some justified, some the vented frustration of a busy man. But I'd never seen a man strike a boy with such apparent relish as Galen had. I strove to keep my face impassive, and to look at him without appearing to stare. For I knew that if I glanced away I'd be accused of not paying attention.

Satisfied, Galen nodded to himself, and then resumed his lecture. To master the Skill, he must first teach us to master ourselves. Physical deprivation was his key. Tomorrow, we were to arrive before the sun was over the horizon. We were not to wear shoes, socks, cloaks, nor any woollen garment. Heads were to be uncovered. The body must be scrupulously clean. He exhorted us to imitate him in his eating and living habits. We would avoid meat, sweet fruit, seasoned dishes, milk, and 'frivolous foods'. He advocated porridges and cold water, plain breads and stewed root vegetables. We would avoid all unnecessary conversation, especially with those of the other sex. He counselled us long against any sort of 'sensual' longings, in which he included desiring food, sleep or warmth. And he advised us that he had arranged for a separate table to be set for us in the hall, where we might eat appropriate food and not be distracted by idle talk. Or questions. The last phrase he added almost like a threat.

He then put us through a series of exercises. Close the eyes and roll your eyeballs up as far as they would go. Strive to roll them all the way around to look into the back of one's own skull. Feel the pressure this created. Imagine what you might see if you could roll your eyes that far. Was what you saw worthy and correct? Eyes still closed, stand on one leg. Strive to remain perfectly still. Find a balance, not just of body, but of spirit. Drive from the mind all unworthy thoughts, and you could remain like this indefinitely.

As we stood, eyes always closed, going through these various exercises, he moved amongst us. I could track him by the sound of the riding crop. 'Concentrate!' he would command us, or 'Try, at least try!' I myself felt the crop at least four times that day. It was a trifling thing, little more than a tap, but it was unnerving to be touched with a lash, even without pain. Then the last time it fell, it was high on my shoulder, and the lash of it coiled against my bare neck while the tip caught me on the chin. I winced, but managed to keep my eyes closed and my precarious balance on one aching knee. As he walked away, I felt a slow drip of warm blood form on my chin.

He kept us all day, releasing us when the sun was a half-copper on the horizon and the winds of night were rising. Not once had he excused us for food, water, or any other necessity. He watched us file past him, a grim smile on his face, and only when we were through the door did we feel free to stagger and flee down the staircase.

I was famished, my hands swollen red with the chill, and my mouth so dry I couldn't have spoken if I had wished to. The others seemed much the same, though some had suffered more acutely than I. I at least was used to long hours, many of them outdoors. Merry, a year or so older than I, was accustomed to helping Mistress Hasty with the weaving. Her round face was more white than red with the cold, and I heard her whisper something to Serene, who took her hand as we went down the stairs. 'It wouldn't have been so bad, if he had paid any attention to us at all,' Serene whispered back. And then I had the unpleasant experience of seeing them both glance back fearfully, to see if Galen had seen them speak to one another.

Dinner that night was the most cheerless meal I had ever endured at Buckkeep. There was a cold porridge of boiled grain, bread, water and boiled, mashed turnips. Galen, uneating, presided over our meal. There was no conversation; I don't think we even looked at one another. I ate my allotted portions, and left the table almost as hungry as I had arrived.

Halfway up the stairs I remembered Smithy. I returned to the kitchen to get the bones and scraps Cook saved for me, and a pitcher of water to refill his dish. They seemed an awful weight as I climbed the stairs. It struck me as strange that a day of relative inactivity out in the cold had wearied me as much as a day of strenuous work.

Once inside my room, Smithy's warm greeting and eager consumption of the meat was like a healing balm. As soon as he had finished eating, we snuggled into bed. He wanted to bite and tussle, but soon gave up on me. I let sleep claim me.

And woke with a jolt to darkness, fearing that I had slept too long. A glance at the sky told me I could beat the sun to the rooftop, but just barely. No time to wash myself or eat or clean up after Smithy, and it was just as well Galen had forbidden shoes and socks, for I had no time to put mine on. I was too tired even to feel a fool as I raced through the keep and up the stairs of the tower. I could see others hurrying before me by wavering torchlight, and when I emerged from the stairwell, Galen's quirt fell on my back.

It bit unexpectedly sharp through my thin shirt. I cried out in surprise as much as pain. 'Stand like a man and master yourself, bastard,' Galen told me harshly, and the quirt fell again. Everyone else had resumed their places of the day before. They looked as weary as I, and most, too, looked as shocked as I felt by Galen's treatment of me. To this day I don't know why, but I went silently to my place and stood there facing Galen.

'Whoever comes last, is late, and will be treated so,' he warned us. It struck me as a cruel rule, for the only way to avoid his quirt tomorrow was to arrive early enough to see it fall on one of my fellows.

There followed another day of discomfort and random abuse. So I see it now. So I think I knew it then, in my heart of hearts. But ever he spoke of proving us worthy, of making us tough and strong. He made it an honour to be standing out in the cold, bare feet going numb against the chill stone. He roused in us a competition, not just against each other, but against his shabby images of us. 'Prove me wrong,' he said over and over again. 'I beg you, prove me wrong, that I may show the King at least one pupil worthy of my time.' And so we tried. How strange now to look back on it all and wonder at myself. But in the space of one day, he had succeeded in isolating us and plunging us into another reality, where all rules of courtesy and common sense were suspended. We stood silently in the cold, in various uncomfortable positions, eyes closed, wearing little more than our undergarments. And he walked among us, dealing out cuts from his silly little whip, and insults from his nasty little tongue. He cuffed occasionally, or shoved, something that is much more painful when one is chilled to the bone.

Those who flinched or wavered were accused of weakness. During the day he berated us with our unworthiness and repeated that he had only consented to try to teach us at the King's behest. The women he ignored, and though he often spoke of past princes and kings who had wielded the Skill in defence of the realm, he never once mentioned the queens and princesses who had done likewise. Nor did he ever once give us an overview of what he was attempting to teach us. There was only the cold and the discomfort of his exercises, and the uncertainty of when we would be struck. Why we struggled to endure it, I don't know. So quickly were we all made accomplices in our own degradation.

The sun finally ventured once again toward the horizon. But Galen had saved two final surprises for us that day. He let us stand, open our eyes and stretch freely for a few moments. Then he gave us a final lecture, this one to warn us against those among us who would undermine the training of all by foolish self-indulgences. He walked slowly among us as he spoke, wending his way in and out of our rows, and I saw many a rolling eye and intake of breath as he passed. Then, for the first time that day, he ventured over to the women's corner of the court.

'Some,' he cautioned us as he strolled, 'think themselves above rules. They think themselves worthy of special attention and indulgences. Such illusions of superiority must be driven from you before you can learn anything. It is hardly worthy of my time for me to have to teach these lessons to such laggards and dolts as need them. It is a shame that they have even found their way into our gathering. But they are among us, and I will honour the will of my king, and attempt to teach them. Even though there is only one way I know to waken such lazy minds.'

To Merry he gave two quick cuts with the quirt. But Serene he shoved down onto one knee, and struck four times. To my shame, I stood there with the rest, as each cut fell, and hoped only that she would not cry out and bring more punishment on herself.

But Serene rose, swayed once, and then stood again, still, looking out over the heads of the girls before her. I breathed a sigh of relief. But then Galen was back, circling like a shark around a fishing-boat, speaking now of those who thought themselves too good to share the discipline of the group, of ones who indulged in meat in plenty while the rest limited ourselves to wholesome grains and pure foods. I wondered uneasily who had been so foolish as to visit the kitchen after hours.

Then I felt the hot lick of the whip on my shoulders. If I had thought he was using the lash to his full capability before, he proved me wrong now.

'You thought to deceive me. You thought I would never know if Cook saved her precious pet a plate of tidbits, didn't you? But I know all that happens in Buckkeep. Don't deceive yourself about that.'

It dawned on me that he was speaking of the meat scraps I'd taken up to Smithy.

'That food wasn't for me,' I protested, and then could have bitten my tongue out.

His eyes glittered coldly. 'You'd lie to save yourself a little just pain. You'll never master the Skill. You'll never be worthy of it. But the King has commanded that I try to teach, and so I will try. Despite you or your low birth.'

In humiliation I took the welts he dealt me. He berated me as each fell, telling the others that the old rules against teaching the Skill to a bastard had been to prevent just such a thing as this.

Afterwards, I stood, silent and shamed, as he went down the rows, dealing a perfunctory swat with the quirt to each of my fellows, explaining as he did so that we all must pay for the failures of the individuals. It did not matter that this statement made no sense, or that the whip fell lightly compared to what Galen had just inflicted on me. It was the idea that they were all paying for my transgression. I had never felt so shamed in my life.

Then he released us, to go down to another cheerless meal, much the same as yesterday's. This time no one spoke on the stairs or at the meal. And afterwards, I went straight up to my room.

Meat soon, I promised the hungry pup that waited for me. Despite my aching back and muscles, I forced myself to clean up the room, scrubbing up Smithy's messes, and then making a trip for fresh strewing reeds. Smithy was a bit sulky at being left alone all day, and I was troubled when I realized I had no idea how long this miserable training would last.

I waited until late, when all ordinary folk of the keep were in their beds, before venturing down to get Smithy's food for him. I dreaded that Galen would find out, but what else was I to do? I was halfway down the big staircase when I saw the glimmering of a single candle being borne toward me. I shrank against the wall, suddenly sure it was Galen. But it was the Fool who came toward me, glowing as white and pale as the wax candle he carried. In his other hand was a pail of food and a beaker of water balanced on top of it. Soundlessly he waved me back to my room.

Once inside, the door shut, he turned on me. 'I can take care of the pup for you,' he told me dryly. 'But I can't take care of you. Use your head, boy. What can you possibly learn from what he's doing to you?'

I shrugged, then winced. 'It's just to toughen us. I don't think it will go on much longer before he gets down to actually teaching us. I can take it.' Then, 'Wait,' I said, as he fed bits of meat to Smithy from the pail. 'How do you know what Galen's been putting us through?'

'Ah, that would be telling,' he said blithely. 'And I can't do that. Tell, that is.' He dumped the rest of the pail out for Smithy, replenished his water, and stood.

'I'll feed the puppy,' he told me. 'I'll even try to take him outside for a bit each day. But I won't clean up his messes.' He paused at the door. 'That's where I draw the line. You'd better decide where you will draw the line. And soon. Very soon. The danger is greater than you know.'

And then he was gone, taking his candle and warnings with him. I lay down and fell asleep to the sounds of Smithy worrying a bone and making puppy growls to himself.

FIFTEEN

The Witness Stones

The Skill, at its simplest, is the bridging of thought from person to person. It can be used a number of ways. During battle, for instance, a commander can relay simple information and commands directly to those officers under him, if those officers have been trained to receive it. One powerfully Skilled can use his talent to influence even untrained minds or the minds of his enemies, inspiring them with fear or confusion or doubt. Men so talented are rare. But, if incredibly gifted with the Skill, a man can aspire to speak directly to the Elderlings, those who are below only the gods themselves. Few have ever dared to do so, and of those who did, even fewer attained what they asked. For it is said, one may ask of the Elderlings, but the answer they give may not be to the question you ask, but to the one you should have asked. And the answer to that question may be one a man cannot hear and live. For when one speaks to the Elderlings, then is the sweetness of using the Skill strongest and most perilous. And this is the thing that every practitioner of the Skill, weak or strong, must always guard against. For in using the Skill, the user feels a keenness of life, an uplifting of being, that can distract a man from taking his next breath. Compelling is this feeling, even in the common uses of the Skill, and addictive to any not hardened of purpose. But the intensity of this exultation when speaking to the Elderlings is a thing for which we have no comparison. Both senses and sense may be blasted forever from a man who uses the Skill to speak to an Elderling. Such a man dies raving, but it is also true he dies raving of his joy.

* * *

The Fool was right. I had no idea of the peril I faced. I plunged on doggedly. I have no heart to detail the weeks that followed. Suffice to say that with each day Galen had us more under his sway, and that he also became more cruel and manipulative. Some few pupils disappeared early on. Merry was one. She stopped coming after the fourth day. I saw her only once after that, creeping about the keep with a face both woebegone and shamed. I learned later that Serene and the other women had shunned her after she had dropped the training, and when they later spoke of her, it was not as if she had failed at a test, but rather had committed some low and loathsome act for which she could never be forgiven. I know not where she went, only that she left Buckkeep and never returned.

As the ocean sorts pebbles from sand on a beach and stratifies them at the tide mark, so did the poundings and caressings of Galen separate his students. Initially, all of us strove to be his best. It was not because we liked or admired him. I do not know what the others felt, but there was nothing in my heart but hate for him, a hatred so strong that it spawned a resolution not to be broken by such a man. After days of his abuse, to wring a single grudging word of acknowledgement from him was like a torrent of praise from any other master. Days of his belittling should have made me numb to his mockery. Instead, I came to believe much of what he said, and tried futilely to change.

We vied constantly with one another to come to his attention. Some emerged clearly as his favourites. August was one, and we were often urged to imitate him. I was clearly his most despised. And yet this did not stop me from burning to distinguish myself before him. After the first time, I was never last on the tower top. I never wavered from his blows. Nor did Serene, who shared my distinction of being despised. Serene became Galen's grovelling follower, never breathing a word of criticism about him after that first lashing. Yet he constantly found fault with her, berated and reviled her, and struck her far more often than he struck any of the other women. This, however, made her only more determined to prove she could withstand his abuse, and she, after Galen, was the most intolerant of any who wavered or doubted in our teaching.

Winter deepened. It was cold and dark on the tower top, save for what light came from the stairwell. It was the most isolated place in the world, and Galen was its god. He forged us into a unit. We believed ourselves élite, superior and privileged to be instructed in the Skill. Even I, who endured mockery and beatings, believed this to be so. Those of us he broke, we despised. We saw only one another for this time, we heard only Galen. At first I missed Chade. I wondered what Burrich and Lady Patience were doing. But as months went by, such lesser occupations no longer seemed interesting. Even the Fool and Smithy came to be almost annoyances to me, so single-mindedly did I pursue Galen's approval. The Fool came and went silently then. There were times, though, when I was sorest and weariest, when the touch of Smithy's nose against my cheek was the only comfort I had, and times when I felt shamed by how little time I was giving to my growing puppy.

After three months of cold and cruelty, Galen had whittled us down to eight candidates. The real training finally began then, and also he returned to us a small measure of comfort and dignity. These seemed by then not only great luxuries, but gifts from Galen to be grateful for. A bit of dried fruit with our meals, permission to wear shoes, brief conversation allowed at the table – that was all, and yet we were grovellingly grateful for it. But the changes were only beginning.

It comes back in crystal glimpses. I remember the first time he touched me with the Skill. We were on the tower top, spaced even further now that there were fewer of us, and he went from one of us to the next, pausing a moment before each, while the rest of us waited in reverent silence. 'Ready your minds for the touch. Be open to it, but do not indulge in the pleasure of it. The purpose of the Skill is not pleasure.'

He wended his way among us, in no particular order. Spaced as we were, we could not see one another's faces, nor did it ever please Galen that our eyes follow his movements. And so we heard only his brief, stern words, then heard the in-drawn gasp of each touched one. To Serene he said in disgust, 'Be open to it, I said. Not cower like a beaten dog.'

And last he came to me. I listened to his words, and as he had counselled us earlier, I tried to let go of every sensory awareness

I had, and be open only to him. I felt the brush of his mind against mine, like a soft tickle on my forehead. I stood firm before it. It grew stronger, a warmth, a light, but I refused to be drawn into it. I felt Galen stood within my mind, sternly regarding me, and using the focusing techniques he had taught us (imagine a pail of purest white wood, and pour yourself into it) I was able to stand before him, waiting, aware of the Skill's elation, but not giving in to it. Thrice the warmth rushed through me, and thrice I stood before it. And then he withdrew. He gave me a grudging nod, but in his eyes I saw not approval but a trace of fear.

That first touch was like the spark that finally kindles the tinder. I grasped what it was. I could not do it yet; I could not send my thoughts out from me, but I had a knowledge that would not fit into words. I would be able to Skill. And with that knowing my resolve hardened, and there was nothing, nothing Galen could have done that would stop me learning it.

I think he knew it, for he turned on me in the days that followed with a cruelty that I now find incredible. Hard words and blows he dealt me, but none could turn me aside. He struck me once in the face with his quirt. It left a visible welt, and it chanced that when I was coming into the dining hall, Burrich was also there. I saw his eyes widen. He started up from his place at table, his jaw clenched in a way I knew too well. But I looked aside from him and down. He stood a moment, glaring at Galen, who returned his look with a supercilious stare. Then, fists clenched, Burrich turned his back and left the room. I relaxed, relieved there would be no confrontation. But then Galen looked at me, and the triumph in his face made my heart cold. I was his now, and he knew it.

Pain and victories mixed for me in the next week. He never lost an opportunity to belittle me. And yet, I knew I excelled at each exercise he gave us. I sensed the others groping after his touch of Skill, but for me it was as simple as opening my eyes. I knew one moment of intense fear. He had entered my mind with the Skill, and given me a sentence to repeat aloud. 'I am a bastard, and I shame my father's name,' I said aloud, calmly. And then he spoke again within my mind. *You draw strength from somewhere, bastard. This is not your Skill. Do you think I will not find the source?* And then I quailed before him, and drew back from his touch, hiding Smithy within my mind. His smile showed all his teeth to me.

In the days that followed, we played a game of hide and seek. I must let him into my mind, to learn the Skill. Once there, I danced on coals to keep my secrets from him. Not just Smithy, but Chade and the Fool did I hide, and Molly and Kerry and Dirk, and other, older secrets I would not reveal even to myself. He sought them all, and I juggled them desperately out of his reach. But despite all that, or perhaps because of it, I felt myself growing stronger in the Skill. 'Don't mock me!' he roared after one session, and then grew infuriated as the other students exchanged shocked glances. 'Attend to your own exercises!' he roared at them. He paced away from me, then spun suddenly and flung himself at me. Fist and boot, he attacked me and, as Molly once had, I had no more thought than to shield my face and belly. The blows he rained on me were more like a child's tantrum than a man's attack. I felt their ineffectiveness and then realized with a chill that I was *repelling* at him. Not so much that he would sense it, just enough that not one of his blows fell exactly as he had intended. I knew, more, that he had no idea what I was doing. When at last he dropped his fists and I dared to lift my eyes, I felt momentarily that I had won, for all the others on the tower top were looking at him with gazes mingled of disgust and fear. He had gone too far for even Serene to stomach. White-faced, he turned aside from me. In that moment, I felt him reach a decision.

That evening in my room, I was horribly tired, but too enervated to sleep. The Fool had left food for Smithy, and I was teasing him with a large beef knuckle. He had set his teeth in my sleeve and was worrying it while I held the bone just out of his reach. It was the sort of game he loved, and he snarled with mock ferocity as he shook my arm. He was near as big as he would get, and I felt with pride the muscles in his thick little neck. With my free hand, I pinched his tail and he spun snarling to this new attack. From hand to hand I juggled his bone, and his eyes darted back and forth as he snapped after it. 'No brain,' I teased him. 'All you can think of is what you want. No brain, no brain.'

'Just like his owner.'

I startled, and in that second Smithy had his bone. He flopped down with it, giving the Fool no more than a perfunctory wag of his tail. I sat down, out of breath. 'I never even heard the door open. Or shut.'

He ignored that and went straight to his topic. 'Do you think Galen will allow you to succeed?'

I grinned smugly. 'Do you think he can prevent it?'

The Fool sat down beside me with a sigh. 'I know he can. So does he. What I cannot decide is if he is ruthless enough. But I suspect he is.'

'So let him try,' I said flippantly.

'I have no choice in that.' The Fool was adamantly serious. 'What I had hoped to do was dissuade you from trying.'

'You'd ask me to give up? Now?' I was incredulous.

'I would.'

'Why?' I demanded.

'Because,' he began, and then stopped in frustration. 'I don't know. Too many things converge. Perhaps if I pluck one thread loose, the knot will not form.'

I was suddenly tired, and the earlier elation of my triumph collapsed before his dour warnings. My irritability won and I snapped, 'If you cannot speak clearly, why do you speak at all?'

He was as silent as if I had struck him. 'That's another thing I don't know,' he said at last. He rose to go.

'Fool,' I began.

'Yes. I am that,' he said, and left.

And so I persevered, growing stronger. I grew impatient with our slow pace of instruction. We went over the same practices each day, and gradually the others began to master what seemed so natural to me. How could they have been so closed off from the rest of the world, I wondered? How could it be so hard for them to open their minds to Galen's Skill? My own task was not to open, but rather to keep closed to him what I did not wish to share. Often, as he gave me a perfunctory touch of the Skill, I sensed a tendril of seeking slinking into my mind. But I evaded it.

'You are ready,' he announced one chill day. It was afternoon, but the brightest stars were already showing in the blue darkness of the sky. I missed the clouds that had yesterday snowed upon us, but had at least kept this deeper cold at bay. I flexed my toes inside the leather shoes that Galen permitted us, trying to warm them to life again. 'Before I have touched you with the Skill, to accustom you to it. Now, today, we will attempt a full joining. You will each reach out to me as I reach out to you. But beware! Most of you have coped with resisting the distractions of the Skill touch, but the power of what you felt was the lightest brush. Today will be stronger. Resist it, but stay open to the Skill.'

And again he began his slow circuit amongst us. I waited, enervated but unafraid. I had looked forward to attempting this. I was ready.

Some clearly failed, and were rebuked for laziness or stupidity. August was praised. Serene was slapped for reaching forth too eagerly. And then he came to me.

I braced as if for a wrestling contest. I felt the brush of his mind against mine, and offered him a cautious reaching of thought. *Like this?*

Yes, bastard. Like this.

And for a moment we were in balance, hovering like children on a see-saw. I felt him steady our contact. Then, abruptly, he slammed into me. It felt exactly as if the air had been knocked out of me, but in a mental rather than physical way. Instead of being unable to get my breath, I was unable to master my thoughts. He rifled through my mind, ransacking my privacy, and I was powerless before him. He had won and he knew it. But in that moment of his careless triumph I found an opening. I grasped at him, trying to seize his mind as he had mine. I gripped him and held him, and knew for a dizzying instant that I was stronger than he, that I could force into his mind any thought I chose to put there. 'No!' he shrieked, and dimly I knew that, at some former time, he had struggled like this with someone he had despised. Someone else who had also won as I intended to. 'Yes!' I insisted. 'Die!' he commanded me, but I knew I would not. I knew I would win, and I focused my will and bore down on my grip.

The Skill does not care who wins. It does not allow anyone to surrender to any one thought, even for a moment. But I did. And when I did, I forgot to guard against the ecstasy that is both the honey and the sting of the Skill. The euphoria rushed over me, drowning me, and Galen, too, sank below it, no longer exploring my mind, but seeking only to return to his.

I had never felt the like of that moment.

Galen had called it pleasure, and I had expected a pleasant sensation, like warmth in winter, or the fragrance of a rose or a sweet taste in my mouth. This was none of these. Pleasure is too physical a word to describe what I felt. It had nothing to do with the skin or body. It suffused me, it washed over me in a wave that I could not repulse. Elation filled me and flowed through me. I forgot Galen and all else. I felt him escape me, and knew it mattered, but could not care. I forgot all except exploring this sensation.

'Bastard!' Galen bellowed, and struck me with his fist on the side of my head. I fell, helpless, for the pain was not enough to jolt me from the entrancement of the Skill. I felt him kick me, I knew the cold of the stones under me that bruised and scraped me, and yet I felt I was held, smothered in a blanket of euphoria that would not let me pay attention to the beating. My mind assured me, despite the pain, that all was well, that there was no need to fight or flee.

Somewhere a tide was ebbing, leaving me beached and gasping. Galen stood over me, dishevelled and sweating. His breath smoked in the cold air as he leaned close over me. 'Die!' he said, but I did not hear the words. I felt them. He let go of my throat and I fell.

And in the wake of the devouring elation of the Skill came now a bleakness of failure and guilt that made my physical pain as nothing. My nose was bleeding, it was painful to breathe, and the force of the kicks he had dealt me had scraped skin from my body as I had slid across the tower stones. The different pains contradicted one another, each clamouring for attention so that I couldn't assess what damage had been done to me. I could not even gather myself together to stand up. Looming over all was the knowledge that I had failed. I was defeated and unworthy and Galen had proven it.

As if from a distance, I heard him shouting at the others, telling them to beware, for this was how he would deal with those so undisciplined that they could not turn their minds from pleasure of the Skill. And he warned them all of what befell such a man, who strove to use the Skill and instead fell under the spell of the pleasure it bore with it. Such a man would become mindless, a great infant, speechless, sightless, soiling himself, forgetting thought, forgetting even food and drink, until he died. Such a one was beyond disgust.

And such a one was I. I sank into my shame. Helplessly, I began to sob. I merited such treatment as he had given me. I deserved worse. Only a misplaced pity had kept Galen from killing me. I had wasted his time, had taken his painstaking instruction and turned it all to selfish indulgence. I fled myself, going deeper and deeper within, but finding only disgust and hatred for myself layered throughout my thoughts. I would be better off dead. Were I to throw myself from the tower roof, it would still not be enough to destroy my shame, but at least I need no longer be aware of it. I lay still and wept.

The others left. As each one passed, they had a word, a gobbet of spittle, a kick or a blow for me. I scarcely noticed. I rejected myself more completely than they could. Then they were gone, and Galen alone stood over me. He nudged me with his foot, but I was incapable of response. Suddenly, he was everywhere, over, under, around and inside me, and I could not deny him. 'You see, bastard,' he said archly, calmly. 'I tried to tell them you were not worthy. I tried to tell them the training would kill you. But you would not listen. You strove to usurp that which had been given to another. Again, I am right. Well. This has not been time wasted if it has done away with you.'

I don't know when he left me. After a time, I was aware that it was the moon looking down on me, and not Galen. I rolled onto my belly. I could not stand, but I could crawl. Not quickly, not even lifting my stomach completely off the ground, but I could scuffle and scrape myself along. With a singleness of purpose, I began to make my way towards the low wall. I thought that I could drag myself up onto a bench, and from there to the top of the wall. And from there. Down. End it.

It was a long journey, in the cold and the dark. Somewhere I could hear a whimpering, and I despised myself for that, too. But as I scraped myself along, it grew, as a spark in the distance becomes a fire as one approaches. It refused to be ignored. It grew louder in my mind, a whining against my fate, a tiny voice of resistance that forbade that I should die, that denied my failure. It was warmth and light, too, and it grew stronger and stronger as I tried to find its source.

I stopped.

I lay still.

It was inside me. The more I sought it, the stronger it grew. It loved me. Loved me even if I couldn't, wouldn't, didn't love myself. Loved me even if I hated it. It set its tiny teeth in my soul and braced and held so that I couldn't crawl any further. And when I tried, a howl of despair burst from it, searing me, forbidding me to break so sacred a trust.

It was Smithy.

He cried with my pains, physical and mental. And when I stopped struggling toward the wall, he went into a paroxysm of joy, a celebration of triumph for us. And all I could do to reward him was to lie still and no longer attempt to destroy myself. And he assured me it was enough, it was a plenitude, it was a joy. I closed my eyes.

The moon was high when Burrich rolled me gently over. The Fool held the torch and Smithy capered and danced about his feet. Burrich gathered me up and stood, as if I were still a child just given into his care. I had a glimpse of his dark face, but read nothing there. He carried me down the long stone staircase, the Fool bearing the torch to light the way. And he took me out of the keep, back to the stables and up to his room. There the Fool left Burrich and Smithy and me, and I do not recall that there had been one word spoken. Burrich set me down on his own bed, and then dragged it, bedstead and all, closer to the fire. With returning warmth came great pain, and I gave my body over to Burrich, my soul to Smithy, and let go of my mind for a long while.

I opened my eyes to night. I knew not which one. Burrich sat next to me still, undozing, not even slumped in his chair. I felt the strictures of bandaging on my ribs. I lifted a hand to touch it, but was baffled by two splinted fingers. Burrich's eyes followed my motion. 'They were swollen with more than cold. Too swollen for me to tell if it were breaks, or just sprains. I splinted them in case. I suspect it's just a sprain. I think if they were broken, the pain of my working on them would have wakened even you.'

He spoke calmly, as if telling me that he had purged a new dog for worms as a preventative against contagion. And just as his steady voice and calm touch had worked on a frantic animal, so it worked on me. I relaxed, thinking that if he were calm, not much could be wrong. He slipped a finger under the bandages supporting my ribs, checking the tightness. 'What happened?' he asked, and turned aside from me to pick up a cup of tea as he spoke, as if the question and my answer were of no great import.

I pushed my mind back over the last few weeks, tried to find a way to explain. Events danced in my mind, slipped away from me. I remembered only defeat. 'Galen tested me,' I said slowly. 'I failed. And he punished me for it.' And with my words, a wave of dejection, shame and guilt swept over me, washing away the brief comfort I had taken in the familiar surroundings. On the hearth, a sleeping Smithy abruptly waked and sat up. Reflexively, I quieted him before he could whine. *Lie down. Rest. It's all right.* To my relief, he did so. And to my greater relief, Burrich seemed unaware of what had passed between us. He offered me the cup.

'Drink this. You need water in you, and the herbs will deaden the pain and let you sleep. Drink it all, now.'

'It stinks,' I told him, and he nodded, and held the cup my hands were too bruised to curl around. I drank it all and then lay back.

'That was all?' he asked carefully, and I knew what he referred to. 'He tested you on a thing he had taught you, and you did not know it. So he did this to you?'

'I could not do it. I didn't have the . . . self-discipline. So he punished me.' Details eluded me. Shame washed over me, drowning me in misery.

'No one is taught self-discipline by beating him half to death.' Burrich spoke carefully, stating the truth for an idiot. His movements were very precise as he set the cup back on the table.

'It was not to teach me . . . I don't think he believes I can be taught. It was to show the others what would happen if they failed.'

'Very little worth knowing is taught by fear,' Burrich said stubbornly. And, more warmly, 'It's a poor teacher who tries to instruct by blows and threats. Imagine taming a horse that way. Or a dog. Even the most knot-headed dog learns better from an open hand than a stick.'

'You've struck me before, when trying to teach me something.'

'Yes. Yes, I have. But to jolt, or warn, or awaken. Not to damage. Never to break a bone or blind an eye or cripple a hand. Never. Never say to anyone that I've struck you, or any creature in my care that way, for it's not true.' He was indignant that I could even have suggested it.

'No. You're right about that.' I tried to think how I could make Burrich understand why I had been punished. 'But this was different, Burrich. A different kind of learning, a different kind of teaching.' I felt compelled to defend Galen's justice. I tried to explain. 'I deserved this, Burrich. The fault was not with his teaching. I failed to learn. I tried. I did try. But like Galen, I believe there is a reason the Skill is not taught to bastards. There is a taint in me, a fatal weakness.'

'Horseshit.'

'No. Think on it, Burrich. If you breed a scrub-mare to a fine stud, the colt you get is as likely to get the weakness of the mother as the fineness of the father.'

The silence was long. Then, 'I doubt much that your father would have lain down beside a woman that was a "scrub". Without some fineness, some sign of spirit or intelligence, he would not. He could not.'

'I've heard it said he was tranced by a mountain witch-woman.' For the first time I repeated a tale I'd heard whispered often.

'Chivalry was not a man to fall for such magickry. And his son is not some snivelling, weak-spirited fool that lies about and whines that he deserved a beating.' He leaned closer, gently prodded just below my temple. A blast of pain rocked my consciousness. 'That's how near you were to losing an eye to this "teaching".' His temper was rising, and I kept my mouth closed. He took a quick turn around the room, then spun to face me.

'That puppy. He's from Patience's bitch, isn't he?'

'Yes.'

'But you haven't . . . oh, Fitz, please tell me that it wasn't your using the Wit that brought this on you. If he did this to you for that, there's not a word I can say to anyone, or an eye I can meet anywhere in the keep or the whole kingdom.'

'No, Burrich. I promise you, this had nothing to do with the pup. It was my failure to learn what I had been taught. My weakness.'

'Quiet,' he ordered me impatiently. 'Your word is enough. I know you well enough to know your promise will always be true. But for the rest, you're making no sense at all. Go back to sleep. I'm going out, but I'll be back soon enough. Get some rest. It's the real healer.'

A purpose had settled on Burrich. My words seemed to have satisfied him finally, settled something for him. He dressed quickly, pulling on boots, changing his shirt for a loose one, and putting only a leather jerkin over it. Smithy stood and whined anxiously as Burrich went out, but could not convey his worry to me. Instead, he came to the bedside and scrabbled up, to burrow into the covers beside me and comfort me with his trust. In the bleak despair that settled over me, he was my only light. I closed my eyes and Burrich's herbs sank me into a dreamless sleep.

I awoke later that afternoon. A gust of cold air preceded Burrich's entry into the room. He checked me over, casually prising open my eyes and then running competent hands down my ribs and over my other bruises. He grunted his satisfaction, then changed his torn and muddied shirt for a fresh one. He hummed as he did so, seeming in a fine mood much at odds with my bruises and depression. It was almost a relief when he left again. Below, I heard him whistling and calling orders to the stable-boys. It all sounded so normal and workaday and I longed for it with an intensity that surprised me. I wanted that back, the warm smell of the horses and dogs and straw, the simple tasks, done well and completely, and the good sleep of exhaustion at the end of a day. I longed for it, but the worthlessness that filled me now predicted that, even at that, I would fail. Galen had often sneered at those who worked such simple jobs about the keep. He had only contempt for the kitchen-maids and cooks, derision for the stable-boys, and the men-at-arms who guarded us with sword and bow, were, in his words, 'ruffians and dolts, doomed to flail away at the world, and control with a sword what they can't master with their minds'. So now I was strangely torn. I longed to return to being what Galen had convinced me was contemptible, yet doubt and despair filled me that I could even do so much as that.

I was abed for two days. A jovial Burrich tended me with banter and good nature that I could not fathom. There was a briskness to his step and a sureness to him that made him seem a much younger man. It added to my dispiritedness that my injuries put him in such fine fettle. But after two days of bed rest, Burrich informed me that only so much stillness was good for a man, and it was time I was up and moving if I wished to heal well. He proceeded to find me many minor chores to perform, none heavy enough to tax my strength, but more than enough to keep me busy, for I had to rest often. I believe that the busyness was what he was after rather than any exercise for me, for all I had done was to lie in bed and look at the wall and despise myself. Faced with my unrelenting depression, even Smithy had begun to turn aside from his food. Despite this, he remained my only real source of comfort. Following me about the stable was the purest enjoyment he'd ever had. Every scent and sight he relayed to me with an intensity that, despite my bleakness, renewed in me the wonder I had first felt when I'd plunged into Burrich's world. Smithy was savagely possessive of me as well, challenging even Sooty's right to sniff me, and earning himself a snap from Vixen that sent him yipping and cowering to my heels.

I begged the next day free for myself, and went into Buckkeep Town. The walk took me longer than it had ever taken me before, but Smithy rejoiced in my slow pace, for it gave him time to snuff his way around every clump of grass and tree on the way. I had thought that seeing Molly would lift my spirits, and give me some sense of my own life again. But when I got to the chandlery she was busy, filling three large orders for outbound ships. I sat by the hearth in the shop. Her father sat opposite me, drinking and glaring at me. Although his illness had weakened him, it had not changed his temperament, and on days when he was well enough to sit up, he was well enough to drink. After a while, I gave up all pretence at conversation, and simply watched him drink and disparage his daughter as Molly bustled frantically about, trying to be both efficient and hospitable to her customers. The dreary pettiness of it all depressed me.

At noon she told her father she was closing the shop while she went to deliver an order. She gave me a rack of candles to carry, loaded her own arms, and we left, latching the door behind us. Her father's drunken imprecations followed us, but she ignored them. Once outside in the brisk winter wind, I followed Molly as she walked quickly to the back of the shop. Motioning for my silence, she opened the back door and set all that she carried inside. My rack of candles, too, were unloaded there, and then we left.

For a bit, we just wandered through the town, talking little. She commented on my bruised face; I said only that I had fallen. The wind was cold and relentless, so the market stalls were near-empty of both customers and vendors. She paid much attention to Smithy, and he revelled in it. On our walk back, we stopped at a tea shop, and she treated me to mulled wine and made so much of Smithy that he fell over on his back and all his thoughts turned into wallowing in her affection. I was struck suddenly by how clearly Smithy was aware of her feelings, and yet she did not sense his at all, except on the shallowest level. I quested gently toward her, but found her elusive and drifting, like a perfume that comes strong and then faint on the same breath of wind. I knew that I could have pushed more insistently against her, but somehow it seemed pointless. An aloneness settled on me, a deadly melancholy that she never had been and never would be any more aware of me than she was of Smithy. So I took her brief words to me as a bird pecks at dry breadcrumbs, and let alone the silences she curtained between us. Soon she said that she could not tarry long, or it would be the worse for her, for if her father no longer had the strength to strike her, he was still capable of smashing his beer mug on the floor or knocking over racks of things to show his displeasure at being neglected. She smiled an odd little smile as she told me this, as if it would be less appalling if somehow we thought of his behaviour as amusing. I couldn't smile and she looked away from my face.

I helped her with her cloak and we left, walking uphill and into the wind. And that suddenly seemed a metaphor for my whole life. At her door, she shocked me with a hug and a kiss on the corner of my jaw, the embrace so brief that it was almost like being bumped in the market. 'Newboy . . .' she said, and then, 'Thank you. For understanding.'

And then she whisked into her shop and shut the door behind her, leaving me chilled and bewildered. She thanked me for understanding her at a time when I had never felt more isolated from her, and everyone else. All the way up to the keep Smithy kept prattling to himself about all the perfumes he'd smelt on her and how she had scratched him just where he could never reach in front of his ears and of the sweet biscuit she'd fed him in the tea shop.

It was mid-afternoon when we got back to the stables. I did a few chores, and then went back up to Burrich's room, where Smithy and I fell asleep. I awoke to Burrich standing over me, a slight frown on his face.

'Up, and let's have a look at you,' he commanded, and I arose wearily and stood quiet while he went over my injuries with deft hands. He was pleased with the condition of my hand, and told me that it might go unbandaged now, but to keep the wrapping about my ribs and to come back to have it adjusted each evening. 'As for the rest of it, keep it clean and dry, and don't pick at the scabs. If any of it starts to fester, come and see me.' He filled a little pot with an unguent that eased sore muscles and gave it to me, by which I deduced that he expected me to leave.

I stood holding the little pot of medicine. A terrible sadness welled up in me, and yet I could find no words to say. Burrich looked at me, scowled and turned away. 'Now stop that,' he commanded me angrily.

'What?' I asked.

'You look at me sometimes with my lord's eyes,' he said quietly, and then as sharply as before, 'Well, what did you think to do? Hide in the stables the rest of your life? No. You have to go back. You have to go back and hold up your head and eat your meals among the keep folk, and sleep in your own room, and live your own life. Yes, and go and finish those damn lessons in the Skill.'

His first commands had sounded difficult, but the last, I knew, was impossible.

'I can't,' I said, not believing how stupid he was. 'Galen wouldn't let me come back to the group. And even if he did, I'd never catch up on all I'd missed. I've already failed at it, Burrich. I failed and that's done, and I need to find something else to do with myself. I'd like to learn the hawks, please.' The last I heard myself say with some amazement, for in truth it had never crossed my mind before. Burrich's reply was at least as strange.

'You can't, for the hawks don't like you. You're too warm and you don't mind your own business enough. Now listen to me. You didn't fail, you fool. Galen tried to drive you away. If you don't go back, you'll have let him win. You have to go back and you have to learn it. But,' and here he turned on me, and the anger in his eyes was for me, 'You don't have to stand there like a carter's mule while he beats you. You've a birthright to his time and his knowledge. Make him give you what is yours. Don't run away. No one ever gained anything by running away.' He paused, started to say more, and then stopped.

'I've missed too many lessons. I'll never . . .'

'You haven't missed anything,' Burrich said stubbornly. He turned away from me, and I couldn't read his tone as he added, 'There have been no lessons since you left. You should be able to pick up just where you left off.'

'I don't want to go back.'

'Don't waste my time by arguing with me,' he said tightly. 'Don't dare to try my patience that way. I've told you what you are to do. Do it.'

Suddenly I was five years old again, and a man in a kitchen backed up a crowd with a look. I shivered, cowed. Abruptly, it was easier to face Galen than to defy Burrich. Even when he added, 'And you'll leave that pup with me until your lessons are done. Being shut up inside your room all day is no life for a dog. His coat will go bad and his muscles won't grow properly. But you'd better be down here each evening to see to both him and Sooty or you'll answer to me. And I don't give a damn what Galen says about that, either.'

And so I was dismissed. I conveyed to Smithy that he was to

stay with Burrich, and he accepted it with an equanimity that surprised me as much as it hurt my feelings. Dispirited, I took my pot of unguent and plodded back up to the keep. I took food from the kitchen, for I had no heart to face anyone at table and went up to my room. It was cold and dark; no fire in the hearth, no candles in the sticks and the fouled reeds underfoot stank. I fetched candles and wood, set a fire, and while I was waiting for it to take some of the chill off the stone walls and floors, I busied myself with taking up the floor rushes. Then, as Lacey had advised me, I scrubbed the room well with hot water and vinegar. Somehow I got the vinegar that had been flavoured with tarragon, and so when I was finished, the room smelt fragrant. Exhausted, I flung myself down on my bed, and fell asleep wondering why I'd never discovered how to open whatever hidden door it was that led to Chade's quarters. But I had no doubt that he would have simply dismissed me, for he was a man of his word and would not interfere until Galen had finished with me. Or until he discovered that I was finished with Galen.

The Fool's candles awoke me. I was completely disoriented, until he said, 'You've just time to wash and eat and still be first on the tower top.'

He'd brought warm water in an ewer, and warm rolls from the kitchen ovens.

'I'm not going.'

It was the first time I'd ever seen the Fool look surprised. 'Why not?'

'It's pointless. I can't succeed. I simply haven't the aptitude and I'm tired of beating my head against the wall.'

The Fool's eyes widened further. 'I thought you had been doing well, before . . .'

It was my turn to be surprised. 'Well? Why do you think he mocked me and struck me? As a reward for my success? No. I haven't even been able to understand what it's about. All the others had already surpassed me. Why should I go back? So Galen can prove even more thoroughly how right he was?'

'Something,' the Fool said carefully, 'is not right here.' He considered for a moment. 'Before, I asked you to give up the lessons. You would not. Do you recall that?'

I cast my mind back. 'I'm stubborn, sometimes,' I admitted.

'And if I asked you now, to continue? To go up to the tower top, and continue to try?'

'Why have you changed your mind?'

'Because that which I sought to prevent came to pass. But you survived it. So I seek now to . . .' His words trailed off. 'It is as you said. Why should I speak at all, when I cannot speak plainly?'

'If I said that, I regret it. It is not a thing one should say to a friend. I do not remember it.'

He smiled faintly. 'If you do not remember it, then neither shall I.' He reached and took both of my hands in his. His grip was oddly cool. A shiver passed over me at his touch. 'Would you continue, if I asked it of you? As a friend?'

The word sounded so odd from his lips. He spoke it without mockery, carefully, as if the saying of it aloud could shatter the meaning. His colourless eyes held mine. I found I could not say no. So I nodded.

Even so, I rose reluctantly. He watched me with an impassive interest as I straightened the clothes I'd slept in, splashed my face, and then tore into the bread he'd brought. 'I don't want to go,' I told him as I finished the first roll and took up the second. 'I don't see what it can accomplish.'

'I don't know why he bothers with you,' the Fool agreed. The familiar cynicism was back.

'Galen? He has to, the King . . .'

'Burrich.'

'He just likes bossing me about,' I complained, and it sounded childish, even to me.

The Fool shook his head. 'You haven't even a clue, have you?'

'About what?'

'About how the stablemaster dragged Galen from his bed, and from thence to the Witness Stones. I wasn't there, of course, or I would be able to tell you how Galen cursed and struck at him at first, but the stablemaster paid no attention. He just hunched his shoulders to the man's blows, and kept silent. He gripped the Skillmaster by the collar, so the man was fair choked, and dragged him along. And the soldiers and guards and stable-boys followed in a stream that became a torrent of men. If I had been there, I could tell you how no man dared to interfere, for it was as if the stablemaster had become as Burrich once was, an iron-muscled man with a black temper that was like a madness when it came on him. No one, then, dared to brook that temper, and that day, it was as if Burrich was that man again. If he limped still, no one noticed it at all.

'As for the Skillmaster, he flailed and cursed, and then he grew still, and all suspected that he turned what he knew upon his captor. But if he did, it had no effect, save that the stablemaster tightened his grip on the man's neck. And if Galen strove to sway others to his cause, they did not react. Perhaps being choked and dragged was sufficient to break his concentration. Or perhaps his Skill is not as strong as it was rumoured. Or perhaps too many remember his mistreatment of them too well to be vulnerable to his wiles. Or perhaps . . .'

'Fool! Get on with it! What happened?' A light sweat cloaked my body and I shivered, not knowing what I hoped for.

'I wasn't there, of course,' the Fool asserted sweetly. 'But I have heard it said that the dark man dragged the skinny man all the way up to the Witness Stones. And there, still gripping the Skillmaster so that he could not speak, he asserted his challenge. They would fight. No weapons, but hands only, just as the Skillmaster had assaulted a certain boy the day before. And the Stones would witness, if Burrich won, that Galen had had no call to strike the boy, nor had he the right to refuse to teach the boy. And Galen would have refused the challenge and gone to the King himself, except that the dark man had already called the Stones to witness. And so they fought, in much the same way that a bull fights a bale of straw when he tosses and stamps and gores it. And when he was done, the stablemaster bent and whispered something to the Skillmaster, before he and all others turned and left the man lying there, with the Stones witness to his whimpering and bleeding.'

'What did he say?' I demanded.

'I wasn't there. I saw and heard nothing of it.' The Fool stood and stretched. 'You'll be late if you tarry,' he pointed out to me, and left. And I left my room, wondering, and climbed the tall tower to the Queen's stripped Garden and was still in time to be the first one there.

SIXTEEN

Lessons

According to ancient chronicles, Skillusers were organized in coteries of six. These groups did not usually include any of exceptional royal blood, but were limited to cousins and nephews of the direct line of ascension, or those who showed an aptitude and were judged worthy. One of the most famous, Crossfire's Coterie, provides a splendid example of how they functioned. Dedicated to Queen Vision, Crossfire and the others of her coterie had been trained by a Skillmaster called Tactic. The partners in this coterie were mutually chosen by one another, and then received special training from Tactic to bind them into a close unit. Whether scattered across the Six Duchies to collect or disseminate information, or when massed as a group for the purpose of confounding and demoralizing the enemy, their deeds became legendary. Their final heroism, detailed in the ballad Crossfire's Sacrifice, was the massing of their strength, which they channelled to Queen Vision during the Battle of Besham. Unbeknownst to the exhausted queen, they gave to her more than they could spare themselves, and in the midst of the victory celebration the coterie was discovered in their tower, drained and dying. Perhaps the people's love of Crossfire's Coterie stemmed in part from their all being cripples in one form or another: blind, lame, harelipped or disfigured by fire were all of the six, yet in the Skill their strength was greater than that of the largest warship, and more of a determinant in the defence of the Queen.

During the peaceful years of King Bounty's reign, the instruction of the Skill for the creation of coteries was abandoned. Existing coteries disbanded due to ageing, death or simply a lack of purpose. Instruction in the Skill began to be limited to princes only, and for a time it was seen as a rather archaic art. By the time of the Red Ship raids, only King Shrewd and his son Verity were active practitioners of the Skill. Shrewd made an effort to locate and recruit former practitioners, but most were aged, or no longer proficient.

Galen, then Skillmaster for Shrewd, was assigned the task of creating new coteries for the defence of the kingdom. Galen chose to set aside tradition. Coterie memberships were assigned rather than mutually chosen. Galen's methods of teaching were harsh, his training goal that each member would be an unquestioning part of a unit, a tool for the King to use as he needed. This particular aspect was designed solely by Galen, and the first Skill coterie he created, he presented to King Shrewd as if it were his gift to give. At least one member of the royal family expressed his abhorrence of the idea. But times were desperate, and King Shrewd could not resist wielding the weapon that had been given into his hand.

Such hate. Oh, how they hated me. As each student emerged from the stairwell onto the tower roof to find me there and waiting, each spurned me. I felt their disdain, as palpably as if each had dashed cold water against me. By the time the seventh and final student appeared, the cold of their hatred was like a wall around me. But I stood, silent and contained, in my accustomed place, and met every eye that was lifted to mine. That, I think, was why no one spoke a word to me. They were forced to take their places around me. They did not speak to each other, either.

And we waited.

The sun came up, and even cleared the wall around the tower, and still Galen had not come. But they kept their places and waited and so I did likewise.

Finally, I heard his halting steps upon the stairs. When he emerged, he blinked in the sun's pale wash, glanced at me, and visibly startled. I stood my ground. We looked at one another. He could see the burden of hatred that the others had imposed on me and it pleased him, as did the bandages I still wore on my temple. But I met his eyes and did not flinch. I dared not.

And I became aware of the dismay the others were feeling. No one could look at him and not see how badly he had been beaten. The Witness Stones had found him lacking, and all who saw him would know. His gaunt face was a landscape of purples and greens washed over with yellows. His lower lip was split in the middle, and cut at the corner of his mouth. He wore a long-sleeved robe that covered his arms, but the flowing looseness of it contrasted so strongly with his usual tightly-laced shirts and tunics that it was like seeing the man in his nightshirt. His hands, too, were purple and knobby, but I could not recall that I had seen bruises on Burrich's body. I concluded that he had used them in a vain attempt to shield his face. He still carried his little whip with him, but I doubted he had the capability to swing it effectively.

And so we inspected one another. I took no satisfaction in his bruises or his disgrace. I felt something akin to shame for them. I had believed so strongly in his invulnerability and superiority that this evidence of his mere humanity left me feeling foolish. That unbalanced his composure. Twice he opened his mouth to speak to me. The third time, he turned his back on the class and said, 'Begin your physical limbering. I will observe you to see if you are moving correctly.'

The ends of his words were soft, spoken through a painful mouth. And as we dutifully stretched and swayed and bowed in unison, he crabbed awkwardly about the tower garden. He tried not to lean on the wall, or to rest too often. Gone was the slap, slap, slap of the whip against his thigh that had formerly orchestrated our efforts. Instead, he gripped it as if afraid he might drop it. For my part, I was grateful that Burrich had made me get up and move. My bound ribs didn't permit me the full flexibility of motion that Galen had formerly commanded from us, but I made an honest attempt at it.

He offered us nothing new that day, only going over what we had already learned, and the lessons came to an early end, before the sun was even down. 'You have done well,' he offered lamely. 'You have earned these free hours, for I am pleased you have continued to study in my absence.' Before dismissing us, he called each of us before him, for a brief touch of the Skill. The others left reluctantly, with many a backward glance, curious as to how he would deal with me. As the numbers of my fellow students dwindled, I braced myself for a solitary confrontation.

But even that was a disappointment. He called me before him, and I came, as silent and outwardly respectful as the others. I stood before him as they had, and he made a few brief passes of his hands before my face and over my head. Then he said in a cold voice, 'You shield too well. You must learn to relax your guard over your thoughts if you are either to send them forth or receive those of others. Go.'

And I left, as the others had, but regretfully. Privately I wondered if he had made a real attempt to use the Skill on me. I had felt no brush of it. I descended the stairs, aching and bitter, wondering why I was trying.

I went to my room, and then to the stables. I gave Sooty a cursory brushing while Smithy watched. Still I felt restless and dissatisfied. I knew I should rest, that I would regret it if I did not. *Stone walk?* Smithy suggested, and I agreed to take him into town. He galloped and snuffled circles around me as I made my way down from the keep. It was a blustery afternoon after a calm morning; a storm was building offshore. But the wind was unseasonably warm, and I felt the fresh air clearing my head, and the steady rhythm of walking soothed and stretched the muscles that Galen's exercises had left bunched and aching. Smithy's sensory prattle grounded me firmly in the immediate world so that I could not dwell on my frustrations.

I told myself it was Smithy who led us so directly to Molly's shop. Puppylike, he had returned to where he had been welcomed before. Molly's father had kept his bed that day, and the shop was fairly quiet. A single customer lingered, talking to Molly. Molly introduced him to me as Jade. He was a mate off some Sealbay trading vessel, not quite twenty, and he spoke to me as if I were ten, smiling past me at Molly all the while. He was full of tales of Red Ships and sea storms. He had a red stone earring in one ear, and a new beard curled along his jaw. He took far too long to select candles and a new brass lamp, but finally he left.

'Close the store for a bit,' I urged Molly. 'Let's go down to the beach. The wind is lovely today.'

She shook her head regretfully. 'I'm behind in my work. I should dip tapers all this afternoon if I have no customers. And if I do have customers, I should be here.'

I felt unreasonably disappointed. I quested toward her, and discovered how much she actually wished to go. 'There's not that much daylight left,' I said persuasively. 'You can always dip tapers this evening. And your customers will come back tomorrow if they find you closed today.'

She cocked her head, looked thoughtful, and abruptly set aside the wicking she held. 'You're right, you know. The fresh air will do me good.' And she took up her cloak with an alacrity that delighted Smithy and surprised me. We closed up the shop and left.

Molly set her usual brisk pace. Smithy frolicked about her, delighted. We talked, in a cursory way. The wind put roses in her cheeks, and her eyes seemed brighter in the cold. And I thought she looked at me more often, and more pensively than she usually did.

The town was quiet, and the market all but deserted. We went to the beach, and walked sedately where we had raced and shrieked but a few years before. She asked me if I had learned to light a lantern before going down steps at night, and that mystified me, until I remembered that I had explained my injuries as a fall down a dark staircase. She asked me if the schoolteacher and the horsemaster were still at odds, and by this I discerned that Burrich and Galen's challenge at the Witness Stones had become something of a local legend already. I assured her that peace had been restored. We spent some little time gathering a certain kind of seaweed that she wanted to flavour her chowder with that evening. Then, because I was winded, we sat in the lee of some rocks and watched Smithy make numerous attempts to clear the beach of gulls.

'So. I hear Prince Verity is to wed,' she began conversationally.

'What?' I asked, amazed.

She laughed heartily. 'Newboy, I have never met anyone as immune to gossip as you seem to be. How can you live right up there in the keep and know nothing of that which is the common talk of the town? Verity has agreed to take a bride, to assure the succession. But the story in town is that he is too busy to do his courting himself, so Regal will find him a lady.'

'Oh, no.' My dismay was honest. I was picturing big bluff Verity paired with one of Regal's sugar-crystal women. Whenever there was a festival of any kind in the keep, Springsedge or Winterheart or Harvestday, here they came, from Chalced and Farrow and Bearns, in carriages or on richly-caparisoned palfreys or riding in litters. They wore gowns like butterflies' wings, ate as daintily as sparrows, and seemed to flutter about and perch always in Regal's vicinity. And he would sit in their midst, in his own silk and velvet hues, and preen while their musical voices tinkled around him and their fans and fancywork trembled in their fingers. 'Prince-catchers', I'd heard them called, noble women who displayed themselves like goods in a store window in the hopes of wedding one of the royals. Their behaviour was not improper, not quite. But to me it seemed desperate, and Regal cruel as he smiled first on this one and then danced all evening with that one, only to rise to a late breakfast and walk yet another through the gardens. They were Regal's worshippers. I tried to picture one on Verity's arm as he stood watching the dancers at a ball, or quietly weaving in his study while Verity pondered and sketched at the maps he so loved. No garden strolls – Verity took his walks along the docks and through the crops, stopping often to talk to the seafolk and farmers behind their ploughs. Dainty slippers and embroidered skirts would surely not follow him there.

Molly slipped a penny into my hand.

'What's this for?'

'To pay for whatever you've been thinking so hard that you've been sitting on the edge of my skirt while I've twice asked you to lift up. I don't think you've heard a word I've said.'

I sighed. 'Verity and Regal are so different, I cannot imagine one choosing a wife for the other.'

Molly looked puzzled.

'Regal will choose someone who is beautiful and wealthy and of good blood. She'll be able to dance and sing and play the chimes. She'll dress beautifully and have jewels in her hair at the breakfast table, and always smell of the flowers that grow in the Rain Wilds.'

'And Verity will not be glad of such a woman?' The confusion on Molly's face was as if I were insisting the sea was soup.

'Verity deserves a companion, not an ornament to wear on his sleeve,' I protested in disdain. 'Were I Verity, I'd want a woman who could do things. Not just select her jewellery or plait her own hair. She should be able to sew a shirt, or tend her own garden, and have something special she can do that is all her own, like scrollwork or herbery.'

'Newboy, the like of that is not for fine ladies,' Molly chided me. 'They are meant to be pretty and ornamental. And they are rich. It isn't for them to have to do such work.'

'Of course it is. Look at Lady Patience and her woman, Lacey. They are always about and doing things. Their apartments are a jungle of the lady's plants, and the cuffs of her gowns are sometimes a bit sticky from her paper-making, or she will have bits of leaves in her hair from her herbery work, but she is still just as beautiful. And prettiness is not all that important in a woman. I've watched Lacey's hands making one of the keep children a fish-net from a bit of jute string. Quick and clever as any webman's fingers down on the dock are her fingers; now that's a pretty thing that has nothing to do with her face. And Hod, who teaches weapons? She loves her silver-work and graving. She made a dagger for her father's birthday, with a grip like a leaping stag, and yet done so cleverly that it's a comfort in the hand, with not a jag or edge to catch on anything. Now that's a bit of beauty that will live on long after her hair greys or her cheeks wrinkle. Someday her grandchildren will look at that work and think what a clever woman she was.'

'Do you think so, really?'

'Certainly.' I shifted, suddenly aware of how close Molly was to me. I shifted, yet did not really move further away. Down the beach, Smithy made another foray into a flock of gulls. His tongue was hanging nearly to his knees, but he was still galloping.

'But if noble ladies do all those things, they'll ruin their hands with the work, and the wind will dry their hair and tan their faces. Surely Verity doesn't deserve a woman who looks like a deckhand?'

'Surely he does. Far more than he deserves a woman who looks like a fat red carp kept in a bowl.'

Molly giggled.

'Someone to ride beside him of a morning when he takes Hunter out for a gallop, or someone who can look at a section of map he's just finished and actually understand just how fine a piece of work it is. That's what Verity deserves.'

'I've never ridden a horse,' Molly objected suddenly. 'And I know few letters.'

I looked at her curiously, wondering why she seemed so suddenly downcast. 'What matter is that? You're clever enough to learn anything. Look at all you've taught yourself about candles and herbs. Don't tell me that came from your father. Sometimes when I come to the shop, your hair and dress smell of fresh herbs and I can tell you've been experimenting to get new perfumes for the candles. If you wanted to read or write more, you could learn. As for riding, you'd be a natural. You've balance and strength . . . look at how you climb the rocks on the cliffs. And animals take to you. You've fair won Smithy's heart away from me . . .'

'Fa!' She gave me a nudge with her shoulder. 'You talk as if some lord should come riding down from the keep and carry me off.'

I thought of August with his stuffy manners, or Regal simpering at her. 'Eda forbid. You'd be wasted on them. They wouldn't have the wit to understand you, or the heart to appreciate you.'

Molly looked down at her work-worn hands. 'Who would, then?' she asked softly.

Boys are fools. The conversation had grown and twined around us, my words coming as naturally as breathing to me. I had not intended any flattery, or subtle courtship. The sun was beginning to dip into the water, and we sat close by one another and the beach before us was like the world at our feet. If I had said at that moment, 'I would,' I think her heart would have tumbled into my awkward hands like ripe fruit from a tree. I think she might have kissed me, and sealed herself to me of her own free will. But I couldn't grasp the immensity of what I suddenly knew I had come to feel for her. It drove the simple truth from my lips, and I sat dumb and half a moment later Smithy came, wet and sandy, barrelling into us so that Molly leaped to her feet to save her skirts, and the opportunity was lost forever, blown away like spray on the wind.

We stood and stretched, and Molly exclaimed about the time, and I felt all the sudden aches of my healing body. Sitting and letting myself cool down on a chill beach was a stupid thing I certainly wouldn't have done to any horse. I walked Molly home and there was an awkward moment at her door before she stooped and hugged Smithy goodbye. And then I was alone, save for a curious pup demanding to know why I went so slowly and insisting he was half-starved and wanting to run and tussle all the way up the hill to the keep.

I plodded up the hill, chilled within and without. I returned Smithy to the stables, and said good night to Sooty, and then went up to the keep. Galen and his fledglings had already finished their meagre meal and left. Most of the keep folk had eaten, and I found myself drifting back to my old haunts. There was always food in the kitchen, and company in the watch-room off the kitchen. Men-at-arms came and went there all hours of the day and night, so Cook kept a simmering kettle on the hook, adding water and meat and vegetables as the level went down. Wine and beer and cheese were also there, and the simple company of those who guarded the keep. They had accepted me as one of their own since the first day I'd been given into Burrich's care. So I made myself a simple meal, not near as scanty as Galen would have provided me, nor yet as ample and rich as I craved. That was Burrich's teaching; I fed myself as I would have an injured animal.

And I listened to the casual talk going on around me, focusing myself into the life of the keep as I hadn't for months. I was amazed at all that I had not known because of my total immersion in Galen's teaching. A bride for Verity was most of the talk. There was the usual crude soldiers' jesting one could expect about such things, as well as a lot of commiseration over his ill-luck in having Regal choose his future spouse. That the match would be based on political alliances had never been in question; a prince's hand could not be wasted on something as foolish as his own choice. That had been a great part of the scandal surrounding

Chivalry's stubborn courtship of Patience. She had come from within the realm, the daughter of one of our nobles, and one already very amicable to the royal family. No political advantage at all had come out of that marriage.

But Verity would not be squandered so. Especially with the Red Ships menacing us all along our straggling coastline. And so speculation ran rife. Who would she be? A woman from the Near Islands, to our north in the White Sea? The islands were little more than rocky bits of the earth's bones thrusting up out of the sea, but a series of towers set amongst them would give us earlier warning of the sea raiders' ventures into our waters. To the southwest of our borders, beyond the Rain Wilds where no one ruled were the Spice Coasts. A princess from there would offer few defensive advantages, but some argued for the rich trading agreements she might bring with her. Days to the south and east over the sea were the many big islands where grew the trees that the boat-builders yearned for. Could a king and his daughter be found there who would trade her warm winds and soft fruits for a keep in a rocky, ice-bounded land? What would they ask for a soft southern woman and her tall-timbered island trade? Furs said some, and grain said another. And there were the mountain kingdoms at our backs, with their jealous possession of the passes that led into the tundra lands beyond. A princess from there would command warriors of her folk, as well as trade links to the ivory workers and reindeer herders who lived beyond their borders. On their southern border was the pass that led to the headwaters of the great Rain River that meandered through the Rain Wilds. Every soldier among us had heard the old tales of the abandoned treasure-temples on the banks of that river, of the tall, carved gods who presided still over their holy springs, and of the flake gold that sparkled in the lesser streams. Perhaps a mountain princess, then?

Each possibility was debated with far more political sophistication than Galen would have believed these simple soldiers capable of commanding. I rose from their midst feeling ashamed of how I had dismissed them; in so short a time Galen had brought me to think of them as ignorant sword-wielders, men of brawn with no brain at all. I had lived among them all my life. I should have known better. No, I *had* known better. But my hunger to set myself higher, to prove beyond doubt my right to that royal magic, had made me willing to accept any nonsense with which he might choose to present me. Something clicked within me, as if the key piece to a wood puzzle had suddenly slid into place. I had been bribed with the offer of knowledge as another man might have been bribed with coins.

I did not think very well of myself as I climbed the stairs to my room. I lay down to sleep with the resolve that I would not let Galen deceive me any longer, nor persuade me to deceive myself. I also resolved most firmly that I would learn the Skill, no matter how painful or difficult it might be.

And so dark and early the next morning, I plunged fully back into my lessons and routine. I attended Galen's every word, I pushed myself to do each exercise, physical or mental, to the extreme of my ability. But as the week, and then the month, wore painfully on, I felt like a dog with his meat suspended just beyond the reach of his jaws. For the others, something was obviously happening. A network of shared thought was building between them, a communication that had them turning to one another before they spoke, that let them perform the shared physical exercises as one being. Sullenly, resentfully, they took turns being partnered with me, but from them I felt nothing, and from me they shuddered and pulled back, complaining to Galen that the force I exerted towards them was either like a whisper or a battering ram.

I watched in near despair as they danced in pairs, sharing control of one another's muscles, or as one walked blindfolded the maze of the coals, guided by the eyes of his seated partner. Sometimes I knew I had the Skill. I could feel it building within me, unfolding like a growing seed, but it was a thing I could not seem to direct or control. One moment it was within me, booming like a tide against rock cliffs, and the next it was gone and all within me was dry, deserted sand. At its strength, I could compel August to stand, to bow, to walk. The next he would stand glaring at me, daring me to contact him at all.

And no one seemed able to reach inside me. 'Drop your guard, put down your walls!' Galen would angrily order me, as he stood before me, vainly trying to convey to me the simplest direction or suggestion. I felt the barest brush of his Skill against me; but I could no more allow him inside my mind than I could stand complacent while a man slid a sword between my ribs. Try as I might to compel myself, I shied from his touch, physical or mental, and the touches of my classmates I could not feel at all.

Daily they advanced, while I watched and struggled to master the barest basics. A day came when August looked at a page, and across the rooftop his partner read it aloud, while another set of two pairs played a chess game in which those who commanded the moves could not physically see the board at all. Galen was well pleased with all of them, save me. Each day he dismissed us after a touch, a touch I seldom felt. Each day I was the last free to go, and he coldly reminded me that he wasted his time on a bastard only because the King commanded him to do so.

Spring was coming on and Smithy grown from a puppy to a dog. Sooty dropped her foal while I was at my lessons, a fine filly sired by Verity's stallion. I saw Molly once, and we walked together almost wordlessly through the market. There was a new stall set up, with a rough man selling birds and animals, all captured wild and caged by him. He had crows and sparrows, a swallow, and one young fox so weak with worms he could scarcely stand. Death would free him sooner than any buyer, and even if I had had the coin for him, he had reached a state where the worm-medicines would only poison him as well as his parasites. It sickened me, and so I stood, questing toward the birds with suggestions of how picking at a certain bright bit of metal might unpin the doors of their cages. But Molly thought I stared at the poor beasts themselves, and I felt her grow cooler and further from me than ever she had been before. As we walked her home, Smithy whined beggingly for her attention, and so won from her a cuddle and a pat before we left. I envied him the ability to whine so well. My own seemed to go unheard.

With spring in the air, all in the seaport braced, for soon it would be raiding weather. I ate with the guards every night now, and listened well to all the rumours. Forged ones had become robbers all along our highways, and the stories of their depravities and depredations were all the tavern talk now. As predators, they were more devoid of decency and mercy than any wild animal could be. It was easy to forget they had ever been human, and to hate them with a venom like nothing else.

The fear of being Forged increased proportionately. Markets carried candy-dipped beads of poison for mothers to give their children in the event the family was captured by raiders. There were rumours that some sea-coast villagers had packed up all their belongings in carts and moved inland, forsaking their traditional occupations as fishers and traders to become farmers and hunters away from the threat of the sea. Certainly the population of beggars within the city was swelling. A Forged one came into Buckkeep Town itself and walked the streets, as untouchable as a mad man as he helped himself to whatever he wanted from the market stalls. Before a second day had passed, he had disappeared, and dark whispers said to watch for his body to wash up on the beach. Other rumours said a wife had been found for Verity among the mountain folk. Some said it was to secure our access to the passes; others that we could not afford a potential enemy at our backs when all along our sea-coast we must fear the Red Ships. And there were yet other whispers that all was not well with Prince Verity. Tired and sick said some, and others sniggered about a nervous and weary bridegroom. A few sneered that he had taken to drink and was only seen by day when his headache was worst.

I found my concern over these last rumours to be deeper than I would have expected. None of the royals had ever paid much mind to me, at least not in a personal way. Shrewd saw to my education and comfort, and had long ago bought my loyalty, so that now I was his without even giving thought to any alternative. Regal despised me, and I had long learned to avoid his narrow glance, and the casual nudges or furtive shoves that had once been enough to send a smaller boy staggering. But Verity had been kind to me, in an absent-minded sort of way, and he loved his dogs and his horse and his hawks in a way I understood. I wanted to see him stand tall and proud at his wedding, and hoped someday to stand behind the throne he would occupy much as Chade stood behind Shrewd's. I hoped he was well, and yet there was nothing I could do about it if he were not, nor any way I could see him. Even if we had been keeping the same hours, the circles we moved in were seldom the same.

It was still not quite full spring when Galen made his announcement. The rest of the keep was making its preparations for Springfest. The stalls in the marketplace would be sanded clean and repainted in bright colours, and tree branches would be brought inside and gently forced so that their blossoms and tiny leaves could grace the banquet table on Springseve. But tender new greens and eggcake with carris seed toppings were not what Galen had in mind for us, nor puppet shows and huntdances. Instead, with the coming of the new season, we would be tested, to be proven either worthy or discarded.

'Discarded,' he repeated, and if he had been condemning those unchosen to death, the attention of his other students could not have been more intent. I tried numbly to understand what it would mean to me when I failed. I had no belief that he would test me fairly, or that I could pass such a test even if he did.

'You shall be a coterie, those of you who prove yourselves. Such a coterie as has never been before, I would think. At the height of Springfest, I myself will present you to your king, and he shall see the wonder of what I have wrought. As you have come this far with me, you know I will not be shamed before him. So I myself will test you, and test you to your limits, to be sure that the weapon I place in my king's hand holds an edge worthy of its purpose. One day from now, I will scatter you, like seeds in the wind, across the kingdom. I have arranged that you will be taken hence, by swift horse, to your destinations. And there each of you will be left, alone. Not one of you will know where any of the others are.' He paused, I think to let each of us feel the tension thrumming through the room. I knew that all the others vibrated in tune, sharing a common emotion, almost a common mind, as they received their instruction. I suspected they heard far more than the simple words from Galen's lips. I felt a foreigner there, listening to words in a language whose idiom I could not grasp. I would fail.

'Within two days of being left, you will be summoned. By me. You will be directed whom to contact, and where. Each of you will receive the information you need to make your way back here. If you have learned, and learned well, my coterie will be here and present on Springseve, ready to be presented to the King.' Again the pause. 'Do not think, however, that all you must do is find your way back to Buckkeep by Springseve. You are to be a coterie, not homing-pigeons. How you come and in what company will prove to me that you have mastered your Skill. Be ready to leave by tomorrow morning.'

And then he released us, one by one, again with a touch for each, and a word of praise for each, save me. I stood before him, as open as I could make myself, as vulnerable as I dared to be, and yet the brush of the Skill against my mind was less than the touch of the wind. He stared down at me as I looked up at him, and I did not need the Skill to feel that he both loathed and despised me. He made a noise of contempt and looked aside, releasing me. I started to go.

'Far better,' he said in that cavernous voice of his, 'if you had gone over the wall that night, bastard. Far better. Burrich thought I abused you. I was only offering you a way out, as close to an honourable way as you were capable of finding. Go away and die, boy, or at least go away. You shame your father's name by existing. By Eda, I do not know how you came to exist. That a man such as your father could fall to such depth as lying with something and letting you become is beyond my mind to imagine.'

As always, there was that note of fanaticism in his voice as he spoke of Chivalry, and his eyes became almost blank with blind idolatry. Almost absent-mindedly, he turned away and walked off. He reached the top of the stairs, and then turned, very slowly. 'I must ask,' he said, and the venom in his voice was hungry with hatred. 'Are you his catamite, that he lets you suck strength from him? Is that why he is so possessive of you?'

'Catamite?' I repeated, not knowing the word.

He smiled. It made his cadaverous face even more skulllike. 'Did you think I hadn't discovered him? Did you think you'd be free to draw on his strength for this test? You won't. Be assured, bastard, you won't.'

He turned and went down the steps, leaving me standing there alone on the rooftop. I had no idea what his final words meant; but the strength of his hatred had left me sickened and weak as if it were a poison he'd put in my blood. I was reminded of the last time all had left me on the tower roof. I felt compelled to walk to the edge of the tower and look down. This corner of the keep did not face the sea, but there were still jagged rocks aplenty at the foot of it. No one would survive that fall. If I could make a second's firm decision, then I could put myself out of it all. And what Burrich or Chade or anyone else might think of it would not be able to trouble me.

A distant echo of a whimper.

'I'm coming, Smithy,' I muttered, and turned away from the edge.

SEVENTEEN

The Trial

The Man Ceremony is supposed to take place within the moon of a boy's fourteenth birthday. Not all are honoured with it. It requires a Man to sponsor and name the candidate, and he must find a dozen other Men who concede the boy is worthy and ready. Living among the men-at-arms, I was aware of the ceremony, and knew enough of its gravity and selectivity that I never expected to participate in it. For one thing, no one knew my birth date. For another, I had no knowledge of who was a Man, let alone if twelve Men existed who would find me worthy.

But on a certain night, months after I had endured Galen's test, I awoke to find my bed surrounded by robed and hooded figures. Within the dark hoods I glimpsed the masks of the Pillars.

No one may speak or write of the ceremony details. This, I think, I may say: as each life was put into my hands – fish, bird and beast – I chose to release it, not to death but back to its own free existence. So nothing died at my ceremony, and hence no one feasted. But even in my state of mind at that time, I felt there had been enough blood and death around me to last a lifetime, and I refused to kill with hands or teeth. My Man still chose to give me a name, so He could not have been totally displeased. The name is in the old tongue, which has no letters and cannot be written. Nor have I ever found any with which I chose to share the knowledge of my Man name. But its ancient meaning, I think, I can divulge here. Catalyst. The Changer.

* * *

I went straight to the stables, to Smithy and then to Sooty. The distress I felt at the thought of the morrow went from mental to physical, and I stood in Sooty's stall, leaned my head against her withers, and felt queasy. Burrich found me there. I recognized his presence and the steady cadence of his boots as he came down the stable walkway, and then he halted abruptly outside Sooty's stall. I felt him looking in at me.

'Well. Now what?' he demanded harshly, and I heard in his voice how weary he was both of me and my problems. Had I been any less miserable, my pride would have made me draw myself up and declare that nothing was wrong.

Instead, I muttered into Sooty's coat, 'Tomorrow Galen plans to test us.'

'I know. He's demanded quite abruptly that I furnish him horses for this idiotic scheme. I would have refused, had he not a wax signet from the King giving him authority. And no more do I know than that he wants the horses, so don't ask it,' he added gruffly as I looked up suddenly at him.

'I wouldn't,' I told him sullenly. I would prove myself fairly to Galen, or not at all.

'You've no chance of passing this trial he's designed, have you?' Burrich's tone was casual, but I could hear how he braced himself to be disappointed by my answer.

'None,' I said flatly, and we were both silent a moment, listening to the finality of that word.

'Well.' He cleared his throat and gave his belt a hitch. 'Then you'd best get it over with and get back here. It's not as if you haven't had good luck with your other schooling. A man can't expect to succeed at everything he tries.' He tried to make my failure at the Skill sound as if it were of no consequence.

'I suppose not. Will you take care of Smithy for me while I'm gone?'

'I will.' He started to turn away, then turned back, almost reluctantly. 'How much is that dog going to miss you?'

I heard his other question, but tried to avoid it. 'I don't know. I've had to leave him so much during these lessons, I'm afraid he won't miss me at all.'

'I doubt that,' Burrich said ponderously. He turned away. 'I doubt that a very great deal,' he said as he walked off between the rows of stalls. And I knew that he knew, and was disgusted, not just that Smithy and I shared a bond, but that I refused to admit it.

'As if admitting it were an option, with him,' I muttered to Sooty. I bade my animals farewell, trying to convey to Smithy that several meals and nights would pass before he saw me again. He wriggled and fawned and protested that I must take him, that I would need him. He was too big to pick up and hug any more. I sat down and he came into my lap and I held him. He was so warm and solid, so near and real. For a moment I felt how right he was, that I would need him to be able to survive this failure. But I reminded myself that he would be here, waiting for me when I returned, and I promised him several days of my time for his sole benefit when I returned. I would take him on a long hunt, such as we had never had time for before. (Now) he suggested, and (soon) I promised. Then I went back up to the keep to pack a change of clothes and some travelling food.

The next morning had much of pomp and drama to it and very little sense, to my way of thinking. The others to be tested seemed excited and elated. Of the eight of us who were setting out, I was the only one who seemed unimpressed by the restless horses and the eight covered litters. Galen lined us up and blind-folded us as three-score or more people looked on. Most of them were related to the students, or friends, or the keep gossips. Galen made a brief speech, ostensibly to us, but telling us what we already knew: that we were to be taken to different locations and left; that we must cooperate, using the Skill, in order to make our ways back to the keep; that if we succeeded, we would become a coterie and serve our king magnificently and be essential to defeating the Red Ship Raiders. The last bit impressed our onlookers, for I heard muttering tongues as I was escorted to my litter and assisted inside.

There passed a miserable day and a half for me. The litter swayed, and with no fresh air on my face or scenery to distract me, I soon felt queasy. The man guiding the horses had been sworn to silence and kept his word. We paused briefly that night.

I was given a meagre meal, bread and cheese and water, and then I was reloaded and the jolting and swaying resumed.

At about midday of the following day, the litter halted. Once more I was assisted in dismounting. Not a word was said, and I stood, stiff and headachy and blindfolded in a strong wind. When I heard the horses leaving, I decided I had reached my destination and reached up to untie my blindfold. Galen had knotted it tightly and it took me a moment to get it off.

I stood on a grassy hillside. My escort was well on his way to a road that wound past the base of the hill, moving swiftly. The grass was tall around my knees, sere from winter, but green at the base. I could see other grassy hills with rocks poking out of their sides, and strips of woodland sheltering at their feet. I shrugged and turned to get my bearings. It was hilly country, but I could scent the sea and a low tide to the east somewhere. I had a nagging sense that the countryside was familiar; not that I had been to this particular spot before, but that the lie of the terrain was familiar somehow. I turned, and to the west saw the Sentinel. There was no mistaking the double-jag of its peak. I had copied a map for Fedwren less than a year ago, and the creator had chosen the Sentinel's distinctive peak as a motif for the decorative border. So. The sea over there, the Sentinel there, and, with a suddenly dipping stomach, I knew where I was. Not too far from Forge.

I found myself turning quickly in a circle to survey the surrounding hillside, woodlands and road. No sign of anyone. I quested out, almost frantically, but found only birds and small game and one buck, who lifted his head and snuffed, wondering what I was. For a moment I felt reassured, until I remembered that the Forged ones I had encountered before had been transparent to that sense.

I moved down the hill to where several boulders jutted out from its side, and sat in their shelter. It was not that the wind was cold, for the day promised spring soon. It was to have something firmly against my back, and to feel that I was not such an outstanding target as I had been on top of the hill. I tried to think coolly what to do next. Galen had suggested to us that we should stay quietly where we were deposited, meditating and remaining open in our senses. At sometime in the next two days, he would try to contact me.

Nothing takes the heart out of a man more than the expectation of failure. I had no belief that he would really try to contact me, let alone that I would receive any clear impressions if he did. Nor did I have faith that the drop-off he had chosen for me was a safe location. Without much more thought than that, I rose, again surveyed the area for anyone watching me, then struck out toward the sea-smell. If I were where I supposed myself to be, from the shore I should be able to see Antler Island, and, on a clear day, possibly Scrim Isle. Even one of those would be enough to tell me how far from Forge I was.

As I hiked, I told myself I only wanted to see how long a walk I would have back to Buckkeep. Only a fool would imagine that the Forged ones still represented any danger. Surely winter had put an end to them, or left them too starved and weakened to be a menace to anyone. I gave no credence to the tales of them banding together as cut-throats and thieves. I wasn't afraid. I merely wanted to see where I was. If Galen truly wanted to contact me, location should be no barrier. He had assured us innumerable times that it was the person he reached for, not the place. He could find me as well on the beach as he could on the hilltop.

By late afternoon, I stood on top of rocky cliffs, looking out to sea. Antler Island, and a haze that would be Scrim beyond it. I was north of Forge. The coast-road home would go right through the ruins of that town. It was not a comforting thought.

So now what?

By evening, I was back on my hilltop, scrunched down between two of the boulders. I had decided it was as good a place to wait as any. Despite my doubts, I would stay where I had been left until the contact time was up. I ate bread and salt-fish, and drank sparingly of my water. My change of clothes included an extra cloak. I wrapped myself in this and sternly rejected all thoughts of making a fire. However small, it would have been a beacon to anyone on the dirt road that passed the hill.

I don't think there is anything more cruelly tedious than unremitting nervousness. I tried to meditate, to open myself up to Galen's Skill, all the while shivering with cold and refusing to admit that I was scared. The child in me kept imagining dark, ragged figures creeping soundlessly up the hillside around me, Forged folk who would beat and kill me for the cloak I wore and the food in my bag. I had cut myself a stick as I made my way back to my hillside, and I gripped it in both hands, but it seemed a poor weapon. Sometimes I dozed despite my fears, but my dreams were always of Galen gloating over my failure as Forged ones closed in on me, and I always woke with a start, to peer wildly about to see if my nightmares were true.

I watched the sunrise through the trees, and then dozed fitfully through morning. Afternoon brought me a weary sort of peace. I amused myself by questing out toward the wildlife on the hillside. Mice and songbirds were little more than bright sparks of hunger in my mind, and rabbits little more, but a fox was full of lust to find a mate and further off a buck battered the velvet off his antlers as purposefully as any smith at his anvil. Evening was very long. It was surprising just how hard it was for me to accept, as night fell, that I had felt nothing, not the slightest pressure of the Skill. Either he hadn't called or I hadn't heard him. I ate bread and fish in the dark and told myself it didn't matter. For a time, I tried to bolster myself with anger, but my despair was too clammy and dark a thing for anger's flames to overcome. I felt sure Galen had cheated me, but I would never be able to prove it, not even to myself. I would always have to wonder if his contempt for me had been justified. In full darkness, I settled my back against a rock, my stick across my knees, and resolved to sleep.

My dreams were muddled and sour. Regal stood over me, and I was a child sleeping in straw again. He laughed and held a knife. Verity shrugged, and smiled apologetically at me. Chade turned aside from me, disappointed. Molly smiled at Jade, past me, forgetting I was there. Burrich held me by the shirt-front and shook me, telling me to behave like a man, not a beast. But I lay down on straw and an old shirt, chewing at a bone. The meat was very good, and I could think of nothing else.

I was very comfortable until someone opened a stable door and left it ajar. A nasty little wind came creeping across the stable floor to chill me, and I looked up with a growl. I smelled Burrich and ale. Burrich came slowly through the dark, with a muttered, 'It's all right, Smithy,' as he passed me. I put my head down as he began to climb his stairs.

Suddenly there was a shout and men falling down the stairs. They struggled as they fell. I leaped to my feet, growling and barking. They landed half on top of me. A boot kicked at me, and I seized the leg above it in my teeth and clamped my jaws. I caught more boot and trouser than flesh, but he hissed in anger and pain, and struck at me.

A knife went into my side.

I set my teeth harder and held on, snarling around my mouthful. Other dogs had awakened and were barking, the horses were stamping in their stalls. *Boy! Boy!* I called for help. I felt him with me, but he didn't come. The intruder kicked me, but I wouldn't let go. Burrich lay in the straw and I smelled his blood. He did not move. I heard old Vixen flinging herself against the door upstairs, trying vainly to get to her master. Again and then again the knife plunged into me. I cried out to my Boy a last time, and then I could no longer hold on. I was flung off the kicking leg, to strike the side of a stall. I was drowning, blood in my mouth and nostrils. Running feet. Pain in the dark. I hitched closer to Burrich. I pushed my nose under his hand. He did not move. Voices and light coming, coming, coming . . .

I awoke on a dark hillside, gripping my stick so tightly my hands were numb. Not for a moment did I think it a dream. I couldn't stop feeling the knife between my ribs, and tasting the blood in my mouth. Like the refrain of a ghastly song, the memories came again and again, the draught of cold air, the knife, the boot, the taste of my enemy's blood in my mouth, and the taste of my own. I struggled to make sense of what Smithy had seen. Someone had been at the top of Burrich's stairs, waiting for him. Someone with a knife. And Burrich had fallen, and Smithy had smelled blood . . .

I stood and gathered my things. Thin and faint was Smithy's warm little presence in my mind. Weak, but there. I quested carefully, and then stopped when I felt how much it cost him to acknowledge me. *Still. Be still. I'm coming.* I was cold and my knees shook beneath me, but sweat was slick on my back. Not once did I question what I must do. I strode down the hill to the dirt road. It was a little trade road, a pedlars' track, and I knew that if I followed it, it must intersect eventually with the coast-road. I would follow it, I would find the coast-road, I would get myself home. And if Eda favoured me, I would be in time to help Smithy. And Burrich.

I strode, refusing to let myself run. A steady march would carry me further faster than a mad sprint through the dark. The night was clear, the trail straight. I considered, once, that I was putting an end to any chance of proving I could Skill. All I had put into it – time, effort, pain – all wasted. But there was no way I could have sat down and waited another full day for Galen to try and reach me. To open my mind to Galen's possible Skill touch, I would have had to clear it of Smithy's tenuous thread. I would not. When it was all put in the balances, the Skill was far outweighed by Smithy. And Burrich.

Why Burrich, I wondered. Who could hate him enough to ambush him? And right outside his own quarters. As clearly as if I were reporting to Chade, I began to assemble my facts. Someone who knew him well enough to know where he lived; that ruled out some chance offence committed in a Buckkeep town tavern. Someone who had brought a knife; that ruled out someone who just wanted to give him a beating. The knife had been sharp, and the wielder had known how to use it. I winced again from the memory.

Those were the facts. Cautiously, I began to build assumptions upon them. Someone who knew Burrich's habits and had a serious grievance against him, serious enough to kill over. My steps slowed suddenly. Why hadn't Smithy been aware of the man up there waiting? Why hadn't Vixen been barking through the door? Slipping past dogs in their own territory bespoke someone well practised at stealth.

Galen.

No. I only wanted it to be Galen. I refused to leap to the conclusion. Physically, Galen was no match for Burrich and he knew it. Not even with a knife, in the dark, with Burrich half-drunk and surprised. No. Galen might want to, but he wouldn't do it. Not himself.

Would he send another? I pondered it, and decided I didn't know. Think some more. Burrich was not a patient man. Galen was the most recent enemy he'd made, but not the only one. Over and over I re-stacked my facts, trying to reach a solid conclusion. But there simply wasn't enough to build on.

Eventually I came to a stream, and drank sparingly. Then I walked again. The woods grew thicker, and the moon was mostly obscured by the trees lining the road. I didn't turn back. I pushed on, until my trail flowed into the coast-road like a stream feeding a river. I followed it south, and the wider highway gleamed like silver in the moonlight.

I walked and pondered the night away. As the first creeping tendrils of dawn began to put colour back into the landscape, I felt incredibly weary, but no less driven. My worry was a burden I couldn't put down. I clutched at the thin thread of warmth that told me Smithy was still alive, and wondered about Burrich. I had no way of knowing how badly he'd been injured. Smithy had smelled his blood, so the knife had scored at least once. And the fall down the staircase? I tried to set the worry aside. I had never considered that Burrich could be injured in such a way, let alone what I would feel about it. I could come up with no name for the feeling. Just hollow, I thought to myself. Hollow. And weary.

I ate a bit as I walked and refilled my waterskin from a stream. Midmorning clouded up and rained on me for a bit, only to clear as abruptly by early afternoon. I strode on. I had expected to find some sort of traffic on the coast-road, but saw nothing. By late afternoon, the road had veered close to the cliffs. I could look across a small cove and down onto what had been Forge. The peacefulness of it was chilling. No smoke rose from the cottages, no boats rode in the harbour. I knew my route would take me right through it. I did not relish the idea, but the warm thread of Smithy's life tugged me on.

I lifted my head to the scuff of feet against stone. Only the reflexes of Hod's long training saved me. I came about, staff at the ready, and swept around me in a defensive circle that cracked the jaw of the one that was behind me. The others fell back. Three others. All Forged, empty as stone. The one I had struck was rolling and yelling on the ground. No one paid him any mind except me. I dealt him another quick jolt to his back. He yelled louder and thrashed about. Even in that situation, my action surprised me. I knew it was wise to make sure a disabled enemy stayed disabled, but I knew I could never have kicked at a howling dog as I did at that man. But fighting these Forged ones was like fighting ghosts: I felt no presence from any of them; I had no sense of the pain I'd dealt the injured man, no echoes of his anger or fear. It was like slamming a door, violence without a victim, as I cracked him again, to be sure he would not snatch at me as I leaped over him to a clear space in the road.

I danced my staff around me, keeping the others at bay. They looked ragged and hungry, but I still felt they could outrun me if I fled. I was already tired, and they were like starving wolves. They'd pursue me until I dropped. One reached too close and I struck him a glancing blow to the wrist. He dropped a rusty fish-knife and clutched his hand to his heart, shrieking over it. Again, the other two paid no attention to the injured one. I danced back.

'What do you want?' I demanded of them.

'What do you have,' one of them said. His voice was rusty and hesitant, as if long unused, and his words lacked any inflection. He moved slowly around me, in a wide circle that kept me turning. Dead men talking, I thought to myself, and couldn't stop the thought from echoing through my mind.

'Nothing,' I panted, jabbing to keep one from moving any closer. 'I don't have anything for you. No money, no food, nothing. I lost all my things, back down the road.'

'Nothing,' said the other, and for the first time I realized she had been a woman, once. Now she was this empty malevolent puppet, whose dull eyes suddenly lit with avarice as she said, 'Cloak. I want your cloak.'

She seemed pleased to have formulated this thought, and it made her careless enough to let me crack her on the shin. She glanced down at the injury as if puzzled, and then continued to limp after me.

'Cloak,' echoed the other. For a moment they glared at one another in dull realization of their rivalry. 'Me. Mine,' he added.

'No. Kill you,' she offered calmly. 'Kill you, too,' she reminded me, and came close again. I swung my staff at her, but she leaped back, and then made a snatch at it as it went by. I turned, just in time to whack the one whose wrist I had already damaged. Then I leaped past him and raced down the road. I ran awkwardly, holding onto my staff with one hand as I fought the fastening of my cloak with the other. At last it came undone and I let it fall from me as I continued to run. The rubberiness in my legs warned me that this was my last gambit. But a few moments later, they must have reached it, for I heard angry cries and screams as they quarrelled over it. I prayed it would be enough to occupy all four of them and kept running. There was a bend in the road, not much but enough to take me out of their sight. I continued to run and then trotted for as long as I could before daring to look back. The road shone wide and empty behind me. I pushed myself on, and when I saw a likely spot, I left the road.

I found a savagely nasty thicket of brambles and forced my way into the heart of it. Shaking and exhausted, I crouched down on my heels in the thick of the spiny bushes and strained my ears for any sound of pursuit. I took short sips from my water-skin, and tried to calm myself. I had no time for this delay; I had to get back to Buckkeep; but I dared not emerge.

It is still inconceivable to me that I fell asleep there, but I did.

I came awake gradually. Groggy, I felt sure I was recovering from a severe injury or long illness. My eyes were gummy, my mouth thick and sour. I forced my eyelids open and looked around me in bewilderment. The light was ebbing, and an overcast defeated the moon.

My exhaustion had been such that I had leaned over into the thorn bushes and slept despite a multitude of jabbing prickles. I extricated myself with much difficulty, leaving bits of cloth, hair and skin behind. I emerged from my hiding-place as cautiously as any hunted animal, not only questing as far as my sense would reach, but also snuffing the air and peering all about me. I knew that my questing would not reveal to me any Forged ones, and hoped that if any were nearby, the forest animals would have seen them and reacted. But all was quiet.

I cautiously emerged onto the road. It was wide and empty. I looked once at the sky, and then set out for Forge, staying close to the edge of the road, where the shadows of the trees were thickest. I tried to move both swiftly and silently, and did neither as well as I wanted. I had stopped thinking of anything except vigilance and my need to get back to Buckkeep. Smithy's life was the barest tendril in my mind. I think the only emotion still active in me was the fear that kept me looking over my shoulder and scanning the woods to either side as I walked.

It was full dark when I arrived on the hillside overlooking Forge. For some time I stood looking down on it, seeking for any signs of life, then I forced myself to walk on. The wind had come up, and fitfully granted me moonlight. It was a treacherous boon, as much deceiver as revealer. It made shadows move at the corners of abandoned houses, and cast sudden reflections that glinted like knives from puddles in the street. But no one walked in Forge. The normal inhabitants had abandoned it not long after that fateful raid, and evidently the Forged ones had as well, once there were no more sources of food or comfort there. The town had never really rebuilt itself after the raid, and a long season of winter storms and tides had nearly completed what the Red Ships had begun. Only the harbour looked almost normal, save for the empty slips. The sea-walls still curved out into the bay like protective hands cupping the docks. But there was nothing left to protect.

I threaded my way through the desolation that was Forge. My skin prickled as I crept past sagging doors on splintered frames in half-burnt buildings. It was a relief to get away from the mouldy smell of the empty cottages and to stand on the wharves overlooking the water. The road went right down to the docks and curved along the cove. A shoulder of roughly-worked stone had once protected the road from the greedy sea, but a winter of tides and storms without the intervention of man was breaking it down. Stones were working loose, and the sea's driftwood battering rams, abandoned now by the tide, cluttered the beach below. Once carts of iron ingots had been hauled down this road to waiting vessels. I walked along the sea-wall, and saw that what had appeared so permanent from the hill above would withstand perhaps one or two more winter seasons without maintenance before the sea reclaimed it.

Overhead, stars shone intermittently through scudding clouds. The evasive moon cloaked and revealed herself as well, occasionally granting me glimpses of the harbour. The shushing of the waves was like the breathing of a drugged giant. It was a night from a dream, and when I looked out over the water, the ghost of a Red Ship cut across the moonpath as it put into Forge harbour. Her hull was long and sleek, her masts bare of canvas as she came slipping into port. The red of her hull and prow was shiny as fresh-spilled blood, as if she cut through runnels of gore instead of saltwater. In the dead town behind me, no one raised a shout of warning.

I stood like a fool, limned on the sea-wall, shivering at the apparition, until the creak of oars and the silver of dripping water off an oar's edge made the Red Ship real.

I flung myself flat to the causeway, then slithered off the smooth road surface into the boulders and driftwood cluttered along the sea-wall. I could not breathe for terror. All my blood was in my head, pounding, and no air was in my lungs. I had to set my head down between my arms and close my eyes to regain control of myself. By then the small sounds even a stealthy vessel must make came faint but distinct across the water to me. A man cleared his throat, an oar rattled in its lock, something heavy thudded to the deck. I waited for a shout or command to betray that I had been seen. But there was nothing. I lifted my head cautiously, peering through the whitened roots of a driftwood log. All was still save the ship coming closer and closer as the rowers brought her into harbour. Her oars rose and fell in near-silent unison.

Soon I could hear them talking in a language like to ours, but so harshly spoken I could barely get the meaning of the words. A man sprang over the side with a line and floundered ashore. He made the ship fast no more than two shiplengths away from where I lay hidden among the boulders and logs. Two others sprang out, knives in hands, and scrambled up the sea-wall. They ran along the road in opposite directions, to take up positions as sentries. One was on the road almost directly above me. I made myself small and still. I held onto Smithy in my mind the way a child grips a beloved toy as protection against nightmares. I had to get home to him, therefore I must not be discovered. The knowledge that I must do the first somehow made the second seem more possible.

Men scrabbled hastily from the ship. Everything about them

bespoke familiarity. I could not fathom why they had put in here until I saw them unloading empty water casks. The casks were sent hollowly rolling down the causeway, and I remembered the well I had passed. The part of my mind that belonged to Chade noted how well they knew Forge, to put in almost exactly opposite that well. This was not the first time this ship had stopped here for water. 'Poison the well before you leave,' that corner of my mind suggested. But I had no supplies for anything like that, and no courage to do anything except remain hidden.

Others had emerged from the ship and were stretching their legs. I overheard an argument between a woman and a man. He wished permission to light a fire with some of the driftwood, to roast some meat. She forbade it, saying they had not come far enough, and that a fire would be too visible. So they had raided recently, to have fresh meat, and not too far from here. She gave permission for something else that I did not quite understand, until I saw them unload two full kegs. Another man came ashore with a whole ham on his shoulder, which he dropped with a meaty slap onto one of the upright kegs. He drew a knife and began to carve off chunks of it while another man broached the other keg. They would not be leaving for some time. And if they did light a fire, or stay until dawn, my log's shadow would be no hiding-place at all. I had to get out of there.

Through nests of sandfleas and squiggling piles of seaweed, under and between logs and stones, I dragged my belly through sand and pebbled gravel. I swear that every root snag caught at me, and every shifted slab of stone blocked my way. The tide had changed. The waves broke noisily against the rocks, and the flying spray rode the wind. I was soon soaked. I tried to time my movement with the sound of the breaking waves, to hide my small sounds in theirs. The rocks were toothed with barnacles, and sand packed the gouges they made in my hands and knees. My staff became an incredible burden, but I would not abandon my only weapon. Long after I could no longer see or hear the raiders, I dared not stand, but crept and huddled still from stone to log. At last I ventured up onto the road and crawled across it. Once in the shadow of a sagging warehouse, I stood, hugging the wall, and peered about me.

All was silent. I dared to step out two paces onto the road, but even there I could see nothing of the ship or the sentries. Perhaps that meant they could not see me either. I took a calming breath. I quested after Smithy the way some men pat their pouches to be sure their coin is safe. I found him but faint and quiet, his mind like a still pool. 'I'm coming,' I breathed, fearful of stirring him to an effort. And I set forth again.

The wind was relentless, and my salt-wet clothing clung and chafed. I was hungry, cold, and tired. My wet shoes were a misery, but I had no thought of stopping. I trotted like a wolf, my eyes continually shifting, my ears keen for any sound behind me. One moment, the road was empty and black before me. In the next, the darkness had turned to men. Two before me, and when I spun about, another behind me. The slapping waves had covered the sound of their feet, and the dodging moon offered me only glimpses of them as they closed the distance around me. I set my back to the solid wall of a warehouse, readied my staff, and waited.

I watched them come, silent and skulking. I wondered at that, for why did they not raise a shout, why did not the whole crew come to watch me taken? But these men watched one another as much as they watched me. They did not hunt as a pack, but each hoped the others would die killing me and leave the bounty for the picking. Forged ones, not raiders.

A terrible coldness welled up in me. The least sound of a scuffle would bring the raiders, I was sure. So if the Forged ones did not finish me, the raiders would. However, when all roads lead to death, there is no point in running down any of them. I would take things as they came. There were three of them. One had a knife. But I had a staff, and was trained to use it. They were thin, ragged, at least as hungry as I, and as cold. One, I think, was the woman from the night before. As they closed on me, so silently, I guessed they were aware of the raiders and feared them as much as I. It was not good to consider the desperation that would prompt them still to attack me. Then in the next breath, I wondered if Forged ones felt desperation or anything else. Perhaps they were too dulled to realize the danger.

All of the stealthy arcane knowledge Chade had given me, all of Hod's brutally elegant strategies for fighting two or more opponents, went to the wind. For as the first two stepped into my range, I felt the tiny warmth that was Smithy ebbing in my grasp. 'Smithy!' I whispered, a desperate plea that he somehow stay with me. I all but saw a tail tip stir in a last effort at a wag. Then the thread snapped and the spark blinked out. I was alone.

A black flood of strength surged through me like a madness. I stepped out, thrust the end of my staff deep into a man's face, drew it quickly back, and continued a swing that went through the woman's lower jaw. Plain wood sheared the lower half of her face away, so forceful was my blow. I whacked her again as she fell, and it was like hitting a netted shark with a fish-bat. The third drove into me solidly, thinking, I suppose, to be inside my staff's range. I didn't care. I dropped my stick and grappled with him. He was bony and he stank. I drove him onto his back, and his expelled breath in my face stank of carrion. Fingers and teeth, I tore at him, as far from human as he was. They had kept me from Smithy as he was dying. I did not care what I did to him so long as it hurt him. He reciprocated. I dragged his face along the cobbles, I pushed my thumb into an eye. He sank his teeth into my wrist, and clawed my cheek bloody. And when at last he ceased to fight against my strangling grip, I dragged him to the sea-wall and threw his body down onto the rocks.

I stood panting, my fists still clenched. I glared toward the raiders, daring them to come, but the night was still, save for the waves and wind and the soft gargling of the woman as she died. Either the raiders had not heard, or they were too concerned with their own stealth to investigate sounds in the night. I waited in the wind for someone to care enough to come and kill me. Nothing stirred. An emptiness washed through me, supplanting my madness. So much death in one night, and so little significance save to me.

I left the other broken bodies on top of the crumbling sea-wall for the waves and the gulls to dispose of. I walked away from them. I had felt nothing from them when I killed them. No fear, no anger, no pain, not even despair. They had been things. And as I began my long walk back to Buckkeep, I finally felt nothing from within myself. Perhaps, I thought, Forging is a contagion and I have caught it now. I could not bring myself to care.

Little of that journey stands out in my mind now. I walked all the way, cold, tired and hungry. I encountered no more Forged ones, and the few other travellers I saw on that stretch of road were no more anxious than I to speak to a stranger. I thought only of getting back to Buckkeep. And Burrich. I reached Buckkeep two days into the Springfest celebration. The guards at the gate tried to stop me at first. I looked at them.

'It's the fitz,' one gasped. 'It was said you were dead.'

'Shut up,' barked the other. He was Gage, long known to me, and he said quickly, 'Burrich's been hurt. He's up at the infirmary, boy.'

I nodded and walked past them.

In all my years at Buckkeep, I had never been to the infirmary. Burrich and no one else had always treated my childhood illnesses and mishaps. But I knew where it was. I walked unseeing through the knots and gatherings of merrymakers, and suddenly felt as if I were six years old and come to Buckkeep for the very first time. I had hung onto Burrich's belt. All that long way from Moonseye, with his leg torn and bandaged. But not once had he put me on another's horse, or entrusted my care to another. I pushed myself through the people with their bells and flowers and sweet cakes to reach the inner keep. Behind the barracks was a separate building of whitewashed stone. There was no one there, and I walked unchallenged through the antechamber and into the room beyond.

There were clean strewing-reeds on the floor, and the wide windows let in a flood of spring air and light, but the room still gave me a sense of confinement and illness. This was not a good place for Burrich to be. All the beds were empty, save one. No soldier kept to bed in Springfest days, save that they had to. Burrich lay, eyes closed, in a splash of sunlight on a narrow cot. I had never seen him so still. He had pushed his blankets aside and his chest was swathed in bandages. I went forward quietly and sat down on the floor beside his bed. He was very still, but I could feel him, and the bandages moved with his slow breathing. I took his hand.

'Fitz,' he said, without opening his eyes. He gripped my hand hard.

'Yes.'

'You're back. You're alive.'

'I am. I came straight here, as fast as I could. Oh, Burrich, I feared you were dead.'

'I thought *you* were dead. The others all came back days ago.' He took a ragged breath. 'Of course, the bastard left horses with all the others.'

'No,' I reminded him, not letting go of his hand. 'I'm the bastard, remember?'

'Sorry.' He opened his eyes. The white of his left eye was mazed with blood. He tried to smile at me. I could see then that the swelling on the left side of his face was still subsiding. 'So. We look a fine pair. You should poultice that cheek. It's festering. Looks like an animal scratch.'

'Forged ones,' I began, and could not bear to explain more. I only said, softly, 'He set me down north of Forge, Burrich.'

Anger spasmed his face. 'He wouldn't tell me. Nor anyone else. I even sent a man to Verity, to ask my prince to make him say what he had done with you. I got no answer back. I should kill him.'

'Let it go,' I said, and meant it. 'I'm back and alive. I failed his test, but it didn't kill me. And as you told me, there are other things in my life.'

Burrich shifted slightly in his bed. I could tell it didn't ease him. 'Well. He'll be disappointed over that.' He let out a shuddering breath. 'I got jumped. Someone with a knife. I don't know who.'

'How bad?'

'Not good, at my age. A young buck like you would probably just give a shake and go on. Still, he only got the blade into me once. But I fell, and struck my head. I was fair senseless for two days. And, Fitz. Your dog. A stupid, senseless thing, but he killed your dog.'

'I know.'

'He died quickly,' Burrich said, as if to be a comfort.

I stiffened at the lie. 'He died well,' I corrected him. 'And if he hadn't, you'd have had that knife in you more than once.'

Burrich grew very still. 'You were there, weren't you,' he said at last. It was not a question, and there was no mistaking his meaning.

'Yes,' I heard myself saying, simply.

'You were there, with the dog that night, instead of trying for the Skill?' His voice rose in outrage.

'Burrich, it wasn't like . . .'

He pulled his hand free of mine and turned as far away from me as he could. 'Leave me.'

'Burrich, it wasn't Smithy. I just don't have the Skill. So let me have what I do have, let me be what I am. I don't use this in a bad way. Even without it, I'm good with animals. You've forced me to be. If I use it, I can . . .'

'Stay out of my stables. And stay away from me.' He rolled back to face me, and to my amazement, a single tear tracked his dark cheek. 'You failed? No, Fitz. I failed. I was too soft-hearted to beat it out of you at the first sign of it. "Raise him well," Chivalry said to me. His last command to me. And I failed him. And you. If you hadn't meddled with the Wit, Fitz, you'd have been able to learn the Skill. Galen would have been able to teach you. No wonder he sent you to Forge.' He paused. 'Bastard or no, you could have been a fit son to Chivalry. But you threw it all away. For what? A dog. I know what a dog can be to a man, but you don't throw your life over for a . . .'

'Not just a dog,' I cut in almost harshly. 'Smithy. My friend. And it wasn't only him. I gave up the wait and came back for you. Thinking you might need me. Smithy died days ago. I knew that. But I came back for you, thinking you might need me.'

He was silent so long I thought he wasn't going to speak to me. 'You needn't have,' he said quietly. 'I take care of myself.' And harsher, 'You know that. I always have.'

'And me,' I admitted to him. 'And you've always taken care of me.'

'And small damn good that did either of us,' he said slowly. 'Look what I've let you become. Now you're just . . . Go away. Just go away.' He turned away from me again, and I felt something go out of the man.

I stood slowly. 'I'll make you a wash from helena leaves for your eye. I'll bring it this afternoon.'

'Bring me nothing. Do me no favours. Go your own way, and be whatever you will. I'm done with you.' He spoke to the wall. In his voice was no mercy for either of us.

I glanced back as I left the infirmary. He had not moved, but even his back looked older, and smaller.

That was my return to Buckkeep. I was a different creature from the naïf who had left. Little fanfare was made over my not being dead as supposed. I made no opportunity for anyone to do so. From Burrich's bed, I went straight to my room. I washed and changed my garments. I slept, but not well. For the rest of Springfest, I ate at night, alone in the kitchens. I penned one note to King Shrewd, suggesting that raiders might regularly be using the wells at Forge. He made no reply to me about it, and I was glad of it. I sought no contact with anyone.

With much pomp and ceremony, Galen presented his finished coterie to the King. One other besides myself had failed to return. It shames me now that I cannot recall his name, and if I ever knew what became of him, I have forgotten it. Like Galen, I suppose I dismissed him as insignificant.

Galen spoke to me only once the rest of that summer, and that was indirectly. We passed one another in the courtyard, not long after Springfest. He was walking and talking with Regal. As they passed me, he looked at me over Regal's head and said sneeringly, 'More lives than a cat.'

I stopped and stared at them until both were forced to look at me. I made Galen meet my eyes; then I smiled and nodded. I never confronted Galen about his attempt to send me to my death. He never appeared to see me after that; his eyes would slide past me, or he would exit a room when I entered it.

It seemed to me that I had lost everything when I lost Smithy. Or perhaps in my bitterness I set out to destroy what little was left to me. I sulked about the keep for weeks, cleverly insulting anyone foolish enough to speak to me. The Fool avoided me. Chade didn't summon me. I saw Patience thrice. The first two times I went to answer her summons, I made only the barest efforts to be civil. The third time, bored by her chatter about rose cuttings, I simply stood up and left. She did not summon me again.

But there came a time when I felt I had to reach out to someone. Smithy had left a great gap in my life. And I had not expected that my exile from the stables would be as devastating as it was.

Chance encounters with Burrich were incredibly awkward as we both learned painfully to pretend not to see each other.

I wanted, achingly, to go to Molly, to tell her everything that had befallen me, all that had happened to me since I first came to Buckkeep. I imagined in detail how we could sit on the beach while I talked, and that when I had finished, she would not judge me or try to offer advice, but would just take my hand and be still beside me. Finally, she would know everything, and I would not have to hide anything from her any more. I dared imagine no more beyond that. I longed desperately, and feared with the fear known only to a boy whose love is two years older than he is. If I took her all my woes, would she think me a hapless child and pity me? Would she hate me for all that I had never told her before? A dozen times that thought turned my feet away from Buckkeep Town.

But some two months later, when I did venture into town, my traitorous feet took me to the chandlery. I happened to have a basket with me, and a bottle of cherry wine in it, and four or five brambly little yellow roses, obtained at great loss of skin from the Women's Garden where their fragrance overpowered even the thyme beds. I told myself I had no plan. I did not have to tell her everything about myself. I did not even have to see her. I could decide as I went along. But in the end all decisions had already been made, and they had nothing to do with me.

I arrived just in time to see Molly leaving with Jade. Their heads were close together, and she leaned toward him as they spoke in soft voices. Outside the door of the chandlery, he stooped to look into her face. She lifted her eyes to his. When the man reached a hesitant hand to gently touch her cheek, Molly was suddenly a woman, one I did not know. The two years' age difference between us was a vast gulf I could never hope to bridge. I stepped around the corner before she could see me, and turned aside, my face down. They passed me as if I were a tree or a stone. Her head leaned on his shoulder, and they walked slowly. It took forever for them to be out of sight.

That night I got drunker than I had ever been, and awoke the next day in some bushes halfway up the keep road.

EIGHTEEN

Assassinations

Chade Fallstar, a personal adviser to King Shrewd, made an extensive study of Forging during the period just preceding the Red Ship wars. From his tablets, we have the following: 'Netta, the daughter of the fisherman Gill and the farmer Ryda, was taken alive from her village Goodwater on the seventeenth day after Springfest. She was Forged by the Red Ship Raiders and returned to her village three days later. Her father was killed in the same raid, and her mother, having five younger children, was little able to deal with Netta. She was, at the time of her Forging, fourteen summers old. She came into my possession some six months after her Forging.

'When first brought to me, she was dirty, ragged and greatly weakened owing to starvation and exposure. At my direction, she was washed, clothed and housed in chambers convenient to my own. I proceeded with her as I might have done with a wild animal. Each day I brought her food with my own hands, and stayed by her while she ate. I saw to it that her chambers were kept warm, her bedding clean, and that she was provided with the amenities a woman might expect; water for washing, brushes and combs, and all that is otherwise needful. In addition, I saw to it that she was furnished with sundry supplies for needlework, for I had discovered that prior to Forging, she had had a great fondness for doing such fancywork, and had created several artful pieces. My intention in all this was to see if, under gentle circumstances, a Forged one might not return to a semblance of the person she had formerly been.

'Even a wild animal might have become a little tamer under these

circumstances. But to all things Netta reacted with indifference. She had lost not only the habits of a woman, but even the good sense of an animal. She would eat to satiation, with her hands, and then let fall to the floor whatever was excess, to be trodden underfoot. She did not wash, nor care for herself in any way. Even most animals soil only one area of their dens, but Netta was like a mouse that lets her droppings fall everywhere, with no care for bedding.

'She was able to speak, in a sensible way, if she chose to or wanted some item badly enough. When she spoke by her own choice, it was usually to accuse me of stealing from her, or to utter threats against me if I did not immediately give her some item she wanted. Her habitual attitude toward me was suspicious and hateful. She ignored my attempts at normal conversation, but by withholding food from her, I was able to elicit answers in exchange for food. She had clear memory of her family, but had no interest in what had become of them. Rather, she answered those questions as if answering questions about yesterday's weather. Of her Forging time, she said only that they had been held in the belly of a ship, and that there had been little food and only enough water to go around. She had been fed nothing unusual that she recalled, nor had she been touched in any way that she remembered. Thus she could furnish to me no clue as to the mechanism of Forging itself. This was a great disappointment to me, for I had hoped that by learning how a thing was done, a man could discover how to undo it.

'I endeavoured to bring human behaviour back to her by reasoning with her, but to no avail. She appeared to understand my words, but would not act on them. Even when given two loaves of bread, and warned that she must save one for the morrow or go hungry, she would let her second loaf fall to the floor, tread upon it, and on the morrow eat her own dropped leavings careless of what dirt clung to them. She evinced no interest in her needlework or in any other pastime, not even the bright toys of a child. If not eating or sleeping, she was content merely to sit or lie, her mind as idle as her body. Offered sweets or pastries, she would indulge until she vomited, and then eat more.

'I treated her with sundry elixirs and herbal teas. I fasted her, I steamed her, I purged her body. Hot and cold dousings had no effect other than to make her angry. I caused her to sleep a full day and a night, to no change. I so charged her with elfbark that she could not sleep for two nights, but this only made her irritable. I spoiled her with *kindnesses for a time, but as when I treated her with the harshest restrictions, it made no difference in how she regarded me. If hungry, she would make courtesies and smile pleasantly when commanded to, but as soon as food was furnished, all further commands and requests were ignored.*

'She was viciously jealous of territory and possessions. More than once she attempted to attack me, for no more reason than that I had ventured too close to food she was eating, and once because she suddenly decided she wished to have a ring I was wearing. She regularly killed the mice her untidiness attracted, snatching them up with amazing swiftness and dashing them against the wall. A cat that once ventured into her chambers met with a similar fate.

'She seemed to have little sense of the time that had passed since her Forging. She could give good account of her earlier life, if commanded when hungry, but of the days since her Forging, all was as one long "yesterday" to her.

'From Netta, I could not learn if something had been added to her or taken away to Forge her. I did not know if it was a thing consumed or smelled or heard or seen. I did not know if it was even the work of a man's hand and art, or the work of a sea-demon such as some Farlanders claim to have power upon. From a long and weary experiment, I learned nothing.

'To Netta I gave a triple sleeping-draught one evening with her water. I had her body bathed, her hair groomed, and sent her back to her village to be decently buried. At least one family could put finis to a tale of Forging. Most others must wonder, for months and years, what has become of the one they once held dear. Most are better off not knowing.'

There were, at that time, over one thousand souls known to have been Forged.

Burrich had meant what he said. He had nothing more to do with me. I was no longer welcome down at the stables and kennels. Cob especially took savage pleasure in this. Although he was often gone with Regal, when he was about the stables he would often step to block my entry. 'Allow me to bring you your horse, Master,' he would say obsequiously. 'The stablemaster prefers that grooms handle animals within the stables.' And so I must stand, like some incompetent lordling, while Sooty was saddled and brought for me. Cob himself mucked out her stall, brought her feed and groomed her, and it ate at me like acid to see how quickly she welcomed him back. She was only a horse, I told myself, and not to be blamed. But it was one more abandonment.

I had too much time, suddenly. Mornings had always been spent working for Burrich. Now they were mine. Hod was busy training green men for defence. I was welcome to drill with them, but it was all lessons I had learned long ago. Fedwren was gone for the summer, as he was every summer. I could not think of a way to apologize to Patience, and I did not even think about Molly. Even my forays to the taverns in Buckkeep had become solitary ones. Kerry had apprenticed to a puppeteer, and Dirk gone for a sailor. I was idle and alone.

It was a summer of misery, and not just for me. While I was lonely and bitter and out-growing all my clothes, while I snapped and snarled at any foolish enough to speak to me, and drank myself insensible several times a week, I was still aware of how the Six Duchies were racked. The Red Ship Raiders, bolder than ever before, harried our coastline. This summer, in addition to threats, they finally began to make demands. Grain, cattle, the right to take whatever they wished from our seaports, the right to beach their boats and live off our lands and people for the summer, their choice of our folk for slaves . . . each demand was more intolerable than the last, and the only things more intolerable than the demands were the Forgings that followed each refusal by the King.

Common folk were abandoning the seaport and waterfront towns. One could not blame them, but it left our coastline even more vulnerable. More soldiers were hired, and more, and so the levies were raised to pay them, and folk grumbled under the burden of the taxes and their fear of the Red Ship Raiders. Even stranger were the Outislanders who came to our shore in their family ships, their raiding vessels left behind, to beg asylum of our people, and to tell wild tales of chaos and tyranny in the Out Islands where the Red Ships now ruled completely. They were a mixed blessing, perhaps. They were cheaply hired as soldiers, though few really trusted them. But at least their tales of the Out Islands under Red Ship domination were harrowing enough to keep anyone from thinking of giving in to the Raiders' demands.

About a month after my return, Chade opened his door to me. I was sullen over his neglect of me, and went more slowly up his stairs than ever I had before. But when I got there, he looked up from crushing seeds with a pestle with a face full of weariness. 'I am glad to see you,' he said, with nothing of gladness in his voice.

'That's why you were so swift to welcome me back,' I observed sourly.

He stopped his grinding. 'I'm sorry. I thought perhaps you would need time alone, to recover yourself.' He looked back to his seeds. 'It has not been an easy winter and spring for me, either. Shall we try to put the time behind us, and go on?'

It was a gentle, reasonable suggestion. I knew it was wise.

'Have I any choice?' I asked sarcastically.

Chade finished grinding his seed. He scraped it into a finely-woven sieve and put it over a cup to drip. 'No,' he said at last, as if he had considered it well. 'No, you haven't, and neither have I. In many things, we have no choice.' He looked at me, his eyes running up and down me, and then poked at his seed again. 'You,' he said, 'will stop drinking anything but water or tea for the rest of the summer. Your sweat stinks of wine. And for one so young, your muscles are lax. A winter of Galen's meditations has done your body no good at all. See that you exercise it. Take it upon yourself, as of today, to climb to Verity's tower four times a day. You will take him food, and the teas I will show you how to prepare. You will never show him a sullen face, but will always be cheerful and friendly. Perhaps a while of waiting on Verity will convince you that I have had reasons for my attention not being centred on you. That is what you will do each day you are at Buckkeep. There will be some days when you will be fulfilling other assignments for me.'

It had not taken many words from Chade to awaken shame in myself. My perception of my life crashed from high tragedy to juvenile self-pity in a matter of moments. 'I have been idle,' I admitted.

'You have been stupid,' Chade agreed. 'You had a month in

which to take charge of your own life. You behaved like . . . a spoiled brat. I have no wonder that Burrich is disgusted with you.'

I had long ago stopped being surprised at what Chade knew. But this time, I was sure he did not know the real reason, and I had no desire to share it with him.

'Have you discovered yet who tried to kill him?'

'I haven't . . . tried, really.'

Now Chade looked disgusted, and then puzzled. 'Boy, you are not yourself at all. Six months ago you would have torn the stables apart to know such a secret. Six months ago, given a month's holiday, you would have filled each day. What troubles you?'

I looked down, feeling the truth of his words. I wanted to tell him everything that had befallen me; I wanted not to say a word of it to anyone. 'I'll tell you all I do know of the attack on Burrich.' And I did.

'And the one who saw all this,' he asked when I had finished. 'Did he know the man who attacked Burrich?'

'He didn't get a good look at him,' I hedged. Useless to tell Chade that I knew exactly how he smelled, but had only a vague visual image.

Chade was quiet for a moment. 'Well, as much as you can, keep an ear to the earth. I should like to know who has grown so brave as to try to kill the King's stablemaster in his own stable.'

'Then you do not think it was just some personal quarrel of Burrich's?' I asked carefully.

'Perhaps it was. But we will not jump to conclusions. To me, it has the feel of a gambit. Someone is building up to something, but has missed their first block. To our advantage, I hope.'

'Can you tell me why you think so?'

'I could, but I will not. I want to leave your mind free to find its own assumptions, independent of mine. Now come. I will show you the teas.'

I was more than a bit hurt that he asked me nothing about my time with Galen or my test. He seemed to accept my failure as a thing expected. But as he showed me the ingredients he had chosen for Verity's teas, I was horrified by the strength of the stimulants he was using.

I had seen little of Verity, though Regal had been in only too much evidence. He had spent the last month coming and going, always just returning, or just leaving, and each cavalcade seemed richer and more ornate than the one before. It seemed to me that he was using the excuse of his brother's courting to feather himself more brightly than any peacock. Common opinion was that he must go so, to impress those with whom he negotiated. For myself, I saw it as a waste of coin that could have gone on defences. When Regal was gone, I felt relief, for his antagonism toward me had taken a recent bound, and he had found sundry small ways to express it.

The brief times when I had seen Verity or the King, they had both looked harassed and worn. But Verity especially had seemed almost stunned. Impassive and distracted, he had noticed me only once, and then smiled wearily and said I had grown. That had been the extent of our conversation. But I had noticed that he ate like an invalid, without appetite, eschewing meat and bread as if they were too great an effort to chew and swallow, instead subsisting on porridges and soups.

'He is using the Skill too much. That much Shrewd has told me. But why it should drain him so, why it should burn the very flesh from his bones, he cannot explain to me. So I give him tonics and elixirs, and try to get him to rest. But he cannot. He dares not, he says. He tells me that all his efforts are necessary to delude the Red Ship navigators, to send their ships onto the rocks, to discourage their captains. And so he rises from bed, and goes to his chair by a window, and there he sits, all the day.'

'And Galen's coterie? Are they of no use to him?' I asked the question almost jealously, almost hoping to hear they were of no consequence.

Chade sighed. 'I think he uses them as I would use carrier-pigeons. He has sent them out to the towers, and he uses them to convey warnings to his soldiers, and to receive from them sightings of ships. But the task of defending the coast he trusts to no one else. Others, he tells me, would be too inexperienced; they might betray themselves to those they Skilled. I do not understand. But I know he cannot continue much longer. I pray for the end of summer, for winter storms to blow the Red Ships home. Would there were someone to spell him at this work. I fear it will consume him.'

I took that as a rebuke for my failure and subsided into a sulky silence. I drifted around his chambers, finding them both familiar and strange after my months of absence. The apparatus for his herbal work was, as always, cluttered about. Slink was very much in evidence, with his smelly bits of bones in corners. As always, there was an assortment of tablets and scrolls by various chairs. This crop seemed to deal mostly with Elderlings. I wandered about, intrigued by the coloured illustrations. One tablet, older and more elaborate than the rest, depicted an Elderling as a sort of gilded bird with a man-like head crowned with quillish hair. I began to piece out the words. It was in Piche, an ancient native tongue of Chalced, the southernmost duchy. Many of the painted symbols had faded, or flaked away from the old wood, and I had never been fluent in Piche. Chade came to stand at my elbow.

'You know,' he said gently. 'It was not easy for me, but I kept my word. Galen demanded complete control of his students. He expressly stipulated that no one might contact you or interfere in any way with your discipline and instruction. And, as I told you, in the Queen's Garden, I am blind and without influence.'

'I knew that,' I muttered.

'Yet I did not disagree with Burrich's actions. Only my word to my king kept me from contacting you.' He paused cautiously. 'It has been a difficult time, I know. I wish I could have helped you. And you should not feel too badly that you—'

'Failed.' I filled in the word while he searched for a gentler one. I sighed, and suddenly admitted my pain. 'Let's leave it, Chade. I can't change it.'

'I know.' Then, even more carefully, 'But perhaps we can use what you learned of the Skill. If you can help me understand it, perhaps I can devise better ways to spare Verity. For so many years, the knowledge has been kept too secret . . . there is scarcely a mention of it in the old scrolls, save to say that such and such a battle was turned by the King's Skill upon his soldiers, or such and such an enemy was confounded by the King's Skill. Yet there is nothing of how it is done, or . . .'

Despair closed its grip on me again. 'Leave it. It is not for bastards to know. I think I've proved that.'

A silence fell between us. At last Chade sighed heavily. 'Well. That's as may be. I've been looking into Forging as well, over these last few months. But all I've learned of it is what it is not, and what does not work to change it. The only cure I've found for it is the oldest one known to work on anything.'

I rolled and fastened the scroll I had been looking at, feeling I knew what was coming. I was not mistaken.

'The King has charged me with an assignment for you.'

That summer, over three months, I killed seventeen times for the King. Had I not already killed, out of my own volition and defence, it might have been harder.

The assignments might have seemed simple. Me, a horse, and panniers of poisoned bread. I rode roads where travellers had reported being attacked, and when the Forged ones attacked me, I fled, leaving a trail of spilled loaves. Perhaps if I had been an ordinary man-at-arms, I would have been less frightened. But all my life I had been accustomed to relying on my Wit to let me know when others were about. To me, it was tantamount to having to work without using my eyes. And I swiftly found out that not all Forged ones had been cobblers and weavers. The second little clan of them that I poisoned had several soldiers among them. I was fortunate that most of them were squabbling over loaves when I was dragged from my horse. I took a deep cut from a knife, and to this day I bear the scar on my left shoulder. They were strong and competent, and seemed to fight as a unit, perhaps because that was how they had been drilled, back when they were fully human. I would have died, except that I cried out to them that it was foolish to struggle with me while the others were eating all the bread. They dropped me, I struggled to my horse, and escaped.

The poisons were no crueller than they had to be, but to be effective even in the smallest dosage, we had to use harsh ones. The Forged ones did not die gently, but it was as swift a death as Chade could concoct. They snatched their deaths from me eagerly, and I did not have to witness their frothing convulsions, or even see their bodies by the road. When news of the fallen

Forged ones reached Buckkeep, Chade's tale that they had probably died from eating spoiled fish from spawning streams had already spread as a ubiquitous rumour. Relatives collected the bodies and gave them proper burial. I told myself that they were probably relieved, and that the Forged ones had met a quicker end than if they had starved to death over winter. And so I became accustomed to killing, and had nearly a score of deaths to my credit before I had to meet the eyes of a man, and then kill him.

That one, too, was not so difficult as it might have been. He was a minor lordling, holding lands outside Turlake. A story reached Buckkeep that he had, in a temper, struck the child of a servant, and left the girl a witling. That was sufficient to raise King Shrewd's lip. But the lordling had paid the full blood-debt, and by accepting it the servant had given up any form of the King's justice. But some months later there came to court a cousin of the girl's, and she petitioned for private audience with Shrewd.

I was sent to confirm her tale, and saw how the girl was kept like a dog at the foot of the lordling's chair, and more, how her belly had begun to swell with child. And so it was not too difficult, as he offered me wine in fine crystal and begged the latest news of the King's Court at Buckkeep, for me to find a time to lift his glass to the light and praise the quality of both vessel and wine. I left some days later, my errand completed, with the samples of paper I had promised Fedwren, and the conveyed wishes of the lordling for a good trip home. The lordling was indisposed that day. He died, in blood and madness and froth, a month or so later. The cousin took in both girl and child. To this day, I have no regrets, for the deed or for the choice of slow death for him.

And when I was not dealing death to Forged ones, I waited on my lord Prince Verity. I remember the first time I climbed all those stairs to his tower, balancing a tray as I went. I had expected a guard or sentry at the top. There was none. I tapped at the door, and receiving no answer, entered quietly. Verity was sitting in a chair by a window. A summer wind off the ocean blew into the room. It could have been a pleasant chamber, full of light and air on a stuffy summer day. Instead it seemed to me a cell. There was the chair by the window, and a small table next to it.

In the corners and around the edges of the room the floor was dusty and littered with bits of old strewing-reeds. And Verity, chin slumped to his chest as if dozing, except that to my senses the room thrummed with his effort. His hair was unkempt, his chin bewhiskered with a day's growth. His clothing hung on him.

I pushed the door shut with my foot and took the tray to the table. I set it down and stood beside it, quietly waiting. And in a few minutes he came back from wherever he had been. He looked up at me with a ghost of his old smile, and then down at his tray. 'What's this?'

'Breakfast, sir. Everyone else ate hours ago, save yourself.'

'I ate, boy. Early this morning. Some awful fish soup. The cooks should be hung for that. No one should face fish first thing in the morning.' He seemed uncertain, like some doddering gaffer trying to recall the days of his youth.

'That was yesterday, sir.' I uncovered the plates. Warm bread swirled with honey and raisins, cold meats, a dish of strawberries and a small pot of cream for them. All were small portions, almost a child's serving. I poured the steaming tea into a waiting mug. It was flavoured heavily with ginger and peppermint, to cover the ground elfbark's tang.

Verity glanced at it, and then up to me. 'Chade never relents, does he?' Spoken so casually, as if Chade's name were mentioned everyday about the keep.

'You need to eat, if you are to continue,' I said neutrally.

'I suppose so,' he said wearily, and turned to the tray as if the artfully-arranged food were yet another duty to attend to. He ate with no relish for the food, and drank the tea in a manful draught, as a medicine, undeceived by ginger or mint. Halfway through the meal he paused with a sigh, and gazed out of the window for a bit. Then, seeming to come back again, he forced himself to consume each item completely. He pushed the tray aside, and leaned back in the chair as if exhausted. I stared. I had prepared the tea myself. That much elfbark would have had Sooty leaping over the stall walls.

'My prince?' I said, and when he did not stir, I touched his shoulder lightly. 'Verity? Are you all right?'

'Verity,' he repeated as in a daze. 'Yes. And I prefer that to "sir" or "my prince" or "my lord". This is my father's gambit, to send you. Well. I may surprise him yet. But, yes, call me Verity. And tell them I ate. Obedient as ever, I ate. Go on, now, boy. I have work to do.'

He seemed to rouse himself with an effort, and once more his gaze went afar. I stacked the dishes as quietly as I could onto the tray and headed toward the door. But as I lifted the latch, he spoke again.

'Boy?'

'Sir?'

'Ah-ah!' he warned me.

'Verity?'

'Leon is in my rooms, boy. Take him out for me, will you? He pines. There is no sense in the both of us shrivelling like this.'

'Yes, sir. Verity.'

And so the old hound, past his prime now, came to be in my care. Each day I took him from Verity's room, and we hunted the back hills and cliffs and the beaches for wolves that had not run there in a score of years. As Chade had suspected, I was badly out of condition, and at first it was all I could do to keep up even with the old hound. But as the days went by, we regained our tone, and Leon even caught a rabbit or two for me. Now that I was exiled from Burrich's domain, I did not scruple to use the Wit whenever I wished. But as I had discovered long ago, I could communicate with Leon, but there was no bond. He did not always heed me, nor even believe me all the time. Had he been but a pup, I am sure we could have bonded to one another. But he was old, and his heart given forever to Verity. The Wit was not dominion over beasts, but only a glimpse into their lives.

And thrice a day I climbed the steeply winding steps, to coax Verity to eat, and to a few words of conversation. Some days it was like speaking to a child or a doddering oldster. On others, he asked after Leon, and quizzed me about matters down in Buckkeep Town. Sometimes I was absent for days on my other assignments. Usually, he seemed not to have noticed, but once, after the foray in which I took my knife wound, he watched me awkwardly load his empty dishes onto the tray. 'How they must laugh in their beards, if they knew we slay our own.'

I froze, wondering what answer to make to that, for as far as I knew, my tasks were known only to Shrewd and Chade. But Verity's eyes had gone afar again, and I left silently.

Without intending to, I began to make changes around him. One day, while he was eating, I swept the room, and later that evening brought up a sackful of strewing-reeds and herbs. I had worried that I might be a distraction to him, but Chade had taught me to move quietly. I worked without speaking, and Verity acknowledged neither my coming nor going. But the room was freshened, and the ververia blossoms mixed in with the strewing herbs were an enlivening herb. Coming in once, I discovered him dozing in his hard-backed chair. I brought up cushions, which he ignored for several days, and then one day had arranged to his liking. The room remained bare, but I sensed he needed it so, to preserve his single-mindedness. So what I brought him were the barest items of comfort, no tapestries or wall hangings, no vases of flowers or tinkling wind chimes, but flowering thymes in pots to ease the headaches that plagued him, and on one stormy day, a blanket against the rain and chill from the open window.

On that day I found him sleeping in his chair, limp as a dead thing. I tucked the blanket around him as if he were an invalid, and set the tray before him, but left it covered, to keep the good heat in the food. I sat down on the floor next to his chair, propped against one of his discarded cushions, and listened to the silence of the room. It seemed almost peaceful today, despite the driving summer rain outside the open window, and the gale wind that gusted in from time to time. I must have dozed, for I woke to his hand on my hair.

'Do they tell you to watch over me so, boy, even when I sleep? What do they fear, then?'

'Naught that I know, Verity. They tell me only to bring you food, and see as best I can that you eat it. No more than that.'

'And blankets and cushions, and pots of sweet flowers?'

'My own doing, my prince. No man should live in such a desert as this.' And in that moment, I realized we were not speaking aloud, and sat bolt upright and looked at him.

Verity, too, seemed to come to himself. He shifted in his comfortless chair. 'I bless this storm, that lets me rest. I hid it from three of their ships, persuading those who looked to the sky that it was no more than a summer squall. Now they ply their oars and peer through the rain, trying to keep their courses. And I can snatch a few moments of honest sleep.' He paused. 'I ask your pardon, boy. Sometimes, now, the Skilling seems more natural than speaking. I did not mean to intrude on you.'

'No matter, my prince. I was but startled. I cannot Skill myself, except weakly and erratically. I do not know how I opened to you.'

'Verity, boy, not your prince. No one's prince sits still in a sweaty shirt, with two days of beard. But what is this nonsense? Surely it was arranged for you to learn the Skill? I remember well how Patience's tongue battered away my father's resolve.' He permitted himself a weary smile.

'Galen tried to teach me, but I had not the aptitude. With bastards, I am told it is often . . .'

'Wait,' he growled, and in an instant was within my mind. 'This is faster,' he offered, by way of apology, and then, muttering to himself, 'What is this, that clouds you so? Ah!' and was gone again from my mind, and all as deft and easy as Burrich taking a tick off a hound's ear. He sat long, quiet, and so did I, wondering.

'I am strong in it, as was your father. Galen is not.'

'Then how did he become Skillmaster?' I asked quietly. I wondered if Verity were saying this only to somehow make me feel my failure less.

Verity paused as if skirting a delicate subject. 'Galen was Queen Desire's . . . pet. A favourite. The Queen emphatically suggested Galen as apprentice to Solicity. Often I think our old Skillmaster was desperate when she took him as apprentice. Solicity knew she was dying, you see. I believe she acted in haste, and towards the end, regretted her decision. And I do not think he had half the training he should have had before becoming "master". But there he is; he is what we have.'

Verity cleared his throat and looked uncomfortable. 'I will speak as plainly as I can, boy, for I see that you know how to hold your tongue when it is wise. Galen was given that place as a plum, not because he merited it. I do not think he has ever fully grasped what it means to be the Skillmaster. Oh, he knows the position carries power, and he has not scrupled to wield it. But Solicity was more than someone who swaggered about secure in a high position. Solicity was advisor to Bounty, and a link between the King and all who Skilled for him. She made it her business to seek out and teach as many as manifested real talent and the judgement to use it well. This coterie is the first group Galen has trained since Chivalry and I were boys. And I do not find them well-taught. No, they are trained, as monkeys and parrots are taught to mimic men, with no understanding of what they do. But they are what I have.' Verity looked out of the window and spoke softly. 'Galen has no finesse. He is as coarse as his mother was, and just as presumptuous.' Verity paused suddenly, and his cheeks flushed as if he had said something ill-considered. He resumed more quietly. 'The Skill is like language, boy. I need not shout at you to let you know what I want. I can ask politely, or hint, or let you know my wish with a nod and a smile. I can Skill a man, and leave him thinking it was all his own idea to please me. But all that eludes Galen, both in the use of the Skill and the teaching of it. Privation and pain are one way to lower a man's defences; it is the only way Galen believes in. But Solicity used guile. She would have me watch a kite, or a bit of dust floating in a sunbeam, focusing on it as if there were nothing else in the world. And suddenly, there she would be, inside my mind with me, smiling and praising me. She taught me that being open was simply not being closed. And going into another's mind is mostly done by being willing to go outside of your own. Do you see, boy?'

'Somewhat,' I hedged.

'Somewhat,' he sighed. 'I could teach you to Skill, had I but the time. I do not. But tell me this: were your lessons going well, before he tested you?'

'No. I never had any aptitude . . . wait! That's not true! What am I saying, what have I been thinking?' Though I was sitting, I swayed suddenly, my head bounding off the arm of Verity's chair. He reached out a hand and steadied me.

'I was too swift, I suppose. Steady now, boy. Someone had misted you. Befuddled you, much as I do Red Ship navigators and steersmen. Convince them they've taken a sighting already and their course is true when really they are steering into a cross-current. Convince them they've passed a point they haven't sighted yet. Someone convinced you that you could not Skill.'

'Galen.' I spoke with certainty. I almost knew the moment. He had slammed into me that afternoon, and from that time, nothing had been the same. I had been living in a fog, all those months . . .

'Probably. Though if you Skilled into him at all, I'm sure you've seen what Chivalry did to him. He hated your father with a passion, prior to Chiv turning him into a lapdog. We felt badly about it. We'd have undone it, if we could have worked out how to do it, and escape Solicity's detection. But Chiv was strong with the Skill, and we were all but boys then, and Chiv was angry when he did it. Over something Galen had done to me, ironically. Even when Chivalry was not angry, being Skilled by him was like being trampled by a horse. Or ducked in a fast-flowing river, more like. He'd get in a hurry, barge into you, dump his information and flee.' He paused again, and reached to uncover a dish of soup on his tray. 'I suppose I've always assumed you knew all this. Though I'm damned if there's any way you could have. Who would have told you?'

I seized on one piece of information. 'You could teach me to Skill?'

'If I had time. A great deal of time. You're a lot like Chiv and I were, when we learned. Erratic. Strong, but with no idea of how to bring that strength to bear. And Galen has . . . well, scarred you, I suppose. You've walls I can't begin to penetrate, and I am strong. You'd have to learn to drop them. That's a hard thing. But I could teach you, yes. If you and I had a year, and nothing else to do.' He pushed the soup aside. 'But we don't.'

My hopes crashed again. This second wave of disappointment engulfed me, grinding me against stones of frustration. My memories all re-ordered themselves, and in a surge of anger, I knew all that had been done to me. Were it not for Smithy, I'd have dashed my life out at the base of the tower that night. Galen had tried to kill me, just as surely as if he'd had a knife. No one would even have known of how he'd beaten me, save his loyal coterie. And while he'd failed at that, he had taken from me the chance to learn Skilling. He'd crippled me, and I would . . . I leaped to my feet, furious.

'Whoa. Be slow and careful. You have a grievance, but we cannot have discord within the keep itself right now. Carry it with you until you can settle it quietly, for the King's sake.' I bowed my head to the wisdom of his counsel. He lifted the cover from a small roast fowl, dropped it again. 'Why would you want to learn this Skill anyway? It's a miserable thing. No fit occupation for a man.'

'To help you,' I said without thinking, and then found it true. Once it would have been to prove myself a true and fit son to Chivalry, to impress Burrich or Chade, to increase my standing in the keep. Now, after watching what Verity did, day after day, with no praise or acknowledgement from his subjects, I found I only wanted to help him.

'To help me,' he repeated. The storm winds were slackening. With exhausted resignation, he lifted his eyes to the window. Take the food away, boy. I've no time for it now.'

'But you need strength,' I protested. Guiltily, I knew he had taken time with me he should have taken for food and sleep.

'I know. But I have no time. Eating takes energy. Odd to realize that. I have none extra to give to that just now.' His eyes were questing afar now, staring through the sheeting rain that was just beginning to slacken.

'I'd give you my strength, Verity. If I could.'

He looked at me oddly. 'Are you sure? Very sure?'

I could not understand the intensity of his question, but I knew the answer. 'Of course I would.' And more quietly, 'I am a King's man.'

'And of my own blood,' he affirmed. He sighed. For a moment he looked sickened. He looked again at the food, and again out of the window. 'There is just time,' he whispered. 'And it might be enough. Damnation to you, Father. Must you always win? Come here, then, boy.'

There was an intensity to his words that frightened me, but I obeyed. When I stood by his chair, he reached out a hand. He placed it on my shoulder, as if he needed assistance to rise.

I looked up at him from the floor. There was a pillow under

my head, and the blanket I had brought up earlier had been tossed over me. Verity stood, leaning out of the window. He was shaking with effort, and the Skill he exerted was like battering waves I could almost feel. 'Onto the rocks,' he said with deep satisfaction, and whirled from the window. He grinned at me, an old, fierce grin that faded slowly as he looked down on me.

'Like a calf to the slaughter,' he said ruefully. 'I should have known that you didn't know what you were talking about.'

'What happened to me?' I managed to ask. My teeth chattered against each other, and my whole body shook as with a chill. I felt I would rattle my bones out of their joints.

'You offered me your strength. I took it.' He poured a cup of the tea, then knelt to hold it to my mouth. 'Go slowly. I was in a hurry. Did I say earlier that Chivalry was a bull with his Skill? What must I say about myself then?'

He had his old bluff heartiness and good nature back. This was a Verity I had not seen for months. I managed a mouthful of the tea, and felt the elfbark sting my mouth and throat. My shivering eased. Verity took a casual gulp from the mug.

'In the old days,' he said conversationally, 'a king would draw on his coterie. Half a dozen men or more, and all in tune with one another, able to pool strength and offer it as needed. That was their true purpose. To provide strength to their king, or to their own key man. I don't think Galen quite grasps that. His coterie is a thing he has fashioned. They are like horses and bullocks and donkeys, all harnessed together. Not a true coterie at all. They lack the singleness of mind.'

'You drew strength from me?'

'Yes. Believe me, boy, I would not have, except that I had a sudden need, and I thought you knew what you offered. You yourself named yourself as a King's man, the old term. And as close as we are in blood, I knew I could tap you.' He set the mug down on the tray with a thump. Disgust deepened his voice. 'Shrewd. He sets things in motion, wheels turning, pendulums swaying. It is no accident that you are the one to bring me my meals, boy. He was making you available to me.' He took a swift turn about the room, then stopped, standing over me. 'It will not happen again.'

'It was not so bad,' I said faintly.

'No? Why don't you try to stand then? Or even sit up? You're just one boy, alone, not a coterie. Had I not realized your ignorance and drawn back, I could have killed you. Your heart and breath would just have stopped. I'll not drain you like this, not for anyone. Here.' He stopped and without effort lifted me and placed me in his chair. 'Sit here a bit. And eat. I don't need it now. And when you are better, go to Shrewd for me. Say that I say you are a distraction. I wish a kitchen-boy to bring my meals, from now on.'

'Verity,' I began.

'No,' he corrected me. 'Say "my prince". For in this, I am your prince, and I will not be questioned on it. Now eat.'

I bowed my head, miserable, but I did eat, and the elfbark in the tea worked to revive me faster than I had expected. Soon I could stand, to stack the dishes on the tray, and then to carry them to the door. I felt defeated. I lifted the latch.

'FitzChivalry Farseer.'

I halted, frozen by the words. I turned slowly.

'It's your name, boy. I wrote it myself, in the military log, on the day you were brought to me. Another thing I had thought you knew. Stop thinking of yourself as the bastard, FitzChivalry Farseer. And be sure that you see Shrewd today.'

'Goodbye,' I said quietly, but he was already staring out of the window again.

And so high summer found us all. Chade at his tablets, Verity at his window, Regal courting a princess for his brother, and I, quietly killing for my king. The Inland and Coastal Dukes took sides at the council tables, hissing and spitting at one another like cats over fish. And over it all was Shrewd, keeping each piece of web as taut as any spider, and alert to the least thrumming of a line. The Red Ships struck at us, like ratfish on beef bait, tearing away bits of our folk and Forging them. And the Forged folk became a torment to the land, beggars or predators or a burden to their families. Folk feared to fish, to trade, or to farm the rivermouth plains by the sea. And yet the taxes had to be raised to feed the soldiers and the watchers who seemed unable to defend the land despite their growing numbers. Shrewd had grudgingly released me from my service to Verity. My king had not called for me in over a month when one morning I was abruptly summoned to breakfast.

'It's a poor time to wed,' Verity objected. 'I have no time for it. Let us be but promised for a year or so. Surely that will be enough for you.'

I looked at the sallow, fleshless man who shared the King's breakfast table and wondered if this were the bluff, hearty prince from my childhood. He had worsened so much in just a month. He toyed with a bit of bread, set it down again. The outdoors had gone from his cheeks and eyes; his hair was dull, his musculature slack. The whites of his eyes were yellowed. Burrich would have wormed him if he'd been a hound.

Unasked, I said, 'I hunted with Leon two days ago. He took a rabbit for me.'

Verity turned to me, a ghost of his old smile playing on his face. 'You took my wolfhound for rabbits?'

'He enjoyed it. He misses you, though. He brought me the rabbit, and I praised him but it didn't seem to satisfy him.' I couldn't tell him how the hound had looked at me, *not for you* as plain in his eyes as in his bearing.

Verity picked up his glass. His hand quivered ever so slightly. 'I am glad he gets out with you, boy. It's better than . . .'

'The wedding,' Shrewd cut in, 'will hearten the people. I am getting old, Verity, and the times are troubled. The people see no end to their troubles, and I do not dare promise them solutions we do not have. The Outislanders are right, Verity. We are not the warriors who once settled here. We have become a settled people – a settled people who can be threatened in ways that nomads and rovers have no care for. And we can be destroyed in those same ways. When settled people look for security, they look for continuity.'

Here I looked up sharply. Those were Chade's words, I'd bet my blood on it. Did that mean that this wedding was something Chade was helping to engineer? My interest became keener, and I wondered again why I had been summoned to this breakfast.

'It's a matter of reassuring our folk, Verity. You have not Regal's charm, nor the bearing that let Chivalry convince anyone that he could take care of any matter. This is not to slight you; you have as much talent for the Skill as I have ever seen in our line, and in many eras your soldierly skills in tactics would have been more important than Chivalry's diplomacy.'

This sounded suspiciously like a rehearsed speech to me. I watched Shrewd pause. He put cheese and preserves on some bread and bit into it thoughtfully. Verity sat silent, watching his father. He seemed both attentive and bemused, like a man trying desperately to stay awake and be alert when all he can think of is putting his head down and closing his eyes. My brief experiences of the Skill and the split concentration it demanded to resist its enticements while bending it to one's will made me marvel at Verity's ability to wield it every day.

Shrewd glanced from Verity to me and back to his son's face. 'Putting it simply, you need to marry. More, you need to beget a child. It would put heart into the people. They would say, "well, it cannot be as bad as all that, if our prince does not fear to marry and have a child. Surely he would not be doing that if the whole kingdom were on the verge of crumbling."'

'But you and I would still know better, wouldn't we, Father?' There was a hint of rust in Verity's voice, and a bitterness I had never heard there before.

'Verity,' Shrewd began, but his son cut in.

'My king,' he said formally. 'You and I do know that we are on the brink of disaster. And now, right now, there can be no slackening of our vigilance. I have no time for courting and wooing, and even less time for the more subtle negotiations of finding a royal bride. While the weather is fine, the Red Ships will raid. And when it turns poor, and the tempests blow their ships back to their own ports, then we must turn our minds and our energies to fortifying our coastlines, and training crews to manage raiding ships of our own. That is what I want to discuss with you. Let us build our own fleet, not fat merchant ships to waddle about tempting raiders, but sleek warships, such as we once had and our oldest shipwrights still know how to make. And let us take this battle to the Outislanders, yes, even through the storms of winter. We used to have such sailors and warriors amongst us. If we begin to build and train now, by next spring we could at least hold them away from our coast, and possibly by winter we could . . .'

'It will take money. And money does not flow fastest from terrified men. To raise the funds we need, we need to have our merchants confident enough to continue trading and farmers unafraid to pasture their flocks on the coast meadows and hills. It all comes back, Verity, to your taking a wife.'

Verity, so animated when speaking of warships, leaned back in his chair. He seemed to sag in on himself, as if some piece of structure inside him had given way. I almost expected to see him collapse. 'As you will, my king,' he said, but as he spoke he shook his head, denying the affirmation of his own words. 'I will do as you see wise. Such is the duty of a prince to his king and to his kingdom. But as a man, Father, it is a bitter and empty thing, this taking of a woman selected by my younger brother. I will wager that having looked on Regal first, when she stands beside me, she will not see me as any great prize.' Verity looked down at his hands, at the battle and work scars that now showed plainly against their paleness. I heard his name in his words when he said softly, 'Always I have been your second son. Behind Chivalry, with his beauty, strength and wisdom. And now behind Regal, with his cleverness and charm and airs. I know you think he would be a better king to follow after you than I. I do not always disagree with you. I was born second and raised to be second. I had always believed my place would be behind the throne, not upon it. And when I thought that Chivalry would follow you to that high seat, I did not mind it. He gave me great worth, my brother did. His confidence in me was like an honour; it made me a part of all he accomplished. To be the right hand of such a king was better than to be king of many a lesser land. I believed in him as he believed in me. But he is gone. And I tell you nothing surprising when I say to you that there is no such bond between Regal and me. Perhaps there are too many years; perhaps Chivalry and I were so close we left no room for a third. But I do not think he has been seeking for a woman who can love me. Or one who . . .'

'He has been seeking a queen!' Shrewd interrupted harshly. I knew then that this was not the first time this had been argued, and sensed that Shrewd was most annoyed that I had been privy to these words. 'Regal has been seeking a woman, not for you, or himself, or any such silliness. He has been seeking a woman to be queen of this country, of these Six Duchies. A woman who can bring to us the wealth and the men and the trade agreements that we need now, if we are to survive these Red Ships. Soft hands and a sweet scent will not build your warships, Verity. You must set aside this jealousy of your brother; you cannot fend off the enemy if you do not have confidence in those who stand behind you.'

'Exactly,' Verity said quietly. He pushed his chair back.

'Where do you go?' Shrewd demanded irritably.

'To my duties,' Verity said shortly. 'Where else have I to go?'

For a moment, even Shrewd looked taken aback. 'But you've scarcely eaten . . .' he faltered.

'The Skill kills all other appetites. You know that.'

'Yes.' Shrewd paused. 'And I know, too, as you do, that when this happens, a man is close to the edge. The appetite for the Skill is one that devours a man, not one that nourishes him.'

They both seemed to have forgotten about me entirely. I made myself small and unobtrusive, nibbling on my biscuit as if I were a mouse in a corner.

'But what does the devouring of one man matter, if it saves a kingdom?' Verity did not bother to disguise the bitterness in his voice, and to me it was plain that it was not the Skill alone of which he spoke. He pushed his plate away. 'After all,' he added with ponderous sarcasm, 'it is not as if you do not have yet another son to step in and wear your crown. One unscarred by what the Skill does to men. One free to wed where he will, or will not.'

'It is not Regal's fault that he is unSkilled. He was a sickly child, too sickly for Galen to train. And who could have foreseen that two Skilled princes would not be enough?' Shrewd protested. He rose abruptly and paced the length of the chamber. He stood, leaning on the windowsill and peering out over the sea below. 'I do what I can, son,' he added in a lower voice. 'Do you think I do not care, that I do not see how you are being consumed?'

Verity sighed heavily. 'No. I know. It is the weariness of the

Skill that speaks so, not I. One of us, at least, must keep a clear head and try to grasp the whole of what is happening. For me, there is nothing but the sensing out, and then the sorting, the trying to fix navigator out from oarsman, to scent out the secret fears that the Skill can magnify, to find the faint hearts in the crew and prey upon those first. When I sleep, I dream them, and when I try to eat, they are what sticks in my throat. You know I have never relished this, Father. It never seemed to me worthy of a warrior, to skulk and spy about in men's minds. Give me a sword and I'll willingly explore their guts. I'd rather unman a man with a blade than turn the hounds of his own mind to nipping at his heels.'

'I know, I know,' Shrewd said gently, but I did not think he really did. I, at least, did understand Verity's distaste for his task. I had to admit I shared it, and felt him somehow dirtied by it. But when he glanced at me, my face and eyes were empty of any judgement. Deeper within me was the sneaking guilt that I had failed to learn the Skill, and was no use to my uncle at this time. I wondered if he looked at me, and thought of drawing on my strength again. It was a frightening thought, but I steeled myself to the request. But he only smiled at me kindly, if absently, as if no such thought had ever crossed his mind. And as he rose, and walked past my chair, he tousled my hair as if I were Leon.

'Take my dog out for me, even if it is only for rabbits. I hate to leave him in my rooms each day, but his poor dumb pleading was a distraction from what I must do.'

I nodded, surprised at what I felt emanating from him. A shadow of the same pain I had felt at being separated from my own dogs.

'Verity.'

He turned at Shrewd's call.

'Almost I forgot to tell you why I had called you here. It is, of course, the mountain princess. Ketkin, I think her name was . . .'

'Kettricken. I at least remember that much. A skinny little child, the last time I saw her. So, she is the one you have selected?'

'Yes. For all the reasons we have already discussed. And a day has been set. Ten days before Harvestday. You will have to leave here during the first part of Reaptime in order to reach there in time. There will be a ceremony there, before her own people, binding the two of you and sealing all the agreements and a formal wedding later, when you arrive back here with her. Regal sends word that you must . . .'

Verity had halted, and his face darkened with frustration. 'I cannot. You know I cannot. If I leave off my work here while it is still Reaptime, there will be nothing to bring a bride back to. Always, the Outislanders have been greediest and most reckless in the final month before the winter storms drive them back to their own wretched shore. Do you think it will be any different this year? Like as not I would bring Kettricken back here to find them feasting in our own Buckkeep, with your head on a pike to greet me!'

King Shrewd looked angered, but kept his temper as he asked, 'Do you really think they could press us that greatly if you left off your efforts for twenty days or so?'

'I know it,' Verity said wearily. 'I know it as surely as I know that I should be at my post right now, not arguing here with you. Father, tell them it must be put off. I'll go for her as soon as we've a good coat of snow on the ground, and a blessed gale lashing all ships into their ports.'

'It cannot be,' Shrewd said regretfully. 'They have beliefs of their own, up in the mountains. A wedding made in winter yields a barren harvest. You must take her in the autumn when the lands are yielding, or in late spring, when they till their little mountain fields.'

'I cannot. By the time spring comes to their mountains, it is fair weather here, with Raiders on our doorsills. Surely they must understand that!' Verity moved his head about, like a restless horse on a short lead. He did not want to be here. Distasteful as he found his Skill work, it called to him. He wanted to go to it, wanted it in a way that had nothing to do with protecting his kingdom. I wondered if Shrewd knew that. I wondered if Verity did.

'To understand something is one thing,' the King expounded. 'To insist they flaunt their traditions is another. Verity, this must be done, done now.' Shrewd rubbed his head as if it pained him. 'We need this joining. We need her soldiers, we need her marriage gifts, we need her father at our back. It cannot wait. Could not you perhaps go in a closed litter, unhampered by managing a horse, and continue your Skill work as you travel? It might even do you good, to get out and about a bit, to have a little fresh air and . . .'

'NO!' Verity bellowed the word, and Shrewd turned where he stood, almost as if he were at bay against the windowsill. Verity advanced to the table, and pounded upon it, showing a temper I had never suspected in him. 'No and no and no! I cannot do the work I must do to keep the Raiders from our coast while being rocked and jolted in a horse litter. And no, I will not go to this bride you have chosen for me, to this woman I scarce recall, in a litter like an invalid or a witling. I will not have her see me so, nor would I have my men sniggering behind me, saying, "oh, this is what brave Verity has come to, riding like a palsied old man, pandered off to some woman as if he were an Outislander whore". Where are your wits that you can think such stupid plans? You've been among the mountain folk, you know their ways. Think you a woman of theirs would accept a man who came to her in such a sickly way? Even their royals expose a child if it is born less than whole. You'd spoil your own plan, and leave the Six Duchies to the Raiders while you did it.'

'Then perhaps . . .'

'Then perhaps there is a Red Ship right now, not so far that they cannot see Egg Island, and already the captain of it is discounting the dream of ill omen he had last night, and the navigator is correcting his course, wondering how he could have so mistaken the landmarks of our coastline. Already all the work I did last night while you slept and Regal danced and drank with his courtiers is coming undone, while we stand here and yatter at one another. Father, arrange it. Arrange it any way you wish and can, so long as it does not involve me doing anything save the Skill while fair weather plagues our coast.' Verity had been moving as he spoke, and the slamming of the King's chamber door almost drowned out his final words.

Shrewd stood and stared at the door for some moments. Then he passed his hand across his eyes, rubbing them, but for weariness or tears or just a bit of dust, I could not tell. He looked about the room, frowning when his eyes encountered me, as if I were a thing puzzlingly out of place. Then, as if recalling why I were there, he observed dryly, 'Well, that went well, didn't it? Still, and all, a way must be found. And when Verity rides to claim his bride, you will go with him.'

'If you wish, my king,' I said quietly.

'I do.' He cleared his throat, then turned to look out of his window again. 'The princess has a single sibling, an older brother. He is not a healthy man. Oh, he was well and strong once, but on the Ice Fields he took an arrow through his chest. Passed clean through him, so Regal was told. And the wounds on his chest and back healed. But during the winters, he coughs blood, and in summer he cannot sit a horse nor drill his men for more than half the morning. Knowing the mountain folk, it is full surprising that he is their King-in-Waiting still. Usually they do not tolerate weaklings.'

I thought quietly for a moment. 'Among the mountain people the custom is the same as ours. Male or female, the offspring inherit by the order of their birth.'

'Yes. That is so,' Shrewd said quietly, and I knew that already he was thinking that seven duchies might be stronger than six. This was why I had been summoned to breakfast.

'And Princess Kettricken's father?' I asked. 'How is his health?'

'As hale and hearty as one could wish, for a man of his years. I am sure he will reign long and well for at least another decade, keeping his kingdom whole and safe for his heir.'

'Probably by then, our troubles with the Red Ships will long be over. Verity will be free to turn his mind to other things.'

'Probably,' King Shrewd agreed quietly. His eyes finally met mine. 'When Verity goes to claim his bride, you will go with him. You understand what your duties will be? I trust to your discretion.'

I inclined my head to him. 'As you wish, my king.'

NINETEEN

Journey

To speak of the Mountain Kingdom as a kingdom is to start out with a basic misunderstanding of the area and the folk who people it. It is equally inaccurate to refer to the region as Chyurda, although the Chyurda do make up the dominant folk there. Rather than one stretch of united countryside, the Mountain Kingdom consists of various hamlets clinging to the mountainsides, of small vales of arable land, of trading hamlets sprung up along the rough roads that lead to the passes, and clans of nomadic herders and hunters who range the inhospitable countryside in between. Such a diverse people are unlikely to unite, for their interests are often in conflict. Strangely, though, the only force more powerful than each group's independence and insular ways is the loyalty they bear to the 'King' of the mountain folk.

Traditions tell us that this line was begun by a prophet-judge, a woman who was not only wise, but also a philosopher who founded a theory of ruling the keystone of which is that the leader is the ultimate servant of the people, and must be totally selfless in that regard. There was no definite time when the judge became the king; rather it was a gradual transition, as word of the fairness and wisdom of the holy one at Jhaampe spread. As more and more folk sought counsel there, willing to be bound by the decision of the judge, it was only natural that the laws of that settlement came to be respected throughout the mountains, and that more and more folk adopted Jhaampe laws as their own. And so judges became kings, but, amazingly, retained their self-imposed decree of servitude and self-sacrifice for their people. The Jhaampe tradition is rife with tales of kings and queens who sacrificed themselves *for their folk, in every conceivable way, from fending wild animals off shepherd children to offering themselves as hostages in times of feud.*

Tales have been told that make the mountain folk out to be harsh, almost savage. In truth, the land they dwell in is uncompromising, and their laws mirror this condition. It is true that badly-formed infants are exposed, or, more commonly, drowned or drugged to death. The elderly often choose Sequestering, a self-imposed exile in a family but where cold and starvation end all infirmities. A man who breaks his word may have his tongue notched as well as having to surrender double the value of his original bargain. Such customs may seem quaintly barbaric to those in the more settled of the Six Duchies, but they are peculiarly suited to the world of the Mountain Kingdom.

In the end, Verity had his way. There was no sweetness in the triumph for him, I am sure, for his own stubborn insistence was backed by a sudden increase in the frequency of the raids. In the space of a month, two villages were burned and had a total of thirty-two inhabitants taken for Forging. Nineteen of them apparently carried the now popular poison vials, and chose to commit suicide. A third town, a more populous one, was successfully defended, not by the royal troops, but by a mercenary militia the townsfolk had organized and hired themselves. Many of the fighters, ironically, were immigrant Outislanders, using one of the few skills they had. And the mutterings against the King's apparent inactivity increased.

It did little good to try to explain to them about Verity and the coterie's work. What the people needed and wanted were warships of their own, defending the coastline. But ships take time to build, and the converted merchant ships that were already in the water were tubby, wallowing things compared to the sleek Red Ships that harassed us. Promises of warships by spring were small comfort to farmers and herders trying to protect this year's crops and flocks. And the land-locked duchies were becoming more and more vociferous about paying heavier taxes to build warships to protect a coastline they didn't share. For their part, the leaders of the Coastal Duchies sarcastically wondered how well the inland folk would do without their seaports and trading vessels to outlet their goods. During at least one High Council meeting, there was a noisy altercation in which Duke Ram of Tilth suggested that it would be little loss to cede the Near Islands and Fur Point to the Red Ships if that would slacken their raiding, and Duke Brawndy of Bearns retaliated by threatening to stop all trade traffic along the Bear River and see if Tilth found that as small a loss. King Shrewd managed to bring the council to adjournment before they came to blows, but not before the Farrow Duke had made it clear that he sided with Tilth. The lines of division were being made more sharp with each passing month and each allotment of taxes. Clearly something was needed to rebuild the kingdom's unity, and Shrewd was convinced it was a royal marriage.

So Regal danced his diplomatic steps, and it was arranged that the Princess Kettricken would make her pledges to Regal in his brother's stead, with all of her own folk to witness, and Verity's word would be given by his brother. With a second ceremony to follow, of course, at Buckkeep, with suitable representatives from Kettricken's folk to witness it. And for the nonce, Regal remained in the Mountain Kingdom's capital at Jhaampe. His presence there created a regular flow of emissaries, gifts and supplies between Buckkeep and Jhaampe. Seldom did a week pass without a cavalcade either leaving or arriving. It kept Buckkeep in a constant stir.

It seemed to me an awkward and ungainly way to assemble a marriage. Each would be wed almost a month before glimpsing the other. But the political expedients were more important than the feelings of the principals, and the separate celebrations were planned.

I had long since recovered from Verity tapping my strength. It was taking me longer to grasp completely what Galen's misting of my mind had done to me. I believe I would have confronted him, despite Verity's counsel, except that he had left Buckkeep, in company of a cavalcade bound for Jhaampe, to ride with them as far as Farrow, where he had relatives he wished to visit. By the time he returned, I myself would be on my way to Jhaampe, so Galen remained out of my reach.

Again, I had too much time on my hands. I still tended Leon, but he did not take more than an hour or two of my time each day. I had been able to discover nothing more about the attack on Burrich, nor did Burrich show any signs of relenting on my ostracism. I had made one jaunt into Buckkeep Town, but when I chanced to wander by the chandlery, it was shuttered and silent. My inquiries at the shop next door brought me the information that the chandlery had been closed for ten days or more, and that unless I wished to buy some leather harness, I could go elsewhere and stop bothering him. I thought of the young man I had last seen with Molly, and bitterly wished them no good of each other.

For no other reason than that I was lonely, I decided to seek out the Fool. Never before had I tried to initiate a meeting with him. He proved more elusive than I had ever imagined.

After a few hours of randomly wandering the keep, hoping to encounter him, I made brave enough to go to his chamber. I had known for years where it was, but had never gone there before, and not simply because it was in an out of the way part of the keep. The Fool did not invite intimacy, except of the kind he chose to offer, and only when he chose to offer it. His chambers were a tower-top room. Fedwren had told me that it had once been a map room, and had offered an unobstructed view of the land surrounding Buckkeep, but later additions to Buckkeep had blocked the views, and higher towers supplanted it. It had outlived its usefulness for anything, save chambers for a Fool.

I climbed to it, that one day toward the beginning of harvest-time. It was already a hot and sticky day. The tower was a closed one, save for arrow slits that did little more than illuminate the dust motes my feet set to dancing in the still air. At first the darkness of the tower had seemed cooler than the stuffy day outside, but as I climbed, it seemed to get hotter and more close, so that by the time I reached the last landing, I felt as if there were no air left to breathe at all. I lifted a weary fist and pounded on the stout door. 'It's me, Fitz!' I called, but the still, hot air muffled my voice like a wet blanket smothering a flame.

Shall I use that as an excuse? Shall I say I thought perhaps he could not hear me, and so I went in to see if he was there? Or shall I say that I was so hot and thirsty that I entered to see if his chambers offered any hint of air or water? Why doesn't matter, I suppose. I put my hand to the door-latch, and it lifted and I went inside.

'Fool?' I called, but I could feel he wasn't there. Not as I usually felt folk's presence or absence, but by the stillness that met me. Yet I stood in the door and gawked at a soul laid bare.

Here was light, and flowers, and colours in profusion. There was a loom in the corner, and baskets of fine, thin thread in bright, bright hues. The woven coverlet on the bed, and the drapings on the open windows were unlike anything I had ever seen, woven in geometric patterns that somehow suggested fields of flowers beneath a blue sky. A wide pottery bowl held floating flowers and a slim silver fingerling swam about the stems and above the bright pebbles that floored it. I tried to imagine the pale cynical Fool in the midst of all this colour and art. I took a step further into the room, and saw something that moved my heart aside in my chest.

A baby. That was what I took it for at first, and without thinking, I took the next two steps and knelt beside the basket that cradled it. But it was not a living child, but a doll, crafted with such incredible art that almost I expected to see the small chest move with breath. I reached a hand to the pale, delicate face, but dared not touch it. The curve of the brow, the closed eyelids, the faint rose that suffused the tiny cheeks, even the small hand that rested on top of the coverlets were more perfect than I supposed a made thing could be. Of what delicate clay it had been crafted, I could not guess, nor what hand had inked the tiny eyelashes that curled on the infant's cheek. The tiny coverlet was embroidered all over with pansies, and the pillow was of satin. I don't know how long I knelt there, as silent as if it were truly a sleeping babe. But eventually I rose, and backed out of the Fool's room, and then drew the door silently closed behind me. I went slowly down the myriad steps, torn between dread that I might encounter the Fool coming up, and burdened with the knowledge that I had discovered one denizen of the keep who was at least as alone as I was.

Chade summoned me that night, but when I went to him, he seemed to have no more purpose in calling me than to see me. We sat almost silently before the black hearth, and I thought he looked older than he ever had. As Verity was devoured so Chade was consumed. His bony hands appeared almost desiccated, and the whites of his eyes were webbed with red. He needed to sleep, but instead had chosen to call me. Yet he sat, still and silent, scarce nibbling at the food he had placed before us. At length, I decided to help him.

'Are you afraid I won't be able to do it?' I asked him softly.

'Do what?' he asked absently.

'Kill the mountain prince. Rurisk.'

Chade turned to look at me full-face. The silence held for a long moment.

'You didn't know King Shrewd had given me this,' I faltered.

Slowly he turned back to the empty hearth, and studied it as carefully as if there were flames to read. 'I'm only the tool-maker,' he said at last, quietly. 'Another man uses what I make.'

'Do you think this is a bad . . . task? Wrong?' I took a breath. 'From what I've been told, he has not that much longer to live anyway. It might almost be a mercy, if death were to come quietly in the night, instead of . . .'

'Boy,' Chade remarked quietly. 'Never pretend we are anything but what we are. Assassins. Not merciful agents of a wise king. Political assassins dealing death for the furtherance of our monarchy. That is what we are.'

It was my turn to study the ghosts of the flames. 'You are making this very hard for me. Harder than it already was. Why? Why did you make me what I am, if you then try to weaken my resolve . . .' My question died away, half-formed.

'I think . . . never mind. Maybe it is a kind of jealousy in me, my boy. I wonder, I suppose, why Shrewd uses you instead of me. Maybe I fear I have outlived my usefulness to him. Maybe, now that I know you, I wish I had never set out to make you what . . .' And it was Chade's turn to fall silent, his thoughts going where his words could not follow them.

We sat contemplating my assignment. This was not the serving of a king's justice. This was not a death sentence for a crime. This was a simple removal of a man who was an obstacle to greater power. I sat still until I began to wonder if I would do it.

Then I lifted my eyes to a silver fruit-knife driven deep into Chade's mantelpiece, and I thought I knew the answer.

'Verity had made complaint, on your behalf,' Chade said suddenly.

'Complaint?' I asked weakly.

'To Shrewd. First, that Galen had mistreated you and cheated you. This complaint he made formally, saying that he had deprived the kingdom of your Skill, at a time when it would have been most useful. He suggested to Shrewd, informally, that he settle it with Galen, before you took matters into your own hands.'

Looking at Chade's face, I could see that the full content of my discussion with Verity had been revealed to him. I was not sure how I felt about that. 'I would not do that, take my own revenge on Galen. Not after Verity asked me not to.'

Chade gave me a look of quiet approval. 'So I told Shrewd. But he said to me that I must say to you, that he will settle this. This time the King works his own justice. You must wait and be satisfied.'

'What will he do?'

'That I do not know. I do not think Shrewd himself knows yet. The man must be rebuked. But we must keep in mind that if other coteries are to be trained, Galen must not feel too badly treated.' Chade cleared his throat, and said more quietly, 'And Verity made another complaint to the King as well. He accused Shrewd and I, quite bluntly, of being willing to sacrifice you for the sake of the kingdom.'

This, I knew suddenly, was why Chade had called me tonight. I was silent.

Chade spoke more slowly. 'Shrewd claimed he had not even considered it. For my part, I had no idea such a thing was possible.' He sighed again, as if parting with these words cost him. 'Shrewd is a king, my boy. His first concern must always be for his kingdom.'

The silence between us stretched long. 'You are saying he would sacrifice me. Without a qualm.'

He did not take his eyes from the fireplace. 'You. Me. Even Verity, if he thought it necessary for the survival of the kingdom.' Then he did turn to look at me. 'Never forget that,' he said.

The night before the wedding caravan was to leave Buckkeep,

Lacey came tapping on my door. It was late, and when she said Patience wished to see me, I foolishly asked, 'Now?'

'Well, you leave tomorrow,' Lacey pointed out, and I obediently followed her as if that made sense.

I found Patience sitting up in a cushioned chair, an extravagantly-embroidered robe on over her nightclothes. Her hair was down about her shoulders, and as I seated myself where she indicated, Lacey resumed the brushing of it.

'I have been waiting for you to come to apologize to me,' Patience observed.

I immediately opened my mouth to do so, but she irritably waved me to silence.

'But, in discussing it with Lacey tonight, I found I had already forgiven you. Boys, I decided, simply have a given amount of rudeness they must express. I decided you meant nothing by it, hence you do not need to apologize.'

'But I am sorry,' I protested. 'I just couldn't decide how to say . . .'

'It's too late to apologize now, I've forgiven you,' she said briskly. 'Besides, there isn't time. I'm sure you should be asleep by now. But as this is your first real venture into court life, I wanted to give you something before you left.'

I opened my mouth, then shut it again. If she wanted to consider this my first real venture into court life, I wouldn't argue with her.

'Sit here,' she said imperiously, and pointed to a spot by her feet.

I went and sat obediently. For the first time, I noticed a small box in her lap. It was of dark wood, and a stag was carved into the lid in bas relief. As she opened it, I caught a whiff of the aromatic wood. She took out an ear stud and held it up to my ear. 'Too small,' she muttered. 'What is the sense of wearing jewellery if no one else can see it?' She held up and discarded several others, with similar comments. Finally she held up one that was like a silver bit of net with a blue stone caught in it. She made a face over it, then nodded reluctantly. 'That man has taste. Whatever else he lacks, he has taste.' She held it up to my ear again, and with absolutely no warning, thrust the pin of it through my earlobe.

I yelped and clapped a hand over my ear, but she slapped it away. 'Don't be such a baby. It only stings for a minute.' There was a sort of clasp that held it behind, and she ruthlessly bent my ear in her fingers to fasten it. 'There. That quite suits him, don't you think, Lacey?'

'Quite,' Lacey agreed over her eternal tatting.

Patience dismissed me with a gesture. As I rose to go, she said, 'Remember this, Fitz. Whether you can Skill or not, whether you wear his name or not, you are Chivalry's son. See that you behave with honour. Now go and get some sleep.'

'With this ear?' I asked, showing her blood on my fingertips.

'I hadn't thought. I'm sorry . . .' she began, but I interrupted her.

'Too late to apologize. I've already forgiven you. And thank you.' Lacey was still giggling as I left.

I arose early the next morning, to take my place in the wedding cavalcade. Rich gifts must be taken as a token of the new bond between the families. There were gifts for the Princess Kettricken herself, a fine-blooded mare, jewellery, fabric for garments, servants, and rare perfumes. And there were the gifts to her family and people. Horses and hawks and worked gold for her father and brother of course, but the more important gifts were the ones offered to her kingdom, for in keeping with the Jhaampe traditions, she was of her people more than she was of her family. And so there was breeding stock, cattle, sheep, horses and fowl, and powerful yew bows such as the mountain folk did not have, and metalworking tools of good Forge iron, and other gifts judged likely to improve the lot of the mountain people. And there was knowledge, in the form of several of Fedwren's best illustrated herbals, several tablets of cures, and a scroll on hawking that was a careful copy of one created by Hawker himself. These last, ostensibly, were my purpose in accompanying the caravan.

They were given into my keeping, along with a generous supply of the herbs and roots mentioned in the herbal, and with seed for growing those that did not keep well. This was not a trivial gift, and I took my responsibility for seeing it well delivered as seriously as I took my other mission. All was carefully wrapped and then placed in a carved cedar chest. I was checking their wrappings a final time before taking the chest down to the court-yard when I heard the Fool behind me.

'I brought you this.'

I turned to find him standing just inside the door of my room. I hadn't even heard the door open. He was proffering a leather drawstring bag. 'What is it?' I asked, and tried not to let him hear either the flowers or the doll in my voice.

'Seapurge.'

I raised my eyebrows. 'A cathartic? As a marriage gift? I suppose some would find it appropriate, but the herbs I am taking can be planted and grown in the mountains. I do not think . . .'

'It is not a wedding gift. It is for you.'

I accepted the pouch with mixed feelings. It was an exception-ally powerful purge. 'Thank you for thinking of me. But I am not usually prone to travellers' ailments, and . . .'

'You are not usually, when you travel, in danger of being poisoned.'

'Is there something you'd like to tell me?' I tried to make my tone light and bantering. I missed the Fool's usual wry faces and mockeries from this conversation.

'Only that you'd be wise to eat lightly, or not at all, of any food you do not prepare yourself.'

'At all the feasts and festivities that will be there?'

'No. Only at the ones you wish to survive.' He turned to go.

'I'm sorry,' I said hastily. 'I didn't mean to intrude. I was looking for you, and I was so hot, and the door wasn't latched, so I went in. I didn't mean to pry.'

His back was to me and he didn't turn back as he asked, 'And did you find it amusing?'

'I –' I could not think of anything to say, of any way to assure him that what I had seen there would stay only within my own mind. He took two steps and was closing the door. I blurted, 'It made me wish there were a place as much me as that place is you. A place I would keep as secret.'

The door halted a handsbreadth short of closed. 'Take some advice, and you may survive this trip. When considering a man's motives, remember you must not measure his wheat with your bushel. He may not be using the same standard at all.'

And the door closed and the Fool was gone. But his last words had been cryptic and frustrating enough that I thought perhaps he had forgiven me my trespass.

I stuffed the seapurge into my jerkin, not wanting it, but afraid to leave it now. I glanced about my room, but as always it was a bare and practical place. Mistress Hasty had seen to my packing, not trusting me with my new garments. I had noticed that the barred buck on my crest had been replaced with a buck with his antlers lowered to charge. 'Verity ordered it,' was all she said when I asked about it. 'I like it better than the barred buck myself. Don't you?'

'I suppose so,' I replied, and that had been the end of it. A name and a crest. I nodded to myself, shouldered my chest of herbs and scrolls, and went down to join the caravan.

As I was going down the steps, I encountered Verity coming up. At first I scarcely knew him, for he was ascending like a crabbed old man. I stepped out of his way to let him pass, and then knew him as he glanced at me. It is a strange thing to see a once-familiar man like that, encountered as a stranger. I marked how his clothes hung on him now, and the bushy dark hair I remembered had a peppering of grey. He smiled absently at me, and then, as if it had suddenly occurred to him, he stopped me.

'You're leaving for the Mountain Kingdom? For the wedding ceremony?'

'Yes.'

'Do me a favour, boy?'

'Of course,' I said, taken aback by the rust in his voice.

'Speak well of me to her. Truthfully, mind you, I'm not asking for lies. But speak well of me. I've always thought that you thought well of me.'

'I do,' I said to his retreating back. 'I do, sir.' But he didn't turn or make a reply, and I felt much as I had when the Fool left me.

The courtyard was a milling of folk and animals. There were no carts this time; the roads into the mountains were notoriously bad, and it had been decided that pack animals would have to suffice for the sake of swiftness. It would not do for the royal entourage to be late for the wedding; it was bad enough that the groom was not attending.

The flocks and herds had been sent on days before. It was expected that our trip would take two weeks, and three had been allowed for it. I saw to fastening the cedar chest onto a pack animal, and then stood beside Sooty and waited. Even in the cobbled courtyard, dust stirred thick in the hot summer air. Despite all the careful planning that had gone into it, the caravan seemed chaotic. I glimpsed Sevrens, Regal's favourite valet. Regal had sent him back to Buckkeep a month ago, with specific instructions about certain garments he wished created. Sevrens was following Hands, dithering and expostulating about something, and whatever it was, Hands was not looking patient about it. When Mistress Hasty had been giving me final instructions on the care of my new garments, she had divulged that Sevrens was taking enough new garments, hats and accoutrements for Regal that he had been allotted three pack animals to carry them. I imagined that caring for the three animals had fallen to Hands, for Sevrens was an excellent valet, but timid around the larger animals. Rowd, Regal's ready man, hulked after both of them, looking ill-tempered and impatient. On one wide shoulder he carried yet another trunk, and perhaps the loading of this additional item was what was fretting Sevrens. I soon lost sight of them in the crowd.

I was surprised to discover Burrich checking the lead-lines on the breeding horses and the Princess's gift mare. Surely whoever was in charge of them could do that, I thought. And then, as I saw him mount, I realized that he, too, would be part of this procession. I looked about to see who was accompanying him, but saw none of the stable-boys I knew, save Hands . . . Cob was already in Jhaampe with Regal. So Burrich had taken this on himself. I was not surprised.

August was there, astride a fine grey mare, waiting with an impassivity that was almost inhuman. Already his time in the coterie had changed him. Once he had been a chubby youth, quiet but pleasant. He had the same black bushy hair as Verity, and I had heard it said that he resembled his cousin as a boy. I reflected that as his Skill duties increased, he would probably resemble Verity even more. He would be present at the wedding, as a sort of window for Verity as Regal uttered the vows on his brother's behalf. Regal's voice, August's eyes, I mused to myself. What did I go as? His poignard?

I mounted Sooty, as much to be up and away from the folk exchanging goodbyes and last-minute instructions as for any other reason. I wished to Eda we could be away and on the road. It seemed to take forever for the straggling line to form and for the tying and strapping of bundles to be accomplished. And then, almost abruptly, the standards were lifted, a horn was blown, and the line of horses, laden pack-animals and folk began to move. I looked up once, to see that Verity had actually come out to stand on top of the tower and watch us depart. I waved up at him, but doubted that he knew me amidst so many. And then we were out of the gates, and winding up the hilly path that led away from Buckkeep and to the west.

Our path would lead us up the banks of the Buck River, which we would ford at its wide shallows near where the borders of Buck and Farrow Duchies touched. From there we would journey across Farrow's wide plains, in baking heat I had never encountered before, until we reached Blue Lake. From Blue Lake, we would follow a river named simply Cold whose origins were in the Mountain Kingdom. From the Cold Ford the trading road began, that led between the mountains and through their shadows and up, ever up, to Storm Pass, and thence to the thick green forests of the Rain Wilds. We would not go as far as that, but would stop at Jhaampe, which was as close to a city as the Mountain Kingdom possessed.

In some ways, it was an unremarkable journey, if one discounts all that inevitably goes with such journeys. After the first three days or so, things settled into a remarkably monotonous routine, varied only by the different countryside we passed. Every little village or hamlet along our road turned out to greet us and delay us, with official best wishes and felicitations for the Crown Prince's wedding festivities.

But after we reached the wide plains of Farrow, such hamlets were few and far between. Farrow's rich farms and trading cities were far to the north of our path, along the Vin River. We travelled Farrow's plains, where people were mostly nomadic herders, creating towns only in the winter months when they settled along the trade routes for what they called 'the green season'. We passed herds of sheep, goats, or horses; or more rarely, the dangerous, rangy swine they called *haragars*, but our contact with the people of that region was usually limited to the sight of their conical tents in the distance, or some herder standing tall in his saddle, holding aloft his crook in greeting.

Hands and I became reacquainted. We would share food and a small cook-fire in the evenings, and he would regale me with tales of Severn's nattering worries of dust getting into silk robes or bugs getting into fur collars and velvet getting chafed to pieces during the long trek. Grimmer were his complaints about Rowd. I myself had no fond memories of the man, and Hands found him an oppressive travelling companion, for he seemed to constantly suspect Hands of trying to steal from the packs of Regal's belongings. One evening Rowd even found his way to our fire, where he laboriously delivered a vague and indirect warning against any who might conspire to steal from his master.

The fair weather held, and if we sweated by day, it was pleasant enough by night. I slept on top of my blanket, and seldom bothered with any other shelter. Each night I checked the contents of my trunk, and did my best to keep the roots from becoming completely desiccated, and to keep the shifting from putting wear on the scrolls and tablets. One night I awoke to a loud whinnying from Sooty, and thought that the cedar chest had been moved slightly from where I placed it. But a brief check of its contents proved that all was in order, and when I mentioned it to Hands, he merely asked if I were catching Rowd's disease.

The hamlets and herds we passed frequently provided us with fresh foods, and were most generous in their allocation of it, so we had little hardship on the journey. Open water was not as plentiful as we could have wished as we crossed Farrow, but each day we found some spring or dusty well to water at, so even that was not as bad as it might have been.

I saw very little of Burrich. He arose earlier than the rest of us, and preceded the main caravan, that his charges might have the best grazing and the cleanest water. I knew he would want his horses in prime condition when they arrived at Jhaampe. August, too, was almost invisible. While he was technically in charge of our expedition, he left the running of it to the captain of his honour-guard. I could not decide if he did this out of wisdom, or laziness. In any event, he kept mostly to himself, although he did allow Sevrens to tend him and share his tent and meals.

For me, it was almost a return to a sort of childhood. My responsibilities were very limited. Hands was a genial companion, and it took very little encouragement to have him telling from his vast store of tales and gossip. I often went for almost the whole day before I would recall that, at the end of this journey, I would kill a prince.

Such thoughts usually came on me when I awoke in the dark part of the night. Farrow's sky seemed to be much thicker with stars than the night over Buckkeep, and I would stare up at them, and mentally rehearse ways to put an end to Rurisk. There was another chest, a tiny one, packed carefully within the bag that held my clothing and personal items. I had compiled it with much thought and anxiety for this assignment must be carried out perfectly. It must be done cleanly, with not even the tiniest suspicion raised. And timing was critical. The prince must not die while we were at Jhaampe. Nothing must cast the slightest shadow upon the nuptials. Nor must he die before the ceremonies were observed at Buckkeep and the wedding safely consummated, for that might be seen as an ill omen for the couple. It would not be an easy death to arrange.

Sometimes I wondered why it had been entrusted to me instead of to Chade. Was it a test of some sort, one that if I failed I would be put to death? Was Chade too old for this challenge, or too valuable to be risked for this? Could he simply not be spared from tending Verity's health? And when I reined my mind away from these questions, I was left wondering whether to use a powder that would irritate Rurisk's damaged lungs so he might cough himself to death. Perhaps I might treat his pillows and bedding with it. Should I offer him a pain remedy, one that would slowly addict him and lure him into a sleeping death? I had a blood-thinning tonic. If his lungs were chronically bleeding already, it might be enough to send him on his way. I had one poison, swift and deadly and tasteless as water, if I could devise a way to be sure he would encounter it at a safely distant time. None of these were thoughts conducive to sleep, and yet the fresh air and the exercise of riding all day were usually sufficient to counter them, and I often awoke eager for the next day of travel.

When we finally sighted Blue Lake, it was like a miracle in the distance. It had been years since I had been so far from the sea for so long, and I was surprised how welcome the sight of water was to me. Every animal in our baggage-train filled my thoughts with the clean scent of water. The country became greener and more forgiving as we approached the great lake, and we were hard put to keep the horses from overgrazing themselves at night.

Hordes of sailing-boats plied their merchant trade on Blue Lake, and their sails were coloured so as to tell not only what they sold but which family they sailed for. The settlements along Blue Lake were built out on pilings into the water. We were well greeted there, and feasted with freshwater fish, which tasted odd to my sea-trained tongue. I felt myself quite the traveller, and Hands and I were nearly overwhelmed with our opinions of ourselves when some green-eyed girls from a grain-trading family came giggling to our fireside one night. They had brought with them small, brightly-coloured drums, each toned differently, and they played and sang for us until their mothers came scolding to find them and lead them home. It was a heady experience, and I did not think of Prince Rurisk at all that night.

West and north we travelled now, ferried across Blue Lake on some flat-bottomed barges I trusted not at all. On the far side, we found ourselves suddenly in forest lands, and the hot days of Farrow became a fond memory. Our path led us through immense stands of cedar, pricked here and there with groves of white paper-birch and seasoned in burned areas with alder and willow. Our horses' hooves thudded on the black earth of the forest trail, and the sweet smells of the autumn were all around us. We saw unfamiliar birds, and once I glimpsed a great stag of a colour and kind I had never seen before or since. Night grazing for the horses was not good, and we were glad of the grain we had bought from the lake people. We lit fires at night, and Hands and I shared a tent.

Our way led steadily uphill now. We wound our way between the steepest slopes, but we were unmistakably making our way up into the mountains. One afternoon we met a deputation from Jhaampe, sent to greet us and guide us on our way. After that, we seemed to travel faster, and every evening we were entertained with musicians, poets and jugglers, and feasted with their delicacies. Every effort was made to welcome us and to honour us. But I found them passing strange and almost frightening in their differences. Often I was forced to remind myself of what both Burrich and Chade had taught me about the courtesies, while poor Hands withdrew almost totally from these new companions.

Physically, most of them were Chyurda, and were as I had expected them to be; a tall, pale people, light of hair and eye, and some with hair as red as a fox. They were a brawny people, the women as well as the men. All seemed to carry a bow or a sling, and they were obviously more comfortable on foot than on horseback. They dressed in wool and leather, and even the humblest wore fine furs as if they were no more than homespun. They strode alongside us, mounted as we were, and seemed to have no difficulty keeping up with the horses all day. They sang as they walked, long songs in an ancient tongue that sounded almost mournful, but were interspersed with shouts of victory or delight. I was later to learn they were singing us their history, that we might know better what kind of a people our prince was joining us to. I gathered that they were, for the most part, minstrels and poets, the 'hospitable' ones, as their language translated it, traditionally sent to greet guests and to make them glad they had come even before they arrived.

As the next two days passed, our trail widened, for other paths and roads fed into it the closer we came to Jhaampe. It became a broad tradeway, sometimes paved with a crushed white stone. And the closer we came to Jhaampe, the greater our procession became, for we were joined by contingents from villages and tribes, pouring in from the outer reaches of the Mountain Kingdom to see their princess pledge herself to the powerful prince from the lowlands. Soon, with dogs and horses and some sort of goat they used as pack-beasts, with wains of gifts and folk of every walk and degree trailing in families and knots behind us, we came to Jhaampe.

TWENTY

Jhaampe

'– and so let them come, the people of who I am, and when they reach the city, let them always be able to say, "this is our city and our home, for however long we wish to stay" – Let there always be spaces left, let – (words obscured) – of the herds and flocks. Then there will be no strangers in Jhaampe, but only neighbours and friends, coming and going as they will.' And the will of the Sacrifice was observed in this, as in all things.

So I read years later, in a fragment from a Chyurda holy tablet, and so finally came to understand Jhaampe. But that first time, as we rode up the hills toward Jhaampe, I was both disappointed and awed at what I saw.

The temples, palaces, and public buildings reminded me of the immense closed blossoms of tulips, both in colour and shape. The shape they owe to the once traditional stretched-hide shelters of the nomads who founded the city; the colour purely to the mountain folk's love of colour in everything. Every building had been recently restained in preparation for our coming and the Princess's nuptials, and thus they were almost garishly bright. Shades of purple seemed to dominate, set off by yellows, but every colour was represented. It is best compared, perhaps, to chancing upon a patch of crocus, pushing up through snow and black earth, for the bare, black rocks of the mountains and the dark evergreens made the brightness of the buildings even more

327

impressive. Additionally, the city itself is built on an area fully as steep as Buckkeep Town, so that when one beholds it from below, the colour and lines of it are presented in layers, like an artful arrangement of flowers in a basket.

But as we drew closer, we were able to see that between and among the great buildings were tents and temporary huts and tiny shelters of every kind. For at Jhaampe, only the public buildings and the royal houses are permanent. All else is the ebb and flow of folk coming to visit their capital city, to ask judgement of the Sacrifice, as they call the king or queen who rules there, or to visit the repositories of their treasures and knowledge, or simply to trade with and visit other nomads. Tribes come and go, tents are pitched and inhabited for a month or two, and then one morning, all is bare, swept earth where they were, until another group moves in to claim the spot. Yet it is not a disorderly place, for the streets are well-defined, with stone stairs set into the steeper places. Wells and bath-houses and streams are located at intervals throughout the city, and the strictest rules are observed about rubbish and offal. It is also a green city, for the outskirts of it are pastures for those who bring their herds and horses with them, with tenting areas defined by the shade trees and wells there. Within the city are stretches of garden, flowers and sculpted trees, more artfully tended than anything I had ever seen in Buckkeep. The visiting folk leave their creations among these gardens, and they may take the form of stone sculptures or carvings of wood, or brightly-painted pottery creatures. In a way, it put me in mind of the Fool's room, for in both places were colour and shape set out simply for the pleasure of the eye.

Our guides halted us at a pasture outside the city, and indicated that it had been set aside for us. After a while it became obvious that they expected we would leave our horses and mules here, and proceed on foot. August, who was the nominal head of our caravan, did not handle this very diplomatically. I winced as he angrily explained that we had brought with us much more than we could be expected to carry into the city, and that many there were too weary from travelling to relish the idea of the uphill walk. I bit my lip and forced myself to stand quietly, to witness the polite confusion of our hosts. Surely Regal had known of these customs; why had he not warned us of them, so we would not begin our visit by appearing boorish and unaccommodating?

But the hospitable folk tending to us swiftly adapted to our strange ways. They bade us rest, and begged us to be patient with them. For a time we all stood about, vainly trying to appear comfortable. Rowd and Sevrens joined Hands and me. Hands had a slosh or two of wine left in a skin, and this he shared, while Rowd grudgingly reciprocated with some smoked meat in strips. We talked, but I confess I paid little attention. I wished I had the courage to go to August, and entreat him to be more adaptable to the ways of this people. We were their guests, and it was already bad enough that the groom had not come in person to carry off his bride. I watched from a distance as August consulted with several elder lords who had come with us, but from the motions of their hands and heads I deduced that they were only agreeing with him.

Moments later, a stream of sturdy Chyurda youths and maidens appeared on the road above us. Bearers had been summoned to help carry our goods into the city, and from somewhere bright tents were conjured for those servants who would stay here to tend the horses and mules. I much regretted to find that Hands would be one of those left behind. I entrusted Sooty to him. Then I shouldered the cedar herb-chest and slung my personal bag from my other shoulder. As I joined the procession of those walking into the city, I smelled meats sizzling and tubers cooking, and saw our hosts setting up an open-sided pavilion, and assembling tables within it. Hands, I decided, would not fare poorly, and almost I wished I had nothing more to do than tend the animals and explore this bright city.

We had not gone far up the winding street ascending into the city before we were met by a flock of litters carried by tall Chyurda women. We were earnestly invited to mount into these litters and be carried into the city, and many apologies were made that we had been wearied by our trip. August, Sevrens, the older lords and most of the ladies of our party seemed only too happy to take advantage of this offer, but for me, it seemed a humiliation to be carried into the city. However, it would have been even ruder to turn down their polite insistence, and so I surrendered my chest to a boy obviously younger than myself, and mounted into a litter borne by women old enough to be my grandmother. I blushed to see how curiously the folk on the streets regarded us, and how they stooped to talk quickly together as we passed. I saw few other litters, and they were inhabited by those obviously old and infirm. I set my teeth and tried not to think what Verity would have felt about this display of ignorance. I tried to look out pleasantly on those we passed, and to let my delight in their gardens and graceful buildings show on my face.

I must have succeeded in this, for presently my litter began to move more slowly, to allow me more time to see things, and the women to point to anything they thought I might have missed noticing. They spoke to me in Chyurda, and were delighted to find I had a crude understanding of their language. Chade had taught me the little he knew, but he had not prepared me for how musical the language was, and it soon became apparent to me that the note of a word was as important as the pronunciation. Fortunately, I had a quick ear for languages, so I blundered manfully into conversation with my bearers, resolved that by the time I spoke to my betters in the palace, I would no longer sound quite so much an outland fool. One woman undertook to give me a commentary on all we passed. Jonqui, her name was, and when I told her mine was FitzChivalry, she muttered it to herself several times as if to fix it in her mind.

With great difficulty, I persuaded my bearers to pause once and let me alight to examine a particular garden. It was not the bright flowers that attracted me, but what appeared to be a sort of willow that was growing in spirals and curls rather than the straight willow I was accustomed to. I ran my fingers along the supple bark of one limb and felt sure I could persuade a cutting to sprout, but dared not take a piece of it, lest it be construed as rude. One old woman stooped down beside me, grinned, and then ran her hand across the tops of a low-growing, tiny-leaved bed of herbs. The fragrance that arose from the stirred leaves was astounding, and she laughed aloud at the delight on my face. I would have liked to linger longer, but my bearers emphatically insisted that we must hurry to catch up with the others before they reached the palace. I gathered there was to be an official welcoming, one I must not miss.

Our procession wound up a terraced street, ever higher, until our litters were set down outside a palace that was a cluster of the bright, bud-like structures. The main buildings were purple tipped with white, putting me in mind of the roadside lupin and beach-pea flowers of Buck. I stood beside my litter, staring up at the palace, but when I turned to my bearers to indicate my pleasure in it, they were gone. They reappeared moments later, robed in saffron and azure, peach and rose, as did the other bearers, and walked among us, offering us basins of scented water and soft cloths to wash the dust and weariness from our faces and necks. Boys and young men in belted blue tunics brought a berry wine and tiny honey cakes. When every guest was washed and greeted with wine and honey, we then were bade to follow them into the palace.

The interior of the palace was as foreign to me as the rest of Jhaampe. A great central pillar supported the main structure, and closer examination showed it to be the immense trunk of a tree, with the swells of its roots still obvious beneath the paving stones around its base. The supports of the gracefully curving walls were likewise trees, and days later I was to find that the 'growing' of the palace had taken almost one hundred years. A central tree had been selected, the area cleared, and then the circle of supporting trees planted and tended, and shaped during their growing by ropes and pruning, so that they all bowed toward the centre tree. At some point all other branches had been lopped away and the treetops interwoven to form a crown. Then the walls had been created, first with a layer of finely-woven fabric, that was then varnished to hardness, and then overlaid with lapping after lapping of sturdy cloth made from bark. The bark-cloth was daubed over with a peculiar local clay, and then coated with a bright layer of resinous paint. I never did discover if every building in the city had been created in this laborious fashion, but the 'growing' of the palace had enabled its creators to give it a living grace that stone could never mimic.

The immense interior was open, not unlike the great hall at Buckkeep, with a similar number of hearths. There were tables

set out, and areas obviously for cooking and weaving and spinning and preserving, and all the other necessities of a great
household. The private chambers seemed to be no more than
curtained alcoves, or rooms like small tents set against the
exterior wall. There were also some elevated chambers, reached
by a network of open wooden stairs, reminding me of tents
pitched on stilt platforms. The supporting legs of these chambers
were natural tree-trunks. My heart sank as I realized how little
privacy there would be for any 'quiet' work I needed to do.

I was shown quickly to a tent chamber. Inside I found my
cedar chest and clothing bag awaiting me, as well as more warm
and scented wash-water and a dish of fruit. I changed quickly
from my dusty travelling clothes into an embroidered robe with
slit sleeves and matching green leggings that Mistress Hasty had
decreed as appropriate. I wondered once more at the threatening
buck embroidered on it, then set it out of my mind. Perhaps
Verity had thought this changed crest less humiliating than the
one that so clearly proclaimed my illegitimacy. In any case, it
would serve. I heard chimes and small drums from the great
central room, and left my chamber hurriedly to find out what
was afoot.

On a dais set before the great trunk and decorated with
flowers and evergreen swags, August and Regal stood before an
old man flanked by two servants in plain white robes. A crowd
had gathered in a great circle around the dais, and I quickly
joined them. One of my litter-bearers, now robed in rose drapings
and crowned with a twining of ivy, soon appeared at my side.
She smiled down at me.

'What is happening?' I made bold to ask.

'Our Sacrifice, er, ah, you say, King Eyod will welcome you.
And he will show to you all his daughter, to be your Sacrifice,
hem, ah, queen. And his son, who will rule for her here.' She
stumbled through this explanation, with many a pause, and many
encouraging nods from me.

With mutual difficulty, she explained that the woman standing
beside King Eyod was her niece and I awkwardly managed a
compliment to the effect that she looked both healthy and
strong. At the moment it seemed the kindest thing I could find

to say of the impressive woman standing so protectively by her king. She had an immense mass of the yellow hair that I was becoming accustomed to in Jhaampe, with some of it braided up and coiled about her head, and some flowing loose down her back. Her face was grave, her bare arms muscular. The man on the other side of King Eyod was older, but still as like to her as a twin, save that his hair was cut severely short at his collar. He had the same jade eyes, straight nose and solemn mouth. When I managed to ask the old woman if he, too, were a relative, she smiled as if I must be a bit dim, and replied that, of course, he was her nephew. She shushed me then, as if I were but a child, for King Eyod was speaking.

He spoke slowly and carefully, but even so, I was glad of my conversations with my litter-bearers, for I was able to make out most of his speech. He greeted us all formally, including Regal, for he said that previously he had greeted him only as the emissary of King Shrewd and now he greeted him as Prince Verity's symbol of his presence. August was included in this greeting, and both were presented with several gifts, jewelled daggers, a precious fragrant oil, and rich fur stoles. When the stoles were placed about their shoulders, I thought with chagrin that both now looked more like decorations than princes, for in contrast to the simple garb of King Eyod and his attendants, Regal and August were decked in circlets and rings, and their garments were of opulently rich fabrics and cut with no regard for either thrift or service. To me, they both appeared foppish and vain, but I hoped that our hosts would merely think their outlandish appearance was part of our foreign customs.

And then, to my personal chagrin, the King summoned forward his male attendant, and introduced him to our assemblage as Prince Rurisk. The woman beside him was, of course, Princess Kettricken, and Verity's betrothed.

And finally, I realized that those who had been our litter-bearers and greeted us with cakes and wine were not the servants, but the women of the royal household, the grandmothers, aunts and cousins of Verity's betrothed, all following the Jhaampe tradition of serving their people. I quailed to think I had spoken to them so familiarly and casually, and again mentally cursed Regal that he had not foreseen to send us more word of their customs rather than the long list of clothing and jewellery he wished brought for himself. The elderly woman beside me, then, was the King's own sister. I think she must have sensed my confusion, for she patted my shoulder benignly and smiled at my blushes as I attempted to stutter an apology.

'For, you have done nothing to shame yourself,' she informed me, and then bade me call her not, 'My lady', but Jonqui.

I watched as August presented to the Princess the jewellery Verity had selected to send her. There was a net of finely-woven silver chain set with red gems to drape her hair, and a silver collar set with larger red stones. There was a silver hoop, wrought like a vine, full of jingling keys, that August explained were her household keys for when she joined her husband at Buckkeep, and eight plain silver rings for her hands. She stood still as Regal himself decked her. I thought to myself the silver with red stones would have looked better on a darker woman, but Kettricken's girlish delight was dazzlingly obvious in her smile, and around me people turned and murmured approvingly to one another to see their princess so adorned. Perhaps, I thought, she might enjoy our outlandish colours and accoutrements.

I was grateful for the briefness of King Eyod's speech that followed, for all he added was that he bade us welcome, and invited us to rest, relax and enjoy the city. If we had any needs, we had but to ask of anyone we encountered, and they would attempt to meet them. Tomorrow at noon would begin the three-day ceremony of the Joining, and he desired that we all be well-rested to enjoy it. Then he and his offspring descended, to mingle as freely with one and all as if we were all soldiers on the same watch.

Jonqui had obviously attached herself to me, and there was no gracious way to escape her company, so I resolved to learn as much as I could as quickly as I could about their customs. But one of her first acts was to present me to the Prince and Princess. They were standing with August, who appeared to be explaining how, through him, Verity would witness his ceremony. He was speaking loudly, as if this would somehow make it easier for them to understand. Jonqui listened for a moment, then apparently decided that August had finished speaking. She spoke as if we were all children brought together for sweetcakes while our parents conversed. 'Rurisk, Kettricken, this young man is most interested in our gardens. Perhaps later we can arrange that he speak with those who tend them.' She seemed to speak especially to Kettricken as she added, 'His name is FitzChivalry.'

August frowned suddenly and amended her introduction. 'Fitz. The bastard.'

Kettricken looked shocked at this soubriquet, but Rurisk's fair face darkened somewhat. Ever so slightly, he turned toward me, putting his shoulder to August. Even so, it was a gesture that needed no explaining in any language. 'Yes,' he said, switching to Chyurda and looking me full in the eye. 'Your father spoke of you to me, the last time I saw him. I was grieved to hear of his death. He did much to prepare the way for the forging of this bond between our folk.'

'You knew my father?' I asked stupidly.

He smiled down at me. 'Of course. He and I were treating together, regarding the use of Bluerock Pass, at Moonseye, north-east of here, when he first learned of you. When our time of talking of passes and trade as envoys were done, we sat down to meat together, and spoke, as men, of what he must next do. I confess, I still do not understand why he felt he must not rule as king. The customs of one folk are not those of another. Still, with this wedding, we shall be closer to making one folk of our peoples. Do you think that would please him?'

Rurisk was giving me his sole attention, and his use of Chyurda effectively excluded August from the conversation. Kettricken appeared fascinated. August's face past Rurisk's shoulder grew very still. Then, with a grim smile of purest hatred for me, he turned aside and rejoined the group around Regal, who was speaking with King Eyod. For whatever reason, I had the complete attention of Rurisk and Kettricken.

'I did not know my father well, but I think he would be pleased to see . . .' I began, but at that moment, Princess Kettricken smiled brilliantly at me.

'Of course, how could I have been so stupid? You are the one they call Fitz. Do not you usually travel with Lady Thyme, King

Shrewd's poisoner? And are you not training as her apprentice? Regal has spoken of you.'

'How kind of him,' I said inanely, and I have no idea what next was said to me, nor what I replied. I could only be thankful I did not reel where I stood. And inside me, for the first time, I acknowledged that what I felt for Regal went beyond distaste. Rurisk frowned a brother's rebuke at Kettricken, and then turned to deal with a servant urgently asking his instructions about something. Around me people conversed genially amid summer colours and scents, but I felt as if my guts had turned to ice.

I came back to myself when Kettricken plucked at my sleeve. 'They are this way,' she informed me. 'Or are you too weary to enjoy them now? If you wish to retire, it will offend no one. I understand that many of you were too weary even to walk into the city.'

'But many of us were not, and would truly have enjoyed the chance to walk leisurely through Jhaampe. I have been told of the Blue Fountains, and look forward to seeing them.' I only faltered slightly as I said this, and hoped it had some bearing on what she had been saying to me. At least it had nothing to do with poison.

'I will be sure you are guided to them, perhaps this evening. But for now, come this way.' And with no more ado or formality than that, she led me away from the gathering. August watched after us as we walked away, and I saw Regal turn and say something in an aside to Rowd. King Eyod had withdrawn from the crowd, and was looking benignly down on all from an elevated platform. I wondered why Rowd had not remained with the horses and other servants, but then Kettricken was drawing a painted screen aside from a door-opening and we were leaving the main room of the palace.

We were outside, in fact, walking on a stone pathway under an archway of trees. They were willows, and their living branches had been interlaced and woven overhead to form a green screen from the noon sun. 'And they shed rain from the path, too. At least, most of it,' Kettricken added as she noted my interest. 'This path leads to the shade gardens. They are my favourites. But perhaps you would wish to see the herbery first?'

'I shall enjoy seeing any and all of the gardens, my lady,' I replied, and this at least was true. Out here, away from the crowd, I would have more chance to sort my thoughts and ponder what to do from my untenable position. It was occurring to me, belatedly, that Prince Rurisk had shown none of the signs of injury or illness that Regal had reported. I needed to withdraw from the situation and re-evaluate it. There was more, much more, going on than I had been prepared for.

But with an effort I pulled my thoughts away from my own dilemma and focused on what the Princess was telling me. She spoke her words clearly, and I found her conversation much easier to follow away from the background chatter of the great hall. She seemed to know much about the gardens, and gave me to understand that it was not a hobby but knowledge that was expected of her as a princess.

As we walked and talked, I constantly had to remind myself that she was a princess, and betrothed to Verity. I had never encountered a woman like her before. She wore a quiet dignity, quite unlike the awareness of station that I usually encountered in those better born than I. But she did not hesitate to smile, or become enthused, or stoop to dig in the soil around a plant to show me a particular type of root she was describing. She rubbed the root free of dirt, then sliced a bit with her belt knife from the heart of the tuber, to allow me to taste its tang. She showed me certain pungent herbs for seasoning meat, and insisted I taste a leaf of each of three varieties, for though the plants were very similar, the flavours were very different. In a way, she was like Patience, without her eccentricity. In another way, she was like Molly, but without the callousness that Molly had been forced to develop to survive. Like Molly, she spoke directly and frankly to me, as if we were equals. I found myself thinking that Verity might find this woman more to his liking than he expected.

And yet, another part of me worried what Verity would think of his bride. He was not a womanizer, but his taste in women was obvious to anyone who had been much around him. And those whom he smiled upon were usually small and round and dark, often with curly hair and girlish laughter and tiny soft hands.

What would he think of this tall, pale woman, who dressed as simply as a servant and declared she took much pleasure in tending her own gardens? As our talk turned, I found she could speak as familiarly about falconry and horse-breeding as any stableman. And when I asked her what she did for pleasure, she told me of her small forge and tools for working metal, and lifted her hair to show me the earrings she had made for herself. The finely-hammered silver petals of a flower clasped a tiny gem like a drop of dew. I had once told Molly that Verity deserved a competent and active wife, but now I wondered if she would much beguile him. He would respect her, I knew. But was respect enough between a king and his queen?

I resolved not to borrow trouble, but to keep my word to Verity instead. I asked her if Regal had told her much of her husband, and she became suddenly quiet. I sensed her drawing on her strength as she replied that she knew he was a King-in-Waiting with many problems facing his realm. Regal had warned her that Verity was much older than she was, a plain and simple man, who might not take much interest in her. Regal had promised to be ever by her, helping her to adapt, and doing his best to see that the court was not a lonely place for her. So she was prepared . . .

'How old are you?' I asked impulsively.

'Eighteen,' she replied, and then smiled to see the surprise on my face. 'Because I am tall, your people seem to think I am much older than that,' she confided to me.

'Well, you are younger than Verity, then. But not so much more than between many wives and husbands. He will be thirty-three this spring.'

'I had thought him much older than that,' she said wonderingly. 'Regal explained they share but a father.'

'It is true that Chivalry and Verity were both sons of King Shrewd's first queen, but there is not that great a span between them. And Verity, when he is not burdened with the problems of state, is not so dour and severe as you might imagine him. He is a man who knows how to laugh.'

She cast me a sideways glance, as if to see if I were trying to put a better face on Verity than he deserved.

'It is true, princess. I have seen him laugh like a child at the puppet shows at Springfest. And when all join in for luck at the fruitpress to make autumn wine, he does not hold back. But his greatest pleasure has always been the hunt. He has a wolfhound, Leon, which he holds dearer than some men hold their sons.'

'But,' Kettricken ventured to interrupt. 'Surely this is as he was, once. For Regal speaks of him as a man older than his years, bent down by the cares of his people.'

'Bent down as a tree burdened by snow, that springs erect again with the coming of spring. His last words to me before I left, princess, were to desire me to speak well of him to you.'

She cast her eyes down quickly, as if to hide from me the sudden lift of her heart. 'I see a different man, when you speak of him.' She paused, and then closed her mouth firmly, forbidding herself the request I heard anyway.

'I have always seen him as a kind man. As kind as one lifted to such a responsibility can be. He takes his duties very seriously, and will not spare himself from what his folk need of him. This it is that has made him unable to come here, to you. He engages in a battle with the Red Ship Raiders, one he couldn't fight from here. He gives up the interests of a man to fulfil his duty as a prince. Not through a coldness of spirit, or a lack of life in himself.'

She gave me a sideways glance, fighting the smile from her face as if what I told her were sweetest flattery such as a princess must not believe.

'He is taller than I am, but only by a bit. His hair is very dark, as is his beard, when he lets it grow. His eyes are blacker still, yet when he is enthused, they shine. It is true there is a scattering of grey in his hair now that you would not have found a year ago. True, also, that his work has kept him from the sun and the wind, so his shoulders no longer tear the seams of his shirts. But my uncle is still very much a man, and I believe that when the danger of the Red Ships has been driven from our shores, he will ride and shout and hunt with his hound once more.'

'You give me heart,' she muttered, and then straightened herself as if she had admitted some weakness. Looking at me gravely, she asked, 'Why does Regal not speak of his brother so? I thought I went to an old man, shaking of hand, too burdened by his duties to see a wife as anything other than another duty.'

'Perhaps he . . .' I began, and could think of no courtier's way to say that Regal was frequently deceptive if it gained him his goal. For the life of me, I had no idea what goal might be served by making Kettricken so dread Verity.

'Perhaps he has . . . been . . . unflattering about other things as well,' Kettricken suddenly supposed aloud. Something seemed to alarm her. She took a breath, and became suddenly franker. 'There was an evening, in my chamber, when we had dined, and Regal had, perhaps, drunk a bit too well. He told tales of you then, saying you had once been a sullen, spoiled child, too ambitious for your birth, but that since the King had made you his poisoner, you seemed content with your lot. He said it seemed to suit you, for even as a boy, you had enjoyed eavesdropping and skulking about and other secretive pursuits. Now, I do not tell you this to make a mischief, but only to let you know what I first believed of you. The next day Regal begged me to believe it had been the fancies of the wine rather than the facts he had shared with me. But one thing he had said that night was too icy a fear for me entirely to lay aside. He said that if the King did send you or Lady Thyme, it would be to poison my brother, so that I might be the sole heir to the Mountain Kingdom.'

'You are speaking too quickly,' I chided her gently, and hoped my smile did not look as dizzy and sickly as I suddenly felt. 'I did not understand all you said.' Desperately I strove to think of what to say. Even as accomplished a liar as I found such a direct confrontation uncomfortable.

'I am sorry. But you speak our language so well, almost like a native. Almost as if you were recalling it, rather than learning it new. I will go more slowly. Some weeks, no, it was over a month ago, Regal came to my chambers. He had asked if he might dine alone with me, that we might get to know one another better, and . . .'

'Kettricken!' It was Rurisk, calling down the path as he came seeking us. 'Regal is asking that you would come and meet the lords and ladies who have come so far to see your marriage.'

Jonqui was at his shoulder, hurrying after him, and as the

second and unmistakable wave of dizziness hit me, I thought she looked too knowing. And, I asked myself, what step would Chade have taken if someone had sent a poisoner to Shrewd's court, to eliminate Verity? All too obvious.

'Perhaps,' Jonqui suddenly suggested, 'FitzChivalry would like to be shown the Blue Fountains now. Litress has said she would gladly take him.'

'Maybe later this afternoon,' I managed to say. 'I find myself suddenly wearied. I think I shall seek my chamber.'

None of them looked surprised. 'Shall I have some wine sent to you?' Jonqui asked graciously. 'Or perhaps some soup? The others will be summoned to a meal soon. But, if you are tired, it is no trouble to bring food to you.'

Years of training came to the fore. I kept my posture straight, despite the sudden fire in my belly. 'That would be most kind of you,' I managed to say. The brief bow I forced myself to make was sophisticated torture. 'I am sure I will rejoin you soon.'

And I excused myself, and I did not run, nor curl in a ball and whimper as I wished to. I walked, with obvious enjoyment of the plantings, back through the garden to the door of the great hall. And the three of them watched me go, and spoke softly together of what we all knew.

I had but one trick left to me, and small hope it would be effective. Back in my room, I dug out the seapurge the Fool had given me. How long, I wondered, had it been since I had eaten the honey cakes? For that was the venue I would have chosen. Fatalistically, I decided I would trust the ewer of water in my room. A tiny part of me said that was foolish, but as wave after wave of giddiness washed over me, I felt incapable of any further thought. With shaking hands I crumbled the seapurge into water. The dried herb absorbed the water and became a green sticky wad, which I managed to choke down. I knew it would empty my stomach and bowels. The only question was, would it be swift enough, or was the Chyurda poison too widespread in me?

I spent a miserable evening that I will not dwell on. No one came to my room with soup or wine. In my moments of lucidity, I decided they would not come until they were sure their poison had had its effect. Morning, I decided. They would send a servant to waken me, and he would discover my death. I had until morning.

It was past midnight when I was able to stand. I left my room as silently as my shaking legs would carry me and went out into the garden. I found a cistern of water there, and drank until I thought I would burst. I ventured further into the garden, walking slowly and carefully, for I ached as if I had been beaten and my head pounded painfully with each step I took. But eventually I stumbled into an area of fruit trees gracefully trained along a wall, and as I had hoped, they were heavy with the harvest. I helped myself, filling my jerkin with a supply. These I would conceal in my room, to give me food I could safely consume. Sometime tomorrow, I would make an excuse to go down and check on Sooty. My saddlebags still held some dried meat and hard bread. I hoped it would be enough to get me through this visit.

And as I made my way back to my room, I wondered what else they would try when they found the poison hadn't worked.

TWENTY-ONE

Princes

Of the Chyurdan herb Carryme, their saying is, 'A leaf to sleep, two to dull pain, three for a merciful grave.'

Towards dawn, I finally dozed, only to be awakened by Prince Rurisk flinging aside the screen that served as door to my chamber. He burst into the room, flourishing a sloshing decanter. The looseness of the garment that fluttered about him declared it a nightrobe. I rolled quickly from the bed and managed to stand, with the bedstead between us. I was cornered, sick and weaponless, save for my belt knife.

'You live still!' he exclaimed in amazement, then advanced on me with his flask. 'Quick, drink this.'

'I would sooner not,' I told him, retreating as he advanced.

Seeing my wariness, he paused. 'You have taken poison,' he told me carefully. 'It is fully a miracle of Chranzuli that you still live. This is a purge, that will flush it from your body. Take it, and you may still live.'

'There is nothing left in my body to purge,' I told him bluntly, and then caught at a table as I began to shake. 'I knew I had been poisoned when I left you last night.'

'And you said nothing to me?' He was incredulous. He turned back to the door, where Kettricken now peeked in timidly. Her hair was in tousled braids, and her eyes red with weeping. 'It is averted, small thanks to you,' her brother told her severely. 'Go

343

and make him a salty broth from some of last night's meat. And bring a sweet pastry as well. Enough for both of us. And tea. Go on now, you foolish girl!'

Kettricken scampered off like a child. Rurisk gestured at the bed. 'Come. Trust me enough to sit down. Before you upset the table with your shaking. I am speaking plainly to you. You and I, FitzChivalry, we have no time for this distrust. There is much we must speak of, you and I.'

I sat down, not out of trust so much as for fear I would otherwise collapse. Without formality, Rurisk sat down on the end of the bed. 'My sister,' he said gravely, 'is impetuous. Poor Verity will find her more child than woman, I fear, and much of that is my fault; I have spoiled her so. But, although that explains her fondness for me, it does not excuse her poisoning of a guest. Especially not on the eve of her wedding to his uncle.'

'I think I would have felt much the same about it at any time,' I said, and Rurisk threw back his head and laughed.

'There is much of your father in you. So would he have said, I am sure. But I must explain. She came to me days ago, to tell me that you were coming to make an end of me. I told her then that it was not her concern, and I would take care of it. But, as I have said, she is impulsive. Yesterday she saw an opportunity and took it. With no regard as to how the death of a guest might affect a carefully-negotiated wedding. She thought only to do away with you before vows bound her to the Six Duchies and made such an act unthinkable. I should have suspected it when she took you so quickly to the gardens.'

'The herbs she gave me?'

He nodded, and I felt a fool. 'But after you had eaten them, you spoke so fair to her that she came to doubt you could be what it was said you were. So she asked you, but you turned the question aside by pretending to not understand. So again she doubted you. Still, it should not have taken her all night to come to me with her tale of what she had done, and her doubts of the wisdom of it. For that, I apologize.'

'Too late to apologize. I have already forgiven you,' I heard myself say.

Rurisk looked at me. 'That was your father's saying, as well.'

He glanced at the door a moment before Kettricken came through it. Once she was within the room, he slid the screen shut and took the tray from her. 'Sit down,' he told her sternly. 'And see another way of dealing with an assassin.' He lifted a heavy mug from the tray and drank deeply of it before passing it to me. He shot Kettricken another glance. 'And if that was poisoned, you have just killed your brother as well.' He broke an apple pastry into three portions. 'Select one,' he told me, and then took that one for himself, and gave the next I chose to Kettricken. 'So you may see there is nothing amiss with this food.'

'I see small reason why you would give me poison this morning after coming to tell me I was poisoned last night,' I admitted. Still, my palate was alive, questing for the slightest mistaste. But there was none. It was rich, flaky pastry stuffed with ripe apples and spices. Even if I had not been so empty, it would have been delicious.

'Exactly,' Rurisk said in a sticky voice, and then swallowed. 'And, if you were an assassin,' here he shot a warning to silence Kettricken, 'you would find yourself in the same position. Some murders are profitable only if no one else knows they were murders. Such would be my death. Were you to slay me now, indeed, were I to die within the next six months, Kettricken and Jonqui both would be shrieking to the stars that I had been assassinated. Scarcely a good foundation for an alliance of peoples. Do you agree?'

I managed a nod. The warm broth in the mug had stilled most of my trembling, and the sweet pastry tasted fit for a god.

'So. We agree that, were you an assassin, there would now be no profit to carrying out my murder. Indeed, there would be a very great loss to you if I died. For my father does not look on this alliance with the favour that I do. Oh, he knows it is wise, for now. But I see it as more than wise. I see it as necessary.

'Tell this to King Shrewd. Our population grows, but there is a limit to our arable soil. Wild game will only feed so many. Comes a time when a country must open itself to trade, especially so rocky and mountainous a country as mine. You have heard, perhaps, that the Jhaampe way is that the ruler is the servant of his people? Well, I serve them in this wise. I marry my beloved

345

younger sister away, in the hopes of winning grain and trade routes and lowland goods for my people, and grazing rights in the cold part of the year when our pastures are under snow. For this, too, I am willing to give you timbers, the great straight timbers that Verity will need to build his warships. Our mountains grow white oak such as you have never seen. This is a thing my father would refuse. He has the old feelings about the cutting of live trees. And like Regal, he sees your coast as a liability, your ocean as a great barrier. But I see it as your father did: a wide road that leads in all directions, and your coast as our access to it. And I see no offence in using trees uprooted by the annual floods and windstorms.'

I held my breath a moment. This was a momentous concession. I found myself nodding to his words.

'So, will you carry my words to King Shrewd, and say to him that it is better to have a live friend in me?'

I could think of no reason not to agree.

'Aren't you going to ask him if he intended to poison you?' Kettricken demanded.

'If he answered yes, you would never trust him. If he answered no, you would probably not believe him, and think him a liar as well as an assassin. Besides, is not one admitted poisoner in this room enough?'

Kettricken ducked her head and a flush suffused her cheeks.

'So come,' Rurisk told her, and held out a conciliatory hand. 'Our guest must get what little rest he can before the day's festivities. And we must back to our chambers before the whole household wonders why we are dashing about in our night-clothes.'

And they left me, to lie back on my bed and wonder. What manner of folk were these that I dealt with? Could I believe their open honesty, or was it a magnificent sham for Eda knew what ends? I wished Chade were here. More and more, I felt nothing was as it seemed. I dared not doze, for I knew if I fell asleep, nothing would wake me before nightfall. Servants came soon with pitchers of warm water and cool, and fruit and cheese on a platter. Reminding myself that these 'servants' might be better born than myself, I treated them all with great courtesy, and later wondered if that might not be the secret of the harmonious household; that all, servants or royalty, be treated with the same courtesy.

It was a day of great festivity. The entries to the palace had been thrown wide open, and folk had come from every vale and dell of the Mountain Kingdom to witness this pledging. Poets and minstrels performed, and more gifts were exchanged, including my formal presentation of the herbals and herb starts. The breeding stock that had been sent from the Six Duchies was displayed, and then gifted forth again to those most in need of it, or most likely to be successful with it. A single ram or bull, with a female or two, might be sent out as a common gift to a whole village. All of the gifts, whether fowl or beast or grain or metal, were brought within the palace, so that all might admire them.

Burrich was there – the first time I had glimpsed him in days. He must have been up before dawn, to have his charges so glossy. Every hoof was freshly oiled, every mane and tail plaited with bright ribbons and bells. The mare to be given to Kettricken was saddled and bridled with harness of finest leather, and her mane and tail hung with so many tiny silver bells that each swish of her tail was a chorus of tinkling. Our horses were different creatures from the small and shaggy stock of the mountain folk, and attracted quite a crowd. Burrich looked weary, yet proud, and his horses stood calmly amidst the clamour. Kettricken spent a deal of time admiring her mare, and I saw her courtesy and deference thawing Burrich's reserve. When I drew closer, I was surprised to hear him speaking in hesitant but clear Chyurda.

But a greater surprise was in store for me that afternoon. Food had been set out on long tables, and all, palace residents and visitors, dined freely. Much had come from the kitchens of the palace, but much more from the mountain folk themselves. They came forward, without hesitation, to set out wheels of cheese, loaves of dark bread, dried or smoked meats, or pickles and bowls of fruit. It would have been tempting, had not my stomach still been so touchy. But the way the food was given was what impressed me. It was unquestioning, this giving and taking between the royalty and their subjects. I noted, too, that there were no sentries or guards of any kind upon the doors. And all mingled and talked as they ate.

At noon precisely a silence fell over the crowd. The Princess Kettricken alone ascended the central dais. In simple language, she announced to all that she now belonged to the Six Duchies and hoped to serve that land well. She thanked her land for all it had ever done for her, for the food it had grown to feed her, the waters of its snows and rivers, the air of the mountain breezes. She reminded all that she did not change her allegiance due to any lack of love for her land, but rather in the hopes of it benefiting both the lands. All kept silent as she spoke, and as she descended from the dais. And then the merriment resumed.

Rurisk came, seeking me out, to see how I did. I assured him I was fully recovered, though in truth I longed to be sleeping. The clothing Mistress Hasty had decreed for me was of the latest court fashion and featured highly inconvenient sleeves and tassles that fell into anything I tried to do or eat, and an uncomfortably snug waist. I longed to be out of the press of people, where I could loosen some laces and get rid of the collar, but knew that if I left now, Chade would frown when I reported to him, and demand that I somehow know all that had happened while I was absent. Rurisk, I think, sensed my need for a bit of quiet, for he suddenly proposed a stroll out to his kennels. 'Let me show you what the addition of some Six Duchies blood a few years back did for my dogs,' he offered.

We left the palace, and walked down a short way to a long, low wooden building. The clean air cleared my head and lifted my spirits. Inside, he showed me a pen where a bitch presided over a litter of red pups. They were healthy little creatures, glossy of coat, nipping and tumbling about in the straw. They came readily, totally unafraid of us. 'These are of Buckkeep lineage, and will hold to a scent even in a downpour,' he told me proudly. He showed me other breeds as well, including a tiny dog with wiry legs, which, he claimed, would clamber right up a tree after game.

We emerged from his kennels and out into the sun, where an older dog slept lazily on a pile of straw. 'Sleep on, old man. You've fathered enough pups that you never need hunt again, except you love it so,' Rurisk told him genially. At his master's voice, the old hound heaved himself to his feet and came to lean affectionately on Rurisk. He looked up at me, and it was Nosy.

I stared at him, and his copper ore eyes returned the look. I quested softly toward him, and for a moment received only puzzlement. And then a flood of warmth, of affection shared and remembered. There was no doubt that he was Rurisk's hound now; the intensity of the bond that had been between us was gone. But he offered me back great fondness and warm memories of when we were puppies together. I went down on one knee, and stroked the red coat gone all bristly with the years, and looked into the eyes that were beginning to show the clouding of age. For an instant, with the physical touch, the bond was as it had been. I knew he was enjoying dozing in the sun, but could be persuaded to go hunting with very little trouble. Especially if Rurisk came along. I patted his back, and drew away from him. I looked up to find Rurisk regarding me strangely. 'I knew him when he was just a puppy,' I told him.

'Burrich sent him to me, in care of a wandering scribe, many years ago,' Rurisk told me. 'He has brought me great pleasure, in company and in hunting.'

'You have done well by him,' I said. We left and strolled back to the palace, but as soon as Rurisk left my side, I went straight to Burrich. As I came up, he had just received permission to take the horses outside and into the open air, for even the calmest beast will grow restive in close quarters with many strangers. I could see his dilemma; while he was taking horses out, he would be leaving the others untended. He looked up warily as I approached.

'With your leave, I will help you move them,' I offered.

Burrich's face remained impassive and polite. But before he could open his mouth to speak, a voice behind me said, 'I am here to do that, master. You might soil your sleeves, or overly weary yourself working with beasts.' I turned slowly, baffled by the venom in Cob's voice. I glanced from him to Burrich, but Burrich did not speak. I looked squarely at Burrich.

'Then I will walk alongside you, if I may, for I have something important we must speak of.' My words were deliberately formal. For a moment longer Burrich gazed at me. 'Bring the Princess's mare,' he said at last, 'and that bay filly. I will take the greys. Cob, mind the rest for me. I shan't be long.'

And so I took the mare's head and the filly's lead-rope, and followed Burrich as he edged the horses through the crowd and out of doors. 'There is a paddock, this way,' he said, and no more. We walked for a bit in silence. The crowd thinned rapidly once we were away from the palace. The horses' hooves thudded pleasantly against the earth. We came to the paddock, which fronted on a small barn with a tack room. For a moment or two, it almost seemed normal to be working alongside Burrich again. I unsaddled the mare, and wiped the nervous sweat from her while he shook out grain into a grain box for them. He came to stand beside me as I finished with the mare. 'She's a beauty,' I said admiringly. 'From Lord Ranger's stock?'

'Yes.' His word cut off the conversation. 'You wished to speak to me.'

I took a great breath, then said it simply. 'I just saw Nosy. He's fine. Older now, but he's had a happy life. All these years, Burrich, I always believed you killed him that night. Dashed out his brains, cut his throat, strangled him – I imagined it a dozen different ways, a thousand times. All those years.'

He looked at me incredulously. 'You believed I would kill a dog for something you did?'

'I only knew he was gone. I could imagine nothing else. I thought it was my punishment.'

For a long time he was still. When he looked back up at me, I could see his torment. 'How you must have hated me.'

'And feared you.'

'All those years? And you never learned better of me, never thought to yourself, "He would not do such a thing"?'

I shook my head slowly.

'Oh, Fitz,' he said sadly. One of the horses came to nudge at him, and he petted it absently. 'I thought you were stubborn and sullen. You thought you had been grievously wronged. No wonder we have been so much at odds.'

'It can be undone,' I offered quietly. 'I have missed you, you know. Missed you sorely, despite all our differences.'

I watched him thinking, and for a moment or two, I thought he would smile and clap me on the shoulder and tell me to go fetch the other horses. But his face grew still, and then stern.

'But for all that, it did not stop you. You believed I had it in me to kill any animal you used the Wit on. But it did not stop you from doing it.'

'I don't see it the way you do,' I began, but he shook his head.

'We are better parted, boy. Better for both of us. There can be no misunderstandings if there are no understandings at all. I can never approve, or ignore, what you do. Never. Come to me when you can say you will do it no more. I will take your word on it, for you've never broken your word to me. But until then, we are better parted.'

He left me standing by the paddock and went back for his other horses. I stood a long time, feeling sick and weary, and not just from Kettricken's poison. But I went back into the palace, walked about, spoke to people and ate, and even endured with silence the mocking, triumphant smiles Cob gave me.

The day seemed longer than any two days in my previous experience. Had not it been for my burning and gurgling stomach, I would have found it exciting and absorbing. The afternoon and early evening were given over to congenial contests of archery, wrestling and foot-races. Young and old, male and female, joined in these contests, and there seemed to be some mountain trad-ition that whoever won on such an auspicious occasion would enjoy luck for a full turn of a year. Then there was more food, and singing, and dancing of dancers, and an entertainment, like a puppet show, but done all with shadows on a screen of silk. By the time folk began to retire, I was more than ready for my bed. It was a relief to close my chamber screen and be alone. I was just pulling off my annoying shirt, and reflecting on what a strange day it had been when there was a tap at my door.

Before I could speak, Sevrens slid open the screen and slipped in. 'Regal commands your presence,' he told me.

'Now?' I asked owlishly.

'Why else would he send me now?' Sevrens demanded.

Wearily I pulled my shirt back on and followed him out of the room. Regal's chambers were in an upper level of the palace, not really a second floor, but more like a wooden terrace built to one side of the great hall. The walls were screens, and there was a sort of balcony where he might stand and look down before descending. These rooms were much more richly decorated. Some of the work was obviously Chyurda, bright birds brushed onto silk panels and figurines carved of amber. But many of the tapestries and statues and hangings looked to me like things Regal had acquired for his own pleasure and comfort. I stood waiting in his antechamber while he finished his bath. By the time he ambled out in his nightshirt, it was all I could do to keep my eyes open.

'Well?' he demanded of me.

I looked at him blankly. 'You summoned me,' I reminded him.

'Yes. I did. I should like to know why it was necessary. I thought you had received some sort of training in this sort of thing. How long were you going to wait before you reported to me?'

I could think of nothing to say. I had never remotely considered reporting to Regal. To Shrewd or Chade, definitely, and to Verity. But to Regal?

'Need I remind you of your duty? Report.'

I hastily gathered my wits. 'Would you hear my observations on the Chyurda as a people? Or information on the herbs they grow? Or . . .'

'I want to know what you are doing about your . . . assignment. Have you acted yet? Have you made a plan? When can we expect results, and of what kind? I scarcely want the Prince dropping dead at my feet, and me unprepared for it.'

I could scarcely credit what I was hearing. Never had Shrewd spoken so bluntly or so openly of my work. Even when our privacy was assured, he circled and danced and left me to draw my own conclusions. I had seen Sevrens go into his other chamber, but had no idea where the man was now or how sound carried in this chamber. And Regal was speaking as if we were discussing shoeing a horse.

'Are you being insolent, or stupid?' Regal demanded.

'Neither,' I rejoined as politely as I was able. 'I am being cautious. My prince.' I added the last in the hopes of putting the conversation on a more formal level.

'You are being foolishly cautious. I trust my valet, and there is no one else here. So report. My bastard assassin.' He said the last words as if he thought them cleverly sarcastic.

I took a breath and reminded myself I was a King's man. And

in this time and place, this was as close to a king as I was going to get. I chose my phrases carefully. 'Yesterday, in the garden, Princess Kettricken told me you had told her I was a poisoner and that her brother Rurisk was my target.'

'A lie,' Regal said decisively. 'I told her nothing of the kind. Either you had clumsily betrayed yourself, or she was merely fishing for information. I hope you have not spoiled all by revealing yourself to her.'

I could have lied much better than he did. I let his remarks slide by, and went on. I gave him a full report, of my poisoning, and of Rurisk and Kettricken's early-morning visit. I repeated our conversation verbatim. And when I was finished, Regal spent a number of minutes looking at his nails before he spoke to me. 'And have you decided on a method and time yet?'

I tried not to show my surprise. 'Under the circumstances, I thought it better to abandon the assignment.'

'No nerve,' Regal observed with disgust. 'I asked Father to send that old whore Lady Thyme. She'd have had him in his grave by now.'

'Sir?' I asked questioningly. That he referred to Chade as Lady Thyme made me nearly certain that he knew nothing at all.

'Sir?' Regal mimicked back at me, and for the first time I realized the man was drunk. Physically, he carried it well. He did not stink of it, but it brought all his pettiness to the surface. He sighed heavily, as if too disgusted for words, then flung himself down on a couch draped with blankets and cushions. 'Nothing has changed,' he informed me. 'You've been given your task. Do it. If you are clever, you can make it appear an accident. Having been so naively open with Kettricken and Rurisk, neither will expect it. But I want it done. Before tomorrow evening.'

'Before the wedding?' I asked incredulously. 'Don't you think the death of the bride's brother might lead her to cancel it?'

'It would be no more than temporary if she did. I have her well in hand, boy. She is easily dazzled. That end of this thing is my concern. Yours is getting rid of her brother. Now. How will you do it?'

'I've no idea.' That seemed a better answer than saying I had no intention. I would return to Buckkeep and report back to

Shrewd and Chade. If they said I had chosen wrongly, then they might do with me as they wished. But I remembered Regal's own voice, from so long ago, quoting Shrewd. 'Don't do what you can't undo, until you've considered what you can't do once you've done it.'

'When will you know?' he demanded sarcastically.

'I don't know,' I hedged. 'These things cannot be done recklessly or sloppily. I need to study the man and his habits, explore his chambers, and learn the habits of his servants. I must find a way to . . .'

'The wedding is two days hence,' Regal interrupted. The focus of his eyes softened. 'I already know all the things you say you must discover. Easiest, then, for me to plan it for you. Come to me tomorrow night, and I will give you your orders. Mind this well, bastard. I do not want you to act before you have informed me. I would find any surprise unpleasant. You would find it deadly.' He lifted his eyes to mine but I kept my face a careful blank.

'You are dismissed,' he told me regally. 'Report to me here, tomorrow night, at the same time. Do not make me send Sevrens to fetch you. He has more important tasks. And do not think my father will not hear of your laxity. He will. He will regret not sending Bitch Thyme to do this little deed.' He leaned back heavily and yawned, and I caught a whiff of wine, and a subtle smoke. I wondered if he were learning his mother's habits.

I returned to my chambers, intending to ponder carefully all my options and formulate a plan. But so weary was I and half-sick still, that I was asleep as soon as my head touched the pillow.

TWENTY-TWO

Dilemmas

In the dream, the Fool stood by my bed. He looked down at me and shook his head. 'Why cannot I speak clearly? Because you make it all a muddle. I see a crossroads through the fog, and who always stands within it? You. Do you think I keep you alive because I am so entranced with you? No. It is because you create so many possibilities. While you live, you give us more choices. The more choices, the more chances to steer for calmer water. So it is not for your benefit, but for the Six Duchies that I preserve your life. And your duty is the same. To live, so that you may continue to present possibilities.'

I awoke in precisely the same quandary I had gone to sleep in. I had no idea of what I was going to do. I lay in my bed, listening to the random sounds of the palace awakening. I needed to talk to Chade. That was not possible. So I lightly closed my eyes and tried to think as he had taught me. 'What do you know?' he would have asked me, and 'What do you suspect?' So.

Regal had lied to King Shrewd about Rurisk's health, and his attitude toward the Six Duchies. Or, possibly, King Shrewd had lied to me about what Regal had said. Or Rurisk had lied about his inclinations toward us. I pondered a moment, and decided to follow my first assumption. Shrewd had never lied to me, that I knew, and Rurisk could have simply let me die instead of rushing to my room. So.

So Regal wanted Rurisk dead. Or did he? If he wanted Rurisk

dead, why did he betray me to Kettricken? Unless she had lied about that. I considered. Not likely. She might wonder if Shrewd would send an assassin, but why would she immediately decide to accuse me? No. She had recognized my name. And known of Lady Thyme. So.

And Regal had said, twice last night, that he had asked his father to send Lady Thyme. But he had likewise betrayed her name to Kettricken. Who did Regal really want dead? Prince Rurisk? Or Lady Thyme, or I, after an assassination attempt was discovered? And how did any of it benefit him, and this marriage he had engineered? And why was he insisting I kill Rurisk, when all the political advantages were to his living?

I needed to talk to Chade. I couldn't. I had to somehow decide this, myself. Unless.

Servants again brought water and fruit. I arose and dressed in my annoying clothes, and ate, and left my chambers. This day was much the same as yesterday. The holiday atmosphere was beginning to wear on me. I attempted to employ my time to advantage, enlarging my knowledge of the palace, its routines and layout. I found Eyod's, Kettricken's, and Rurisk's chambers. I also carefully studied the staircase and support structures to Regal's. I discovered that Cob slept in the stables, as did Burrich. I expected that of Burrich; he would not surrender the care of Buckkeep horses until he left Jhaampe; but why was Cob sleeping there? To impress Burrich, or to watch him? Sevren and Rowd both slept in the antechamber of Regal's apartments, despite a plenitude of rooms in the palace. I tried to study the distribution and schedules of the guards and sentries, but couldn't find any. And all the while I watched for August. It took me the better part of the morning before I could find him in quiet circumstance. 'I need to talk to you. Privately,' I told him.

He looked annoyed, and glanced about to see if anyone were watching us. 'Not here, Fitz. Maybe when we get back to Buckkeep. I've official duties, and . . .'

I had been prepared for that. I opened my hand, to show him the pin the King had given me so many years ago. 'Do you see this? I had it from King Shrewd, a long time ago.

And with it, his promise that if I ever needed to speak to him, I need only show it and I would be admitted to his chambers.'

'How touching,' August observed cynically. 'And had you some reason for telling me this story? To impress me with your importance, perhaps?'

'I need to speak to the King. Now.'

'He isn't here,' August pointed out. He turned to walk away. I took hold of his arm, turned him back to me.

'You can Skill to him.'

He shook me off angrily, and glanced about us again. 'I most certainly cannot. And would not, if I could. Do you think every man who can Skill is allowed to interrupt the King?'

'I have shown you the pin. I promise you, he would not regard this as an interruption.'

'I cannot.'

'Verity, then.'

'I do not Skill to Verity until he Skills to me first. Bastard, you don't understand. You took the training and you failed at it, and you really have not the slightest comprehension of what the Skill is about. It is not like hallooing to a friend across a valley. It is a serious thing, not to be used except for serious purposes.' Again he turned away from me.

'Turn back, August, or regret it long.' I put every ounce of menace I could into my voice. It was an empty threat; I had no real way to make him regret it, other than threatening to tattle to the King. 'Shrewd will not be pleased that you ignored his token.'

August turned slowly back. He glared at me. 'Well. I will do this thing, then, but you must promise to take all blame for it.'

'I will. Will you come to my chambers, then, and Skill for me now?'

'Is there no other place?'

'Your chambers?' I suggested.

'No, that is even worse. Do not take it amiss, bastard, but I do not wish to seem to associate with you.'

'Take it not amiss, lordling, that I feel the same about you.'

In the end, on a stone bench, in a quiet part of Kettricken's herb-garden, August sat down and closed his eyes. 'What message am I to Skill to Shrewd?'

I considered. This would be a game of riddles, if I were to keep August unaware of my true problem. 'Tell him Prince Rurisk's health is excellent, and we may all hope to see him live to old age. Regal still wishes to give him the gift, but I do not think it appropriate.'

August opened his eyes. 'The Skill is an important . . .'

'I know. Tell him.'

So August sat and took several breaths, and closed his eyes. After a few moments, he opened his eyes. 'He says to listen to Regal.'

'That's all?'

'He was busy. And very irritated. Now leave me alone. I fear you've made me a fool before my king.'

There were a dozen witty replies I could have made to that. But I let him walk away. I wondered if he had Skilled to King Shrewd at all. I sat down on the stone bench and reflected that I had gained nothing at all, and wasted much time. The temptation came and I tried it. I closed my own eyes, breathed, focused, opened myself. *Shrewd, my king.*

Nothing. No reply. I doubt that I Skilled at all. I rose and went back into the palace.

Again that day, at noon, Kettricken ascended the dais alone. Her words today were just as simple, as she announced that she was binding herself to the people of the Six Duchies. From this moment hence, she was their Sacrifice, in all things, for any reason that they commanded of her. And then she thanked her own people, blood of her blood, who had raised her and treated her well, and reminded them she did not change her allegiance out of any lack of affection for them, but only in the hopes that it would benefit both peoples. Again the silence held as she descended the steps. Tomorrow would be her day to pledge herself to Verity as a woman to a man. From what I understood, Regal and August would stand beside her tomorrow in Verity's stead, and August would Skill that Verity might see his bride make her pledge to him.

The day dragged for me. Jonqui came and took me to visit the

Blue Fountains. I did my best to be interested and pleasant. We returned to the palace for more minstrels and feasting and that evening's displays of arts by the mountain people. Jugglers and acrobats performed, and dogs did tricks and swordsmen displayed their prowess in staged bouts. Bluesmoke was very much in evidence, and many were indulging, swinging their tiny censers before them as they milled about and talked to one another. I understood that for them, it was like a carris seed cake, a holiday indulgence, but I avoided the trailing smoke of the burn-pots. I had to keep a clear head. Chade had supplied me with a potion to clear the head of wine fumes, but I had and knew of none for smoke. And I was unused to smoke. I found a clearer corner and stood apparently enraptured by a minstrel's song, but watching Regal over his shoulder.

Regal sat at a table, flanked by two brass burners. A very reserved August sat a slight way away from him. From time to time they spoke, August seriously, the prince dismissively. I was not close enough to hear the words, but I saw my name and Skill from August's lips. I saw Kettricken approach Regal, and noted that she avoided being in the direct draught of the smoke. Regal spoke long to her, smiling and languid, and reached once to tap her hand and the silver rings she wore. He seemed to be one of those that the smoke made talkative and boastful. She seemed to teeter like a bird on a branch, now drawing closer to him and smiling, now drawing back and becoming more formal. Then Rurisk came, to stand behind his sister. He spoke to Regal briefly, and then took Kettricken's arm and drew her away. Sevrens appeared and replenished Regal's burners. Regal gave a foolish smile of thanks and said something, indicating the whole hall with a wave of his hand. Sevrens laughed, and left. Shortly afterward, Cob and Rowd arrived to speak to Regal. August rose and stalked indignantly off. Regal glared, and sent Cob to fetch him back. August came, but not graciously. Regal rebuked, and August glowered, then lowered his eyes and conceded. I wished desperately that I were close enough to hear what was said. Something, I felt, was definitely afoot. It might be nothing to do with me and my task. But somehow I doubted it.

I went over my meagre store of facts, feeling sure I was missing the significance of something. But I also wondered if I were not deceiving myself. Perhaps I was over-reacting to everything. Perhaps the safest course was simply to do as Regal told me and let him accept the responsibility. Perhaps I should save time and cut my own throat.

I could, of course, go directly to Rurisk, tell him that, despite my best efforts, Regal still wanted him dead, and beg asylum of him. After all, who would not find attractive a trained assassin who had already turned on one master?

I could tell Regal I was going to kill Rurisk and then simply not do it. I thought carefully about that.

I could tell Regal I was going to kill Rurisk, and then kill Regal instead. The smoke, I told myself. Only the smoke made that sound so wise.

I could go to Burrich and tell him I was really an assassin, and ask his advice about my situation.

I could take the Princess's mare and ride off into the mountains.

'So, are you enjoying yourself?' Jonqui asked as she came up and took my arm.

I realized I was staring at a man juggling knives and torches. 'I shall long remember this experience,' I told her. And then suggested a stroll through the cool of the gardens.

Late that night, I reported to Regal's chamber. Rowd admitted me this time, smiling pleasantly. 'Good evening,' he greeted me, and I walked in as if into a wolverine's den. But the air within the chamber was blue with smoke, and this seemed the source of Rowd's cheerfulness. Regal kept me waiting again, and though I tucked my chin to my chest and breathed shallowly, I knew the smoke was affecting me. Control, I reminded myself, and tried not to feel the giddiness. I shifted in my seat several times, and finally resorted to covering my mouth and nose openly with a hand. It had small effect on screening the smoke.

I looked up as the screen to the inner chamber slid aside, but it was only Sevrens. He glanced at Rowd, then came to sit beside me. After a moment of his silence, I asked, 'Will Regal see me now?'

Sevrens shook his head. 'He is with a . . . companion. But he has trusted me with all you need to know.' He opened his hand on the bench between us, to show me a tiny white pouch. 'He has obtained this for you. He trusts you will approve. A little of this, mixed with wine, will cause death, but not soon. There will not even be symptom of death for several weeks, and then it comes as a lethargy that gradually increases. The man does not suffer,' he added, as if this were my primary concern.

I racked my brains. 'Is this Kex gum?' I had heard of such a poison, but never seen it. If Regal had a source, Chade would want to know.

'I do not know its name, nor does it matter. Only this. Prince Regal says you will have a use for it tonight. You will make an opportunity.'

'What does he expect of me? That I will go to his chambers, knock, and enter with poisoned wine for him? Isn't that a bit obvious?'

'Done that way, of course it is. But surely your training has given you more finesse than that?'

'My training tells me that things like this are not discussed with a valet. I must hear this from Regal, or I do not act.'

Sevrens sighed. 'My master foresaw this. This is his message. By the pin you carry and the crest on your breast, he commands this. Refuse it, and you refuse your king. You will be committing treason, and he will see you hang for it.'

'But I . . .'

'Take it and go. The longer you wait, the later it is, and the more contrived will seem your visit to his chambers.'

Sevrens rose abruptly and left me. Rowd sat like a toad in the corner, eyeing me and smiling. I would have to kill both of them before we returned to Buckkeep, if I were to preserve my usefulness as an assassin. I wondered if they knew that. I smiled back at Rowd, tasting smoke in the back of my throat. I took my poison and left.

Once at the base of Regal's staircase, I retreated to the wall where it was most shadowed, and clambered as swiftly as I could up one of the supports of Regal's chamber. Clinging like a cat, I snugged myself up to the supports of the chamber floor and waited. And waited. Until between the smoke whirling in my head and my own weariness and the lingering effects of Kettricken's herbs, I wondered if I were dreaming all of it. I wondered if my clumsy trap would yield me nothing. I considered, finally, that Regal had told me he had specifically requested Lady Thyme. But Shrewd had sent me instead. I recalled how Chade had puzzled over that. And finally, I recalled his words to me. Had my king given me up to Regal? And if he had, what did I owe to any of them? Eventually, I saw Rowd depart, and after what seemed a very long time, return with Cob.

I could hear little through the floor, but enough to know Regal's voice. My evening's plans were being divulged to Cob. When I was certain of it, I wriggled out of my hiding-place, clambered down and retreated to my own room. There I made certain of some specialized supplies. I reminded myself, firmly, that I was a King's man. I had told Verity so. I left my chamber and walked softly through the palace. In the great hall, the common folk slept on mats on the floor, in concentric circles around the dais, to have reserved the best viewing of their princess's pledging tomorrow. I walked among them and they did not stir. So much trust, so ill-placed.

The chambers of the royals were at the extreme rear of the palace, farthest from the main entry. There were no guards. I walked past the door that led to the bedroom of the reclusive King, past Rurisk's door, and to Kettricken's. Her door was decorated with hummingbirds and honeysuckle. I thought how much the Fool would have liked it. I tapped lightly and waited. Slow moments passed. I tapped again.

I heard the scuff of bare feet on wood, and the painted screen slid open. Kettricken's hair had been freshly braided, but fine strands had already pulled free around her face. Her long white nightrobe accented her fairness, so that she seemed as pale as the Fool. 'Did you need something?' she asked sleepily.

'Only the answer to a question.' The smoke still twined through my thoughts. I wanted to smile, to be witty and clever before her. Pale beauty, I thought. I pushed the impulse aside. She was waiting. 'If I killed your brother tonight,' I said carefully, 'what would you do?'

She did not even draw back from me. 'I would kill you, of course. At least, I would demand it done, in justice. As I am pledged to your family now, I could not take your blood myself.'

'But would you go on with the wedding? Would you still marry Verity?'

'Would you like to come in?'

'I haven't time. Would you marry Verity?'

'I am pledged to the Six Duchies, to be their queen. I am pledged to their people. Tomorrow, I pledge to the King-in-Waiting. Not to a man named Verity. But even were it otherwise, ask yourself, which is the most binding? I am bound already. It is not just my word, but my father's. And my brother's. I would not want to marry a man who had ordered my brother's death. But it is not the man I am pledged to. It is the Six Duchies. I am given there, in the hopes of it benefiting my people. There I must go.'

I nodded. 'Thank you, my lady. Forgive my disturbing your rest.'

'Where do you go now?'

'To your brother.'

She remained standing in her door as I turned and walked to her brother's chamber. I tapped and waited. Rurisk must have been restive, for he opened the door much more quickly.

'May I come in?'

'Certainly.' Gracious, as I had expected. The edge of a giggle teased at my resolve. Chade would not be proud of you just now, I counselled myself, and refused to smile.

I entered and he closed the door behind me. 'Shall we have wine?' I asked him.

'If you wish it,' he said, puzzled but polite. I seated myself on a chair while he unstoppered a carafe and poured for us. There was a censer on his table, too, still warm. I had not seen him indulge earlier. He probably had thought it more safe to wait until he was alone in his chamber. But you never can tell when an assassin will come calling with a pocket full of death. I pushed down a silly smile. He filled two glasses. I leaned forward, and showed him my twist of paper. Painstakingly, I tipped it into his wine, picked up the glass and swirled it to see it well dissolved. I handed it to him.

'I've come to poison you, you see. You die. Then Kettricken kills me. Then she marries Verity.' I lifted my glass and sipped from it. Apple wine. From Farrow, I guessed. Probably part of the wedding gifts. 'So what does Regal gain?'

Rurisk eyed his wine with distaste, and set it aside. He took my glass from my hand. He drank from it. There was no shock in his voice as he said, 'He's rid of you. I gather he does not value your company. He has been very gracious to me, extending many gifts to me as well as to my kingdom. But if I were dead, Kettricken would be left sole heir to the Mountain Kingdom. That would benefit the Six Duchies, would it not?'

'We cannot protect the land we already have. And I think Regal would see it as benefiting Verity, not the kingdom.' I heard a noise outside the door. 'That will be Cob, coming to catch me in the act of poisoning you,' I surmised. I rose, went to the door, and opened it. Kettricken pushed past me into the room. I closed the screen quickly behind her.

'He's come to poison you,' she warned Rurisk.

'I know,' he said gravely. 'He put it in my wine. That's why I'm drinking his.' He refilled the glass from the carafe, and offered it to her. 'It's apple,' he cajoled when she shook her head.

'I don't see any humour in this,' she snapped. Rurisk and I looked at one another and grinned foolishly. Smoke.

Her brother smiled benignly. 'It's like this. FitzChivalry realized tonight he is a dead man. Too many people have been told he is an assassin. If he kills me, you kill him. If he doesn't kill me, how can he go home and face his king? Even if his king forgives him, half the court will know he's an assassin: that makes him useless. Useless bastards are a liability to royalty.' Rurisk finished his lecture by draining the rest of the glass.

'Kettricken told me that even if I killed you tonight, she would still pledge to Verity tomorrow.'

Again, he was not surprised. 'What would she gain by refusing? Only the enmity of the Six Duchies. She would be forsworn to your people, a great shame to our people. She would become outcast, to the good of no one. It would not bring me back.'

'And would not your people rise up at the thought of giving her to such a man?'

'We would protect them from such knowledge. Eyod and my sister would, anyway. Shall a whole kingdom rise to war over the death of one man? Remember, I am Sacrifice here.'

For the first time, I dimly understood what that meant.

'I may soon be an embarrassment to you,' I warned him. 'I was told it was a slow poison. But I looked at it. It is not. It is a simple extract of deadroot, and actually rather swift, if given in sufficient quantity. First, it gives a man tremors.' Rurisk extended his hands on the table, and they trembled. Kettricken looked furious with both of us. 'Death follows swiftly. And I expect I am supposed to be caught in the act and disposed of along with you.'

Rurisk clutched at his throat, then let his head loll forward on his chest. 'I am poisoned!' he intoned theatrically.

'I've had enough of this,' Kettricken spat, just as Cob tore the door open.

''Ware treachery!' he cried. He went white at the sight of Kettricken. 'My lady princess, tell me you have not drunk of the wine! This traitorous bastard has poisoned it!'

I think his drama was rather spoiled by the lack of response. Kettricken and I exchanged looks. Rurisk rolled from his chair onto the floor. 'Oh, stop it,' she hissed at him.

'I put the poison in the wine,' I told Cob genially. 'Just as I was charged to do.'

And then Rurisk's back arched in his first convulsion.

The blinding realization of how I had been duped took but an instant. Poison in the wine. A gift of Farrow apple wine, probably given this very evening. Regal had not trusted me to put it there, but it was easy enough to accomplish, in this trusting place. I watched Rurisk arch again, knowing there was nothing I could do. Already, there was the spreading numbness in my own mouth. I wondered, almost idly, how strong the dose had been. I had only had a sip. Would I die here, or on a scaffold?

Kettricken herself understood, a moment later, that her brother was truly dying. 'You soulless filth!' she spat at me, and then sank down at Rurisk's side. 'To lull him with jests and smoke, to smile with him as he dies!' Her eyes flashed to Cob. 'I demand his death. Tell Regal to come here, now!'

I was moving for the door, but Cob was faster. Of course. No smoke for Cob this night. He was faster and more muscular than I, clearer of head. His arms closed around me and he bore me down to the floor. His face was close to mine as he drove his fist into my belly. I knew this breath, this scent of sweat. Smithy had scented this, before he died. But this time the knife was in my sleeve and very sharp and treated with the swiftest poison Chade knew. After I put it into him, he managed to hit me twice, good solid punches, before he fell back, dying. Goodbye, Cob. As he fell I suddenly saw a freckly stable-boy saying, 'Come along now, there's some good fellows.' It could have gone so many different ways. I had known this man; killing him killed a part of my own life.

Burrich was going to be very upset with me.

All those thoughts had taken but a fraction of a second. Cob's outflung hand had not struck the floor before I was moving for the door.

Kettricken was even faster. I think it was a brass water-ewer. I saw it as a white burst of light.

When I came to myself, everything hurt. The most immediate pain was in my wrists, for the cords that knotted them together behind my back were unbearably tight. I was being carried. Sort of. Neither Rowd nor Sevrens seemed to care much if parts of me dragged. Regal was there, with a torch, and a Chyurda I didn't know leading the way with another. I didn't know where I was, either, except that we were outdoors.

'Is there nowhere else we can put him? No place especially secure?' Regal was demanding. There was a muttered reply, and Regal said, 'No, you are right. We do not want to raise a great outcry right now. Tomorrow is soon enough. Not that I think he will live that long.'

A door was opened and I was flung headlong to an earthen floor barely cushioned by straw. I breathed dust and chaff. I could not cough. Regal gestured with his torch. 'Go to the Princess,' he instructed Sevrens. 'Tell her I will be there shortly. See if there is anything we can do to make the Prince more comfortable. You, Rowd, summon August from his chambers. We will need his Skill, so that King Shrewd may know how he has succoured a scorpion.

I will need his approval before the bastard dies. If he lives long enough to be condemned. Go on, now. Go.'

And they left, the Chyurda lighting their way for them. Regal remained, looking down on me. He waited until their footfalls were distant before he kicked me savagely in the ribs. I cried out wordlessly, for my mouth and throat were numb. 'It seems to me we have been here before, have we not? You wallowing in straw, and me looking down on you, wondering what misfortune had brought you into my life? Odd, how so many things end as they begin.

'And so much of justice is a circle, also. Consider how you fall to poison and treachery. Just as my mother did. Ah, you start. Did you think I did not know? I knew. I know much you do not think I know. Everything from the stench of Lady Thyme to how you lost your Skill when Burrich would no longer let you tap his strength. He was swift enough to abandon you, when he saw it might otherwise cost him his life.'

A tremor shook me. Regal threw back his head and laughed. Then he gave a sigh and turned. 'A pity I cannot stay and watch. But I have a princess to console. Poor thing, pledged to a man she already hates.'

Either Regal left then, or I did. I am not clear. It was as if the sky opened up and I flowed out into it. 'Being open,' Verity told me, 'is simply not being closed.' Then I dreamed, I think, of the Fool. And of Verity, sleeping with his arms wrapped around his head, as if to keep his thoughts in. And of Galen's voice, echoing in a dark, cold chamber. 'Tomorrow is better. When he Skills now, he scarce has any sense of the room he sits in. We do not have enough bond for me to do this from a distance. A touch will be required.'

There was a squeaking in the dark, a disagreeable mouse of a mind that I did not know. 'Do it now,' it insisted.

'Do not be foolish,' Galen rebuked it. 'Shall we lose it all now, for the sake of haste? Tomorrow is soon enough. Let me worry about that part. You must tidy things there. Rowd and Sevrens know too much. And the stablemaster has annoyed us too long.'

'You leave me standing in a bloodbath,' the mouse squeaked angrily.

'Wade through it to a throne,' Galen suggested.

'And Cob is dead. Who will see to my horses on the way home?'

'Leave the stablemaster, then,' Galen said in disgust. And then, considering, 'I will do him myself, when you get home. I shall not mind. But the others were better done quickly. Perhaps the bastard poisoned other wine, in your quarters. A pity your servants got into it.'

'I suppose. You must find me a new valet.'

'We will have your wife do that for you. You should be with her now. She has just lost her brother. You must be horrified at what has come to pass. Try to blame the bastard rather than Verity. But not too convincingly. And tomorrow, when you are as bereaved as she, well, we shall see what mutual sympathy leads to.'

'She is big as a cow and pale as a fish.'

'But with the mountain lands, you will have a defensible inland kingdom. You know the Coastal Duchies will not stand for you, and Farrow and Tilth cannot stand alone between the mountains and the Coastal Duchies. Besides, she need not live longer than her first child's birth.'

'FitzChivalry Farseer,' Verity said in his sleep. King Shrewd and Chade played at dice-bones together. Patience stirred in her sleep. 'Chivalry?' she asked softly. 'Is that you?'

'No,' I said. 'It's no one. No one at all.'

She nodded and slept on.

When my eyes focused again, it was dark and I was alone. My jaws trembled, and my chin and shirt-front were wet with my own saliva. The numbness seemed less. I wondered if that meant the poison wouldn't kill me. I doubted that it mattered; I would have small chance to speak on my own behalf. My hands had gone numb. At least they didn't hurt any more. I was horribly thirsty. I wondered if Rurisk was dead yet. He had taken a lot more of the wine than I had. And Chade had said it was quick.

As if in answer to my question, a cry of purest pain rose to the moon. The ululation seemed to hang there, and to pull my heart out with it as it rose. Nosy's master was dead.

I flung myself toward him, wrapped the Wit around him. I

know, I know, and we shivered together as one he had loved passed beyond reach. The great aloneness wrapped us together.

Boy? Faint, but true. A paw and a nose, and a door edged open. He padded toward me, his nose telling me how bad I smelled. Smoke and blood and fear sweat. When he reached me, he lay down beside me, and put his head on my back. With the touch came the bond again. Stronger now that Rurisk was gone.

He left me. It hurts.

I know. A long time passed. *Free me?* The old dog lifted his head. Men cannot grieve as dogs do. We should be grateful for that. But from the depths of his anguish, he still rose, and set worn teeth to my bonds. I felt them loosen, a strand at a time, but had not even the strength to pull them apart. Nosy turned his head to set his back teeth to them.

At last the thongs parted. I pulled my arms forward. That made everything hurt differently. I still could not feel my hands, but I could roll over and get my face out of the straw. Nosy and I sighed together. He put his head on my chest and I wrapped a stiff arm around him. Another tremor shook me. My muscles clenched and unclenched themselves so violently that I saw dots of light. But it passed, and I still breathed.

I opened my eyes again. Light blinded me, but I did not know if it was real. Beside me, Nosy's tail thumped the straw. Burrich slowly sank down beside us. He put a gentle hand on Nosy's back. As my eyes adjusted to his lantern, I could see the grief in his face. 'Are you dying?' he asked me. His voice was so neutral, it was like hearing a stone speak.

'I'm not sure.' That was what I tried to say. My mouth still wasn't working very well. He rose and walked away. He took the lantern with him. I lay alone in the dark.

Then the light came back and Burrich with a bucket of water. He lifted my head and sloshed some into my mouth. 'Don't swallow it,' he cautioned me, but I couldn't have made those muscles work anyway. He washed out my mouth twice more, and then half-drowned me trying to get me to drink some. I fended off the bucket with a wooden hand. 'No,' I managed.

After a bit, my head seemed to clear. I moved my tongue against my teeth, and could feel them. 'I killed Cob,' I told him.

'I know. They brought his body out to the stables. No one wanted to tell me anything.'

'How did you know to find me?'

He sighed. 'I just had a feeling.'

'You heard Nosy.'

'Yes. The howling.'

'That isn't what I meant.'

He was quiet a long time. 'Sensing a thing isn't the same as using a thing.'

I couldn't think of anything to say back to that. After a while I said, 'Cob is the one who knifed you on the stairs.'

'Was he?' Burrich considered. 'I had wondered why the dogs barked so little. They knew him. Only Smithy reacted.'

My hands screamed suddenly to life. I folded them to my chest and rocked over them. Nosy whined.

'Stop it,' Burrich hissed.

'Just now, I can't help it,' I replied. 'It all hurts so badly, I'm spilling out all over.'

Burrich was silent.

'Are you going to help me?' I asked finally.

'I don't know,' he said softly, and then, almost pleadingly, 'Fitz, what are you? What have you become?'

'I am what you are, I told him honestly. 'A King's man. Burrich, they're going to kill Verity. If they do, Regal will become King.'

'What are you talking about?'

'If we stay here while I explain it all, it will happen. Help me get out of here.'

He seemed to take a very long time to think about it. But in the end, he helped me to stand and I held onto his sleeve as I staggered out of the stables and into the night.

TWENTY-THREE

The Wedding

The art of diplomacy is the luck of knowing more of your rival's secrets than he knows of yours. Always deal from a position of power. These were Shrewd's maxims. And Verity abided by them.

'You have to get August. He's the only hope Verity has.'

We were sitting in the greyness before dawn on a hillside above the palace. We had not gone far. The terrain was steep, and I was in no condition for hiking. I was beginning to suspect that Regal's kick had renewed Galen's old damage to my ribs. Every deep breath stabbed me. Regal's poison still sent tremors through me, and my legs buckled often and unpredictably. Alone, I could not stand, for my legs would not support me. I could not even cling to a tree-trunk and hold myself upright: there was no strength in my arms. Around us in the dawn forest birds called, squirrels were gathering stores for the winter and insects chirred. It was hard, in the midst of all that life, to wonder how much of this damage was permanent. Were the days and strength of my youth already spent, and nothing left to me but trembling and weakness? I tried to push the question from my mind, to concentrate on the greater problems facing the Six Duchies. I stilled myself, as Chade had taught me. Around us, the trees were immense, with a presence like peace. I understood why Eyod would not cut them for timber. Their needles were soft beneath us, the fragrance soothing. I wished I could just lie back and sleep, like Nosy at my side. Our pains still mingled together, but at least Nosy could escape his in sleep.

'What makes you think August would help us?' Burrich asked. 'If I could get him out here.'

I pulled my thoughts back to our dilemma. 'I don't think he's involved with the rest of it. I think he is still loyal to the King.' I had presented my information to Burrich as my own careful conclusions. He was not a man likely to be convinced by phantom voices overheard in my head. So I could not tell him that Galen had not suggested killing August, and therefore he was probably ignorant of the plot. I was still not sure myself of what I had experienced. Regal could not Skill. Even if he could, how could I have overheard Skilling between two others? No, it had to be something else, some other magic. Of Galen's devising? Was he capable of a magic that strong? I did not know. So much I did not know. I forced myself to set it all aside. For now, it fitted the facts I had, better than any other supposition I could imagine.

'If he's loyal to the King, and has no suspicions of Regal, then he is loyal to Regal as well,' Burrich pointed out as if I were a witling.

'Then we'll have to force him, somehow. Verity must be warned.'

'Of course. I'll just walk in, put a knife to August's back, and march him out of there. No one will bother us.'

I floundered for ideas. 'Bribe someone to lure him out here. Then jump him.'

'Even if I knew someone bribable, what would we use?'

'I have this.' I touched the earring in my ear.

Burrich looked at it and almost jumped. 'Where did you get that?'

'Patience gave it to me. Just before I left.'

'She had no right!' And then, more quietly, 'I thought it went to his grave with him.'

I was silent, waiting.

Burrich looked aside. 'It was your father's. I gave it to him.' He spoke quietly.

'Why?'

'Because I wanted to, obviously.' He closed the topic.

I reached up and began to unfasten it.

'No,' he said gruffly. 'Keep it where it is. But it is not a thing to be spent in a bribe. These Chyurda can't be bribed anyway.'

I knew he was right about that. I tried to think of other plans. The sun was coming up. Morning, when Galen would act. Perhaps had already acted. I wished I knew what was going on in the palace below. Did they know I was missing? Was Kettricken preparing to pledge herself to a man she would hate? Were Sevrens and Rowd dead yet? If not, could I turn them against Regal by warning them?

'Someone's coming!' Burrich flattened himself. I lay back, resigned to whatever happened. I had no physical fight left in me. 'Do you know her?' Burrich breathed.

I turned my head. Jonqui, preceded by a little dog that would never climb a tree for Rurisk again. 'The King's sister.' I didn't bother whispering. She was carrying one of my nightshirts, and an instant later the tiny dog was leaping joyously around us. He romped invitingly at Nosy, but Nosy just looked at him mournfully. An instant later, Jonqui strode up to us.

'You must come back,' she said to me without preamble. 'And you must hurry.'

'Hard enough to come back,' I told her, 'without hurrying to my death.' I was watching behind her for other trackers. Burrich had risen and taken a defensive posture over me.

'No death,' she promised me calmly. 'Kettricken has forgiven you. I have been counselling her since last night, but only lately convinced her. She has invoked her kin-right to forgive kin for injury to kin. By our law, if kin forgive kin, no other can do otherwise. Your Regal sought to dissuade her, but only made her angry. "Here, while I am in this palace, I can still invoke the law of the Mountain People," she told him. King Eyod agreed. Not because he does not mourn Rurisk, but because the strength and wisdom of Jhaampe law must be respected, by all. So, you must come back.'

I considered. 'And have you forgiven me?'

'No,' she snorted. 'I do not forgive my nephew's murderer. But I cannot forgive you for what you did not do. I do not believe you would drink wine you had poisoned. Not even a little. Those of us who know best the dangers of poisons tempt them least.

373

You would have just pretended to drink, and never spoken of poison at all. No. This was done by someone who believes himself very clever, and believes others are very stupid.'

I felt rather than saw Burrich lower his guard. But I couldn't completely relax. 'Why can't Kettricken just forgive me and let me go away? Why must I come back?'

'There is no time for this!' Jonqui hissed, and it was the closest I had seen to an angry Chyurda. 'Shall I take months and years to teach you all I know about balances? For a pull, a push, for a breath, a sigh? Do you think no one can feel how power slews and tilts just now? A princess must endure being bartered away like a cow. But my niece is not a playing-piece to be won in a dice game. Whoever killed my nephew clearly wished you to die also. Shall I let him win that toss? I think not. I do not know whom I wish to win; until I do, I will let no player be eliminated.'

'That's logic I understand,' Burrich said approvingly. He stooped and hauled me suddenly to my feet. The world rocked alarmingly. Jonqui came to put her shoulder under my other arm. They walked and my feet marionetted across the ground between them. Nosy heaved himself to his feet and followed. And so we returned to the palace at Jhaampe.

Burrich and Jonqui took me right through the people gathered throughout the grounds and palace to my room. Actually, I excited little interest. I was just an outlander who had had too much wine and smoke last night. People were too absorbed in finding good places from which to view the dais to worry about me. There was no air of mourning, so I assumed the word of Rurisk's death had not been released. When we finally entered my room, Jonqui's placid face darkened.

'I did not do this! I only took a nightshirt, to give Ruta a scent.'

'This' was the disassembly of my room. It had been thoroughly if not discreetly done. Jonqui immediately set to putting things right, and after a moment Burrich helped her. I sat in a chair and tried to make sense of the situation. Nosy, unnoticed, curled up in a corner. Unthinkingly, I extended comfort to him. Burrich immediately glanced at me, then at the woebegone dog. He looked away. When Jonqui left to fetch wash-water and food for me, I asked Burrich, 'Have you found a tiny wooden chest? Carved with acorns?'

He shook his head. So they had taken my poison-cache. I would have liked to prepare another dagger, or even a powder to fling. Burrich could not always be beside me to protect me, and I certainly couldn't fend off an attacker, or run away in my present condition. But my trade-tools were gone. I would have to hope I wouldn't need them. I suspected Rowd was the one who had been here, and wondered if this had been his last act. Jonqui returned with water and food, and then excused herself. Burrich and I shared wash-water, and with some help I managed to change into clean, if simple, clothes. Burrich ate an apple. My stomach quailed at the mere thought of food, but I drank the water, cold from the well, that Jonqui had brought me. Getting my throat muscles to swallow still took conscious effort, and I felt as if the water sloshed unpleasantly inside me. But I suspected it was good for me.

I felt each moment ticking by, and wondered when Galen would make his move.

The screen slid aside. I looked up, expecting Jonqui again, but August entered on a wave of contempt. He spoke immediately, anxious to do his errand and depart. 'I do not come here of my own volition. I come at the bidding of the King-in-Waiting, Verity, to speak his words for him. This is his message, exactly. He is grieved beyond telling by . . .'

'You Skilled to him? Today? Was he well?'

August seethed at my question. 'He was scarcely well. He is grieved beyond telling at Rurisk's death, and at your betrayal. He bids you draw strength from those around you loyal to you, for you will need it to face him.'

'Is that all?' I asked.

'From the King-in-Waiting, Verity, it is. Prince Regal bids you attend upon him, and swiftly, for the time of the ceremony is only hours away, and he must be attired for it. And your cowardly poison, no doubt meant for Regal, has found poor Sevrens and Rowd. Now Regal must do with an untrained valet. It will take him longer to dress. So do not keep him waiting. He is in the steams, to try to restore himself. You may find him there.'

'How tragic for him. An untrained valet,' Burrich said acidly.

August puffed up like a toad. 'It is scarcely humorous. Have not you lost Cob as well to this scoundrel? How can you bear to aid him?'

'If your ignorance were not protecting you, August, I might dispel it.' Burrich stood, looking dangerous.

'You, too, will face charges,' August warned him as he retreated. 'I am to say to you, Burrich, that King-in-Waiting Verity is not unaware of how you attempted to help the bastard escape, serving him as if he were your king instead of Verity. You will be judged.'

'Did Verity say so?' Burrich asked curiously.

'He did. He said you were once the best of King's men to Chivalry, but apparently you had forgotten how to aid those who truly serve the King. Recall it, he bids you, and assures you of his great wrath if you do not return to stand before him and receive what your deeds merit.'

'I recall it only too well. I will bring Fitz to Regal.'

'Now?'

'As soon as he has eaten.'

August glowered at him and left. Screens cannot be effectively slammed, but he tried.

'I have no stomach to eat, Burrich,' I protested.

'I know that. But we need time for this. I marked Verity's choice of words, and found more in them than August did. Did you?'

I nodded, feeling defeated. 'I understood also. But it is beyond me.'

'Are you sure? Verity does not think so, and he knows of such things. And you told me that was why Cob tried to kill me, because they suspected you of drawing on my strength. So Galen believes you can do it, too.' Burrich crossed to me, and went down stiffly on one knee. His bad leg stretched awkwardly behind him. He took my lax hand and placed it on his shoulder. 'I was King's man to Chivalry,' he told me quietly. 'Verity knew it. I have no Skill myself, you understand. But Chivalry gave me to understand that for such a taking, it was not as important as the friendship between us. I have strength, and there were some few times that he needed it, and I gave it willingly. So I have withstood this before, in worse circumstances. Try, boy. If we fail, we fail, but at least we will have tried.'

'I don't know how. I don't know how to Skill, and I certainly don't know how to tap someone else's strength to do it. And even if I did, if I succeeded, I might kill you.'

'If you succeed, our king may live. That is what I am sworn to. And you?' He made it all seem so simple.

So I tried. I opened my mind, I reached for Verity. I tried, with no idea how, to draw strength from Burrich. But all I heard was the twittering of birds outside the palace walls, and Burrich's shoulder was only a place to rest my hand. I opened my eyes. I didn't have to tell him I'd failed; he knew. He sighed heavily.

'Well. I suppose I take you to Regal,' he said.

'If we did not go, we would be forever curious as to what he wanted,' I added.

Burrich did not smile. 'You have a fey mood on you,' he said. 'You sound more like the Fool than yourself.'

'Does the Fool talk to you?' I asked curiously.

'Sometimes,' he said, and took my arm to help me up.

'It seems as if the closer I walk to death,' I told him, 'the funnier everything seems.'

'To you, perhaps,' he said crossly. 'I wonder what he wants.'

'To bargain. There can be nothing else. And if he wants to bargain, we may be able to gain something.'

'You speak as if Regal follows the same rules of common sense as the rest of us. I've never known him to do that. And I've always hated court intrigue,' Burrich complained. 'I'd rather clean stalls.' He pulled me again to my feet.

If I had ever wondered how deadroot felt to its victim, I knew it now. I did not think I would die of it. But I did not know how much of a life it would leave me either. My legs trembled under me, and my grip was uncertain. I could feel random muscle-twitches throughout my body. Neither my breath, nor the beating of my heart was predictable. I longed to be still, where I could listen to my own body and decide what had been done to it. But Burrich guided my steps patiently, and Nosy drooped along behind us.

I had not been to the steams before, but Burrich had. A separate tulip bud enclosed a bubbling hot spring, tamed to use as a bath. A Chyurda stood outside it; I recognized him as the torch-bearer from the night before. If he thought anything odd about my reappearance, he did not show it. He stepped aside as if expecting us, and Burrich dragged me up the steps to enter.

Clouds of steam fogged the air, carrying a mineral scent with them. We passed a stone bench or two; Burrich walked carefully on the smooth tile floor as we approached the source of the steam. The water rose in a central spring, with bricked sides built up around it to contain it. From there it was channelled in troughs to other, smaller baths, varying the heat by the length of the trough and the depth of the pond. The steam and the noise of the falling water filled the air. I did not find it pleasant; I laboured just to breathe already. My eyes adjusted to the dimness, and I saw Regal soaking in one of the larger baths. He looked up at our approach.

'Ah,' he said, as if well-pleased. 'August told me Burrich would bring you. Well. I suppose you know the Princess has forgiven your murder of her brother? And in this place, at least, by doing so she preserves you from justice. I think it a waste of time, but local customs must be honoured. She says she considers you part of her kin-group now, and so I must treat you as kin. She fails to understand you were not born of a lawful union, and hence have no kin-rights at all. Ah, well. Will you dismiss Burrich and join me in the springs? It might ease you. You look very uncomfortable, held up like a shirt on the washing-line.' He spoke so genially, so affably, as if unaware of my hatred.

'What do you wish to tell me, Regal?' I kept my voice flat.

'Will not you send Burrich away?' he asked again.

'I am not a fool.'

'One could argue that, but very well. I suppose I must send him away, then.'

The steam and the noise of the waters had cloaked the Chyurda well. He was taller than Burrich, and his cudgel was already in motion as Burrich turned. If he hadn't been supporting my weight, he could have avoided it. Burrich turned his head, but the cudgel hit his skull with a terrible, sharp sound, like an axe biting wood. Burrich fell, and I with him. I landed half in one of the smaller ponds. It was not scalding, but nearly so. I managed to roll out of it, but could not regain my feet. My legs would not obey me.

Burrich beside me lay very still. I reached a hand toward him, but could not touch him.

Regal stood up, and motioned to the Chyurda. 'Dead?'

The Chyurda stirred Burrich with a foot, gave a curt nod.

'Good.' Regal was briefly pleased. 'Drag him back behind that deep tank in the corner. Then you may go.' To me, he said, 'It's unlikely anyone will be coming in here until after the ceremony. They're too busy jostling for positions. And back in that corner . . . well, I doubt if he'll be found before you are.'

I could make no response. The Chyurda stooped and seized Burrich by the ankles. As he dragged him away, the dark brush of his hair feathered a trail of blood on the tiles. A dizzying mixture of hatred and despair rolled with the poison through my blood. A cold purpose rose and set in me. I could not hope to live now, but it did not seem important. Warning Verity did. And avenging Burrich. I had no plans, no weapons, no possibilities. So play for time, Chade's counsels advised me. The more time you create for yourself, the better the chance that something will present itself. Delay him. Perhaps someone will come to see why the Prince is not dressing for the wedding. Perhaps someone else will want to use the steams before the ceremony. Engage him somehow.

'The Princess . . .' I began.

'Is not a problem,' Regal finished for me. 'The Princess did not forgive Burrich. Only you. What I have done to him is well within my rights. He is a traitor. He must pay. And the man disposing of him was most fond of his Prince Rurisk. He has no objections to any of this.'

The Chyurda left the steams without a glance back. My hands scrabbled weakly on the smooth tile floor but found no purchase. Regal busily dried himself all the while. When the man was gone, he came to stand over me. 'Aren't you going to call for help?' he asked brightly.

I took a breath, pushed down my fear. I mustered as much contempt for Regal as I could find. 'To whom? Who would hear me over the water?'

'So you save your strength. Wise. Pointless, but wise.'

'Do you think Kettricken will not know what happened?'

'She will know you went to the steams, unwisely in your condition. You slipped beneath the hot, hot water. Such a shame.'

'Regal, this is madness. How many bodies do you think you can leave in your wake? How will you explain Burrich's death?'

'To your first question, quite a few, as long as they are not people of consequence.' He stooped over me, and gripped my shirt. He dragged me while I thrashed weakly, a fish out of water. 'And to your second, well, the same. How much fuss do you think anyone will raise over a dead stableman? You are so obsessed with your plebeian self-importance that you extend it to your servants.' He dumped me carelessly half on top of Burrich. His still-warm body sprawled face-down on the floor. Blood was congealing on the tiles around his face, and still dripping from his nose. A slow bubble of blood formed on his lips, broke with his faint exhalation. He lived yet. I shifted to conceal it from Regal. If I could survive, Burrich might have a chance also.

Regal noticed nothing. He tugged my boots off and set them aside. 'You see, bastard,' he said as he paused to catch his breath. 'Ruthlessness creates its own rules. So my mother taught me. People are intimidated by a man who acts with no apparent regard for consequences. Behave as if you cannot be touched and no one will dare to touch you. Look at the whole situation. Your death will anger some people, yes. But enough to make them take actions that would affect the security of the whole Six Duchies? I think not. Besides, your death will be eclipsed by other things. I'd be a fool not to take this opportunity to remove you.' Regal was so damnably calm, and superior. I fought him, but he was surprisingly strong for the indulgent life he led. I felt like a kitten as he shook me out of my shirt. He folded my clothes neatly and set them aside. 'Minimal alibis will work. If I made too much effort to appear guiltless, people might think I cared. They might start then to pay attention themselves. So, I simply know nothing. My man saw you enter with Burrich after I had left. And I go now to complain to August that you never came to talk with me so that I might forgive you, as I had promised Princess Kettricken. I will reprimand August most severely for not bringing you himself.' He looked around. 'Let's see. A nice deep hot one. Right here.' I clutched at his throat as he levered me up to the edge, but he shook me off easily.

'Goodbye, bastard,' he said calmly. 'Pardon my haste, but you have quite delayed me. I must rush to dress myself. Or I shall be late for the wedding.'

And he tumbled me in.

The pool was deeper than I was tall, designed to be neck-high on a tall Chyurda. It was painfully hot to my unprepared body. It drove the air from my lungs and I sank. I pushed feebly off the bottom and managed to get my face above water. 'Burrich!' I wasted my breath on a shout to someone who could not aid me. The water closed on me again. My arms and legs would not work together. I blundered into a wall and pushed myself under before I could once again surface and gasp in some air. The hot water was loosening my already flaccid muscles. I think I would still have been drowning even if the water had been only knee-deep.

I lost count of how many times I floundered to the surface, to gasp a breath. The smooth, worked stone of the walls eluded my palsied grip, and my ribs stabbed with pain each time I tried for a deep breath. My strength was flowing out of me, lassitude flowing in. So warm, so deep. Drowned like a puppy, I thought to myself as I felt the darkness closing. *Boy?* someone queried, but all was black.

So much water, so hot and so deep. I could not find a bottom any more, let alone a side. I struggled feebly against the water, but there was no resistance. No up, no down. No use fighting to stay alive inside my body. Nothing left to protect, so drop the walls, and see if there is one last service you can render your king. The walls of my world fell away from me, and I sped forth like an arrow finally released. Galen had been right. There was no distance in Skilling, no distance at all. Buckkeep was right here, and *Shrewd!* I shrieked in desperation. But my king was intent upon other things. He was closed and walled to me, no matter how I stormed around him. No help there.

My body was failing, my thread to it was tenuous. One last chance. *Verity, Verity!* I cried. I found him, flailed at him, but could find no purchase, no grip. He was elsewhere, open to someone else, closed to me. *Verity!* I wailed, drowning in despair.

And suddenly it was as if strong hands gripped mine as I scrabbled up a slippery cliff, gripped and held tight and drew me in when I would have slipped away.

Chivalry! No, it can't be, it's the boy! Fitz?

You imagine things, my prince. There is no one there. Attend to what we do now. Galen, calm and insidious as poison as he pushed me aside. I could not withstand him; he was too strong.

Fitz? Verity, unsure now as I grew weaker.

From I knew not where, I found strength. Something gave way before me, and I was strong. I clung to Verity like a hawk on his wrist. I was there with him. I saw with Verity's eyes: the freshly-decked throne room, the Book of Events on the great table before him, laid open to receive the recording of Verity's marriage. Around him, in their best finery and most costly jewels, the few honoured ones who had been invited to witness Verity witnessing his bride's pledge through August's eyes. And Galen, who was supposed to be offering his strength as a King's man, was poised beside and slightly behind Verity, waiting to drain him dry. Shrewd, in crown and robe upon his throne, was all unknowing, his Skill burned and dulled away years ago by misuse, and him too proud to admit it.

Like an echo, I saw through August's eyes as Kettricken stood pale as a wax candle on a dais before all her people. She was telling them, simply and kindly, that last night Rurisk had finally succumbed to the arrow-wound he had taken on the Ice Fields. She hoped to please his memory by pledging herself as he had helped arrange, to the King-in-Waiting of the Six Duchies. She turned to face Regal.

In Buckkeep, Galen's claw of a hand settled on Verity's shoulder.

I broke into his link with Verity, pushed him aside. *Beware Galen, Verity. Beware a traitor, come to drain you dry. Touch him not.*

Galen's hand tightened on Verity's shoulder. Suddenly all was a sucking vortex, draining, trying to pull everything out of Verity. And there was not much left to take. His Skill was so strong because he let it take so much from him so fast. Self-preservation would have made another man hold back some of his strength. But Verity had been spending his recklessly, every day, to keep the Red Ships from his shores. So little left now for this ceremony, and Galen was absorbing it. And growing stronger as he did so. I clung to Verity, fighting desperately to reduce the loss. *Verity!* I cried to him. *My prince.* I sensed a brief rallying in him, but all was growing dim before his eyes. I heard a stirring of alarm as he sagged and caught at the table. Faithless Galen kept his grip on him, bent over him as he went to one knee, murmuring solicitously, 'My prince? Are you quite all right?'

I flung my strength to Verity, reserves I had not suspected in myself. I opened up and let go of them, just as Verity did when he Skilled. 'Take it all. I would die anyway. And you were always good to me when I was young.' I heard the words as clearly as if I had spoken them, and felt the breaking of a mortal bond as strength flowed into Verity through me. He waxed suddenly strong, beast-strong, and angry.

Verity's hand rose to grip Galen's. He opened his eyes. 'I shall be fine,' he said to Galen, aloud. He looked around the room as he rose to his feet again. 'I but worried about you. You seemed to tremble. Are you sure you are strong enough for this? You must not attempt a challenge that is beyond you. Think what might happen.' And as a gardener pulls a weed from the earth, Verity smiled, and pulled from the traitor all that was in him. Galen fell, clutching his chest, an empty man-shaped thing. The onlookers rushed to attend him, but Verity, replete now, lifted his eyes to the window and focused his mind afar.

August. Attend me well. Warn Regal his half-brother is dead. Verity boomed like the sea, and I felt August quail at the strength of the Skilling. *Galen was too ambitious. He attempted that which was beyond his skill. A pity the Queen's bastard could not be content with the position she gave him. A pity my younger brother could not dissuade his half-brother from his misplaced ambitions. Galen overstepped his position. My younger brother should take heed of what comes of such recklessness. And August. Be sure you tell Regal privately. Not many knew Galen was the Queen's bastard and his half-brother. I am sure he would not want scandal to soil his mother's name, or his. Such family secrets should be well-guarded.*

And then, with a force that put August on his knees, Verity pushed through him to stand before Kettricken in her mind. I sensed his effort to be gentle. *I await you, my Queen-in-Waiting. And by my name, I swear to you I had naught to do with your brother's death. I knew nothing of it, and I grieve with you. I would not want you to come to me, thinking his blood on my hands.* Like a jewel opening was the light in Verity's heart as he exposed it to her that she might know she had not been given to a murderer. Selflessly, he made himself vulnerable to her, giving trust to build trust. She swayed, but stood. August fainted. That contact was gone.

And then Verity was shoving at me. *Back, get back, Fitz. That's too much, you'll die. Back, let go!* And he cuffed me like a bear, and I slammed back into my silent, sightless body.

TWENTY-FOUR

The Aftermath

In the Great Library at Jhaampe there is a tapestry that is rumoured to contain a map through the mountains to the Rain Wilds. Like many Jhaampe maps and books, the information contained was considered so valuable that it was encoded in the form of riddles and visual puzzles. Figured on the tapestry, among many images, are the forms of a dark-haired, dark man, stout and muscular and bearing a red shield, and, in the opposite corner, a golden-skinned being. The golden-skinned creature had been the victim of moths and fraying, but it is still possible to see that in the scale of the tapestry, it is much larger than a human, and possibly winged. Buckkeep legend has it that King Wisdom sought and found the Elderlings' homeland by a secret path through the Mountain Kingdom. Could these figures represent an Elderling and King Wisdom? Does this tapestry record the path through the Mountain Kingdom to the Elderlings' homeland in the Rain Wilds?

Much later I learned how I had been found, leaning against Burrich's body on the tile floor of the steams. I was shaking as with an ague, and could not be roused. Jonqui found us, though how she knew to look in the steams I will never know. I will always suspect that she was to Eyod as Chade was to Shrewd, not as assassin perhaps, but as one who had ways of knowing or finding out almost anything that happened within the palace. However it was, she took command of the situation. Burrich and I were isolated in a chamber separate from the palace, and I suspect that for a while no one from Buckkeep knew where we were or if we lived. She tended us herself with the aid of one old manservant.

I awoke some two days after the wedding. Four of the most miserable days of my life were spent lying in bed, limbs atwitch but not at my command. I dozed often, in a deadened way that was not pleasant, and either dreamed vividly of Verity, or sensed him trying to Skill to me. The Skill dreams conveyed no sense to me, other than that he was concerned for me. I grasped only isolated bits of knowledge from them, such as the colour of the curtains in the room he Skilled from, or the feel of a ring on his finger that he absently twisted as he tried to reach me. Some more violent jerk of my muscles would shake me from my dreams, and my spasming would torment me until, exhausted, I dozed again.

My periods of alertness were as bad, for Burrich lay on a pallet in the same room, breathing hoarsely, but doing little more than that. His features were swollen and discoloured such that he was barely recognizable. From the beginning, Jonqui gave me little hope for him, either that he would live, or that he would be himself if he did survive.

But Burrich had cheated death before. The swelling gradually subsided, the purpling faded, and when he did awaken, he proceeded to recover himself swiftly. He had no memories of anything that occurred after he took me from the stable. I told him only what he needed to know. It was more than it was safe for him to know, but I owed it to him. He was up and about before I was, though at first he had times of dizziness and headaches. But before long Burrich was getting to know the Jhaampe stables and exploring the town at his leisure. In the evenings he would return, and we had many long, quiet conversations. We both avoided topics where we knew we would disagree, and there were areas, such as Chade's teachings, where I could not be open with him. Mostly, though, we talked about dogs he had known and horses he'd trained, and sometimes he spoke, a little, of his early days with Chivalry. One evening I told him about Molly. He was quiet for a time, and then told me that he'd heard the owner of the Beebalm Chandlery had died in debt, and that his daughter who had expected to inherit it had gone to live with relatives in a village instead. He did not remember which village, but knew someone who would know. He did not mock me, but told me seriously that I should know my own mind before I saw her again.

August never Skilled again. He was carried from the dais that day, but as soon as he recovered from his faint, he demanded to see Regal immediately. I trust he delivered Verity's message. For while Regal did not come to visit either Burrich or me during our convalescence, Kettricken did, and she mentioned that Regal was most concerned that we recover quickly and completely from our accidents, for as he had promised her, he had forgiven me completely. She told me how Burrich had slipped and struck his head trying to pull me from the pool when I went into a seizure. I do not know who concocted that tale. Jonqui herself, perhaps. I doubt if even Chade could have come up with a better one. But Verity's message was the end of August's leadership of the coterie, and all Skilling as far as I know. I do not know if he was too afraid after that day, or if the talent was blasted out of him by that force. He left court, and went to Withywoods, where Chivalry and Patience had once ruled. I believe he became wise.

Following her wedding, Kettricken joined with all of Jhaampe in a month of mourning for her brother. From my sickbed, I was aware of it mostly as chimes, chantings, and great burnings of incense. All Rurisk's possessions were given away. To me Eyod himself came, and brought a simple silver ring his son had worn. And the head of the arrow that had pierced his chest. He did not say much to me, except to tell me what the objects were, and that I should cherish these reminders of an exceptional man. He left me to wonder why these items had been selected for me.

At the end of a month, Kettricken set her mourning aside. She came to bid Burrich and me a swift recovery, and to bid us farewell until she saw us at Buckkeep. The brief moment of Skilling from Verity had eliminated all her reservations about him. She spoke of her husband with a quiet pride, and went willingly to Buckkeep, knowing herself given to an honourable man.

It was not for me to ride alongside her at the head of that homeward procession, or to enter Buckkeep preceded by horns and tumblers and children ringing bells. That was Regal's place, and he put a gracious face on it. Regal appeared to take Verity's warning to heart. I do not think Verity ever completely forgave him. But he dismissed Regal's plottings as if they were nasty boyish tricks, and I think that cowed Regal more than any public reprimand could have. The poisoning was eventually blamed on Rowd and Sevrens by those who knew of it. Sevrens had, after all, obtained the poison, and Rowd had delivered the gift of apple wine. Kettricken pretended to be convinced that it was a misplaced ambition by servants on behalf of an unknowing master. And Rurisk's death was never openly spoken of as a poisoning. Nor did I become known as an assassin. Whatever was in Regal's heart, his outward demeanour was that of a younger prince graciously escorting his brother's bride home.

I had a long convalescence. Jonqui treated me with herbs she said would rebuild what had been damaged. I should have tried to learn her herbs and techniques, but my mind could not seem to hold things any better than my hands could. I remember little of that time. My recovery from the poisoning was frustratingly slow. Jonqui sought to make it less tedious by arranging time for me in the Great Library, but my eyes wearied quickly and seemed as prone to trembling disorders as my hands. I spent most days lying in my bed, thinking. For a time I wondered if I wanted to return to Buckkeep. I wondered if I could still be Shrewd's assassin. I knew that if I returned, I would have to sit down the table from Regal and look up to see him at my king's left hand. I would have to treat him as if he had never tried to kill me, nor used me in the poisoning of a man I had admired. I spoke of it frankly one evening to Burrich. He sat and listened quietly. Then he said, I cannot imagine it will be easier for Kettricken than it would be for you. Nor for me, to look at a man who has tried to kill me twice, and call him "My prince". You must decide. I should hate to have him think he had frightened us away. But if you decide we are going elsewhere, then we shall.' I think I finally guessed then what the earring signified.

Winter was no longer a threat, but a reality, when we left the mountains. Burrich, Hands and I returned much later to Buckkeep than the others, for we took our time on the journey. I tired easily, and my strength was still very unpredictable. I would crumple at odd moments, falling from the saddle like a sack of grain. Then they would stop to help me re-mount, and I would force myself to

go on. Many nights I awoke shaking, without even the strength
to call out. These lapses were slow to pass. Worst, I think, were
the nights when I could not waken, but dreamed only of endlessly
drowning. From one such dream I woke to Verity standing over me.

You're enough to wake the dead, he told me genially. *We must
find a master for you, to teach you some control if nothing else.
Kettricken finds it a bit peculiar that I dream so often of drowning. I
suppose I should be grateful you slept well on my wedding night at least.*

'Verity?' I said groggily.

Go back to sleep, he told me. *Galen is dead, and I've put Regal
on a shorter leash. You've nothing to fear. Go to sleep, and stop dreaming
so loudly.*

Verity, wait! But my act of groping after him broke the tenuous
Skill contact, and I had no choice but to do as he had advised.

We travelled on, through increasingly unpleasant weather. We all
looked forward to getting home long before we arrived there. Burrich
had, I believe, overlooked Hands' abilities until that trip. Hands had
a quiet competence that inspired trust in horses as well as dogs.
Eventually he easily replaced both Cob and me in the Buckkeep
stables, and the friendship that grew between Burrich and Hands
caused me to be more aware of my aloneness than I care to admit.

Galen's death was considered a tragic thing at Buckkeep court.
Those who had known him least spoke mostly kindly about him.
Obviously the man had overstrained himself, for his heart to fail
him so young. There was some talk of naming a warship after
him, as if he were a fallen hero, but Verity never recognized the
idea and it never came to pass. His body was sent back to Farrow
for burial, with all honour. If Shrewd suspected anything of what
had gone on between Verity and Galen, he kept it well hidden.
Neither he nor even Chade ever mentioned it to me. The loss
of our Skillmaster, with not even an apprentice to replace him,
was no trivial thing, especially with the Red Ships on our horizons.
That was what was openly discussed, but Verity flatly refused to
consider Serene or any of the others Galen had trained.

I never found out if Shrewd had given me over to Regal. I
never asked him, nor even mentioned my suspicions to Chade.
I suppose I didn't want to know. I tried not to let it affect my
loyalties. But in my heart, when I said, *My king,* I meant Verity.

The timbers Rurisk had promised came to Buckkeep even more slowly than I did, for they had to be dragged overland to the Vin River before they could be rafted down to Turlake, and thence down the Buck River to Buckkeep. They arrived by midwinter and were all Rurisk had said they would be. The first completed warship was named after him. I think he would have understood that, but not quite approved of it.

King Shrewd's plan had succeeded. It had been many years since Buckkeep had had a queen of any kind, and Kettricken's arrival stirred interest in court life. The tragic death of her brother on her wedding eve, and the brave way she had continued despite it captured the imagination of the people. Her unmistakable admiration for her new husband made Verity a romantic hero even to his own folk. They were a striking couple; her youth and pale beauty setting off Verity's quiet strength. Shrewd displayed them at balls that attracted every minor noble from every duchy, and Kettricken spoke with intense eloquence of the need for all to band together to defeat the Red Ship Raiders. So Shrewd raised his monies, and even in the storms of winter, the fortification of the Six Duchies began. More towers were constructed, and folk volunteered to man them. Shipwrights vied for the honour of working on the warships, and Buckkeep Town was swollen with volunteers to man the ships. For a brief time that winter, folk believed in the legends they created, and it seemed the Red Ships could be defeated by sheer will alone. I mistrusted that mood, but watched as Shrewd promoted it, and wondered how he would sustain it when the realities of the Forgings began again.

Of one other I must speak, one dragged into that conflict and intrigue only by his loyalty to me. To the end of my days, I will bear the scars he gave me. His worn teeth sank deeply into my hand several times before he managed to drag me from that pool. How he did it, I will never know. But his head still rested on my chest when they found us; his mortal bonds to this world broken. Nosy was dead. I believe he gave his life freely, recalling that we had been good to one another, when we were puppies. Men cannot grieve as dogs do. But we grieve for many years.

EPILOGUE

'You are wearied,' my boy says. He is standing at my elbow and I do not know how long he has been there. He reaches forward slowly, to lift the pen from my lax grip. Wearily I regard the faltering tail of ink it has tracked down my page. I have seen that shape before, I think, but it was not ink then. A trickle of drying blood on the deck of a Red Ship, and mine the hand that spilled it? Or was it a tendril of smoke rising black against a blue sky as I rode too late to warn a village of a Red Ship Raid? Or poison swirling and unfurling yellowly in a simple glass of water, poison I had handed someone, smiling all the while? The artless curl of a strand of woman's hair left upon my pillow? Or the trail a man's heels left in the sand as we dragged the bodies from the smouldering tower at Sealbay? The track of a tear down a mother's cheek as she clutched her Forged infant to her despite his angry cries? Like Red Ships, the memories come without warning, without mercy. 'You should rest,' the boy says again, and I realize I am sitting, staring at a line of ink on a page. It makes no sense. Here is another sheet spoiled, another effort to set aside.

'Put them away,' I tell him, and do not object as he gathers all the sheets and stacks them haphazardly together. Herbery and history, maps and musings, all a hodge-podge in his hands as they are in my mind. I can no longer recall what it was I set out to do. The pain is back, and it would be so easy to quiet it. But that way lies madness, as has been proven so many times before me. So instead I send the boy to find two leaves of Carryme, and ginger root and peppermint to make a tea for me. I wonder if one day I will ask him to fetch three leaves of that Chyurdan herb.

Somewhere, a friend says softly, 'No.'